A SONG OF VICTORY

RACHAEL C. DUNCAN

A Song of Victory
by Rachael C. Duncan

Published in the United States by Wolfpack Publishing, Las
Vegas

CKN Christian Publishing
An Imprint of Wolfpack Publishing
5130 S. Fort Apache Road 215-380
Las Vegas, NV 89148

cknchristianpublishing.com

Paperback ISBN: 978-1-63977-017-5
eBook ISBN: 978-1-63977-016-8
LCCN: 2021953516

NOTE FROM THE AUTHOR

When I began researching my first novel, I was blown away by the vast amount of resources available concerning anything and everything biblical! It was thrilling to discover such a wealth of information regarding topics that have always intrigued me. Because I am called to write Bible-based novels, please allow me to state this simple disclaimer: The novels I write are categorized as biblical fiction, which means I have taken some literary license in instances where the Bible story itself remains silent or unclear. I do this by studying the Bible and delving into both historical and archaeological resources. As you can imagine, there's a lot of controversy and differing opinions regarding certain biblical characters, settings, dates, etc. so I do my very best not to contradict the Word of God (my #1 source!), and then I ask the Lord to help me fill in the blanks in a way that will reach my readers, touch their hearts, draw them closer to Him, and bring these beautiful Bible stories to life for them, inspiring them to dive head-first into the precious Word of God!

Thank you for purchasing this novel. I hope you are blessed page after page!

Blessings in Jesus,
Rachael C. Duncan

A SONG OF VICTORY

CHAPTER 1

Julia

It had taken no time at all for her to fall in love with Barabbas.

Now, it would seem, she would have the rest of her life to regret that careless mistake.

Julia sighed dismally as she strolled comfortably alongside her dearest friend, Melina, upon an elevated balcony overlooking Jerusalem's bustling Upper Market, her mind clouded with thoughts. She scarcely noticed the beauty surrounding them as she fixated upon her recent troubles.

Even so, the clean, spring air was crisp as the sky stretched forth like an endless sea of sapphire blue. The sun rose in regal fashion rather like a majestic sphere of shimmering gold, bathing the fresh earth beneath in a cheerful hue of radiant light.

The day was full of promise, beckoning both hopeful anticipation and new beginnings.

If only it were a simple thing to banish the worries that so easily crowd one's thoughts, plaguing the heart and mind, Julia thought wistfully, her cascading chestnut hair fluttering in the gentle morning breezes. Modestly, she adjusted her head covering, wishing she could tear it away and lift her face heavenward, basking in the warm, promising sunlight!

"At times, I truly believe I live with a perfect stranger," she lamented, covering her teary hazel-colored eyes with delicate hands.

Melina touched her friend's shoulder with a gentle hand, her soft features glowing with compassion. "Oh, my poor Julia. It can't be as bad as that... can it?"

"Worse!" Julia shook her head vehemently, wondering how their innocent conversation had veered in the direction of her offensive husband. "To live with a perfect stranger would be a relief. Barabbas may be a stranger to me, but he's far from perfect!"

Melina paused mid-step, turning to look her friend in the eyes. "I've yet to meet a *perfect* stranger. We are all miserable sinners, Julia. But God is faithful. He will work this situation out for your good."

Julia forced a smile, hoping to convince Melina that her softly spoken words of conviction had encouraged her when, in fact, they hadn't.

There were days when Julia felt the Lord's presence so vividly she was certain she could reach out and touch Him. Then there were other days – like today – when, despite the magnificent beauty surrounding her, her spirit remained unsettled.

"We live in the same house, Melina, but Barabbas and I scarcely know one another. We seldom speak two words to each other. Perhaps we've simply discovered it is better to remain in silence than to spend the evenings in bitter argument." She sighed, remembering numerous occasions when overtures of kindness toward her husband were met with harsh cruelties or stony silence. Perhaps the stony silence wasn't so bad after all. Wasn't a cold shoulder better than being verbally dismembered by an accusatory husband?

Sensing Julia's troubled thoughts, Melina took her hand and smiled warmly. "You have great faith in your Maker, Julia. I see it often. But there are days when the enemy of our souls comes against us in order to distract and discourage us. Most often, I find that those are the times when the Lord is preparing us to do a mighty work through Him. Don't allow the enemy to blow you off course, Julia. Stand firm. Trust in God's promises and trust Him to work mightily in and through you, despite the enemy's relentless advances."

Julia's heart responded to Melina's exhortation. She was right, after all. The devil was the great deceiver of men, and his mission was to steal, kill, and destroy.

Well, he has certainly succeeded in stealing, killing, and destroying my joy today... And annihilating it. And tearing it to shreds. And stomping all over it. But no more!

Setting her jaw firmly, Julia resolved to stay her mind on the Word of God. After all, one overcame evil with good.

And what is good? God is good, she reminded herself firmly. His Word is good. And obedience to His commandments will result in my ultimate good.

"How quickly I allow myself to get distracted!" Julia confessed, laughing in relief. "Forgive my dismal company, Melina. Your reminder is exactly what I needed."

"We all have those days," Melina said, always merciful.

"How is life in the palace these days?" Julia asked lightly, looping her arm through her friend's as they walked along the glistening, stone-paved balcony.

Melina smiled wanly. "As always, there's never a dull moment." Her expression sobered. "I've missed Joanna terribly. She has joined an entourage of women who follow Jesus, ministering financially and attending to the needs of Jesus and His disciples."

"I miss my Joanna too," Julia added with a smile, thinking of her jovial, no-nonsense nursemaid who still served in her father's resplendent villa. "Does your Joanna return often?"

"As often as possible."

"Her husband must miss her terribly."

"Chuza encourages her to go. As overseer of Herod's Jerusalem estate, he is an incredibly busy man and they have little time together anyway. But he believes God has placed him there for a reason, and he also believes that God has called him to support the ministry of Jesus financially since the Lord has given him so much. It is a blessing that he permits his wife to minister in that way. He says God gives to us so that we can bless others."

Julia smiled her understanding. "My father has always believed the same." Her features softened as she considered her father – one of Jerusalem's wealthiest merchant princes – and his outrageous generosity toward others. Marriage to a poor man had certainly opened her eyes to the abundance the Lord had showered upon her childhood home. Sadly, those blessings had to be stripped away before she could recognize the privileges she had enjoyed.

Oh, Lord God, I am convinced I must be the most stubborn of all Your children. Help me, Lord!

"Sometimes I find myself longing to join Joanna, wishing I possessed the freedom to follow Jesus through the cities, towns, and countryside, drinking in His teachings and basking in the glory of His presence," Melina said, a beatific smile upon her serene face. "But then I remind myself that God has placed me exactly where I am for a reason. He has a purpose and a plan for each of His children. But, oh, how I long to meet Jesus!"

"He is magnificent, Melina," Julia said with great feeling. "Despite the mixed reaction He elicits from the people."

"Just imagine, the Son of God walking among us," Melina said, her eyes alight. "When I begin to despair that I have not yet seen Him, a still voice within reminds me that He has seen me. He knows me somehow, even if I have yet to meet Him." She offered a sheepish smile. "I suppose you must think I sound crazy indeed."

Julia smiled knowingly. "Not in the least. Nothing is impossible with God, Melina. He sees you and He knows you intimately."

"Isn't it strange how desperately one can long for someone they have never met?"

"The desire of our soul is for Your name and for the remembrance of You," Julia reminded her, quoting the ancient prophet Isaiah. "God created us to long for Him, Melina. And He promises that if you delight yourself in Him, He will give you the desires of your heart."

Melina's countenance brightened as she considered Julia's words.

The women remained in comfortable silence for several moments, each one contemplating her own thoughts.

"Trouble is brewing on the palace grounds. I can sense it, though I am uncertain as to how it will manifest itself."

Melina's sober observance drew Julia back to the present. "What kind of trouble?"

"There is always tension in the palace, but lately it has been so thick it fairly crackles in the air. Do you know what I'm trying to say?"

Julia nodded apprehensively, her skin prickling. "Are you in danger?"

"God will protect me. And if it is His will that I perish, then nothing can change that and I must trust Him."

Julia admired Melina's steadfast faith. "What is happening in the palace?"

"I wish I knew." Melina lowered her voice, knowing that certain death would surely follow if her comments were overheard by the wrong set of ears. "Herod's stepdaughter, Salome, is in hysterics over her upcoming union with Philip. Nothing that I say or do can soothe her now. Honestly, I fear she may do something desperate."

Julia's lips curved in mischief. "Am I wrong to assume that, if she did, she would be doing poor Philip a very great favor?"

"Julia!" Melina shook her head chidingly. "If Salome should perish now, she would do so without knowledge of the Savior."

"Well, the knowledge is there. It's her motivation to act upon the knowledge that's a bit lacking," Julia inserted ruefully.

With a soft smile, Melina tactfully overlooked her friend's snide comment. "That aside, Herod's birthday approaches, and Herodias has pestered him incessantly. Somehow, she has convinced him to celebrate his birthday at Machaerus."

Julia blanched. "The Black Fortress?"

"I cannot understand her motives, or Herod's capitulation. The decadence of Herod Antipas is no secret. Wouldn't a banquet in honor of Herod's birth be far more comfortable in his luxury palace here in Jerusalem or even in Tiberias? Why Machaerus?"

"Have you ever been there?"

Melina shuddered. "Whatever you may have heard about it is true. That fortress has earned its reputation."

"It certainly doesn't sound like a cheery place for a celebration."

"It is far more befitting for a funeral," Melina admitted, shivering slightly.

Perched upon a precipitous rocky cliff on the eastern side of the Dead Sea, the prison fortress hovered above the harsh desert landscape like a fearsome bird of prey, guarding against fierce Arabian bandits and brigands. The massive military outpost could be seen as far north as Alexandrium and even as far south as Masada.

"It's not entirely without its charm," Melina said with a sigh, pausing to rest her arms upon the smooth, cool stone wall enclosing the meandering balcony. "The palace itself is rather exquisite, but the atrocities that are committed there..." she shuddered, her emerald eyes gazing beyond the glistening marble structures of Jerusalem as if she glimpsed a disturbing future. "The prison is a frightful place, and the tortures are horrific. It's as if a dark presence has settled there and it is loath to depart from its stronghold."

"Is it true that John the Baptizer remains imprisoned there?"

Melina's eyes moistened, and she nodded sadly. "It is. Julia, I fear for him."

Julia joined her friend at the limestone wall. "Herod will have to release him soon, Melina. The only reasons Herod could produce for his arrest were weak, vague excuses. The people love John and will demand his release."

Melina blinked back tears, her heart going out to the fiery prophet chained in a rat-infested cell. For a year now, the man who had given his life to serve the Lord had been grossly mistreated, abused, and beaten. It hurt her heart to even consider it, and she lifted up yet another silent prayer on his behalf.

"Sadly, Julia, the people have already forgotten about him," Melina replied in response to Julia's heartfelt proclamation. "Herodias knew what she was doing when she ordered John arrested – even as I fear she knows what she is doing now. She sees how fickle the heart of man can be. She knew the populace would eventually forget about John, turning instead to other amusements. Vain, foolish amusements."

Julia looked to her friend, her expression troubled. "And when they do?"

"Then Herodias will be free to do as she pleases." There was a long, thoughtful pause as the two young women contemplated the gravity of John's sad plight.

"Do you suppose," Julia ventured slowly, her tone guarded, "that John is the reason Herodias desires to return to Machaerus?"

Melina exhaled slowly. "I can only pray that it is not."

"But John's offense against her was committed years ago. Surely she has forgotten all about it by now..."

"Herodias has a long memory, Julia. And when she considers herself wronged, she never forgets. Even after she extracts her vengeance, she relishes her victims' misfortune for years to come."

Julia wrinkled her nose, disgusted. "How on earth do you a serve a witch like that and keep your sweet disposition, Melina? Had I been her maidservant, I would have been flayed for smacking her upside the head with a Grecian urn my first day in her presence."

Melina held back an amused smile. "Only by the grace of God, Julia. Your prayers help tremendously. And I remind myself that God loves her – despite her wicked heart. His will is that none should perish, and that includes Herodias."

"I'd imagine her perishing would be good riddance," Julia quipped, annoyed.

Melina caught herself before a laugh could escape her lips. "You sound like my friend, Elias, the head cook. If Herodias does indeed perish, it will be by her own will. God continues to reach for her, to call her unto Himself. I pray for her and for Salome without ceasing."

Julia shook her head in a good-natured manner,

awed. "Will I ever have a faith like yours?"

"Oh, Julia, I am the weakest of women. There are times when I can scarcely hold my tongue in their presence. But God is good, and He provides the strength I need to get through each day of service..." she paused, allowing a small smile to curve her delicate lips. "Speaking of which, I suppose I must return. Elias is expecting a bounty of fresh herbs and spices from the Upper Market, and I imagine he is rather impatient to receive them!"

Julia wished they could stay for hours, basking in the glory of the day. "Meeting you today was like a breath of fresh air, Melina. Thank you for your encouragement."

"Wait." Melina caught her friend's arm, a sense of urgency in her expression that gave Julia pause.

Julia looked to Melina, a question in her eyes.

Melina bit her lower lip, a sense of urgency apparent in her strained features. "I believe the Lord has spoken to me, Julia. Spiritual forces are at work, moving through the city, whispering in the wind, stirring within the hearts and minds of this nation."

Julia stared at Melina, her heart pounding more and more rapidly.

"Evil men are the ready instruments of the enemy of God, and this is especially apparent from my perspective in Herod's fortress. God is working mightily through His Son, Jesus, and the enemy will not stand by complacently and watch. Be alert, be on guard, and stand firm in your faith. No matter what happens."

Julia nodded, her eyes somber, her palms sweating. Melina's warning resounded deeply within her heart.

As both women embraced and reluctantly parted ways, Julia purposed in her heart to heed Melina's warning. Perhaps it was God's grace that had prompted her friend to speak to her so plainly.

As if in response to Melina's urgent warning, a chill breeze picked up speed and rustled the fabric of Julia's simple garments, tugging at her shawl and her lush, long hair. Clasping her shawl tightly about her shoulders, Julia took the limestone stairway that would lead her to the ground level, cautiously eyeing her busy surroundings.

She was determined to heed Melina's warning, beseeching her faithful God for the strength to carry it out.

Be alert, be on guard, and stand firm in your faith. No matter what happens.

No matter what happens?

Julia couldn't help but wonder what the future held for her and for those she loved.

CHAPTER 2

Melina

Herod's Jerusalem palace was truly magnificent with its breathtaking gardens bursting with vibrant spring color, impressive pillared, marble porticoes, remarkably intricate stonework, dizzying frescoes swirling with geometric designs and patterns, enormous, comfortable bedchambers, luxurious ritual baths, and green garden groves overflowing with fountains and streams sheltered beneath the verdant canopy of sprawling leaves, flowering branches, and towering palms. The place reeked of unharnessed, limitless luxury, unbridled licentiousness, and raw, unrestrained power.

Melina wondered all the more why Herodias was so determined to leave it all behind for a dark prison fortress on the brink of civilization.

Something was indeed amiss.

"Where have you been?"

Melina entered Salome's audacious chambers with the caution of a graceful, reluctant doe approaching a snarling panther. "I do apologize for the delay, my lady, but I was sent to the Upper Market to purchase – "

"I don't care!" Salome interrupted, flipping her luxuriant black hair over one shoulder with a practiced air of disdain. "What takes you so long, anyway?"

Melina wasn't entirely sure how to respond to her young mistress's imperious demands. After all, Salome wouldn't care that, in a thoughtless moment of uncharacteristic liberality, Herod Antipas had allowed Melina this wondrous sliver of freedom, encouraging her to enjoy the scenery and fresh air on her trips to the market. The only thing Salome seemed to care about was, well, Salome. An unimportant servant girl's desire to enjoy the briefest respite in the fresh air and sunshine were of little consequence to the spoiled and demanding princess.

"When will you begin packing my belongings?"

For once, Melina appreciated Salome's impatience. This second question would prove easier to answer than the first. "Your mother, Lady Herodias, has instructed me to begin the preparations for your journey next week, my lady. I assure you that everything will be in order when you leave for Machaerus." She hid a smile of anticipation. Despite her unease about Herodias' silent scheming, perhaps she would enjoy a bit of peace and quiet in Salome's absence.

Seemingly satisfied with Melina's response, Salome turned to gaze at her own bright reflection in the gilded bronze mirror at her vanity. She sat in an elegant straight-backed chair, her perfect posture bespeaking both royalty and entitlement. She puckered her richly painted lips slightly, as if about to blow a kiss to some unfortunate bystander, her green eyes narrowing slightly beneath long, tilted black lashes. "Be sure to include my finest gowns. Herod's celebrations have been known to drag on for days, and I want an adequate wardrobe close at hand."

Melina could have reminded Salome that she possessed overflowing closets, billowing with expensive, imported gowns and finery, at each of her palace destinations. She could have also mentioned that the gowns would simply be returning to the Jerusalem palace within a few short weeks, as Herod would be expected to return to the Holy City for the ensuing Passover feast. But she refrained, knowing it would make little difference to Salome.

"As you wish, my lady."

"Oh, and Melina?"

Melina paused, a faint warning tingling upon her skin at Salome's unusual use of her given name. Having been in the middle of straightening the tousled Egyptian sheets upon Salome's unmade canopy bed, she straightened stiffly and turned to face her mistress, hands folded before her in a submissive stance.

"Be sure to pack your own belongings as well."

A small gasp escaped Melina's lips, and her hand flew to her throat, unbidden. Stunned, she attempted to gather her wits before Salome detected her hidden panic. Surely Salome didn't expect her to accompany her to Machaerus!

"My lady?" she managed, her voice squeaking slightly.

Salome arched a slender brow. "You object?"

Melina knew she treaded upon dangerous waters. She swallowed her own protests, her heart racing. "Of course not, my lady. I am simply surprised. Your stepfather usually insists I remain in Jerusalem to oversee the chores and kitchen expenditures –"

"Well, I hardly think the palace will fall apart in your brief absence," Salome snapped sharply, her tone dangerous. "I hope you haven't forgotten the fact that you are expendable – one stupid maidservant, easily replaced."

Melina lowered her head, clasping her hands nervously.

"Well?" Salome demanded imperiously.

"I haven't forgotten, my lady," Melina acquiesced, feeling small and very unimportant. Silently, she reminded herself that she was of great worth in the eyes of her loving Creator, despite her low status in popular Roman society.

"Good. Besides, I want you with me, and Herod would be a miserable wretch to refuse me this one small request before he sentences me to a life of drudgery in marriage to a dull man old enough to be my grandfather."

Melina winced at her mistress's blatant disrespect. Had Salome forgotten that her betrothed was an able ruler, a man reputed to care greatly for his subjects? Wouldn't he demonstrate the same thoughtful care toward Salome, his future wife? Perhaps the arrogant young royal should consider herself rather fortunate.

"I suppose that's why Herod has honored my request," Salome spewed bitterly, interrupting Melina's tumultuous thoughts. "Well that, and the fact that we will be returning to Jerusalem shortly after his birthday celebration. For some ridiculous, unknown reason, Herod Antipas trusts your presence in the palace. I daresay he is foolish enough to believe everything *would* fall apart without your staid presence here."

Despite her inner turmoil, Melina hid another smile. It would seem that Salome greatly desired her *staid presence* as well, despite her cutting insults.

"Now," Salome said in an authoritative tone, her mind returning to the business at hand, "You must bring for yourself only the most basic necessities. We needn't weigh down another beast or chariot with the unnecessary indulgences of a worthless serving wench. That would be absurd."

Oh, yes, absurd! Melina thought with a hint of annoyance. *And this coming from the woman who insists I pack her entire wardrobe, only to re-pack it and bring it back to Jerusalem in a matter of weeks!* Sighing, Melina repented silently, recognizing her own impatience and dislike toward the young woman God had called her to serve. And she was running out of time – Salome would soon be sent to Galilee to become Philip's wife. And then who could possibly share the love of God with the unhappy young woman?

But, Lord, she makes it so difficult!

"Do you understand my orders?" Salome spoke slowly, as if questioning a particularly slow child.

Melina forced a breezy smile, determined not to be ruled by her strong dislike for this demanding, imperious woman. After all, if she were to live by her own volatile emotions, then how would she be any different from Salome? As a child of God, Melina understood that her body was the Lord's temple, to be disciplined and exercised on a daily basis. By the grace of God, she would learn to die by her own fleshly desires so that she might live for Him.

Salome looked annoyed. "Why are you smiling like that? A moment ago, you looked about ready to faint."

Melina clung to the courage the Lord supplied. After all, if she were to contemplate her present circumstances, she would have great cause for fear and dismay.

"Well?" Salome crossed her arms, miffed.

More impatient demands. Naturally.

"It will be an honor to serve you on your journey, my lady," Melina responded, attempting to convince herself as well as Salome. After all, she had to trust that God was in control of her life.

And if God saw fit to send her to the harshest and most imposing prison fortress in the region, so be it. Everything He did was for a purpose.

Still, a hollow ache numbed the pit of her stomach, and her skin prickled as sweat beaded her fair brow. Closing her eyes, she recalled the dank, dark prison in which she had once stood, heard the iron grates slamming with thuds of terrible finality, remembered the screams of tortured prisoners and the swinging of an ax upon an elevated chopping block.

Machaerus was a place of death and untried executions. How many innocents had perished there, trapped within the impenetrable walls of the infamous Black Fortress?

Returning to her tasks, Melina pulled the plush bedcovers over Salome's rumpled bed, thankful that her mistress had returned to a thorough inspection of her own dazzling reflection in the enormous oval mirror. Now she could be alone with her thoughts and beseech the Lord in silent prayer.

Lord God, send your angels roundabout to guard me and protect me. May I accomplish Your will wherever I am sent.

Carefully smoothing the lush bedcovers, a nagging thought plagued Melina as she unwillingly contemplated frightening possibilities and worst-case scenarios... She attempted to shove her concerns far from her mind, and yet they persisted.

What if Herod decided to leave her at Machaerus? What if she were never permitted to return to Jerusalem, her home, her place of safety?

And then another thought, even more disturbing than the first, clouded her troubled mind. If she were sentenced to remain in that bleak desert fortress, she might never see Julia, her dearest friend, again. Nor would she be greeted by the easy smile nor teasing brown eyes of Malchus, the man with whom she had fallen deeply in love. What exactly would he have to say about this?

Biting her lower lip, Melina suppressed a shudder and continued about her chores. She imagined that question was best left unanswered.

CHAPTER 3

Malchus

The enchanting solitude of the magnificent garden peristyle tucked safely within the enormous, sprawling house belonging to Caiaphas, high priest of Israel, was balm to Malchus' troubled spirit. All four sides of the breathtaking, open-air courtyard were sheltered by impressive marble columns that bespoke aristocratic opulence, affluence, and indulgence. Flowering shrubs and ivy tendrils wound about graceful Grecian urns and climbed smooth, arched trellises. Delicate marble benches scattered about the lovely, tiled garden invited weary servants to rest their tired bodies and aching, sandaled feet.

Malchus sat with his head in his hands, tense as he attempted to empty his mind of the harried tasks he had been forced to accomplish that day. Caiaphas had proven particularly demanding in recent weeks. New lines had appeared around the eyes and mouth of the aging priest, his forehead creased as his features contorted in his usual fearsome scowl.

Nothing was as it should be. Caiaphas remained in a constant state of unpredictable tension, which unsettled the entire household staff and resulted in constant bickering among the servants, heaping additional strain upon relationships that were already tenuous and volatile.

The ministry of a traveling Rabbi named Jesus continued to grow at an alarming rate, further agitating Caiaphas and his ever-loyal Sanhedrin. Both the Pharisees and Sadducees – two religious sectors that were typically at odds – had united against the controversial teachings of Jesus, even as many in Judea claimed the Man to be the long-awaited Messiah.

To make matters worse, Melina – the love of his life – was becoming more and more entrenched in her religious convictions regarding the mysterious Carpenter of Galilee. Malchus had professed his love for her, his desire to marry her, and yet she held back. And Malchus suspected that the teachings of this Jesus had something to do with her hesitance to marry him which, of course, would fulfill his wildest dreams. The thought galled, driving a hard wedge between himself and the annoyingly practical teachings of the respected Rabbi.

One needn't have perfect vision to see that this Jesus incited rebellion and unrest wherever He happened to be. Is that what Melina desired for their future? Violent uprisings, political unrest, possible incarceration for their association with a controversial new sect, or worse? Wasn't Melina the least bit disturbed that multiple attempts had been made upon the life of this Man named Jesus? Somehow, He had escaped without a scratch every single time.

What was His secret?

And for the love of all that was good, why was Melina so drawn to the Teacher? Was she simply determined to shatter his own cherished hopes and dreams of a peaceful future with the woman he loved? Resentment began creeping into the corners of his tortured mind, despite his desperation to shut it out.

Why, oh why, was she being so difficult?

Malchus would have liked to blame Julia for Melina's fascination with the dangerous Rabbi. After all, he needed a worthy target by which he might vent his wrath. But he knew that blaming Julia would be unfair. As thoughtless and unpredictable as Julia could be, it had been Melina – not Julia – who had first sought the truth about Jesus.

The truth! What on earth was truth, anyway? God was true, he knew that now beyond all doubt. But had God truly placed His mark of approval upon this Jesus who seemed to tempt fate at every turn?

He certainly hoped not.

"I thought I would find you here."

Malchus winced, recognizing the voice even before Mara emerged from the dark enclave behind a row of marble pillars.

All he wanted was a moment – one simple, little moment – for himself! Was that too much to ask?

Malchus released a low chuckle, frustration evident as he lifted his face toward the woman approaching him with both reluctance and grace.

"How do you fare this evening, Malchus?"

Evening? Malchus gazed up at the open rectangle above the evenly spaced columns and realized stars were beginning to dust the dusky sky. Where had the time gone?

Mara hesitated when she reached his marble bench. After an awkward pause, Mara sat beside Malchus on the bench, their shoulders brushing slightly as she did so.

Malchus visibly stiffened even as he inwardly longed to restore their broken friendship. Mara had mothered him as a small boy when he had been forced into a life of service in a dangerous, tenuous household.

And yet he couldn't bring himself to trust her again.

"What draws you from your state of newfound matrimonial bliss in order to seek out my own miserable company?"

"Ah, dry humor combined with biting sarcasm that cuts straight to the quick," Mara mused, surprisingly undaunted. "You sound more like your cousin every day."

Malchus' eyes darkened at the mere mention of Alexander, his ambitious and self-gratifying kinsman. "You would compare me to that foul cretin?" he remarked incredulously. "And you say *my* accusations cut to the quick."

Mara managed a stilted laugh, wishing she hadn't mentioned the swarthy newcomer to Caiaphas' estate. She still felt uncomfortable when she recalled Alexander's brazen advances. He had urged her not to marry Lucius, indicating that he himself would be a better match.

Considering her deteriorating marriage with Lucius, she wondered if perhaps Alexander had been correct in his assessment. She had been certain that marriage would fulfill her deepest longings, and yet her union with a Roman soldier had resulted in nothing but misery and disillusionment. Whereas Lucius had been ravenous for her *before* their vows had transpired, he now possessed little to no interest in her.

What had changed? Was it simply the hunt that had drawn Lucius? Now she was a mere conquest, and perhaps he was in search of more interesting endeavors.

Her heart constricted at the thought. She wanted to make her marriage work! She really did. And that's where Malchus came in... *If* he didn't insist upon being a stubborn lout as she feared he might!

"I have come seeking a favor," Mara stated plainly, knowing that Malchus' suspicious mind would immediately detect her subterfuge if she attempted to dance around the subject.

"So, I gathered."

Mara gritted her teeth, irritated. She wished to call him an arrogant hypocrite straight to his face but restrained herself. After all, she needed his cooperation tonight.

"Despite the fact that you despise my very existence, will you please hear me out?"

Malchus gave her a sardonic look of amusement.

Mara plunged ahead anyway. "When will you see Melina again?"

Startled by her direct question, Malchus shifted uncomfortably. "I hardly think my social life is any of your concern."

"As if you had one," Mara snorted rather gracelessly. She caught herself mid-insult and forced an apologetic smile. "I'm sorry. I just really need to know."

"Why?"

"Why must you make everything so difficult?" Mara huffed, exasperated.

"I'm sorry, but I must be sure that my activities will not be monitored by anyone reporting back to that wolf you married."

Mara bristled. "I haven't spoken a word to Lucius regarding his assignment since the day we were married."

"Then perhaps that explains his sudden loss of interest in you."

Mara jumped to her feet, her eyes flashing angrily. "You are cruel, Malchus."

"Your *husband* is cruel, Mara. What else do you call someone who betrays his own comrades for a few extra shillings?"

"I did not come to discuss my husband!" That's why she needed Melina. Melina would know what to do. Perhaps she would even beseech the Lord on Mara's behalf. God always listened to Melina.

He had never seemed interested in listening to *her.*

Even as rebellious thoughts surfaced, Mara knew such thinking was accusatory and unfair. Perhaps she was the one who had failed to listen to the Lord, not the other way around. She had closed her ears to Him.

But even if she had severed her own line of communication with the Almighty, perhaps He would listen to the intercession of one who had remained faithful.

It was the only hope she possessed for her disintegrating marriage.

The two old friends measured each other for a

long moment, Mara's eyes blazing as Malchus' narrowed in suspicion.

"Why do you wish to see Melina?"

Mara considered a thousand different responses the stubborn young man might accept but decided to simply speak the truth. "Melina is unlike anyone I have ever met. There is no guile in her."

Malchus smiled faintly. "Melina is indeed a young woman without guile – I couldn't agree with you more. So, then you understand why I cannot allow you to corrupt the purity of her nature."

Mara's hands balled into fists at her sides. "She is a grown woman, Malchus, and you are neither her father nor her husband. Whether or not she desires to speak with me is her decision to make, not yours!"

Malchus rose slowly from his bench, his eyes meeting Mara's in challenge. "But she is the woman I love deeply, and I refuse to knowingly allow poisonous influences to corrupt her sweet nature."

"If her nature is as sweet as you suggest, then I doubt it could be so easily corrupted!"

Malchus studied Mara with an even greater dislike. Once, he had considered this maidservant a sweet woman of pure conduct. It had simply taken one foul influence to completely corrupt that innocent nature.

He refused to allow such a thing to happen to Melina.

With flashing eyes, Mara continued to study Malchus, the only sound between them the gentle bubbling of a lonely fountain. She lifted a brow, her face pinched with displeasure. "Look, Malchus, I needn't your permission to seek out a friend. If I wish to speak with Melina, then I shall speak to her.

I was simply trying to be thoughtful and civilized in the way I went about it – for your sake."

Malchus arched a sardonic brow. "Thoughtful and civilized? Is that how you describe your recent behavior?"

"Forget it, Malchus. I should have known you'd refuse to be reasonable. I will speak to Melina myself, with or without your permission." Turning sharply on her heel, Mara stalked angrily from the garden respite, her long brown braid trailing down her rigid back.

Malchus stared after her, clenching and un-clenching his fists at his sides. His blood pounded heavily in his temples as he unsuccessfully attempt-ed to curb his exasperation.

Mara had forsaken her morals and her heritage to marry a Gentile soldier who simply used her to further his own agenda. And several months of abiding with a ruthless man had sharpened Mara's once cheerful features, hardening her mouth and eyes, and evoking a harshness about her person that hadn't been there before.

He didn't like it one bit. Shaking his head in dis-may, he wondered what had happened to the kind woman he had once respected and adored.

In the midst of his great displeasure, Malchus hadn't the slightest idea that another pair of eyes watched with silent intensity as Mara hastened past the last row of towering pillars, her gait graceful despite her obvious agitation.

Leaning against a stately pillar encompassed in shadow, his body tensed like a poised viper, Alex-ander folded strong arms across his chest, his broad shoulders rising and falling with his own rapid breathing, his dark eyes boring into the unknowing back of the only woman he had ever truly wanted.

Black fury swelled within his chest until he longed to throw back his head and bellow out his rage. Instead, he remained taut and still, his eyes burning like two smoldering coals in the enveloping darkness.

With a sardonic curve of his lips, he supposed the oppressive and all-encompassing blackness mirrored the state of his own wicked soul.

CHAPTER 4

Julia

It had been one week since Melina's fateful warning upon the balcony overlooking the Upper Market. Despite her busyness as she tended to the never-ending household chores, cared for the unruly goats Barabbas had purchased, and ministered to the poor at the Pool of Bethesda, Melina's gentle exhortation continued to swirl about Julia's troubled mind in a maddening repetitive cycle.

Be alert, be on guard, and stand firm in your faith. No matter what happens.

Melina's words aroused a faint memory she almost wished to forget, for she was reminded of a dream of many nights past… a troubling dream, of raging waters churning up angry foam, followed by scorching heat and devouring flames. In her dream, the Lord had taken her by the hand and walked beside her, guiding her through it. His presence was surely comforting, but that did not change the terrifying truth: she would pass through the raging waters. She would go through the fire.

But at least she would not go alone.

"Julia!"

Lost in her silent reverie, Julia realized her feet had already carried her to her destination, the Upper Market, where Melina waited with shining eyes.

"You look troubled," Melina observed softly after the two women embraced.

Julia had no desire to cloud the joy of their meeting with a gloomy composure. "I'm fine, really!"

Melina arched a slender brow. "Are you?"

"Truly," Julia assured her, squeezing her friend's arm and leading her toward the inviting shade of the colonnades. "I've just been rather deep in thought lately, that's all."

Melina's pale green eyes sobered. "Julia, there's something I must tell you. But I should wait until Malchus arrives. He needs to know, too –"

"What do I need to know?"

Both women spun around, surprised by Malchus' swift and silent entrance.

"Malchus!" Melina's face grew warm when the handsome young man took her hand and kissed it.

Julia watched her two friends, amused. She resisted the urge to tease them both, though she was sorely tempted to do so.

Despite his air of casual ease, it was obvious Melina's words had troubled Malchus. "So?" he pried, he eyes intentionally playful. "Have you some grand announcement to make, Melina?"

"Yes."

Melina squared her shoulders bravely, and Julia's stomach tightened in knots as she sensed the gravity of whatever her friend was about to tell them.

"Let me guess," Malchus grinned, tweaking Melina's arm playfully. "You've decided to marry me!"

Melina's face bloomed with color, and Julia couldn't help it when a laugh escaped her lips. "We know it's bound to happen eventually," she teased. "Why fight it?"

"My thoughts exactly," Malchus said with great conviction, his brown eyes playful.

"If only the news were as joyous as that," Melina said quietly, forcing a brave smile.

Julia and Malchus sobered.

"What is it, Melina?" Malchus' eyes were serious, clouded with concern.

Melina bit her lower lip. "Before I say anything, just know it is only for a very short time. Just a matter of weeks, and –"

"Excuse me! I'm sorry to interrupt, but I must speak with Melina."

Three pairs of eyes turned in question toward the unexpected interruption.

Mara stood several paces away with an air of forced confidence even as her nervously twisting hands revealed her uncertainty.

"Mara!" Melina hurried to the tall woman, embracing her and then holding her at arms' length. "What a pleasant surprise!"

Feeling awkward and undoubtedly sensing Malchus' angry eyes upon her, Mara took a step back. "I didn't know how to find you, so I followed Malchus again." Her eyes darted briefly toward Malchus, but the expression on his face was anything but welcoming.

"You needn't ever feel the need to shadow someone to meet with us," Melina said warmly. "If you had asked Malchus, he would have been happy to have you join us!"

Again, Mara's eyes flitted to Malchus'. "Yes, I forget how kind and generous he is," she said pointedly. "I should have simply asked him. Malchus would never be unreasonable."

Julia noticed a muscle in Malchus' jaw twitch and suspected Melina was slightly mistaken in her assumption. She hid an amused grin as ominous undercurrents flowed between Mara and Malchus, yet gentle Melina was completely oblivious.

"In case you hadn't noticed, Mara, we were in the midst of a very important discussion. Perhaps you can arrange to meet with Melina another time," Malchus ground out through clenched teeth.

"Nonsense!" Melina exclaimed, her eyes bright. "Mara has traveled all this way to meet with us. It would be a shame for her to have wasted the time."

"Yes, we wouldn't want her wasting anyone's time," Malchus sighed under his breath. What about his precious time with Melina? Mara seemed to have no qualms about wasting that!

"Tell me, what's on your mind, Mara?" Melina's eyes glowed with compassion.

Again, Mara's dark eyes darted accusingly toward Malchus. "Perhaps we could speak alone."

Alone! Malchus' blood boiled. He had but once a week to visit the woman he loved. How dare this selfish, spiteful woman infringe upon that! He wanted to put his foot down but knew he would hurt Melina by doing so. She had compassion upon every single one of God's creatures, wretched as they might be. If he were to turn a troubled woman away, Melina would never forgive him!

Melina turned pleading eyes upon him. "Malchus, Julia, would you be willing to give us a moment?"

"Julia can stay," Mara said stoutly.

The nerve! Malchus' hands balled into fists. First, Mara intrudes upon his sacred meeting! Next, she insists the others stay while sending him along on his merry way!

"Now, see here –"

Sensing Malchus' ire, Julia touched his shoulder. "A walk will do us both good, Malchus. Come along. Let's give them some time."

Malchus stiffened, torn between his love for Melina and his angst toward Mara. "Ten minutes. I'll give you ten minutes, Mara, then I expect to resume my important conversation with Melina."

"Another shining example of your kindness and generosity," Mara said curtly.

Malchus turned on his heels and stalked away without another word, leaving Mara to wonder what form of vengeance he might inflict upon her at a later date.

Sensing the tension between the two old friends for the first time, Melina looked to Julia with questioning eyes.

Shrugging, Julia slipped after Malchus, leaving Melina alone with the troubled maidservant.

CHAPTER 5

Julia and Malchus returned in precisely ten minutes.

Melina was offering Mara a farewell embrace. The woman had tears in her eyes, and her shoulders drooped in a dejected fashion as she left the Upper Market without a second glance at Malchus or Julia.

"Well?" Malchus demanded, an edge to his tone. "What was that all about?"

Melina sighed, her expression troubled. "Mara asked me not to divulge the details, but she is very unhappy in her marriage and needs our prayers."

"Mara? Unhappy to be married to a pompous, arrogant lout who runs around with other women and ignores her very existence?" Malchus said, his brows raised in mock surprise. "If only we had warned her."

Melina shook her head sadly. "We always think we can change people, Malchus. Unfortunately, we can't. Only God can. And Mara is discovering that the hard way."

Julia sighed in commiseration. "Poor girl. I understand what she is going through."

"I fear whatever sage advice you may have offered

our dear little Mara fell upon deaf ears, Melina. Mara is stubborn as a mule and always will be," Malchus said bitterly.

"There is hope for her, Malchus. She recognizes her folly and desires a way out."

"That's exactly what she desires, Melina – a way out. And an easy one, at that," Malchus put in bitterly. "Repentance is the last thing on her mind."

"But these are the very things that drive us to our knees, Malchus. When awakened to our own inadequacies and shortcomings, we are prompted to recognize our need for a Savior."

"I agree with Melina, Malchus. That's exactly what happened to me when I married Barabbas," Julia added thoughtfully. "Before, I thought I knew what I wanted and what I was doing. But after I failed miserably, I turned to God and He restored me. My marriage is still difficult, but the Lord walks me through it. He sustains me."

"Though she doesn't know it yet, Mara seeks the Lord – not a perfect marriage. No person on this earth can fill our longing and desperate need for our Creator. Mara longs for Him, even though the enemy of her soul has convinced her that it is simply marital happiness she seeks." Melina explained. "But there is still time to convince her otherwise. And what a time to seek the Savior, when the Son of God walks among us!"

Warning bells went off in Malchus' mind, and he responded far more harshly than he intended. "Melina, by all means, share the Word of God with her till Kingdom come. But whatever you do, do *not* tell her about your convictions regarding that Prophet Jesus you are so enamored with."

Melina stared at Malchus, stunned.

Feeling as if she were intruding upon a private argument between her two friends, Julia cleared her throat uncomfortably and considered fleeing the scene.

"It's for your own good, and I need you to trust me about this," Malchus insisted, realizing he had startled both women with his vehement outburst.

"But, Malchus," Melina said, a look of confusion tightening her soft features, "I believe Jesus is the Son of God. How can I keep that to myself? Shall I hoard a priceless treasure while others perish by the wayside?"

Malchus ran his hand through his dark, wavy hair, exasperated. "You don't know everything that woman is involved in."

"I know she seeks the truth about God, and that includes His Son, Jesus, who has come to earth to redeem His people. Wouldn't you wish Mara to be counted among them?"

"And what if she doesn't wish to be? Melina, listen to me. Don't say a word to her about Jesus. Do you understand? Your life could be in jeopardy if you do."

The color drained from Melina's face, but the strength of her convictions was still evident in her eyes.

Julia drew alongside her friend and took her hand, willing her strength and support. "Malchus, I think you need to tell us the whole story."

Malchus released a frustrated sigh. "Mara's husband, Lucius, reports directly to Caiaphas. And Caiaphas has entrusted him with the task of hunting down those who follow this Jesus."

"But why?" Julia's eyes sparked angrily.

"Because Caiaphas detests Jesus. He burns with jealousy against the Man – against His miracles and His great following. My concern is that, eventually, Caiaphas will take action against the followers of this new sect." Malchus turned to Melina, his eyes pleading. "Melina, I love you. I can't lose you."

Melina remained thoughtfully silent, the color slowly returning to her face.

"Now do you understand why I've asked you to be silent?"

After a long pause, Melina offered the slightest nod.

Malchus breathed a sigh of desperate relief. "Then you will do as I ask and leave the matter alone?"

Melina looked to Malchus, her eyes filled with sadness and pity. "I understand your concern, Malchus, and I appreciate your desire to protect me. But I cannot keep silent about Jesus."

Malchus couldn't believe what he was hearing. "Surely you understand how serious this is!"

"I do. But the prospect of Mara losing her soul is far more serious to me."

"For heaven's sake, Melina! It would be by her own choice!"

"And I am to stand silently by?"

Julia reached out and touched Malchus' arm, sensing his rising frustration. "Malchus, surely the high priest has far better things to do than track down a humble maidservant who has done nothing but serve her masters well."

"Spoken like a woman who knows next to nothing about my master."

Melina's eyes filled with sympathy. "Caiaphas is

simply your earthly master, Malchus. But we serve a powerful Master who holds the entire universe in His hands. Nothing can happen without His permission. His will prevails in our lives, despite the wicked intentions of evil men."

"And what if those evil men seek to end your life? What then?"

"What men intend for evil, our God can use for good, Malchus."

"Oh, Melina!"

Saddened to her very core, Melina took Malchus' hand and gazed into his dark brown eyes, willing him to grasp the strength and conviction she possessed. "Please don't worry about me, Malchus. God is in control, and I am not afraid."

"The little lamb needn't fear the roaring beast to get eaten."

A soft chuckle escaped Melina's lips.

Julia's gaze flitted from her friend's sweet, serene features to the taut expression of the troubled manservant. She sensed the tension between them growing, and it pained her to watch.

Couldn't Malchus see that he was driving a wedge between himself and Melina by his pathetic lack of faith? Julia wanted to shake him but doubted it would do any good.

It would seem Mara wasn't the only one as stubborn as a mule.

Malchus reached for Melina, drawing her closer to him, his insides trembling in the most unpleasant way. What if he lost her? How could he live without her? Didn't she care if her life was in danger? He would do everything in his power to protect her, to save her. He just couldn't lose her.

For whoever desires to save his life will lose it, but whoever loses his life for My sake and the gospel's will save it... The silent admonition whispered its way into Malchus' heart, troubling him beyond reason. Where had he heard such impossible words? When he remembered they had been spoken by Jesus Himself, causing an uproar among Caiaphas' stern-faced lackeys, he stiffened.

"I would feel so much better if you would simply promise not to speak of Him."

Melina gazed up into his eyes, a smile in her own. "But I have already spoken of Him."

"For the love of –"

"Please, don't be angry, Malchus. Mara has known about my faith long before this. I spoke to her about it before she even married Lucius."

Julia's lips tipped up in a rueful grin. "She did. I was there."

Malchus ran a nervous hand through his abundant hair and turned away, his heart pounding. What was this tightening pain in his chest? Was he actually *angry* at Melina? The thought shocked and surprised him. He couldn't fathom the depth of his own feelings.

Assuming it was safest to simply change the subject, Julia quipped brightly, "Melina, weren't you going to tell us something?" Whatever it was, surely Malchus would receive it better than Melina's refusal to keep silent.

Sensing the dark direction of Malchus' thoughts, Melina cringed when she remembered the subject she had yet to broach with him.

Malchus turned his head, gazing at Melina as if awaiting the killing blow.

"I am being assigned to Machaerus to tend to Salome during Herod's birthday feast."

The silence that followed was deafening.

After a long, awkward pause, Malchus said quietly, "For how long?"

"Only for a few weeks. Herod must return for the Passover feast."

Fear for Melina washed over Julia like a roiling tide, but she refrained from speaking her concerns aloud. It would only worsen the tense situation between her two friends.

But *Machaerus?* How could a delicate flower like Melina possibly survive in such a merciless environment?

"When can we see you again, Melina?" Julia asked quickly, eager to see her friend safe and sound once the entire ordeal was behind them.

"Shall we plan to meet again the week after Passover? I can't imagine Herod could spare me before that."

"I'll be here," Julia said firmly, her gaze traveling to Malchus. His eyes grazed hers briefly, and she attempted to silently convey her message as clearly as possible: *If you refuse to support her in this, Malchus, so help me –*

"Malchus?" Melina touched his arm, troubled. "Say something."

Malchus' jaw remained rigid, his Adam's apple bobbing slightly as he swallowed. Apparently, her words were difficult to digest.

The truth was, Malchus was unnerved. He was losing her. He hated the idea of so much land between them, even as he sensed that the distance between them was growing steadily even now, as they stood face to face. Swallowing his anger, he said quietly, "I won't remind you that these treacherous journeys wouldn't be required if you would accept my earnest proposal of marriage. Then you would be nestled safely with me at a beautiful estate."

"Safe beneath the watch and care of a violent man whom you loathe?" The words escaped Melina's lips before she was even aware of them. Her heart constricted at the look that Malchus gave her.

Biting her lower lip, she reached for him. "Malchus, I'm sorry. But we have to believe that God is the one orchestrating our circumstances. His will is our place of safety, be it a frightful desert fortress or the house of a corrupt high priest."

"How can you be so sure it is God arranging this? What if His plan *does* include me, Melina? Is that really so hard to believe?"

"I pray that it might be so."

"Then make it so!"

"Only if God allows," Melina whispered, her eyes brimming with tears.

"And how exactly will God communicate that to you, Melina? A banner in the sky? A message in the clouds? A chorus of singing angels? A trumpet blast in the heavenlies?"

Melina lowered her gaze, encompassed by a peace she could not understand. "Most often, Malchus, it is a still small voice that gets me. I have yet to hear any singing angels or blasting trumpets."

Malchus gave a slow nod, his eyes conveying the hopelessness he felt. "Well, then, do keep your ears open and listen well. A voice like that could be easily missed." Gently grazing Melina's soft cheek with the back of his hand, he met her gaze briefly before turning on his heels and walking away.

Melina watched his stiffly retreating back, tears trickling down her cheeks.

Julia took her hand again, desperate to console her friend. "It's going to be all right, Melina. He'll come around."

"This wasn't the farewell I had anticipated."

"It never is," Julia said sadly. "But God is merciful. He works in our hearts. He will do so with Malchus."

"Why is he so determined to reject the Son of God?"

"I don't think he intends to reject Him," Julia mused thoughtfully. "I think he is afraid of Him."

"But why?"

"Only God knows his heart, Melina. We can both pray for him. God will hear and He will act."

Melina nodded, a wobbly smile gracing her lips. "Can we pray right now, Julia?"

"You know we can!"

Clasping their hands and bowing their heads, the two young women prayerfully sought their faithful Creator.

"Lord God," Melina prayed fervently, "You are the only stable thing in this unstable world. You are our Rock, our Anchor, our Place of safety. Protect me, Father, as I travel to a dangerous place. Be with Julia in my absence and give her strength and peace. And be with our brother, Malchus. Turn His heart toward Your Son, Jesus..." she paused, her voice catching slightly as tears coursed down her cheeks. "Stagger him by the power of Your love... No matter what it takes."

CHAPTER 6

Melina

The journey to Machaerus proved every bit as treacherous as the prison fortress itself. Roman roads were neatly paved yet designed to cross over the most expedient route rather than the simplest or safest.

Melina was at her wit's end as she attempted to pacify her inconsolable young mistress. Despite her comfortable conditions within a specially enclosed chariot, Salome was inexorable. Bitter tirades poured from her mouth, battering Melina like an angry flood.

Salome's complaints were many, and solutions were often completely out of Melina's control. It was too hot. Too dusty. The roads were too bumpy. Too uneven. She couldn't rest. She couldn't sleep. She was too tired. Too hungry. Too thirsty. Too stiff. Too sore.

In a fit of frustration, Salome would demand that Melina accompany her in the chariot to tend to her countless needs. Moments later, the angry princess would swing open the door, loudly commanding her "insolent" maid to walk.

"You're no good to me!" Salome had shrieked on more than one occasion. "No good to me at all! Why did I even request your presence here?"

Melina had wondered if any human being on earth would be capable of meeting every single one of Salome's impossible and harsh demands.

Now, Melina sat within the enclosed chariot beside her brooding mistress, fanning the young woman's face with a small palm frond that provided little relief.

"Mother was a fool to insist we come here," Salome ground out, her delicate forehead beaded with sweat. "We can thank her for suffering this miserable heat."

Melina fanned a bit harder, bracing herself for Salome's next outrage. She supposed she would soon be on foot again, walking alongside her mistress's jouncing carriage. Her eyes traveled toward her own sandaled feet. She wasn't surprised to see that they were sunburnt and swollen, her leather sandal straps chafing against tender flesh until her feet were nearly raw. Painful blisters begged for her attention.

Grimacing slightly, Melina prayed that Salome would not sentence her to walk again soon.

Impatiently, Salome flicked aside the crimson curtain draped delicately over the open window. "We've nearly reached the dreadful place."

Melina's heart nearly stopped as she caught her first glimpse of a looming hilltop, the dangerous fortress perched atop the sheer incline like a fierce bird of prey. A narrow road paved in white limestone wound its way about the mountainous hilltop, and suddenly, walking didn't seem so disagreeable as Melina imagined Salome's gilded chariot pitching over the side of that ridiculously narrow road clinging to the very brink of the cliff face.

Another thought overlapped her first, this one even more disturbing. She envisioned a man shackled at the feet and wrists, his sandaled feet chafed even worse than her own, the shackles biting painfully into his wrists and ankles. He walked with his head down, his arms secured behind his back, the merciless desert sun beating heavily upon his dejected form. Severe guards walked in step before and behind him, escorting him to an unjust, undeserved fate.

Melina's heart constricted within her chest as tears sprang to her eyes.

John the Baptizer.

She was about to enter the compound that had housed the innocent man far too long. Would she be privileged to meet the fiery prophet whom she had heard so much about? Was there any possibility he might be set free?

Bowing her head, Melina closed her eyes and prayed it would be so.

***

Julia

Julia laughed briskly as she brushed fine, freshly milled flour from her bare arms, hands, and the front of her garment. It had been an extremely enjoyable afternoon. She never tired of milling grain with her dear friend and neighbor, Deborah. The hard work was invigorating and energizing, the conversation uplifting and restoring.

Deborah scooped several generous mounds of flour into a sack before carefully tying the heavy bundle and handing it to Julia.

"There you are, my dear," the older woman beamed, her gray eyes shining.

Julia accepted the heavy sack, eager to bake fresh loaves before her husband returned home. "Thank you, Deborah," she said, her eyes dancing. "I can smell the bread baking already!"

Julia cherished these moments with Deborah, for they were growing more and more sparse. Deborah's husband, Isaac, believed they were called to actively participate in the ministry of Jesus, resulting in much travel and less time at home.

Deborah's expression sobered, and she took Julia's arm before the young woman could duck out the low doorframe.

"Julia, I must speak with you a moment before you depart."

Julia's stomach clenched, for she detected a hint of concern in Deborah's previously cheerful tone.

"Come, sit with me a moment," Deborah said invitingly, patting the wooden bench beside her.

Julia did as commanded. When she met Deborah's gaze, she was unsettled by the sadness reflected in the deep gray eyes.

"Is everything all right?" Julia asked weakly, concern washing over her.

"Oh, I'm sure it is, my dear," Deborah replied reassuringly, patting the younger girl's knee as a grandmother might. "God is in control, after all."

Julia braced herself for whatever Deborah might say next.

Deborah released a long sigh, clearly considering the best way to broach a difficult topic.

"Isaac believes that Jesus has reached a crucial point in His ministry. He has sent out disciples all over the known world to share the Gospel."

Julia nodded her understanding. It was no secret that, apart from the famous twelve that seemed to accompany the Teacher wherever He went, Jesus possessed many more disciples eager to carry out His orders and share the Good News with lost souls.

"Isaac is a skilled sailor, and naturally his skills are needed in the ministry right now. Disciples must travel to spread the word, and Isaac feels called to volunteer his services. He can assist in taking these men wherever they are called to travel. This would be a full-time venture, I'm afraid, and as his wife, I believe I am called to accompany him."

Julia's throat constricted. Blinking back tears, she lowered her head so that Deborah wouldn't witness her private struggle.

Her dear, beloved Deborah was leaving her.

What on earth would she do without this dear woman's love, guidance, and counsel?

The older woman tipped up Julia's chin, her own eyes gleaming with tears. "Now," she said shakily, "I've spoken with my husband, for there is no doubt in my mind that the Lord placed me right here to minister to you, child. Even so, Isaac is certain he is not mistaken. Despite my own misgivings, I know what the Scriptures say. If a husband and wife reach an impasse as we have, the wife is called to submit. I don't like it, not one bit. But I cannot forsake the commands of my Lord."

Julia nodded, holding back tears. "How long will you be away?"

"Isaac's decision isn't final yet, dear one. He is still seeking the Lord about it, as am I. But I felt you needed to be aware of the situation – most importantly, because you can join us in prayer as we seek the Lord's will in this."

Julia managed a slow nod. Her hands felt like lead her lap, her heart equally heavy.

Draping a protective arm about the younger woman, Deborah smiled and offered a reassuring squeeze. "Remember, God is in control, Julia. He always knows what He is doing. I can't stand the idea of being away from you for such a long time, but – "

"*To everything there is a season, a time for every purpose under heaven,*" Julia whispered, her eyes shining through her tears. Even now, the unfailing love of her Savior washed over her, comforting and reassuring. "If the Lord has called you to minister elsewhere for a time, then who am I to object? You are afraid to accompany your husband because you believe you were called to help me, and so you were. You were here for me when I needed you, Deborah, and the Lord knew I would need your steady hand and wise guidance. But the Lord may have other things in store for you now – another season. His will is always best, even when we don't understand it."

Deborah took Julia's hand and squeezed it. "That doesn't mean I'm not hoping the Lord will change my husband's mind!"

Julia laughed, silently committing her cause to the Lord and purposefully refusing to waste any time fretting over the situation. "How can I argue with that?"

Deborah joined her in tearful laughter.

"But we shall pray for God's will, even above our own," Julia said, forcing another smile.

"Yes," Deborah agreed, her eyes determined. "We must pray for an answer."

Bowing their heads, the two women clasped trembling hands and sought their Lord.

CHAPTER 7

Melina

Machaerus was in a state of uproar.

The staff scurried about the compound like frantic, frightened mice as Herodias oversaw the preparations for Herod's fabulous birthday celebration and feast. As difficult to please as her stubborn daughter, Herodias released a flood of commands that nearly ran the servants ragged in their desperate attempts to accomplish her bidding in time for the lavish feast she would host in honor of the tetrarch, Herod Antipas.

Deliveries of fresh flowers, wine, and rich, edible delicacies flooded the compound as servants hastened to and fro, attempting to care for the recently acquired goods. Herodias observed the chaos with an expression of grim amusement, her slender brows arched antagonistically.

Melina was relieved to be somewhat cloistered from the household panic and frenzied activity – especially after discovering that Porcius was now the overseer at Machaerus. His harsh threats of years past still rang loudly in Melina's ears. He had never been popular in Jerusalem, and perhaps that was why Herod had chosen to relocate him, assigning Chuza to the Jerusalem estate. Unlike Chuza, who governed the magnificent estate with calm authority and surprising humility, Porcius had lorded his power over those beneath him with an uncompromising iron fist. The man was pompous and fearsome as ever, and Melina decided that Machaerus fit him like a glove.

Dismissing her troubling thoughts about Porcius, Melina attempted to acquaint herself with Salome's royal chamber. Surprisingly, Salome's suite in Machaerus rivaled her private quarters in Jerusalem. Overflowing with garish, gilded furniture, elegant marble statues, hanging chandeliers, plush Oriental rugs, and a massive canopy bed, the suite left little to be desired.

Still, Salome found fault with nearly everything. The air was stale. The gold, silver, and bronze furnishings needed polishing. The surfaces were not adequately dusted. She couldn't find anything she was looking for.

It seemed that nothing suited her.

Busily unpacking Salome's vast array of lavish gowns, Melina lost track of her mistress's long list of complaints. She couldn't possibly keep up with them, anyway. She prayed as she worked, her senses tingling as she considered her close proximity to the famous prophet she longed to meet.

Rather like the grand palace in Jerusalem, this compound bore the garish stamp of Herod the Great. The prison and fortress itself were harsh and imposing. Protected on three sides by sloping ravines, Machaerus had become the first line of defense against eastern invaders, and it was quite effective. Soaring watchtowers and a sea of rigid sentries warned invaders against a fatal mistake.

Buried within the heart of this ruthless compound was a magnificent pleasure palace rivaling those of Jerusalem, Tiberias, and Herodium. Guests were delighted by the luxurious chambers, heated baths, and a sprawling garden carefully maintained by specially designated household staff despite the stifling heat and fierce desert climate. Cloistered at the center of the ostentatious palace was a stately peristyle courtyard surrounded by magnificent marble pillars. Bright scarlet paint emphasized the size and beauty of the Grecian pillars enclosing the open-air peristyle, beautifully corresponding with the rare, fiery red tiles covering the roofed sections. Underfoot, breathtaking golden and marble tiles swirled in dizzying geometric patterns, reflecting the dazzling sunlight like a sea of freshly hammered gold.

According to Salome, Herod's celebration would take place in the lavish peristyle courtyard. Melina imagined that Herod's guests would be quite impressed once everything was in order. The peristyle would fairly gleam in the firelight, illuminating the sprawling banquet table piled high with golden goblets of wine and platters burdened with rich delicacies and refreshments.

Carefully hanging the last gown, Melina took a deep breath and attempted to calm her frayed nerves. As if Salome's incessant whining and impossible demands weren't enough to set her completely on edge, the wicked grin Herodias had worn while overseeing the celebratory feast had Melina's stomach in constant knots.

Herodias was far too composed. Too confident. The gleam in her eyes was predatory, her smile avaricious.

Something wasn't right.

"I know what to do!"

Melina nearly jumped a foot when Salome slammed open her enormous double doors, barreling into the vast chamber like a stampeding bull.

Taking a deep breath to steady herself, Melina straightened and forced a smile. This was the first time Salome had looked pleased since leaving Jerusalem. "My lady?"

Closing the intricate double doors behind her, Salome pressed her back against the gilded bronze surface, her emerald eyes twinkling conspiratorially.

"Melina, you'll never believe what I'm about to do!"

Heart hammering, Melina hoped all the color hadn't gone out of her face. The fact was, she probably wouldn't have any trouble at all believing whatever ridiculous, far-fetched scheme Salome had concocted. The princess' behavior far surpassed the realm of *unbelievable*, bordering downright maniacal.

Before Melina could form a response, Salome released a delighted squeal, bounding away from the closed doors and reaching for Melina's arm. Drawing her handmaiden into a lovely enclave overlooking the impressive peristyle courtyard, Salome leaned forward and whispered conspiratorially, "I've found a way out of marrying that filthy old goat!"

Melina's eyes widened as she stared at her mistress in stunned disbelief. "Philip?" she managed weakly after what seemed to be an eternity of silence.

Salome clapped her delicate hands ecstatically, giggling like a young girl. "Yes, Philip. Who else? Isn't it marvelous?"

"But, my lady —"

Salome's eyes narrowed dangerously before Melina could complete her protest.

"But... but how?" Melina finished lamely, realizing any argument she might present would prove futile and only excite Salome's wrath.

Salome's eyes danced in gleeful anticipation. "I'll tell you, only because I'll simply burst at the seams if I don't tell *someone!* But you are not to speak a word about this to anyone upon pain of death! Do you hear me?"

Melina swallowed nervously and nodded dumbly, wishing to stop her ears and flee the room.

Gazing out the enormous arched windows overlooking the elegant courtyard, a slow smile transformed Salome's exotic features. She watched as servants scurried about the tiled peristyle, arranging a sprawling triclinium-style banquet table. Herod's guests would recline upon plush settees surrounding the enormous L-shaped table, which enclosed the center of the courtyard to create a central stage where the entertainers would perform up close and personal, delighting the dinner guests.

"As you can imagine, Mother has lined up a rather impressive repertoire of entertainers to please the guests at tomorrow's banquet."

Melina attempted to hide her grimace. She had no doubt Herodias had arranged for an impressive repertoire to dazzle her guests. The Romans were famous for their obscene and vile entertainments, and Herod's thirst for new talent was infamous. It was rumored he had even enjoyed the early preaching of John the Baptizer, for John's fiery outbursts had provided a unique diversion completely unlike anything Herod had ever witnessed.

"But," Salome continued, interrupting Melina's train of thought, "she has been unable to locate entertainers worthy to present the final performance..." her voice trailed off as her eyes danced with salacious mischief. "As you know, the grand finale must be quite a show – we want to give the guests a performance they will never forget, something they'll talk about for *years* to come..."

Melina's pulse quickened, for she sensed she wouldn't like whatever Salome had to say next.

"And *that*," Salome continued, her lips tipping in a wicked smile, "is exactly what I intend to give them!"

Melina stared at Salome, her heart pounding. "My lady?"

"You know I love my mother more than anything on this earth and I would do anything for her, Melina. There's nothing I wouldn't do for that woman. But as much I love her, she is an ignorant fool. She's asked me to dance the final performance tomorrow night! Me! Her own husband will be groveling at my feet. Can you imagine her naïveté?"

Attempting to hide her alarm, Melina struggled to appear composed. Herodias was many things, but she was not naïve. The woman was a skilled manipulator, a master deceiver. Despite Salome's confident assessment, Melina felt certain that Herod's malignant wife was carrying out a carefully conceived and well-crafted plan.

"So, I am to dance tomorrow night, and believe me, it'll be unlike anything Herod has ever seen! I know how to get what I want. I've bewitched a hundred men before this," Salome rushed on, her cheeks flushed with feverish excitement.

"But, my lady," Melina fumbled weakly, her heart pounding, "wouldn't such a dance besmirch your reputation before your approaching union with Philip?"

"You stupid child, didn't you hear anything I said?" Salome chided her in annoyance. "That's the whole point! This is my chance to free myself from a completely unwanted marriage! Philip will be scandalized once word gets out about my performance. But just in case that's not enough to force him to break the engagement, I have a foolproof plan to drive the nail into the coffin."

Melina was having trouble following Salome's wicked scheme. "And what is that, my lady?" she asked faintly, hoping Salome's idea would prove too fanciful or far-fetched to work.

"Herod becomes a blundering idiot when intoxicated. I've seen him fawn all over dozens of dancing girls, making a complete fool of himself and infuriating my mother. If particularly pleased with a woman, he grovels at her feet, insisting that he grant her any wish. Oh, it's sickening. I've seen him do it a hundred times."

Melina hid another grimace. Unfortunately, she'd witnessed the same sad episode on numerous occasions.

"Well," Salome continued, her lovely face coming alive with excitement as the plan unfolded in her mind. "I will completely *mesmerize* Herod and his guests until they're groveling at *my* feet! Considering the exciting performance I'm about to deliver, I wouldn't be surprised if Herod offers me half his kingdom! The stupid, drunken wretch."

Melina stared at Salome, her eyes wide in shock.

"Well, he can keep his miserable kingdom," Salome snorted, tossing her lush black hair over her shoulder. "I don't want it."

Melina imagined the citizens of Herod's domain would be grateful.

"But I'll tell him what I do want: Herod can repay me by breaking my engagement to Philip and granting me the freedom to marry whomever I choose, *if* I choose to marry at all."

"But, my lady," Melina managed, warning bells going off in her mind, "do you think it will work?"

"Of course, it will work! I know exactly what to expect from Herod. And he wouldn't dare refuse me after swearing an oath before a hundred guests! I suppose his insufferable pride will actually prove useful to me for once."

"But what will your mother say?"

"My mother is the one who asked me to dance in the first place!"

"But is she expecting the type of dance you plan to perform?"

Salome grinned, twisting a strand of silky hair between two slender fingers. "I doubt anyone on earth will be expecting the show I'll display tomorrow night."

Melina shook her head frantically, terror gripping her for a reason she couldn't quite comprehend. She had to convince Salome to reconsider her actions! Didn't she realize her safety – possibly her very life – was at stake? How would Philip respond if alerted to the vile actions of his betrothed? And what if Herodias burned with envy when Herod responded to Salome's wicked advances? "My lady, I beg you to consider –"

"No, no, I don't want to hear your prudish protests. I swear, Melina, I detest your ridiculously rigid sense of morality."

"But, my lady –"

"Now go! I have to prepare for my performance, and I don't need you in here watching me rehearse and casting judgment all over the fun I'm about to have!"

"But, my lady –"

"Go!" Salome gave Melina a good, hard shove toward the gilded double doors, dismissing her.

"What shall I do in my absence, my lady?" Melina asked, her voice trembling.

"I don't care. Do anything you wish. Take the afternoon off and enjoy yourself, for all I care. Just stay out of my way!"

Before Melina could protest further, Salome had shoved her into the outer corridor and slammed the double doors behind her with a resounding *thud*.

Covering her face with her hands, Melina attempted to still her own frightened trembling. Something was terribly, terribly wrong. And she felt completely helpless to discover what was amiss, much less to do anything about it.

"Precious Lord, what should I do?"

Entirely unexpectedly, the answer came.

Squaring slender shoulders, Melina resolved to obey despite her quaking fear.

She knew exactly what she must do.

CHAPTER 8

Tunneling deep beneath the grand hallways and impressive chambers of Herod's pleasure palace, the ruthless underground prison of Machaerus was a dreadful place. Rows of stone holding cells and iron grates appeared to writhe beneath dancing shadows cast by flickering torches. Armed sentries stood at the alert, the tips of their iron spears glistening in the eerie firelight.

Despite the fact that she had seen it once before as a young girl, Melina was completely unprepared for the rancor and wretchedness of this merciless dungeon. The smoky haze lingering in the air burned her eyes, and repugnant odors of mold and rotting earth mingling with the stench of the decaying flesh of dead rodents and the unpleasant smell of unbathed men assaulted her senses. The extremely poor ventilation within the underground chamber was a breeding ground for all manner of fetid odors. Melina found herself taking short, shallow breaths, and for a brief moment, she was certain she would vomit, for the environment was so intensely dark and repulsively oppressive she could hardly breathe.

Roman prisons were certainly not designed for the long-term housing of prisoners. As Roman justice was infamously swift and merciless, prisons were ordinarily used to hold criminals for a very brief period of time while they awaited trial. Many times, prisoners were crowded into small rooms and shackled together rather than given individual cells. More often than not, a swift execution followed a prisoner's trial. It was unlikely the prisoner would ever return to his cell.

Taking these things into account, Melina wondered how on earth John the Baptizer had survived these wretched living conditions for an entire year. Melina wondered if he would have preferred a trial followed by a swift execution. How could any human being stomach this horrid dungeon for an entire year? It was unthinkable.

Wrapping her arms about her own slender body, Melina attempted to stifle her fierce shuddering as a neatly uniformed guard led her down a dark chamber lined with empty holding cells. Silently, she thanked God the soldiers on duty had maintained a sense of honor in their treatment of her. Down here, deep within the bowels of the earth, she supposed they could do anything they wished to a helpless, unchaperoned maid. Rather than taking advantage of her or mocking her fear-soaked entreaty, this soldier had simply accepted her timid request without so much as lifting a brow in question.

Thankfully, having only just arrived at Machaerus, Melina hadn't been recognized as Salome's handmaiden. She had a sneaking suspicion that servants were not typically granted entrance in the prison.

Lost in thought, Melina's breath caught in her throat when bold fingers brushed roughly and unexpectedly against her bare arm. The gruff laughter of crude men grated upon her raw nerves. Startled and frightened, she nearly plowed into the guard ahead of her.

The guard turned to see what the commotion was about.

Melina had been so lost in her troubled thoughts she hadn't noticed the men crusted in filth behind the prison bars to her left. One of them leered at her with bulbous eyes, his lips curling to reveal yellowing teeth.

Repulsed that the vile criminal had dared touch her, she hurried to catch up with the guard, who cast a menacing glare in the prisoner's direction.

The leering smile vanished from the prisoner's dirt-encrusted features at the sight of the soldier's cold eyes.

Melina forced herself to pay far more attention to her surroundings. She had no desire to be caught off guard in such an unpleasant manner again.

The soldier's hob-nailed sandals echoed loudly upon the cold stone floor as he led Melina toward the end of the filthy chamber and paused before a set of unforgiving iron bars.

The most dangerous criminals were often kept within the furthest reaches of Roman prisons. Surely the soldiers didn't consider John a threat!

"You have a visitor." The soldier tapped the iron grate roughly, then turned on his heels and disappeared into the flickering shadows.

Melina stood alone at the prison cell.

A lone man, shackled at the wrists and cuffed to a

crumbling wall at the opposite end of the cell, slowly turned his head.

Melina's breath caught in her throat as she gazed into the ghostly eyes of the infamous prophet, John the Baptizer.

***

Mara

It was late, and Mara was weary.

Soul-weary.

She'd been on her feet all day, yet she dreaded the idea of returning to the small abode she shared with her husband, Lucius. The home was one of many outbuildings scattered about Caiaphas' estate. Somehow, she felt as if she remained beneath the watchful gaze of her cruel master even when she entered the confines of her new home. It was as if the very walls had eyes. And ears.

Why had Caiaphas insisted she and her husband live on his property? Did he simply desire his chief of security to remain close at hand?

Somehow, she sensed there was more to it than that, though she couldn't possibly fathom the true motives of the high priest. Caiaphas was a closed book in every way. Only God knew what went on in the mind of that man. And that was probably a very good thing.

Mara sighed as she scrubbed a large cook pot, her back aching and her feet begging for a moment of respite as she stooped over the heavy appliance. Despite her weariness, she preferred the busyness of the kitchen to the aching silence of her new home.

The first few weeks of marriage had been painfully eye-opening. Lucius was seldom home. Caiaphas kept him extremely busy, and she hadn't the slightest idea what her husband did with his free time after completing his assignments.

He certainly wasn't spending it with her!

When Mara considered the liberties he had taken with her before their union, she grew anxious. If a man hadn't the slightest qualm about compromising a woman's purity *before* marriage, then why would he feel obligated to maintain purity and fidelity *within* marriage? Lucius insisted it was official business that kept him away all night multiple times a week.

Still, niggling doubts and fears plagued her days and haunted her nights.

She longed for peace. Joy. Contentment.

She thought of Melina. The young woman's circumstances were very much like her own. Like Mara, Melina belonged to the household of a powerful, notorious man. Her life was not her own. She was not free to make her own decisions. Her entire existence was spent catering to the desires of selfish people.

And yet, unlike Mara... Melina was at peace. Joyful. Content.

What was her secret? How did Melina walk through life with a smile on her face and joy in her heart, regardless of her circumstances? Even as Mara longed for whatever it was that Melina possessed, she convinced herself that it was impossible. After all, what she needed was an entirely different set of circumstances – or a personality transplant.

Perhaps if she had been born with Melina's temperament, she would be happy and content to serve others cheerfully and walk through life with an attitude of serene acceptance.

But she wasn't like Melina.

Mara was certain she could never be happy in her present condition.

Just as you were certain you could never be happy without a husband?

Mara paused mid-scrub, her heart pounding.

Like a gentle admonition, the thought whispered its way into her mind, quietly prompting her to examine her thoughts and actions.

Yes, Mara had been certain her life would finally have meaning if she were privileged to wed. And now here she was – a married woman – every bit as unhappy as she was before. Perhaps even more so!

Clearly, her own clawing, grasping attempts to capture her own happiness had failed. Miserably.

Tossing aside the dirty scrub cloth, Mara buried her face in her hands, shaking her head in an attempt to clear the confusion.

"I see you are bursting with desire to run home and straight into the arms of your waiting husband."

Mara froze, her fingers tightening over her face, her spine rigid.

"Oh, but that's right. I doubt he'll be home. He seldom is. If I should see him at his favorite brothel this evening, I'll be sure to pass along your fond regards."

Mara turned and gazed into the glittering eyes of her nemesis, facing his searing sarcasm head-on.

"Alexander. What a surprise, though I regret to say it isn't a pleasant one."

Alexander released a rough laugh, his expression

taut, his dark eyes dancing in critical amusement.

How she loathed him!

Alexander was the embodiment of masculine grace – tall, strong, powerfully built. With a commanding air, Alexander was charismatic and deceptively charming at times. His arresting presence exuded confidence, capturing the attention of those around him.

He was so handsome that Mara looked away. She was a married woman, after all... even if unhappily so. Returning her attention to the pot she had scoured, she said carelessly, "I'm shocked to see you here. You've seldom spoken two words to me since..."

"Since you wed?" Alexander arched a sardonic brow. "Well, my dear, it would hardly be proper."

"And since when has that stopped you?"

Another harsh laugh.

"If you'll excuse me," Mara said briskly, gathering up her shawl, "I must be returning home."

"You weren't in a hurry a minute ago."

"Well, now I am."

"Amazing how much can change in the blink of an eye."

Mara slipped her shawl over her head, disturbed by his observation.

"Speaking of your wedding, it was a lovely event. Despite the fact that your husband looked positively panic-stricken, you received an excellent turnout."

Mara stiffened, fully aware that he was mocking her. The lack of guests attending the ceremony had been pathetic indeed.

"I don't recall issuing you an invitation," she said curtly,

"And yet I doubt the others failed to attend for the same reason," he responded coolly. "I wonder why they were so reluctant to support your union with a man who uses his brute force like a battering ram. Tell me, does he treat you as gently as the innocents he bullies and interrogates?"

"Lucius does his job," Mara ground out, exasperated. "He is a Roman soldier. At times, force is required." Why was she even having this conversation?

"So, I suppose when he grasped an elderly merchant by the throat last week, lifted him off his feet, and flung him into a pile of his own merchandise, Lucius was simply doing his job?"

Mara paled. Had Lucius really done such a thing?

Alexander's mouth tipped ruefully. "I thought not."

"What do you do?" Mara demanded angrily. "Walk around town stalking people to satiate your own morbid curiosity?"

"At times. But most often, if I follow anyone, it's to garner information that might prove profitable or possibly even save my own neck sometime in the future. It pays to be one step ahead of your superiors – both literally and figuratively speaking."

"By your own admission, you blackmail others for profit. And yet you have the nerve to accuse my husband for his faults?"

"I observe and wield information wisely. And my targets are ruthless men – pompous windbags and hypocritical louts who wield their power and influence like a sword. Your husband devours orphans and widows. There is a vast difference between what he does and what I do."

Even as he spoke the words, Alexander was surprised by a twinge of conscience.

Just as you want men to do to you, you also do to them likewise. The widely circulated words had been spoken by the Prophet, Jesus. Alexander had stumbled upon His teachings while attempting to trap his cousin, Malchus, in his defection. Now, curiosity drew Alexander any time the Rabbi spoke. At first, he was simply entertained. Now, he was thoughtfully disturbed.

But he kept going back. Why? He was frustrated by his own weak capitulation. He knew he endangered his coveted position among Caiaphas' staff each time he visited the traveling Rabbi.

Reaching for the basket she had brought from home, Mara draped the corner of her shawl over one shoulder and prepared to leave. "I'm not going to listen to this," she huffed angrily. She turned to make her grand exit.

Mara was shocked when Alexander took her by the arm, swinging her around to face him. "You did a foolish thing, Mara," he said, his face so close to hers she could smell his spice-scented breath. "I offered you freedom, but you chained yourself to a man who doesn't love you."

His words hurt, and Mara hated the tears that sprang to her eyes. She detested giving Alexander the satisfaction. "You don't know what you're talking about."

"On the contrary, I know exactly what I'm talking about. And you know I'm right."

Mara stared at him, willing a response but coming up empty.

"Should your devoted husband decide to end this

farce you call a marriage," he said, his voice dark and dangerously tempting, "you know where to find me." He smiled, a taunting smile that unnerved her to the very core. "And you needn't worry, my dear. I won't say *I told you so.*"

That being said, Alexander turned sharply on his heel and left the room, leaving her to stand alone and ponder his disturbing message.

CHAPTER 9

Melina

Melina's throat constricted at the sight of the mighty prophet enveloped in darkness, chained within a reeking, rotting prison cell.

Her dear friend, Joanna, had described John the Baptizer as a powerful, robust man with broad shoulders, a barrel chest, and an extremely muscular build. His appearance, she had said, was truly wild, for the animal skins he wore emphasized his dramatic form.

This man now meeting her gaze with vacant eyes was little more than a frail wraith. Her throat constricting, Melina realized that an entire year of forced inactivity and near-starvation had taken its toll.

It was no secret that Roman prisons were designed to torture prisoners both physically and psychologically in order to elicit a prompt confession. For the first time, Melina understood just how effective the system was. She imagined most men would confess to any crime just to escape this wretched place.

And yet John had remained staunch, unbending, for hundreds of days on end. How on earth had he done so?

"John," she whispered, her voice catching.

How long had she waited for this moment? And now, she felt nothing but sorrow and defeat. Her heart was breaking inside her chest. She was powerless to help this man.

"Have we met, child?" His voice was unexpectedly deep and rich.

"I wish we had. My name is Melina, and I am the handmaiden of Herodias' daughter, Salome."

"A believer in the lion's den," he mused, painfully adjusting his position. He was clearly in terrible pain, his body enduring unnatural, cramped positions for days at a time due to the unforgiving shackles he wore.

"I have been praying for you for over a year now." *Although it hasn't appeared to do any good at all,* she thought silently, immediately ashamed and shaken by her bitter response. *But why, God? This is Your faithful servant! Why must he endure this evil?*

"Your prayers are not in vain."

Melina's head came up in surprise. It was as if John had sensed the direction of her wayward thoughts.

"If our Lord does wound, it is only that He might heal. What men intend for evil, God works for good."

Melina was amazed by the unshakeable faith of this man. "Your faith is strong, praise God," she breathed, awed. "John, what can I do to help you?"

"Pray for me. Pray for strength to endure."

"I have prayed for you for so long, but –"

"Persist in your prayers. *Be strong and of good courage.*"

Melina stared at the imprisoned prophet, amazed. She had come to minister to John, and yet here he was – ministering to her despite his chains!

Lowering her head and blinking back tears, she found herself utterly ashamed. She had come to strengthen John, not to wrestle with her own faith!

"Will there be a trial, John? Will you be set free?"

"I am already free."

Melina stared at the heavy cast-iron chains biting into the raw, bleeding flesh around his swollen wrists and ankles.

Somehow, John managed a low chuckle. "I wrestled with my faith as well, daughter. And it would surely seem that God had indeed abandoned me – if this was, in fact, the end. But it is not. It is only the beginning."

Melina stared at John, mystified by his words.

"God sent me to be the forerunner for the Savior, the Christ. Do you know Him?"

Melina's eyes sobered, and she whispered reverently, "Jesus Christ, Son of God."

"Amen, and praise God," John breathed. "God sent me to bear the message, to proclaim the acceptable year of the Lord. By God's grace, I accomplished His good purpose. I was sent to bear witness of the Light, and now I must step back. *He must increase, but I must decrease.*"

Melina nodded slowly, reluctant to speak. It was obvious that John was far ahead of her in his own walk with the Lord. What could she possibly say to strengthen him?

"In a moment of despair, I doubted God's will. I

sent my disciples to question Jesus. Was He truly the One, the Messiah to set His people free? If so, why was His forerunner rotting in a miserable dungeon while wicked men walked free? But while alone in this cell, I had nothing but time to commune with God. And I have learned that the Messiah has come to free us from our sin, not from earthly captors like the Romans. This world is fleeting – it will end in fire and be no more. This is why we are not to grow attached to this world. Consider other prophets before me – unflinchingly, they faced gruesome deaths because they did not fear those who kill the body but cannot kill the soul. They will dwell in perfection for all eternity with a loving Father who has wiped every tear from their eyes."

"Then you have no fear of death?" Melina asked, hardly comforted.

"I welcome it. I long to be released from this frail body, to see the Lord coming with ten thousands of His saints to carry us all home. There, we will never lose a loved one. Never again shall we fear wicked men, for they will be no more. There, we will walk with Jesus in peace and safety for all eternity."

Melina marveled at his words. "You are a man of incredible faith."

"No, I am but a weak man who serves an incredible God."

"I will do as you say, John. I will pray for you without ceasing. May God continue to strengthen you in your faith."

"My time is near. I sense it in my spirit. *Though He slay me, yet will I trust in Him.* He has never failed me in life. He will not fail me in death."

"May I pray with you now?"

"Yes. Though I daresay our time together draws short. Never have the guards permitted a visit to last even this long. Perhaps the new soldier who escorted you here possesses a shred of mercy."

For John's sake, Melina certainly hoped so.

"God has been gracious to grant us this time together," she said, tears in her eyes.

"Our God is gracious in all things."

Melina longed to take John's frail hands as she prayed, but his chains were too short to reach her, and the thick iron grate prevented her from going to him. Instead, she reached one slender arm through the grate, stretching her hand toward John. Her other hand she extended heavenward, beseeching their gracious God.

"Oh, dear God, Father of mercy, grant Your grace and peace to this willing servant, John. Restore his soul, Father. Lead him along Your paths of righteousness for Your name's sake, oh God."

John's deep voice joined hers, and he spoke with a deep, unshakeable love for his God that tugged at Melina's heartstrings. "*Though I walk through the valley of the shadow of death, I will fear no evil; for You are with me; Your rod and Your staff, they comfort me. You prepare a table before me in the presence of my enemies.*"

Melina squeezed her eyes shut as tears trickled down her cheeks. Even as the enemies of God prepared an exquisite banquet table far above John's miserable cell, God was working in heaven on behalf of His saint. One day, every knee would bow before God the Father, and that included Herod Antipas and his murderous wife, Herodias. One day, the wicked would be judged, and even the infamous

Herod Antipas would be forced to give an account before God.

Nothing was hidden from the sight of God. John would receive an eternal reward for his faithfulness, while the wicked would receive their dues on the Day of Judgment.

"Lord God," Melina entreated, her voice growing in strength as she and the faithful prophet communed with their Maker, "May goodness and mercy follow John all the days of his life. May he dwell in Your house forever."

Hours passed, and yet the guard did not return. Amazed, Melina strengthened her brother through prayer and exhortation, thanking God for this incredible gift of ministry.

And even as she prayed, it was as if the darkness lifted. The prison cell grew just a bit lighter. The atmosphere softened. Fear was scattered along with the darkness.

Melina could not see them, but she imagined they were surrounded by angels of light as she knelt in prayer before the thick iron grate, ministering to her brother in chains.

CHAPTER 10

Julia

Julia wondered how Melina fared at Machaerus. She missed her friend and prayed for her incessantly.

Bring her safely back to Jerusalem, Lord. Fill her with the power of Your Holy Spirit. Guide her every step. Protect her from wicked men.

Placing her broom in the storage room at the back of the small house, Julia was startled by a loud screech just behind her.

Maaaaaa! Maaaa!

Spinning around, Julia found herself looking directly into the challenging eyes of Eve, the female goat. It was as if the rebellious little she-goat dared Julia to defy her wishes.

Maaaa!

Julia shook her head and clicked her tongue chidingly. "You stubborn thing!" she lectured, securing the storage room door. "How did you get out of your pen... again?"

Deborah had once laughingly remarked that

goats were skilled escape artists, but Julia hadn't believed it until recently. Little Eve had become rather emboldened, regularly escaping from her pen and tempting Adam to follow her reprehensible behavior.

Right on cue, Adam entered the open doorway, his little hooves pounding on the earthen floor. He gazed up at Julia in question.

Maaaaa?

Julia couldn't help but laugh, for his shrill cry did indeed sound like a question.

"You silly goat! You should be ashamed – following Eve's example of disobedience! Didn't you ever read about what happened to your namesake?"

The male goat gazed up at her intently.

"And Eve, you should be ashamed as well – leading your husband astray in such a disgraceful manner!"

Maaaaaaaaaa!

Laughing, Julia went about her chores, ignoring Adam and Eve as they settled comfortably in the warm house. Once, she would have been utterly horrified at the prospect of two wild goats roaming about her home. Now, with her husband often away, she welcomed the company.

What on earth would Barabbas say if he discovered she had been allowing them to sleep in the house? The corners of her mouth tipped up in a mischievous grin. Hopefully, he wouldn't find out! She imagined this was a secret best kept between herself and the stubborn little goats.

Smiling at the two small creatures sleeping peacefully in the corner, Julia prayed for Melina as she prepared to bake loaves of bread to distribute to the needy gathered at the Pool of Bethesda.

Somehow, she sensed her prayers were especially urgent today. She determined to seek the Lord fervently on behalf of her closest friend.

***

Melina

Melina was utterly appalled, repulsed by the show of drunken licentiousness and blatant debauchery brazenly displayed by the guests at Herod's long-awaited birthday feast.

The servants had indeed outdone themselves, for the magnificent palace courtyard was positively resplendent, spilling over with drunken and carousing guests, all of them politicians, nobles, high officers, and the chief men of Galilee and beyond. Here, all inhibitions and pretenses were cast to the wind. One would have never known these men occupied positions of power and authority as they delighted in lascivious, corrupt entertainment and partook of the opulent feast stretching over the never-ending, three-sided banquet table. Exquisitely dressed women draped themselves over their escorts as they lounged comfortably upon plush settees, their long, tapered fingers encircling golden goblets of rich, imported wine. Their behavior was so ridiculously provocative that Melina blushed in sheer embarrassment.

Had these guests not the slightest sense of modesty nor speck of common decency?

According to Salome, only the best-looking men-servants and the loveliest maidservants had been selected to attend the prestigious guests at Herod's banquet. Melina supposed she should be honored.

Instead, she was scandalized and nauseated.

The atmosphere was thick with the smoke of hundreds of fiery torches, as well as the cloying scent of burning incense. Herodias had spared no expense in the arrangements, importing the finest delicacies from the farthest reaches of the empire and a vast selection of the choicest wines from the celebrated vineyards of Italy. The aromas of the impressive feast mingled with the smoky fumes and the strong, overpowering scent of the incense as guests reclined, swishing the wine in their goblets and reaching across the table to help themselves to whatever edible excesses they desired.

Herod Antipas observed the mayhem with an air of grimness as he sat enthroned upon a massive gilded chair on an elevated dais, his own lavishly excessive banquet table spread before him. Several lovely handmaidens attended him, and Melina noticed that they replenished his goblet with alarming regularity. Melina wondered at the amount of wine the tetrarch had consumed. Was he even aware of the fact that his goblet was rapidly refilled before he had scarcely emptied the contents? He appeared to be brooding and preoccupied rather than comfortable and relaxed as he observed the feverish state of the festivities.

Dressed in queenly, imported finery, her luxuriant black hair braided and pinned in an elaborate Roman stye, Herodias lounged dutifully beside her husband on her own settee in a seemingly relaxed position. Even so, Melina sensed the woman's tension all the way across the enormous marble courtyard. The woman was watching, waiting, biding her time… for what?

Troubled, Melina dipped a glittering golden tray, allowing several guests to grasp new goblets brimming with sparkling wine. The madness of the celebration was positively deafening as guests laughed, cajoled, and teased one another. Others offered crude shouts of encouragement to the thinly veiled, ill-clad dancing girls twisting and turning before them.

Raucous laughter grating upon her already worn nerves, Melina straightened after her tray was emptied of its contents. She prayed she wouldn't have to stomach this depravity much longer. She had been on her feet for hours, serving guests and desperately avoiding the bold stares of Herod's salacious friends. Already, the guests had been dazzled by a dizzying array of exotic dancers, daring acrobats, skilled musicians, and several despicably crude professional storytellers. Melina had wished to stop her ears and flee as the guests howled and guffawed in response to the storytellers' shocking narratives. Instead, she had intentionally drowned out the obscene tales of gods and goddesses, jilted lovers, and amorous escapades, deliberately tuning out the vulgarity encompassing her.

Didn't Rome once pride itself upon a devout sense of honor and virtue? What was honorable or virtuous about these entertainers' stories? Whatever happened to morality, propriety, modesty, and decency? Even if these people refused to acknowledge the God of the universe, surely they must understand that such excessive moral decay would certainly lead to ruin!

Averting her eyes as dancing girls awed the guests

with suggestive dance numbers, Melina silently recited memorized passages of Scripture to keep her mind stayed upon other things.

Turn away my eyes from looking at worthless things, she prayed desperately, drawing comfort from the ancient Psalm, *and revive me in Your way.*

Surely the evening must be drawing to a close! She had long since lost count of entertainers and of the number of trays and platters she had delivered throughout the course of the evening. The full moon rose high overhead, draped in sheets of wispy night clouds and declaring the lateness of the hour.

Fleetingly, Melina allowed her eyes to scan the entirety of the richly decorated palace grounds. Guests filled every nook and cranny, some standing in tight clusters, others lurking within the shadows of towering columns, still others lounging about the magnificent banquet table, whetting rather than sating their indulgent appetites.

But Salome was nowhere in sight.

Was Herod insulted that his stepdaughter had snubbed him, failing to make an appearance at his birthday celebration? Remembering Salome's manipulative scheme, Melina's stomach tied in frantic knots. Perhaps the tetrarch would forgive the wayward princess if her performance pleased him. But what if he were repulsed or scandalized instead? Would Salome be punished? Would her betrothal to Philip be dissolved, as she hoped?

Wincing as she recalled Salome's careless words, Melina wondered what kind of performance the young woman planned to present. Melina knew Salome was a skilled dancer, for she had been trained by the best and most sought-after instructors from an early age. The finest tutors and the very best instructors were naturally selected to equip a young woman of Salome's class.

Melina's heart nearly stopped along with the heavy drum beat that ceased without warning. Gracefully, the dancing girls fled the scene, disappearing behind gauzy scarlet tapestries sectioning off the courtyard from evenly spaced pillared porticoes.

Clearly, the dance number had ended.

Melina steeled herself to endure yet another dreadful performance. Retrieving several empty trays from the banquet table, she prepared to take them to the kitchen. Perhaps she could avoid the next unwanted number if she lingered in the kitchen a bit. Already, the head cook had accused her of loitering and threatened to throw her out of the kitchen. But perhaps he would be too occupied with his duties to notice her presence this time…

Without warning, the hair rose at the back of her neck as skillful musicians assumed the next song. Mesmerizing Middle Eastern music floated enchantingly over the courtyard as musicians lifted pan flutes to their lips, while others pounded incessant, repetitive beats upon cymbals and drums. The music was hypnotic in nature, mysterious and unsettling. Even as Melina longed to slip away unnoticed, the music beckoned her to remain, nailing her feet in place despite her misgivings.

Unexpectedly, the music picked up speed, the feverish drumbeat pounding in time with Melina's own racing heart. As if in response to the erratic music bursting forth from countless ancient instruments, the raging fire upon the torches leaped with a chill breeze that billowed through the courtyard. Several guests cried out, surprised.

Herod leaned forward in his gilded chair.

For a moment, Melina felt faint as smoke streaked across the courtyard, stinging her eyes and assaulting her senses. At the other end of the courtyard, the crimson tapestries parted.

Melina had never seen a woman so brazen, so bold. Smiling coyly, the cloaked dancer stepped boldly through the sheer tapestries and onto the tiled courtyard, her form emanating a dark and disturbing presence. It was as if the girl was emboldened and empowered by some terrible force beyond herself. Marching in time with the deafening drumbeat, the young woman released the clasp of her majestically flowing cape, revealing a shocking costume that glittered in the firelight. Holding the cape between two delicate fingers, she lifted it and released her grasp. The wind caught the gauzy material and snatched it away, carrying it off with the angry breeze.

Melina stared, stunned and repulsed. Then, for the briefest moment, the heavily painted emerald eyes of the shameless performer spanned the vast distance of the courtyard, resting upon Melina. Catching her breath, Melina stifled a gasp as the young woman's ruby lips tipped in a triumphant grin.

Melina's entire body stiffened in swift recognition.

Salome!

The grand finale had commenced.

CHAPTER 11

Julia

Julia awoke with a start.

Pushing herself up to a sitting position upon her hard sleeping pallet, she tucked a wayward strand of dark hair behind her ear and listened thoughtfully.

Silence reigned.

Something had awakened her, she felt sure of it. Yet her ears detected nothing but absolute silence and stillness. It was as if the entire world slept.

Stroking Eve's soft hide, she smiled contentedly as the two young goats nestled together beside her own sleeping pallet. They slept peacefully, their sides rising and falling gently as they slumbered.

Nestling beneath her thin blanket, Julia rested her head upon her own folded hands and prepared to go back to sleep.

But sleep evaded her.

Rising from her sleeping pallet, she tiptoed over to the open window and rested her arms upon the sill. The full moon, suspended majestically in space, flooded her small home with silver light. It was a beautiful moon, pulling her thoughts toward its Creator.

A thought occurred to her. How often had the Lord awakened her during the night when desperate prayer was required? Instantly, she thought of Melina.

Folding her hands, Julia bowed her head and sought the God of creation. "Lord God, protect Your daughter, Melina. She is in the lion's den tonight, but You already know this, Father. Protect her from the forces of evil. May no weapon formed against her prosper. Lord, grant her comfort and hope. Fill her with strength and remind her that You are her hope, the God of her salvation."

***

Melina

Melina turned away from the disturbing scene, her stomach roiling as her temples throbbed with the steady drumbeat. She could not bring herself to look upon her young mistress. Her conscience would not permit it.

Clutching the empty trays to her heart, Melina attempted to still her fierce trembling as Salome exploded into action behind her, eliciting shouts of awe and cries of delight from Herod's guests.

Lord God, take me from this vile place, Melina pled silently, tears welling in her soft green eyes.

Behold, God is my salvation, I will trust and not be afraid...

The words of an ancient prophet crept into her

heart, and she determined to cling to the promise. She would trust rather than fear. God was with her. Even in this wicked place, God reigned. Evil men might triumph for a time, but in due time her God would triumph over them with a shout, with the voice of an archangel, and with the trumpet of God. On that blessed day, the will of God would triumph over the will of wicked men with a resounding song of victory.

An explosion of strident cheers drew Melina's thoughts back to the present. Clearly, the guests were delighted by Salome's performance, for the crowd was rapturous, elated with euphoria. Men shouted and cheered, some standing upon the banquet table and crying out her name. Others applauded madly and whistled their approval.

While Salome danced, Melina chanced a look toward the tetrarch and his wife, concerned for her young mistress. What did *they* think of their daughter's performance?

Herodias lounged comfortably, her sharp eyes glittering, a catlike smile playing about the corners of her lips.

Melina was stunned. Surely Herodias was not *pleased* with her daughter's display!

Herodias tilted her elegant head to one side, observing her husband's response.

Antipas gripped his goblet in a white-knuckled hand, his chiseled jaw firmly set. His eyes were not upon his stepdaughter, but rather observing the hysterical audience. They were delirious in their delight, noisily shouting encouragement and begging Salome to prolong the performance.

Sensing Melina's curious gaze, Herodias' cruel

eyes met the servant girl's. Lifting one bejeweled finger, the woman beckoned Melina to come to her.

Heart dropping to the pit of her stomach, Melina passed her empty trays to a fellow maidservant before swallowing her fear and approaching the terrible woman.

"She is magnificent, is she not?" Herodias purred once Melina reached the dais.

Unwilling to agree, Melina opted for respectful silence.

The music continued to blare loudly, resonating deeply within her chest. She felt as if her own heartbeat were altered by the intensity of the booming drums. She folded her hands before her, silently awaiting orders.

"Wait here," Herodias commanded her. "Salome will need someone to tend her after such a vigorous performance."

Melina had no doubt about that.

Ignoring the handmaiden's presence, Herodias turned heavily lashed eyes to her husband. "She has your men eating out of the palm of her hand."

Herod remained tight-lipped and grim.

"Your popularity is steadily declining in both Judea and Galilee."

Herod stiffened, a muscle twitching in his jaw. Clearly, he did not need to be reminded.

"But after tonight, these powerful men will be groveling at your feet. The greatest men of Rome know precisely how to win over the populace – bread and circuses. You would do well to emulate their tactics, my sweet," Herodias purred, her tone hypnotic. The advice was offered sagely, sweetly. As if she harbored great concern for her husband's office. "Just look at your men, my love. They are utterly captivated. You owe our daughter a great debt."

Melina's insides churned with hidden anger. Fleetingly, she wondered if Herodias was now privy to Salome's deception. Did she intend to assist her daughter in the betrayal of Philip? Melina had no doubt that Herodias harbored ulterior motives, whatever they might be. The disturbing thought made her knees go weak.

Boom, chucka-lucka-lucka-BOOM!

The music slammed to an intense stop, and Melina was caught off guard when Salome swept into her field of vision, gliding into an overly dramatic curtsy upon the steps of the elevated dais directly before the fearsome tetrarch.

The entire courtyard erupted in fierce, hysterical applause. Men shouted and cheered, whistling madly and pumping fists violently into the air.

Melina longed to clasp trembling hands over her ears, for the sound was deafening. It was as if the very earth shook beneath the roar of Herod's guests.

Slowly, provocatively, Salome lifted her head and met the gaze of Herod Antipas, her lips tipping in a knowing smile.

A man at the banquet table exploded to his feet, lifting his goblet high. "To Salome!" he cheered, rocking slightly in his drunken state.

The courtyard erupted with the toast. "To Salome! To Salome!"

"And to Herod Antipas, may he live forever!" Another man shouted

"To Herod Antipas!"

Melina winced, her ears ringing amidst the tumult and mayhem.

Herodias turned her head slowly toward her husband, a smile gracing her hard mouth. "You see? They worship you."

Herod offered a curt nod. Whether it was in acknowledgement to the audience or to his wife, Melina hadn't the slightest idea.

"Do not deny their wishes, and they will serve you with reckless abandon, my husband. Serve their passions and their lusts, and their allegiance will be yours forever."

Tingles skittered up Melina's spine, for Herodias had captured the gaze of an unfamiliar man standing among the guests near the banquet table. The ruthless woman offered a subtle nod, and the stranger lifted his goblet high.

"May Salome, daughter of our great and mighty tetrarch, be honored before all!" the unfamiliar man shouted breathlessly, and, instantly, a chorus of voices joined his.

"Honor Salome! Honor Salome! What will be done for the woman who pleases the mighty tetrarch?" The crowd's mad hysteria was deafening.

Herod's jaw tightened. Even in his drunken state, he sensed something was not quite right. Even so, the whispered words of his wife rang in his ears, taunting and tormenting his troubled soul.

Serve their passions and their lusts, and their allegiance will be yours forever.

It was Rome's way. And he could not deny it. It worked like a charm.

"Honor Salome! Honor Salome! Honor Salome!"

Melina's heart pounded furiously in her chest, her body breaking out in a cold sweat. The crowd of guests rocked and swayed like a mighty sea, and

Melina feared that Herod Antipas was about to be swept away in its fierce wake.

"Honor Salome! Honor Salome! Honor Salome! Honor Salome!"

Herod lifted a bejeweled hand, and the chant was cut short in an instant. Enigmatically, he lowered his gaze to his young stepdaughter.

Salome was breathless, her body slick with sweat. Even so, she drew herself to her full height, carrying herself with the grace and pride of a queen. Boldly, she met Herod's gaze, her eyes gleaming with malice. Her impossible plan was about to unfold. She had the power to plot her own destiny. Drunk with the power she held in her hands, she awaited Herod's predictable response.

And just as Melina feared, Herod was goaded by his desire to please his subjects and garner approval. Dismissing his own gnawing uneasiness, he extended a hand toward his shameless stepdaughter.

"Ask me whatever you wish, and I will give it to you."

The crowd exploded with shouts of approval.

"Even up to half my kingdom," Herod added almost reluctantly, his eyes nervously scanning the unruly crowd.

The avaricious gleam reflected in Herodias' eyes was not lost on Melina. The woman met the gaze of the strange man hidden amidst the guests, and they exchanged subtle, knowing smirks.

Melina's heart began to beat even more rapidly.

Something was terribly wrong.

Bowing her head, Melina began to pray unlike she had ever prayed before.

CHAPTER 12

Completely unexpectedly, Herodias stood and addressed the audience. "The lovely Salome will take a moment to contemplate Herod's gracious offer." Turning her attention to her daughter, Herodias lowered her voice. "Come, Salome. Your maid will help you freshen up."

Salome's eyes flashed, fearful her plan was about to be thwarted. "But, Mother, I already know what to ask –"

"Come." Herodias' tone was dangerous.

Even Salome knew better than to press her further. Balling her hands into angry fists, she followed her mother from the dais.

Melina trailed respectfully behind them, praying as she went.

"Mother!" Salome nearly shrieked the moment they had stepped beyond the crimson tapestries. "How could you humiliate me before all those guests? Now it looks as if I'm a child, incapable of making a decision for myself! I already know what I want!"

"I'm sure you do," Herodias replied, her tone cool

and challenging.

Melina accepted the damp cloth and basin another servant offered her and began to gently dab Salome's slick forehead.

"That's good enough, Melina. I must get out there before Herod changes his mind!"

"He shan't change his mind. The mob won't allow it," Herodias said with cool rationale. "He's sworn an oath to you before a hundred guests. Now tell me, darling, what shall you ask of Herod?"

Salome bit her lower lip, suddenly insecure. She hadn't planned on an interrogation before presenting her request to Herod. Her mother possessed the power to destroy her carefully crafted plan.

"You needn't look fearful, darling. What is it?"

Melina lowered her gaze as she accepted the elaborate robe another servant presented to her. Carefully, she slipped it over Salome's slender shoulders, relieved to cover the girl's disgraceful costume.

"Well?" Herodias was growing dangerously impatient.

"I will ask Herod to abolish my betrothal."

The room grew very still.

"You foolish girl." Herodias' reprimand cut like a knife.

Salome's eyes sparked. "I won't marry him, Mother. He's a disgusting old man."

"He is a very rich old man, and if the gods smile upon you, he will soon die, leaving you with a small fortune!"

Melina cringed at her callous speech.

"I cannot stomach the thought of marrying him!"

"It is a smart move, Salome. I consented to this betrothal because I love you and want nothing but the best for you. You must trust my judgment."

Tears sprang to Salome's eyes. Biting her lower lip, she looked away.

Melina almost felt sorry for Salome as she secured a bejeweled belt around her mistress's slender waist.

"Listen carefully, my daughter, and I will tell you what you must do."

"But, Mother –"

"Listen to me!"

Salome stilled, her eyes wet with tears.

Desperately, Melina attempted to slow her rapidly beating heart. The strain was unbearable.

"Salome, my precious daughter, do you love me?"

Having helped Salome to the best of her ability, Melina took several steps back, averting her gaze and folding her hands subserviently. Her entire being quaked, for she knew Herodias' ulterior motives were about to be revealed.

"Mother, you know I love you."

"More than anything?"

"More than anything."

"Enough to avenge any wrong committed against me?"

Salome lifted her gaze, cautious. "You know I would do anything for you, Mother."

"Then this is the opportune time, my daughter."

"What shall I ask for?" Salome asked hesitantly, struggling with her own fierce emotions.

"That pestilent prophet defamed my good name and destroyed my reputation. I have yet to be avenged."

Melina's entire being went cold.

"Tell Herod what we want, my sweet, and I will repay you in due time. Haven't I always? Do you trust me?"

Salome searched her mother's face, uncertain.

"You go out there, my darling, and tell Herod exactly what you desire – the head of John the Baptizer on a platter."

"No!" The cry of protest escaped Melina's lips before she even recognized her own voice.

Herodias swung around to face her and slapped her so hard that she reeled backward. "Shut up! Do you hear me? You have no right to speak."

Melina knew that to defy her orders could result in certain death, yet in that moment, she didn't care. She rushed to Salome and took her hands. "My lady, I beg you, don't do this! Don't bring this sin upon your head –"

Herodias slapped her again, knocking her off her feet. "Speak again, you fool, and I swear you will have great cause to regret it."

Melina pushed herself up to a sitting position on the marble floor, her head ringing from the blow. She touched her throbbing face, trembling, and beseeched Salome with a look of earnest appeal.

Confused, Salome looked to her mother, then to her maidservant hunkered down on the marble floor.

Herodias stepped in front of Melina, obscuring her from her daughter's field of vision. She tipped her daughter's chin, forcing Salome to look into her eyes.

Salome swallowed hard, her exotic features clouded with disappointment.

"I will make it up to you, my daughter. I swear it."

Taking a deep breath, Salome squared slender shoulders and lifted her proud head. "I will do it."

Melina bowed her head as tears spilled over both cheeks. How could any human being possibly be so cruel? Melina could sense the evil in the marble chamber like a malevolent presence. It emanated from Herodias like the light trailing from a falling star.

"Wise girl. You will not regret it."

Salome hung her head.

"Let us go, my daughter," Herodias said, her tone soothing. She stroked the dark hair back from her daughter's face. "All will be well. I promise."

Painfully, Melina drew herself up and followed her mistress as she emerged from the scarlet tapestries.

The guests cheered madly the moment Salome made her appearance.

"You wait here, or I shall have you flogged," Herodias snarled, wrenching Melina by the arm and leaving her to stand beside a marble pillar on the outskirts of the courtyard. It would be just like the worthless girl to plead before Herod and all his guests, begging him to spare the wretched prophet. And her husband was probably fool enough to grant the maid's appeal, shaming himself before all his guests.

Seething, Herodias resumed her calm position upon the settee nearest her husband, casually reaching for her goblet, her fierce emotions hidden from the sea of onlookers below.

Melina remained stationed by the marble pillar, trembling as Salome swept before Herod and honored him with another dramatic curtsy.

"Well?" Herod demanded, clearly annoyed by the delay. "What do you wish?"

Salome straightened, lifting her eyes boldly. A daring smile swept across her face. She knew her request would greatly trouble her stepfather, and she relished his discomfort. Let him squirm. Let him boil in his own blood. He deserved every ounce of his discomfort.

"I shall present to you, my request!" She stated grandly, turning to engage the crowd, which in turn went wild.

Herod surveyed the scene grimly, his jaw set, body tense.

"I want you to give me at once the head of John the Baptizer on a platter!"

The crowd erupted in raucous shouts and cheers as wine-sodden, drunken guests jumped to their feet and screamed their approval.

Fueled by their passion and bloodlust, Salome wheeled around to face Herod Antipas, thrusting her balled fist into the air. "HE DESERVES TO DIE!"

Herod paled, his entire body going rigid. Clearly, he had not expected such a gruesome request from a seemingly civilized and cultured young woman.

"You heard the girl!" Herodias said grimly, as if disturbed herself by the request. She turned to several armed guards flanking the nearest entrance. "Do her bidding. Now!"

Clicking their heels sharply, the soldiers disappeared through the elegantly arched entryway to commit the grisly deed.

"You!"

Melina almost fainted when Herodias pointed a finger in her direction and shouted at her from the dais.

"Go and retrieve the platter for your mistress."

CHAPTER 13

Mara

"Troubled?"

Mara was astonished when Malchus strode calmly into the garden peristyle, the moonlight streaming over his handsome features.

Sitting sedately upon a curved marble bench, her hands folded quietly in her lap, she glanced up at him, her defenses rising. Malchus seldom spoke to her unless posing some new accusation against her or her new husband.

"Malchus? What are you doing up so late?"

"I could ask you the same question. Shouldn't you be home with your husband?"

Ashamed, Mara lowered her gaze. She was too tired to bother with a cheerful, composed pretense. "He isn't home."

"Oh."

Malchus' answer was flat, emotionless.

Well, at least he isn't taunting me, Mara thought snidely. She preferred Malchus' indifference to his critical and sometimes searing imputations. She had finally accepted the cold, hard truth: their friendship was lost forever, never to be restored.

Unwittingly, she had erected a wall between them the fateful day she had agreed to aid Lucius in his dishonest subterfuge, and Malchus' own anger and resentment had only strengthened that wall, bit by bit, brick by invisible brick.

Surprisingly, Malchus lowered himself beside her on the bench. Resting his elbows on his knees, he folded his hands and waited in silence.

"I suppose you are going to say that I am constantly planting myself in the midst of your own garden respite?" Mara sighed, preparing to leave. Malchus had been the first to discover the serenity of this quiet garden peristyle, making it no secret that he resented Mara's constant intrusion.

"No, I'm not."

Mara lifted a brow in question. "What, then?"

"You look unusually troubled tonight."

"Since when do you care?" Mara hated herself for her nasty retort, but it escaped her mouth before she was even aware of it. Since when had she become so habited to spiteful behavior that she was scarcely aware of her own responses? Just what, exactly, was she becoming?

Angry tears welled in her eyes. It was all Lucius' fault. He was a miserable husband! She resented him and all the pain he had caused her.

Melina had been right all along. A hasty marriage hadn't been the answer to her problems.

Melina.

Mara buried her face in her hands, inexplicably troubled.

"Mara, what's going on?"

"I'm so afraid."

"Of Lucius?" Malchus' jaw twitched, betraying his anger.

"Would you just forget about Lucius for once? He is not the source of *all* my troubles, you know."

"You could've fooled me."

"Why are you even here?"

Malchus sighed, exasperated. Frankly, he wasn't even sure what had prompted him to step into the peristyle when, in passing, he had noticed Mara's dejected form.

"What are you afraid of?" he asked, dodging her question.

"You wouldn't understand even if I told you."

"Try me."

Mara dared another glance at him. He seemed genuinely interested, concerned. Twisting her hands nervously in her lap, she said softly, "I can't stop thinking about Melina. I'm afraid something might be wrong."

Her whispered admission was like a punch in the gut. Malchus leaped to his feet, his blood cold. "What do you mean?" he demanded harshly.

Mara recoiled from his demand. "I don't really understand it myself, Malchus," she explained, attempting to pacify his rising temper. "I am unsettled in spirit. And I cannot stop thinking about her."

"Perhaps your God is urging you to pray for the girl."

Neither Mara nor Malchus were terribly surprised when Alexander stepped into the shadowed peristyle, his manner commanding and confident. They had both eventually acclimated to his annoying habit of seemingly materializing out of thin air.

Unsettled by Alexander's powerful presence, Mara lowered her gaze. "What would a Gentile know about a Jewish God?"

"Enough. I've dwelt here in Jerusalem for some time now."

"And I suppose that makes you the expert," Malchus said wryly.

Alexander paused once he reached the bench, folding his strong arms over his chest. "You faithless Jews. You claim to serve an invisible God who speaks to His people, then you are surprised when He actually addresses you."

Despite the intense dislike Malchus harbored toward his swarthy cousin, he realized that he could not argue with Alexander's logic. "Mara, we must pray for Melina. Now."

"There, that's better," Alexander grinned, his tone tinged with mockery.

"Even if I were to try, God would not listen to me," Mara insisted, her eyes clouded with tears of regret. "I don't even know Him anymore, Malchus."

"Perhaps He will hear if you pray on behalf of another," Alexander offered, disturbed by her tears. "Though I despise His stringent rules of unbending morality, your God possesses great power. I have witnessed it."

"Mara," Malchus reiterated. "We must pray."

"But, Malchus –"

"Try! I'll pray with you."

Bowing her head, Mara held back tears as she prayed to a God she had forsaken. "Oh God, if it's true that You are merciful, please hear me."

"Yes, God, hear us," Malchus reiterated, clenching his eyes shut and willing his heart to slow its incessant pounding. What would he do if something happened to Melina? Was it possible the Spirit of the living God was at work in Mara, urging her to pray for his beloved? Mara hadn't the slightest clue that Melina currently dwelt in the most dangerous fortress of the region, and that knowledge shook Malchus to the very core. It chilled him to consider the possibility of his beloved in danger.

Malchus prayed silently alongside Mara, fervently, unlike he had ever prayed before, silently beseeching the Lord to incline His ear toward them. Momentarily, their differences were entirely forgotten as they united to strengthen a fellow sister in prayer.

Alexander watched grimly, his powerful arms folded over his broad chest. For once, both Mara and Malchus seemed entirely unaware of his presence.

"Lord God," Mara continued, desperate for the Lord to hear her. Even as she prayed, she was surprised at the unfamiliar words that proceeded from her own mouth. It was as if they bubbled forth from her innermost being, supernaturally supplied. "Protect our sweet sister, Melina. Strengthen her in her time of doubt. Surround her with Your angels, Lord. Administer Your peace."

***

Melina

Melina had always known that Herodias was ruthless and bitterly vengeful.

But she had never expected to be on the receiving

end of Herodias' cruel, unbridled hatred. Herodias knew it would tear Melina up inside to retrieve the platter bearing the head of John the Baptizer.

Melina had dared to defy Herodias. And now, true to her malicious and vindictive character, Herodias was making her pay.

Trembling from deep inside, Melina attempted to still her own violent shuddering as she traveled down a torchlit stone corridor leading to the prison. She feared she would never be well again.

Lord God, intervene, she prayed fiercely, tears coursing down her cheeks. *Strike that wicked woman dead, Lord. She is no better than the Jezebel of old, who, along with her wicked daughter Athaliah, destroyed Your holy prophets.*

Melina's cheeks flushed at the extent of her fierce emotions. She was quite certain the Lord would not honor her request to smite Herodias in the presence of her wicked guests.

Oh, God, forgive me! My faith is weak! I fear for John! My heart is filled with loathing toward my wicked mistress. Oh, God, help me!

In that moment, John's words of the previous night returned to her with the strength and intensity of a mighty trumpet blast: *My time is near. I sense it in my spirit. Though He slay me, yet will I trust in Him. He has never failed me in life. He will not fail me in death.*

Oh, God, strengthen John in this hour of darkness! May he fear no evil. Do not fail him, oh God, even in death.

I will never leave him nor forsake him.

Tears coursing down her cheeks, Melina suddenly recognized the precious gift God had bestowed upon her the previous night. God had chosen *her* to minister to the mighty prophet, strengthening him in prayer and preparing him for this very moment.

John himself had stated that he welcomed death. He had accomplished the work God had called him to do. He was weary. Tired. He longed for rest. Melina replayed their conversation over and over in her mind, drawing strength from John's great faith.

It would seem that John had prepared her for this moment as well, even as she had ministered to *him*. How mysterious the ways of her God!

I have learned that the Messiah has come to free us from our sin, not from earthly captors like the Romans, John had stated with great conviction. *This world is fleeting – it will end in fire and be no more. This is why we are not to grow attached to this world. Consider other prophets before me – unflinchingly, they faced gruesome deaths because they did not fear those who kill the body but cannot kill the soul. They will dwell in perfection for all eternity with a loving Father who has wiped every tear from their eyes.*

May you wipe every tear from his eyes, Father, Melina prayed fervently. *May he dwell with You in perfection for all eternity. May these present trials pale in comparison to the wonders You have prepared for him in an unending, everlasting, heavenly home!*

Rounding a sharp corner, Melina nearly collided with a tall, powerfully built Roman soldier. Instantly, she recognized him as the guard who had so graciously allowed her those precious hours with John.

The man stared down at her with a deep, impenetrable gaze.

Melina's stomach lurched, for the man bore a golden platter in the strong, bronzed hands of a warrior.

Recovering to the best of her abilities, Melina clutched her churning stomach and gazed up at the soldier with profound respect.

Somehow, this guard had possessed the foresight to drape a delicate sheet over the platter's gruesome contents.

Why would a Roman soldier honor a Jewish prophet in his grisly death?

Eyes brimming with tears, Melina reached shaking hands toward the burden she had been commanded to bear.

"Come," the soldier commanded, his deep voice resonating with authority.

Stunned, Melina understood that the soldier intended to carry the burden for her. Shakily, Melina touched his muscled forearm. "Thank you," she whispered brokenly.

The soldier resumed his brisk gait, and somehow, Melina's shaky legs bore her weight as she trailed behind him.

Finally pausing before the scarlet curtains – the only barrier standing between Melina and the bloodthirsty crowd – the soldier turned to face her, his eyes boring into hers with an alarming intensity. "He died the victor, triumphing over his foes."

Pressing her hand against her mouth, Melina stifled a sob. Even in her wildest dreams, she never could have imagined that a ruthless Roman soldier would supply comfort in her darkest moment.

When he placed the heavy platter in her hands,

she swayed as the blood drained from her face.

Clamping an iron hand upon her shoulder, the soldier drew her up and strength returned to her weak, trembling legs.

"Be strong and of good courage."

Melina stared at the Roman guard, stunned. Had he overheard her conversation with John? How else could he have known the words by which the prophet had strengthened her?

Gazing down at the heavy tray she bore in her own shaking hands, she reveled in the wonder of this moment. A completely unexpected, other-worldly peace flooded her entire being.

How could it possibly be?

Awed, Melina lifted her eyes to meet the gaze of the exceptional Roman guard. But she stood alone in the vast, empty chamber.

The soldier had vanished without a trace.

CHAPTER 14

Julia

The Passover swept through Jerusalem like a powerful storm as hundreds of thousands of pilgrims flooded the city's swollen borders, their shouts and laughter resonating off the ancient stone walls like the haunted cries of ages past.

Uproarious revelry rocked the ancient city to its very core as both residents and pilgrims scrambled to make last minute preparations for one of the holiest feasts of the year.

For Julia, Passover came and went rather quietly. She was almost disappointed by the lack of grandeur. She observed the feast with Isaac and Deborah, as she had the previous year.

Naturally, Barabbas had refused to participate.

That night, she supposed he was somewhere in the rocky Judean hill country – possibly even in Galilee – drinking with fellow Zealots as they boasted about various conquests.

Julia had found it incredibly challenging to relax

and enjoy the company of her dear neighbors that evening, for she was haunted by memories of another Passover. The fateful night her husband had participated in a violent ambush – an ambush that had cost the life of his closest friend, Dan.

Young, laughing, smiling Dan! It still pained her heart to remember him. She recalled the kind smile he had once offered her... the night before a Roman blade claimed his life.

The blow had been intended for her husband.

And now Barabbas was bent on vengeance, determined to murder the man who had stolen the life of his friend.

Pushing aside painful recollections, Julia reached the uppermost balcony overlooking the Upper Market as the breathtaking city of Jerusalem sprawled out behind her.

Malchus was already there, seated gingerly upon the cool stones, his back pressed against the wall. His mouth tipped up in a rueful grin.

"I'm sorry I'm not Melina," Julia said teasingly, leaning casually against the opposing wall.

"So am I," Malchus grinned, draping one arm lazily behind his head.

Julia rolled her eyes, accustomed to the young man's dry wit. "I'm sure she will arrive any moment."

"One can only hope."

"Until then, I suppose you must suffer my presence alone."

"We all have our burdens to bear."

Julia shook her head, amused. "You must be thrilled at the prospect of seeing Melina again."

"But will she be thrilled to see me? Therein lies the question." They hadn't parted on the best of terms.

"Why wouldn't she be?"

"I wasn't terribly supportive when I learned she planned to journey to Machaerus."

"Frankly, you were quite rude when she told us."

Malchus arched a brow, prepared to strap on his invisible armor if necessary. "Was I supposed to be ecstatic she was placing herself in harm's way?"

"*She* wasn't placing herself *anywhere*, Malchus. She believes her future is in God's hands. *He* decides where she goes and where she stays. This time, He led her to Machaerus."

"And she really believes that He guides our every step? Let me ask you, Julia – was it God that led me, or did my own two feet simply carry me here today by my own decision?"

Folding her arms across her chest, Julia stared at Malchus, incredulous. "Sometimes I wonder if you even believe in God, Malchus."

Malchus was taken aback. "How could you say such a thing? Of course, I believe in God!"

"Perhaps you believe He exists, but you certainly don't seem the least bit convinced that He is in control of our affairs. *A man's heart plans his way, but the Lord directs his steps,* Malchus. When we surrender our lives to God and ask Him to guide us, we must believe that He does."

"And what of free will?"

"That's where the miracle lies," Julia said emphatically. "God allows us the free will to disobey Him. We can walk in the path He carves out for us, or we can choose to walk away from it."

"So, God carved a path for Melina that led her to the Black Fortress? Do you even know what's gone on over there in recent weeks?"

Julia bit her lower lip, saddened. She had heard about the untimely death of John the Baptizer.

"Her master butchered a man she greatly respected, and there she was – right in the thick of it."

"God always provides the strength to endure when we need it. She was not alone, Malchus."

"She'd never have to be alone again if she would marry me," he ground out, immediately regretting his hasty remark.

Julia turned knowing eyes upon him, and he grit his teeth in frustration.

"And that is the heart of the matter, isn't it? Malchus, you cannot resent the Lord simply because He hasn't permitted Melina to immediately accept your proposal."

"She is taking this whole thing entirely too seriously!"   "A lifelong commitment to marriage is a serious thing."

"I doubt God even cares whether we marry or not."

"You're wrong, Malchus," Julia looked at him pointedly. "He cares very much. He loves you too much to allow you to make a mistake you will regret for the rest of your life. Don't you think I know that better than anyone else?"

"Are you saying it would be a mistake to marry Melina?" he asked, defensive.

"Who am I to tell you anything?"

"Clearly, that hasn't stopped you," he shot back, annoyed.

"I mean about whom you marry, Malchus. Frankly, I hope the Lord does bring the two of you together. But it must be in His perfect timing."

Malchus' jaw tightened. Melina had said something similar once before.

To everything there is a season, a time for every purpose under heaven...

"Julia! Malchus!"

Melina emerged from the stone staircase, her emerald eyes alight as joy radiated from her glowing features.

Julia cast Malchus a look of warning: *Behave yourself this time.*

Swallowing his frustration, Malchus rose to his feet as Julia and Melina exchanged a fierce embrace.

Melina turned to look at Malchus, her eyes searching as they gazed into his.

Taking her hands, Malchus squeezed them gently, his heart constricting at the sight of her. She was so lovely, her cheeks flushed with color and her eyes gleaming with joy. "How does it feel to be in Jerusalem again?"

Melina released her breath, laughing happily. "It is a blessed relief!"

"We prayed for you unceasingly," Julia put in emphatically.

"And I felt your prayers – every single one of them," Melina declared with great feeling. Resting a delicate hand upon the cool stone wall, she allowed her gaze to sweep over the bustling city. "God was surely with me in that place."

"What was it like?" Julia asked, her mind brimming with questions.

"As terrible as you might expect," Melina answered honestly, aware of the fact that Malchus wouldn't appreciate her report.

"We heard rumors about your prophet," Malchus

said grimly, carefully watching her expression. "I'm sorry, Melina."

Surprisingly, Melina managed a brave smile. "I met him, Malchus. The night before he was beheaded."

Malchus looked to her in surprise.

"What was he like?" Julia nearly squealed, her interest piqued. "I've heard so many stories about him!"

"I'm afraid he looked nothing like he once did. He was pale and emaciated, chained in a foul, underground prison. I was permitted to visit him there. The soldier that took me to him allowed me to pray with him for hours."

Malchus fidgeted uncomfortably. That was more time than she'd ever been granted to spend with *him.*

"I see now that the Lord gave me a precious gift," Melina explained, tears in her eyes. "He allowed me to strengthen our brother in chains, to prepare him for his ultimate battle." Sensing Julia's sadness, Melina touched her arm. "He was ready to die, Julia. He told me that himself." She smiled, remembering the words of a mysterious messenger. "He died the victor, triumphing over his foes."

Malchus stared at her, incredulous. "He was *beheaded!*"

"Though he died, he will live. He will truly *live,* Malchus! The chosen of our God will dwell in absolute perfection for all of eternity. We needn't fear the second death. John was not afraid."

"And little good his courage did him."

Melina turned troubled eyes to Malchus. "Don't you understand?"

"I understand he received the fate designated to those who follow after the controversial teachings of a controversial Rabbi. What good did it really do for him, Melina? He's dead, gone. If anything, he has his *faith* to thank for his grisly end."

Melina studied him, her eyes awash with tears. "If this life is all we have, then yes, he died in vain. But it doesn't end here, Malchus. No." She took his hand, willing him to believe and understand. "Here, it begins."

Troubled, Malchus looked away from her penetrating gaze.

"I don't understand how Herod Antipas could do such a thing," Julia said angrily. "Does he not fear any repercussions? The people loved John!"

"Sadly, the people have forgotten about him," Melina said quietly.

"Which means there won't be any repercussions for Herod," Malchus said bitterly. "Rumors will abound for a few weeks, until a more interesting scandal arises to absorb the people's attention."

"It is said Herod ordered the execution because he feared John capable of leading an uprising or a rebellion," Julia said, her chagrin evident. "But wouldn't that be rather difficult to do from a prison cell?"

"It's a weak excuse," Melina said sadly. "Herod needed a politically correct reason to justify his actions."

"Then what really happened?" Julia asked, ignoring Malchus' glare.

"Herodias set him up. She used her daughter as a decoy, ordering her to dance for Herod and his guests. In his drunken state, he gratified the crowd's goading to grant Salome anything she wished. Of course, Herodias was at her elbow, dictating exactly what she was to ask for. So, Salome asked that John be executed at once, his head brought to her upon a platter."

"The head of a great prophet, served up on a tray," Malchus mused, disgusted. "You must serve a lovely, dignified woman."

Melina chose not to respond. She hadn't anything polite to say about Herodias or her daughter, Salome.

"Did you witness the beheading?" Julia asked with great pity.

"God is gracious, and He spared me that horror," Melina said softly. "But I was instructed to retrieve the platter and take it to Salome."

Malchus stiffened, protective rage welling up inside him. A curse be upon that dreadful woman and her hateful daughter!

Julia's eyes filled. "Oh, Melina."

"Don't be sorry, Julia," Melina said, her eyes alight.

Malchus turned to study her, moved by the peace in her eyes.

"Yet again, what the wicked intended for evil, God meant for good. By Herodias' cruel order, I witnessed a miracle. Something I will never forget. I have hidden it in my heart, and I will draw upon it for strength when trials arise again."

Malchus lifted a brow in question. "What do you mean, 'again'?"

Julia ignored him, bubbling over with curiosity. "What happened?"

"Do you remember the soldier I mentioned earlier – the one who took me to John? He was waiting for me when I went to retrieve the platter. He carried it for me, and it's a very good thing he did; otherwise, I'm sure I would have humiliated myself by dropping it, sending it clattering to the floor along with its precious cargo. I had never felt so nauseated, so weak. The soldier led me to the courtyard where the celebration raged on. And then he spoke to me: *Be strong and of good courage.* The very words John had spoken to me the previous night! Yet his voice was like a trumpet blast, and strength coursed through my entire body at the sound of it. He handed me the platter, and I accepted it. But when I lifted my eyes to meet his gaze, he was gone."

"Smart man," Malchus muttered.

"No, I mean he was *gone.* He vanished before my eyes!"

Julia stared at her, her dark eyes wide as saucers. "He vanished into thin air?"

"I spoke with several guards in the prison the following day. I described the soldier in great detail and even mentioned him by name, for the day I asked permission to see John, he shared his name after I disclosed my own identity. I found that rather odd, for a soldier."

"And what did the guards say?" Julia asked, leaning forward.

Melina looked to Julia, then to Malchus, chills prickling upon her skin. "They said they knew of no man by that description or that name."

Malchus froze, the hairs on the back of his neck prickling as remembrance of Mara's prayer washed over him. A prayer she had prayed the very night of Herod's birthday celebration…

Surround her with Your angels, Lord. Administer

Your peace.

Surround her with Your angels.

Melina looked to Malchus, her eyes softening as she sensed his inner turmoil. "If that man was a soldier, then I am convinced he belonged to a heavenly army, enlisted to serve the Lord of hosts, the Commander of the armies of heaven."

Malchus let out a low whistle as Julia shook her head in awe.

"Melina," Julia said slowly, "you said he told you his name. What was it?"

"It was a rather odd name for a Roman soldier, but reminiscent of one of the ancient prophets."

"What was it?" Julia asked again.

"Mal'akhi," Melina replied, careful to pronounce the unfamiliar name as he had. A strange sensation swept over her at the look of shock and disbelief exchanged between her two friends.

"What is it?" Melina asked, her heart pounding in her chest.

"The name is Hebrew," Julia said, her eyes wide with wonder and astonishment. "Mal'aki."

Melina waited, pulse racing. "But what does it mean?"

Julia exchanged another glance with Malchus, amazed.

"It means 'messenger of God.'"

CHAPTER 15

Melina

Something broke within Herod Antipas after the senseless murder of John the Baptizer. His behavior became increasingly paranoid and caustic. He grew exceedingly confrontational, eager to inflict pain.

As if his sin had awakened a savage beast.

Herod Antipas had greatly admired John, that was no secret. He had been fascinated by the man, possibly even convicted. And yet the enemy had won the battle for the tetrarch's soul. His day of birth was now the solemn marker of the fateful day he had chosen death rather than life, darkness rather than light.

For on that fateful night, despite the haranguing guests, despite Salome's shocking manipulation, despite his own cursed pride... Herod Antipas could have spared the life of an innocent man.

The fact that he hadn't seemed to gnaw at his very soul. But rather than repenting for his heinous act, Herod became even more hardened and calloused, brooding and withdrawn. It was as if the last thread of mercy he possessed had permanently unraveled.

Calmly, Melina went about her chores, silently beseeching God for protection and the wisdom to escape Herod's ire. As of late, the slightest infraction on the part of a servant was enough to send the ruler into a full-blown rage.

As the ruler's behavior worsened, the palace staff began to fear his sanity was slipping away as well. Especially when he began to insist that Jesus of Nazareth was the reincarnation of John the Baptizer.

Did Herod fear that John had returned to haunt him in the form of a Prophet from Nazareth? Perhaps that explained his increasing paranoia and melodrama.

Fleetingly, Melina wondered if anyone had bothered to remind Herod that Jesus was already walking the earth during John's ministry of baptism and teaching. John had even baptized Jesus in the Jordan River! How, then, could Jesus possibly be the reincarnation of the deceased prophet? Had Herod gone completely mad to assume so?

Sighing, Melina folded soft linen sheets in Salome's bedchamber, contemplating her master's disturbing behavior. She supposed no amount of reason or logic would persuade him.

In all her years of service, she had never seen him in such a state.

To make matters worse, Salome was in a state of near hysteria as her wedding day approached. The young woman alternated between bouts of convulsive sobbing, wild histrionics, or stony silence.

Melina hadn't the slightest idea what to expect from her mistress as she approached her each day.

Despite Salome's constant complaints and frequent fits of rage, Melina found it extremely difficult to conjure up any real sympathy for the girl. Every time Salome would burst into tears, bemoaning the fact that her own mother had thwarted her plans for independence, Melina remembered the moment she had passed the platter to Salome at Herod's birthday feast. Herodias' eyes had glowed with dark fire when Salome tore the sheet off the platter, grinning as she revealed the gruesome contents before the bloodthirsty crowd.

Melina had turned away, determined not to look upon such a disgraceful thing. She would not dishonor the dead prophet by gawking at his corpse. Her stomach had twisted in knots as the crowd applauded in sheer delight, shrieking their approval.

Word must not have reached Philip about the shocking behavior of his betrothed, for the wedding was still imminent. In a few weeks, Salome would be given to him in marriage.

Melina shook her head as she folded the last luxurious sheet.

The poor man. He hadn't the slightest idea what he was about to face!

***

Mara

"I'm leaving."

Mara glanced up from the garment she busily mended, surprised. "Again?"

Lucius glowered at her from across the room, straightening after tying the strap of his military hobnailed sandals. "Don't start."

"Don't start what?" Mara rebutted, her eyes sparking angrily.

"Another interrogation. You seem to forget that's my job, not yours."

"Where are you going?"

"That's none of your concern."

"Well, of course not. I'm only your *wife*, after all."

"Woman, don't start with me." Lucius' tone was dangerous, his eyes menacing. He reached for the leather satchel in which he carried personal belongings.

"More official business, I presume?" Mara asked sharply, setting aside her sewing and rising to her feet.

"I leave in response to orders given by the high priest himself. There, satisfied?"

Not since the day we wed, Mara wished to retort! Somehow, she held her tongue as her husband slung the satchel over his shoulder and pushed open the door of their small home.

"How long will you be gone?" Mara managed as she leaned against the doorpost, fighting for control.

Spring sunlight spilled over her husband the moment he stepped outside. His polished armor fairly glistened in the sunshine.

"Well?" Mara asked, impatient and suspicious. Was it truly necessary for Lucius to be absent as often as he was? "How long?"

Lucius' eyes grazed hers for but a moment, and the guilt she saw reflected there was like a punch in the gut.

"Lucius? How long?"

"As long as it takes." With that, he turned sharply

on his heel and started down the stone path that would lead him toward his new posting... and away from her.

Mara's eyes welled with angry tears.

He hadn't even bothered to kiss her goodbye.

***

Melina

The resounding silence of Salome's abandoned chambers was nearly deafening.

Melina went about her usual duties, airing out the room, fluffing the pillows, straightening the sheets, dusting the surfaces, cleaning the Persian rugs and Babylonian tapestries. Despite Salome's loud absence, Melina still received strict orders to maintain the opulent chambers at all times. If her husband permitted, Salome would visit her family often. Her suite must always be ready for an unexpected arrival.

The month of Sivan had swept in like a tidal wave, and despite her shrill protests, Salome had been carried off in its wake. As promised, she was given in marriage to Philip the tetrarch.

Melina wondered how her young mistress fared as the wife of a respectable ruler in Galilee. She was thankful she had not been required to journey to Galilee for the nuptials and the wedding feast that would surely follow.

Perhaps Salome would learn to love her new husband. Philip was reputed as a kind and gentle ruler, sensitive to the needs of his people. Surely, he would bestow the same tender care upon his wife.

Melina prayed for Philip and Salome as she went about her chores. Even as she hoped Salome would settle comfortably into her wifely duties and be content to love her husband and bear children, Melina doubted that would ever happen. Salome was as restless and dangerous as the violently churning ocean waves.

No matter how kind Salome's aging husband might be, he was sure to grow impatient with her constant complaints, raging temper, and imperious demands.

But despite the impossible odds, Melina determined to pray for both of them each day. No one was entirely outside of God's reach. Perhaps the Lord would shower mercy upon them, and they would recognize His goodness.

***

Mara

It was long after dark when Mara returned home from a hot, sweaty day of miserable work in the kitchen.

She hated returning to an empty house. How was her life any different now than before she wed?

Setting aside the basket she carried on one arm, she felt her way in the dark toward the crude wooden table in the center of the room. She was eager to light the oil lamp to dispel the inky blackness.

A warm glow resonated from the lamp once it was finally lit.

Mara's heart sprang into her throat when a dark figure emerged from the shadows. In one awful instant, a powerful hand clamped over her mouth, smothering her scream.

Terrified, she attempted to wrench away, but a strong arm steadied her.

"By the gods, it's me. Calm down!"

Mara stilled, her eyes narrowing as her panic subsided and she gazed up into an annoyingly handsome face.

Slowly, he removed his hand.

"Alexander! Why are you in my house?"

"Hello, my dear. You're finally home."

"Get out!"

"Yet another warm welcome. I'm flattered."

Shaking with anger, Mara stalked over to the door and swung it open unceremoniously. "I said, get out!"

"If this is the kind of welcome you offer your husband, it's no small wonder he never comes home."

Mara turned to glare at him, her stomach tying in knots at the mischief sparkling in Alexander's dark eyes. What if someone discovered she was alone in a house with a man who was not her husband? What if Lucius heard of it? Would he kill Alexander?

Her tone turned pleading. "Please, you must leave. It's dangerous for you to be here."

Alexander turned teasing eyes upon her. "Oh, yes, I imagine it is."

"Why are you here?" she demanded, trembling with suppressed anger and confusion.

He grinned devilishly, and she immediately regretted voicing the question.

"Alright then," she huffed, reaching for her shawl. "You can leave, or I will."

"My, aren't we bossy."

"It is entirely improper for us to be alone in this house, especially while my husband is away!"

"And that, my dear, is exactly what I wish to discuss."

"How is that any of your business?"

"A woman deserves better, Mara. You deserve better."

Mara's conscience warned her to end the conversation before it even started, but she was curious about what Alexander had to say.

She *did* deserve better. Her life was unfair.

"You shouldn't have to return to a dark, empty house after working all day, Mara. You should be taken into strong arms and warmly embraced, kissed, treasured."

Mara's heart began to beat rapidly like the wings of a trapped bird. Warning bells went off in her mind.

"Lucius isn't the man for you," Alexander stated plainly.

"He is my *husband!*"

"Oh, please. When he insisted upon Roman marriage by *usus*, he made it perfectly clear he had no desire to be bound to you. He's simply using you, Mara. You are an intelligent woman. Surely you know this."

Mara bit her lower lip as the evening breezes wafted through the open door and caressed the curling tendrils of dark hair about her face. "It's already done," she said weakly. "I'm married to him, Alexander."

"But you don't have to be."

The darkness in Alexander's eyes was compelling, and Mara looked away.

"According to Roman law, marriage by *usus* is not binding. Just walk out, Mara. It is your *right* to do so."

Just walk out. How many times had Mara considered doing exactly that? Even so, she hesitated. She was no longer afraid she couldn't live without Lucius. But she was aware of the many blatant sins upon her record. Did she truly wish to add one more to that lengthy list?

"Leave him, Mara," Alexander insisted, drawing closer. "Your happiness is at stake."

Your happiness. Yet hadn't she destroyed her life already chasing her own happiness?

"Walk away, Mara," Alexander said quietly. "You won't be alone if you do."

Never before had Mara faced such blatant temptation. The promise burning within the depths of Alexander's dark eyes was unnerving. It was as if she were being pulled in two opposing directions. The sensation was so intense she feared she would be torn apart.

What on earth should she do? Wasn't Alexander correct in his assessment, after all? She would never be happy if she remained with Lucius.

"Perhaps you simply need a taste of what you are missing, sweet little Mara. Perhaps then you would feel more confident making a final decision." Alexander's tone was lighthearted and teasing, but his offer struck Mara's heart with fear.

Somehow, she was reminded of a serpent in that long-lost garden paradise, whispering into the ear of another woman, telling her of the forbidden pleasures God had kept from her...

You will not surely die... the serpent had promised Eve.

"You won't regret it," Alexander promised Mara, tucking a stray curl behind her ear.

YOU SHALL NOT COMMIT ADULTERY.

The command resounded in Mara's mind like a mighty trumpet blast.

She had already broken many of God's commandments. And though she wasn't entirely sure where she stood with Him now, she feared digging an even deeper ditch for herself. It was going to be hard enough to crawl out of this one.

Perhaps the Lord was delivering her even now, rescuing her in a moment of fierce temptation. Perhaps this was the first step toward freedom, the first step toward climbing out of the pit.

Clutching her shawl tightly about her shoulders, Mara swung the door open even further.

"God has said, 'You shall not commit adultery.'"

Alexander stared at her as if he had been struck. "God says many things. Do you intend to keep every law?"

"Certainly not on my own, but perhaps with His help," she said firmly, drawing a shaky breath. "I haven't the faintest idea about how to please God, Alexander, but I think I must learn. And perhaps you should too."

Alexander simply stared at her, thunderstruck.

"You must leave."

Both shocked and irritated by Mara's uncompromising tone, Alexander brushed silently past her and left the house without another word.

***

Alexander

Moments later, Alexander lowered himself upon a marble bench in the midst of Caiaphas' lovely gardens.

Exhaling in frustration, he closed his eyes and breathed in the cool night air.

This evening certainly had not played out as he had intended.

He was still stunned by Mara's blatant refusal. Anger boiled inside him, for she had crushed his hopes along with his pride.

Annoyed by the deep sense of shame sweeping over him, he attempted to slow his racing heart.

Couldn't Mara see that he was simply looking out for her? That he wanted what was best for her?

Mara would never be happy in her present state. But he could open her eyes to a world of happiness and bliss. She would never regret leaving her husband! Never!

God has said, "You shall not commit adultery."

Alexander's hands curled into fists as Mara's quiet reprimand cut his heart like a knife. It wouldn't be adultery if she divorced her husband first, he wished to argue. After all, it was perfectly legal to get involved in a relationship after ending a marriage! His proposition was not only perfectly logical, it was perfectly legal which made it perfectly moral.

Didn't it?

Groaning in frustration, Alexander raked his fingers through his dark hair in an agitated fashion.

Deep in his gut, he sensed that his motives were far less than honorable. That annoyed him.

He was living to please himself. At Mara's expense. It was his own selfishness, not his concern for Mara, that drove him.

The thought galled.

But what galled even more was the fact that he wouldn't even have considered such things were it not for one Man...

The mysterious Rabbi whose teachings were upending everything he had ever known, turning his perspective inside out.

Annoyed, he dismissed the guilt rising in his chest. If one didn't look out for his own happiness and fulfillment, then how on earth was one to find it? He was simply seeking his own welfare like every other person on this wretched earth. He had a right to do so, as did Mara and anyone else!

Didn't he?

CHAPTER 16

Julia

Uttering a harsh cry, Barabbas shot up like a lightning bolt upon his sleeping pallet.

Frightened, Julia awoke with a start. "Barabbas? What is it?"

Barabbas breathed heavily, his entire body drenched in sweat.

Silver moonlight streamed in the window and slanted across her husband's muscular form. His chest heaved violently as if he struggled to catch his breath.

"Are you sick?" Julia asked groggily, the fog clearing as she sat up beside her husband.

Her inquiry was met by silence.

Her face softened. "Another nightmare?"

Barabbas looked away.

Pity welled up inside Julia. She knew he still dreamed about his family, the cruel way in which their lives were stolen from them.

She wondered at the depth of her husband's scars.

Would he ever recover from that great loss? Even more importantly, would he ever soften his heart toward God and stop blaming Him for that fateful day?

Why had God spared him, knowing that Barabbas would ultimately turn his face from Him?

There had to be a purpose.

Barabbas was a hardened man, walking in the footsteps of his father, a Zealot.

How ironic, Julia thought sadly as she studied her husband's handsome profile in the silver moonlight. *His name, meaning son of the father, fits him all too well. He is very much like his father, who breathed his last upon a Roman cross. If only he would take on the likeness of his heavenly Father and forsake the violence of his earthly one.*

Julia rarely felt any sympathy for her husband. He was stubborn and often cruel, intentionally bucking at the commandments of God in order to accomplish his own will. His heart was set upon vengeance. There was no room in it for anything else.

Barabbas was strong and powerfully built, a man of might like Samson of old. There were times when – much to her dismay – Julia was quite certain he was absolutely fearless, even against his better judgment. He threw himself into the fray with confidence and rage. He welcomed the battle, any battle.

But there were rare moments like this when Julia glimpsed another side of him. She saw a broken-hearted little boy weeping at the foot of a cross with no one to comfort him. Even his mother had fallen prey to the blade of a Roman sword.

How on earth had Barabbas survived the remainder of his childhood? Had he begged or stolen for sustenance? Did he work to support himself? Barabbas never spoke of his childhood.

She imagined he never would.

But tonight, she wished there was something she could do to comfort him, to heal the deep wounds in his soul.

Only You, Lord, she prayed silently, her eyes wet with tears. *Only You can comfort him. Please do so, Lord, and turn his heart to You.*

Barabbas turned to look at her then. Tears trickled down her cheeks. His eyes flickered slightly at the sight of her.

Were her tears for him?

"I'm so sorry, beloved," Julia whispered, her heart breaking. "I would do anything to make it right."

Amazingly, Barabbas' dark eyes softened. There were times when those eyes flashed angry fire, daring anyone to oppose him. Then there were other times, like tonight, when they were so tender, Julia thought that she would melt.

Why couldn't he be this way all the time? Didn't he see how she softened beneath his gaze? When he loved her sweetly, she longed to please him. But she never felt that way when he spoke harshly and ordered her about.

Unexpectedly, Barabbas reached for her and pulled her into his arms. She did not stiffen or recoil this time. Instead, she melted into his strong arms and prayed that God would allow her to comfort him.

***

Julia was uneasy.

Dabbing at her slick forehead with the corner of her shawl, she bent to stir the seasoned lentils in the cook pot dangling over the fire.

The month of Tammuz was typically warm, but this year, it was nearly unbearable. At least the evenings brought some relief, for the air cooled tremendously after sunset.

After stirring the lentils, Julia turned her attention to the vegetables and flatbread she had begun to prepare. Barabbas would be home soon, and he would be hungry.

She must quicken her pace.

But her hands fumbled as she worked. She couldn't stop thinking about her time with Barabbas the previous night.

He had sensed her compassion after he had awakened from his nightmare, and he had been touched. He had been so tender, so gentle with her. In that moment, she had forgotten about their pain and her disillusionment and simply enjoyed her husband.

Now, she felt nothing but regret.

First, one pleasurable night together did not change the character of her husband. He was the same hardened man he had always been. Perhaps by letting her guard down, she had simply made herself more vulnerable, more susceptible to repeated heartbreak.

And secondly, she avoided initiating intimacy with her husband. She was terrified at the prospect of having a child by him. What kind of father would he be? She shuddered even to think of it.

Julia simply couldn't bear to see her own child walking in the footsteps of his father.

Sighing, she arranged the sliced vegetables on layers of flatbread and sprinkled it with crumbled goat cheese.

She supposed she must place her concerns in the hands of the Lord. He was in control. She had to remember that.

As of now, it would seem the Lord had seen fit to close her womb. And for that, she was desperately thankful.

CHAPTER 17

Lucius

Bethany was a wretched little village nestled upon the eastern slope of the Mount of Olives. One of the poorest villages in the region, its advantageous location on the road to Jericho did little to improve its desirability.

Lucius had always detested orders requiring a trip through the squalid little hamlet... until he met Mary.

Mary was an energetic woman with a powerful presence. She wore her sea of abundant black curls in a plaited style, and her apparel was bold and sultry – rather like the woman who wore it.

Not only was this woman gorgeous and talented, she was rich. Apparently, she was a rather acute woman of business, a woman of independent means who conducted her own financial affairs. That was extremely unusual.

Lucius knew very little about her, except for the fact that she was supposedly an easy mark. She was part of the plan, although she wouldn't know that until it was far too late to retreat.

At times, Lucius was plagued with guilt. He suspected that Caiaphas had ordered him to target an orphaned prostitute because she was expendable. Whatever dark plans Caiaphas had for this woman, there would be no husband or father to reckon with once it was finished.

Lucius hoped it wouldn't matter that this woman had relatives in Bethany, a brother and a sister. Apparently, they were the only reason she bothered frequenting the wretched town. He imagined a cosmopolitan woman like herself far preferred bustling, civilized cities like Tiberias, Caesarea, or Magdala.

But today, Lucius pushed aside his guilt and bothersome thoughts, focusing instead on the task at hand.

His heart raced as a beautiful woman with exotic but careworn features emerged from the appointed brothel. She met him with a sultry smile and a close embrace.

"I thought you'd never arrive," she said in her low, breathy tone, her dark eyes gleaming.

Lucius' mouth tipped in a rueful half smile. "I'm here."

At first, he had questioned his ability to carry out this assignment. After all, how was a simple soldier like himself supposed to win the heart of a woman who had known a hundred men before him and kept her heart from every single one of them? In her sight, he was simply another business transaction, another client to aid her in her quest to amass unthinkable wealth.

But it had taken him no time at all to realize that, despite her impenetrable veneer, Mary was far more vulnerable than one might suspect.

What she really desired was love, acceptance. Someone in whom to confide. Someone who treasured her thoughts, her heart, as well as her body. If he could just convince her that he was different from the rest, that he truly loved her for who she was, then his plans would succeed.

A slow grin spread across Lucius' hardened features as Mary took his hand and led him toward the brothel.

He was certainly up for the challenge.

Mary was easy prey for an experienced predator like himself.

***

Malchus

Malchus was irked when Caiaphas ordered him to bring the best wine to the upper terrace where he planned to convene with the captain of the guard.

Balancing a delicate tray on one hand, Malchus climbed the curved marble steps, attempting to mask his rueful expression with a practiced look of insouciance. Servants weren't supposed to have feelings, after all.

But the thought of serving Caiaphas *and* Lucius was rather exasperating. Caiaphas and Lucius upon the same terrace? The situation couldn't possibly get any worse.

Or so he thought.

"She suspects something. She plagued me with

sharp questions the moment I entered the threshold."

Lucius' tone was laced with frustration and unease.

Amused, Malchus paused before climbing the remaining steps and emerging upon the elegant terrace.

Smirking, he knew that Caiaphas would not tolerate Lucius' indolent complaints.

This could get very interesting.

"Of course she suspects something," Caiaphas responded, his tone even. "Your foolish serving wench is responding just as we knew she would. It is all part of the plan."

Again, this elusive plan! What on earth did it entail? Malchus knew it involved Mara, and that concerned him. His conscience pricked, and he wondered if perhaps he should risk speaking with her about it.

Not that she would listen. She never listened to him anymore.

Malchus' train of thought was interrupted when Lucius spoke again, his tone tinged with indignation. "I do wish you would divulge a few more details regarding this plan!"

You and me both, Malchus thought wryly.

"I am under constant interrogation in my own home!" Lucius added, his mounting aggravation evident.

"You are a Roman soldier, trained to withstand the harshest rigors and the heat of battle," Caiaphas mused, his tone tinged with mockery. "And yet you are nettled by the prying questions of one woman?"

The silence that followed crackled with tension.

Malchus savored Lucius' silent fury.

"May I ask a question, Lucius?" the high priest inquired, his tone frightfully composed.

You just did, Malchus thought wryly, enjoying Lucius' discomfort a bit too much.

"You may," Lucius responded, his tone strained.

"Does this marriage mean anything to you? Anything at all?"

Malchus' pulse quickened as he awaited Lucius' response. The silence seemed to stretch on forever.

Eventually, Lucius formed a response.

"You know it means nothing to me."

Malchus grit his teeth, attempting to curb his fury. Hadn't he warned Mara of this all along? The man was a worthless infidel. If only Mara had heeded his valid warning.

"Are you absolutely sure about that?" Caiaphas pressed calmly. "Because I sense that the woman is beginning to mean something to you."

"She is nothing. She means nothing to me."

"And yet you are undone by her questions and accusations?"

"Of course not. She is a constant bur in my side."

"Good. You were trained to operate based on logic and reason, not emotion. Your feelings cannot interfere with this assignment."

"I am a soldier of Rome above all else. You can count on that."

"Rest assured you shall be rewarded. And as promised, I will personally see to the abolition of this undesirable marriage once you have fulfilled your obligations. You have my word it will be arranged."

"My deepest gratitude."

Disgusted by what he was hearing, Malchus hefted the tray a bit higher and prepared to enter the dragon's lair.

If he had any luck at all, Lucius would drink himself into oblivion and topple over the edge of the terrace.

Unfortunately, up to this point, he hadn't possessed the slightest shred of luck.

CHAPTER 18

Joanna

The Upper City slept like a sea of glistening marble beneath the silver moonlight.

Tossing and turning in agitation, Joanna, Julia's former nursemaid, moaned in her sleep as a nightmare gripped her in her unconscious state.

A small, dingy house in a squalid precinct loomed at the forefront of her subconscious mind. Within, she heard a newborn child crying.

The darkness seemed to close in upon the tiny house, as if intent on smothering what little light remained within.

And there was a woman. A young woman, beautiful and afraid. Tears streamed down her pale cheeks as she desperately sought to calm a screaming infant, to no avail.

Joanna awoke with a start, drawing a sharp breath, stifling a cry of despair. Drawing aside her blanket, she arose quietly, her jaw set firmly. Arrangements must be made, but she knew what she must do.

And her kind master, Simon, would surely not forbid her.

***

Julia

Delicately dabbing sweat from her fair brow, Julia was relieved the miserable summer months were nearly behind her.

The month of Elul swept in like a welcome tide. This, too, would be a sweltering month, but it would pass, promising cooler days ahead as autumn approached.

Julia sat heavily upon an unoccupied bench near the Upper Market's colonnades. Despite the fact that the busy marketplace was already bustling with shoppers, Julia prayed Melina would find her there.

She simply hadn't the strength to go any further.

It was this miserable heat! It was suffocating and oppressive. She was certain this invasive heat was the culprit for the misery she had experienced over the past few weeks.

If not for her promise to meet Melina, she would have remained in bed today. Nausea swept over her entire being in vicious waves, nearly rocking her off her feet at times and haunting her with bouts of dizziness.

She was desperate for relief from this heat, this misery.

"Julia!"

Just lifting her head felt like a monumental task, and it took all her strength to force a small smile.

Melina rushed past shoppers in her attempt to

reach Julia, an empty basket bouncing unceremoniously upon her forearm.

"Hello," Julia managed, her voice sounding funny in her own ears.

Worry clouded Melina's soft features the moment her eyes absorbed the image of her friend seated desolately upon the bench. The fact that Julia had failed to rise and enthusiastically embrace her was a disturbing hint that all was not well.

Kneeling before her friend, Melina took both her hands. "Julia, is something wrong?"

Julia managed a weak laugh. "It must be this heat. It just seems to sap all the strength out of me. And it makes me terribly sick to my stomach."

Melina gazed up at her friend with a practiced eye. "It has never affected you this way before."

It took far too much effort to form a logical response, so Julia opted for silence.

Melina tilted her head and studied her lovely friend. Her face was pale, her expression drawn. She had lost a bit of weight. Rising slowly, Melina set aside her basket then seated herself on the bench beside Julia.

"What ails you?" she asked, gently feeling Julia's forehead with the back of her hand. It was warm and clammy.

"Frankly, I'm miserable," Julia managed, closing her eyes against the bright morning sunlight. It hurt her eyes.

Melina shook her head sympathetically. "Oh, Julia, I'm so sorry. You should have said something about this sooner. I could have been praying for you."

"You can pray for me now," Julia managed wryly,

gripping her roiling stomach. "Unceasingly."

"How long have you felt this way?"

"It's worsened this last two weeks or so. Thankfully, it usually passes after a few hours."

"Always in the morning?"

Julia looked to Melina suspiciously, one brow lifted in question. "Yes," she responded slowly. "Why?"

"Well, it's just that…" Melina's voice trailed off and she looked away, wringing her hands nervously in her lap.

"What?" Julia asked, momentarily forgetting her misery as her curiosity got the best of her. "Don't tell me you think I'm dying or suffering some frightful disease!"

"Oh, no!" Melina amended quickly. "Far from it! I just wondered if perhaps…"

"Perhaps what?" Julia hoped she didn't sound as agitated as she felt.

"Well, is it possible that perhaps… perhaps…" Melina lifted her gaze to meet Julia's, clearly nervous to state the obvious. "Well, is it possible you could be with child?"

Julia's stomach dropped to her feet. It took her a moment to realize that her mouth was open. She promptly closed it.

"It's just a thought," Melina stammered blushingly. "Perhaps you should see a physician."

"I don't need a physician!" Julia's stomach roiled in angry response.

"You're certain?" Melina asked shyly, sensing her friend's annoyance. Even so, her concern outweighed Julia's incredulity.

"I cannot be… with child," Julia hissed under her breath, her eyes darting nervously about the crowds milling around the Upper Market.

"But why not?" Melina asked innocently. "You're a married woman. It's only natural to suspect –"

"Oh, Melina, please! I couldn't be!"

Melina touched her shoulder compassionately. "To be with child would be a very great blessing."

Julia buried her face in her hands, panic gripping her. "A blessing? It would be a curse! Who would raise the child? Barabbas?"

"And you, naturally," Melina laughed, attempting to calm her friend.

"Melina, my husband is a Zealot – an outlaw! What kind of father do you suppose he would be?"

"This is why we lay our requests before God, Julia," Melina said with great feeling. She took Julia's hand. "And perhaps we are merely borrowing trouble. You haven't seen a physician. Perhaps you should do so."

Julia looked away, ashamed. "We haven't the funds to pay a physician."

"But surely your father –"

"My father shouldn't have to pay for my husband's incompetence," Julia interrupted impatiently.

"Your father loves you. He would want you to receive the best of care."

"Barabbas would kill me if I went to my father before I told him about the child."

Melina squeezed her hand, sensing her friend's state of agitation. "We will pray about this unceasingly, Julia. God will provide the answers. He knew of your need long before we discovered it."

"Perhaps I will visit my mother," Julia said quietly. "She can keep a confidence, and she will know whether or not a physician is needed. As you said, we may be borrowing trouble."

"Joanna, Chuza's wife, recently told me about a sermon she heard Jesus preach to a large group of people," Melina said gently. "He said, '*Therefore do not worry about tomorrow, for tomorrow will worry about its own things. Sufficient for the day is its own trouble.*'"

"I can't argue with that," Julia stated glumly. "Today's trouble is certainly sufficient."

Melina laughed, a pleasant sound. "The point is that we are not to worry about tomorrow. God has given us *this* moment, this day. And never forget – *This is the day the Lord has made; we will rejoice and be glad in it!* Trust in God and do what He requires of you today, *then* He will show you what needs to be done tomorrow."

Julia stared at Melina, shaking her head in amusement. "Where do you store all this wisdom, Melina? How does it possibly fit in one small person?"

"It isn't *my* wisdom, Julia. It's simply what I've found in the Scriptures. Thank God it is there for all of us!"

Melina's faith was contagious, and Julia couldn't help but catch a bit of it. Fleetingly, she wondered if she would ever have that kind of effect on people. Melina's faith in God was steady and unshakeable. Her joy resonated from deep within, entirely unaffected by circumstance.

Inwardly, Julia determined to learn by her example.

She sensed that she would need an unwavering faith and an unshakeable joy in the days ahead. And perhaps, like Melina, her peace and steadfastness would edify and uplift those around her, as well.

CHAPTER 19

Julia sat across the table from her dear neighbor, Deborah, her hands folded nervously in her lap. She had known this moment would come, but she had hoped against hope that it wouldn't.

"I wish there were some other way," Deborah was saying brokenly, her eyes wet with tears. "But Isaac is certain that God is calling us to follow Jesus from town to town. Isaac believes that Jesus has reached a crucial point in His ministry."

Attempting to hold back tears of her own, Julia bit her lower lip and nodded in resignation. She didn't tell Deborah that she feared she would need her now more than ever. If she did, Deborah would feel even worse about leaving.

Do not worry about tomorrow...

The thought whispered its way gently into Julia's mind, and, squaring her shoulders, she resolved to take the words to heart.

God was in control.

He had a plan.

She, therefore, must trust Him.

Reaching across Julia's crude wooden table, Deborah took her hand. "Isaac assures me this will not be permanent. We will return when Jesus frequents Jerusalem, which means I will still see you often. Jesus always seems to return to Jerusalem for the holy days."

Julia nodded bravely, forcing a smile she was far from feeling. "I understand, Deborah. You have to go wherever God calls you. And when you return, I will be waiting for my beloved friends with open arms."

Deborah smiled through her tears. "I know you will, dear one. I know you will."

Julia feared another bout of nausea was about to overtake her. Or perhaps it was just this miserable heat. Or her great anxiety.

"Can we pray, Julia? Somehow, I still don't have peace about leaving you, even if it's only for a time."

That makes two of us, Julia thought glumly. If her greatest fear was confirmed, then what on earth would she do without Deborah's wise and calming presence?

Do not worry about tomorrow.

Deborah reached across the table and took Julia's other hand. "Let's pray."

Julia bowed her head, quaking inwardly. She was so afraid.

"Lord God of Heaven, how good You are to us! Despite our fears and wavering faith, we ask that you act mightily on our behalf. Make Your will as clear as a sunbeam and guide as by that brilliant light!"

"Yes, Lord," Julia agreed quietly. "May it be so."

"You know my concerns, Lord, and Julia's too. Indeed, you know every inch of our hearts. Lord, make a way for us. Enable Isaac and me to walk in

Your will. Please provide for Julia while we are away. Show her that You, Lord, are *Jehovah Jireh*, the God who provides. You, Lord, are the mighty *El Roi*, the God who sees."

Julia shut her eyes tightly, refusing to allow the tears to escape.

"Lord," Deborah continued, her voice rising in strength as she sought their Maker, "You open doors no one can shut, and shut doors that no one can open. Open a door for us, Lord. Open a door!"

Knock, knock, knock.

Both women froze mid-prayer.

Tentatively, Deborah raised gray eyes toward Julia. "Are you expecting company?"

Julia shook her head, unnerved.

Knock, knock, knock.

Julia rose on shaky legs and went to the door. She swung it open.

Joanna, her beloved nursemaid, stood upon the threshold.

"Joanna!" Julia stared at the pleasant-faced woman in shock. "How I've missed you!"

Joanna's eyes twinkled. "May I come in?"

Julia laughed as she ushered her inside. "Of course! Of course you can! Come in, come in!"

Deborah had risen to her feet, and her eyes traveled to the aging woman, a question in them.

"Forgive me," Julia laughed, drawing Joanna toward the table where Deborah stood. "I've been terribly rude! I'm just taken aback, that's all. Deborah, this is Joanna. She was my nursemaid at my father's house."

Deborah's eyes lit up with respect. "Joanna, it is an honor to meet you!"

"And Joanna, this is Deborah, my dear neighbor and friend."

"I've heard much about you and your husband," Joanna said, firmly grasping Deborah's hand. "My apologies for this intrusion," she added with a broad grin.

"You are never an intrusion!" Julia insisted, her eyes traveling to the one small leather satchel in Joanna's possession. "Have you come to visit?"

Joanna set her satchel on the table, then took Julia's hands in her own. "I'll just get straight to the point," she said in her usual blunt manner.

Julia laughed airily, feeling better already. "You always do."

"The good Lord made it loud and clear I was to get right on over here and help, if you'll have me. I've come to stay for a time, with your permission and blessing, of course."

Julia and Deborah exchanged awed glances, amazed.

Joanna smiled warmly and gave Julia's hands a motherly squeeze.

One look into Joanna's knowing eyes, and Julia realized the woman knew her secret! But how on earth? She herself wasn't quite certain!

One thing of which she was absolutely certain: her God was amazing indeed. It would seem He had quite literally opened a door!

Even so, Julia felt that certain things needed to be said – even if it meant Joanna might retract her kind offer.

"Joanna," she began nervously, her cheeks stained with humiliation, "as desperately as I long to accept your proposal, my husband and I cannot afford to pay household help and –"

"Nonsense!" Joanna interrupted, clicking her tongue chidingly. "I don't want to hear mention of payment again, you hear?"

Julia stared at her, stunned.

"Everything has been arranged. I'm rather a woman of means, if I do say so myself. I've worked for your father for decades, and he is a generous man. His pay has been more than sufficient, and I am a frugal woman. I can support myself, so payment is out of the question. And I have your father's full blessing to remain with you for a time, so that matter has been settled as well."

Julia's heart swelled within her chest, close to bursting with love and gratitude toward this selfless woman. But her emotions plummeted just as quickly when reality struck.

"Oh, Joanna," she moaned, heartbroken. "My husband will never allow this. Never!"

Deborah and Joanna exchanged knowing looks.

"Now listen here, missy," Joanna said, one hand firmly planted upon an ample hip. "God made it perfectly clear this is where I am to be. That being said, your husband has no choice but to allow it. Who is he to defy the Lord?"

"That hasn't stopped him up to this point," Julia groaned in frustration.

"Where is your faith?" Joanna asked pointedly. "I'm not saying your husband won't resist. But if this is the will of God, then no man can stand in His way. You seem to be forgetting that we serve a God who opens doors no one can shut and shuts doors that no one can open – not even Barabbas."

Julia and Deborah exchanged looks of utter

shock. Little chills crept their way up and down Julia's spine.

Joanna had no way of knowing the specific prayer they had offered to God the moment before her arrival! Her words confirmed the fact that God was working – opening the doors He wished to open, and slamming shut the ones He knew were better closed. As they had requested, He was making His will as clear as a sunbeam!

And now, Julia realized, amazed, *I must simply trust the Lord to bring His plan to fruition.*

***

"Absolutely not!" Barabbas' face twisted in rage, sending chills of foreboding scurrying up and down Julia's spine. "I forbid it!"

Humiliated, Julia cast an apologetic glance toward Joanna, who sat calmly at the table.

Surprised, Julia chanced a second glance. Joanna was completely composed. She sat with hands folded comfortably in her lap, smiling faintly as if she were enjoying an evening with friends. Even as Barabbas fumed and raged about her presence there.

"We don't need her, Julia! I don't want her here."

"But why not?"

"Because I don't want a stranger living in my own house!"

"First, she's not a stranger – she helped raise me! And second, why do you even care? It's not as if you are ever home!"

Barabbas flushed with a new wave of fury. He turned to Joanna, his eyes cold. "Get out."

"But, Barabbas –" Julia wept.

"Get out! You are not welcome here."

Unperturbed, Joanna began to rise.

"Wait!" Julia pleaded, tears streaming down her face. "Barabbas, please. She won't be any trouble. She wants to help."

"With what?" Barabbas demanded tautly. "Is it too difficult a task to keep this small home all by yourself?"

"I keep my own home well, and you perfectly know it," Julia retorted, struggling to gain control of her emotions. "But you always hate it when I have to go to the marketplace or run errands alone. Wouldn't you feel better about it if Joanna accompanied me?"

Barabbas considered her logic, though it was obvious he was still annoyed.

"It's only for a time. Can we try it, Barabbas? Please? You'll scarcely notice her presence."

Folding his arms across his broad chest, Barabbas cocked his head to one side and said coolly, "And will she sit there at the table when I return home and desire an evening with my wife?"

Horrified, Julia's color deepened.

"I can make myself scarce anytime, and I can sleep just about anywhere," Joanna quipped, speaking up for the first time. "I'm not looking to cause any trouble between a man and his wife."

"You certainly could have fooled me," Barabbas said through his teeth, earning a glare from Julia. "You say you can sleep anywhere? Fine. You'll sleep on the roof. And you'll only enter this house when granted permission to do so."

Julia blanched, shocked and appalled by her husband's behavior. "Joanna can't sleep on the –"

"Nonsense," Joanna interrupted cheerfully, hoisting her satchel and preparing to retire for the night. "The fresh air will do me good!"

Barabbas watched her go, attempting to recover from his surprise at her cheerful capitulation. "You'll find the ladder propped against the house out back."

"Thank you kindly." Winking at Julia, Joanna slipped out the door before closing it firmly behind her.

Julia stared at Barabbas, aghast. "How can you be so hateful? Her old bones can't endure the night's chill! What if it rains or storms?"

"Then she can go back home where she belongs."

"You're being unfair!"

"She's here, isn't she?"

"Barabbas –"

"Speak another word about this and she'll never set foot in this house again, understand?"

That night, Julia presented a rigid back to her husband as she curled up on her sleeping pallet, tears coursing down her cheeks. She kept thinking about her aging nursemaid, alone and shivering on the decrepit roof. It wasn't fair. It wasn't right.

Joanna had come to serve them at her own expense, and the best they could offer her in return was a cold, hard, lonely roof on which to sleep.

Another thought occurred to Julia – a thought so terrible she covered her face in shame.

What if Joanna discovered that Barabbas served the tyrant force responsible for the death of her beloved husband so many years ago? Surely Joanna would pack her belongings, shake the dust of their home from her feet, and walk out the door to never look back.

Weeping, Julia drew her flimsy blanket to her chin and cried herself to sleep, thinking of one thing only.

Joanna must never, ever find out.

CHAPTER 20

"You've been sleeping on that roof for over a week, Joanna, and it is completely unacceptable!" Julia fumed as she chopped vegetables with a vengeance. "Every time I consider the way my husband treats you –"

"Shah, child," Joanna interrupted, assisting Julia with her supper preparations. "It's rather invigorating sleeping beneath a canopy of stars in the fresh night air. Stop fretting your pretty little head about it!"

"How can I, Joanna? What he is doing isn't right!"

"I don't expect him to be thrilled about my presence here. In his eyes, I am simply an unwanted intrusion."

"That certainly doesn't justify his hatefulness!"

"Julia, a husband and wife need privacy in their own home. When the Lord called me to stay with you for a time, I hadn't realized your house was quite so –" she halted mid-sentence, blushing.

Julia attacked an onion with her cooking knife and threw the pieces into the pot. "It's alright, Joanna, you can say it. *Small*. Our house is terribly, miserably small!"

"I was going to say *cozy*," Joanna amended with a playful grin. "You see, I have no doubt the Lord has called me here. He may have had living arrangements in mind, however, that I hadn't anticipated."

"I can't imagine the Lord would *sentence* you to sleeping on the roof, braving the elements!"

"Ah, dear girl! You forget – the Lord does not sentence us at all. Anything He does to us, He does for our ultimate good."

Julia halted her chopping long enough to pin Joanna down with her own flinty gaze. "And what if the heavens open in the middle of the night? Will that be for your ultimate good as well?"

Joanna laughed blithely. "I'll purchase a canopy."

"But you shouldn't have to!" Julia sighed in frustration as she emptied the last of the vegetables into the pot and hung it over the low fire.

Joanna went to her, turning her by the shoulders in order to look into her eyes. "Julia, my dear girl, you are worried and troubled about many things. But see how the Lord has already provided? He will continue to provide, to meet both our needs."

Julia's eyes filled with tears. Plopping heavily upon the bench, she covered her face with her hands. "I'm ashamed of my lack of faith, Joanna – utterly ashamed. I'm not always like this."

Joanna sat down beside her, wiping her hands on her apron. "I know that, child. We all struggle at times."

"I just haven't felt at all like myself lately."

Joanna placed a heavy hand upon Julia's knee. "And I know *why*, dearest, though you have yet to mention it."

Julia turned tearful eyes toward her nursemaid. "How did you know?"

"I was quite certain the Lord revealed it to me the night He asked me to help you."

Julia shook her head in wonder.

"Does Barabbas know?"

"*I* don't even know for sure!"

Joanna asked several questions, and Julia answered them as accurately as she could.

"Child, I do believe you really are expecting a little one. And what a joy it is to share this special time with you!"

Julia looked away, ashamed. "I'm not ready to tell Barabbas, Joanna. It's too early. Perhaps I will lose the baby, then he will only be disappointed if I tell him."

Joanna's eyes grew serious. "Surely you do not hope for that? A child is a gift from the Lord."

Julia held back tears. "I'm so afraid."

"God will be with you, Julia. Already He has begun making provision for you – long before you even knew you needed it. You must trust Him."

Julia nodded, inwardly striving for the peace she desired.

"Let's visit your mother tomorrow," Joanna suggested as she rose from the bench to stir the vegetables in the pot. "She will want to know right away, I'm thinking."

Julia sighed. If she had married a decent man, this just might be the happiest, proudest moment of her life. Instead, she had disobeyed her Lord and dishonored her parents by marrying a man who opposed God.

At the time, she hadn't even considered the possibly endless repercussions of her rebellion. Now, she nearly quaked in fear at the thought of raising a little one with Barabbas.

"Might I make a suggestion?" Joanna asked as she sprinkled some salt into the cookpot.

Julia nodded glumly.

"You pray for that sweet child of yours, Julia, and pray unlike you ever have before. Pray that your child will follow hard after the Lord all the days of his or her life. There is nothing quite like the power of a praying mother, dear girl."

Julia's eyes welled with tears. She would do as Joanna said, and she would pray unlike ever before.

"Joanna," she asked softly, her voice thick with emotion. "Will you pray for this child too?"

Joanna turned to face her, her lips tipping in a knowing smile. "My dear, sweet girl, I already am!"

Their conversation was interrupted by a faint tap at the door.

Julia rose to answer it. She was pleased to find Deborah standing on the other side.

"Good morning, my dear ladies!" Deborah said cheerfully as she entered the house. "My, something smells wonderful!"

"Well, it should – Julia tells me it's your recipe!" Joanna grinned.

"I'm in a bit of a rush, as Isaac has asked me to purchase a few items from the market," Deborah said with a humble smile. "But an idea occurred to me as I was praying this morning, and I thought I'd ask you both about it."

Julia lifted her brows in question.

"Joanna," Deborah asked earnestly, "this might be a terrible idea, but I wondered if you would be interested in staying at our house while we are away? We are right next-door to Julia, so you would be easily accessible to her at all times. Then all three of you would have a bit more privacy, and I wouldn't worry about our poor little house falling apart in our absence."

Julia and Joanna exchanged looks of surprise, then both women burst out laughing.

Deborah looked back and forth between the two of them as if they had gone mad. "It's a silly suggestion, I know, but –"

"Quite the contrary, Deborah," Joanna gasped, steadying herself at the table. "Your suggestion is simply another answer to prayer!"

Deborah's eyes widened. "How so?"

"Let's just say that Barabbas isn't thrilled about my presence here. He will be relieved not to have me within such close proximity, I imagine. And quite frankly, I don't blame him. It's not right to plant a crotchety old woman like myself right in the midst of a newly married couple!"

"Joanna," Julia interrupted. "You are *not* a crotchety old–"

"I'd be honored to stay in your home, Deborah," Joanna finished grandly. "And thank you for the kind offer!"

Deborah smiled, a look of relief washing over her features. "Then it's all settled! You can move in when we depart three days hence. I'll feel so much better knowing someone is caring for the old place."

Joanna turned to Julia, her eyes twinkling with delight. "You see, dear one? God always provides!"

CHAPTER 21

Malchus

Five days after the most fearsome and sacred day of the Jewish year – the Day of Atonement, which followed the glorious yet deafening Feast of Trumpets – the celebrated Feast of Tabernacles descended upon the numberless sea of pilgrims residing within Jerusalem's ancient borders.

Midway through the esteemed month of Tishri and the last of the highly anticipated autumn festivals, the Feast of Tabernacles was a joyous, week-long occasion, during which all Jewish families constructed a crude *sukkah,* or booth, in which they would dwell for the remainder of the feast in order to commemorate their ancestors' journey through the wilderness. As the Feast of Tabernacles was conducted at the end of the agricultural year when both olives and grapes were plenteously harvested, the feast was also a time to thank the Lord for His provision and to beseech Him for plentiful rain to water the earth the following year.

The *sukkah* erected during the feast also stood as a stark reminder to the people as they forsook the comfort and luxuries of their own homes for the crude shelter of a temporary booth constructed of rough boughs and foliage: one must forsake their own comfortable sins in order to follow God through the wilderness and to the Promised Land.

Malchus' mouth tipped sardonically as his eyes swept the perimeter of his master's lavish *sukkah*. Perched atop an elegant terrace overlooking the Temple compound, the multi-roomed booth of the high priest had been erected by servants rather than Caiaphas himself, who was far too involved in "important" matters to bother with such a menial task. Plush Persian rugs were piled in luxurious stacks upon the floor. Silken tapestries flitted in the warm autumn breezes, concealing the comforts and luxuries within the booth.

It would seem the high priest would have little cause to reflect upon the harsh, relentless wilderness wanderings of his ancestors as he lounged upon plush couches within his own opulent tabernacle.

Malchus was on edge as he stood at attention upon the terrace, awaiting his master's every beck and call. It was nerve-wracking to be within such close proximity of the volatile priest for the course of an entire week. Of course, Caiaphas' presence was also demanded at the Temple compound, and on those occasions, Malchus was exceedingly grateful for the man's absence.

The festivals and holy days were one of the rare occasions when the high priest and his regal wife occupied the same chambers. At times, Malchus forgot the man even had a wife. She was a petite yet robust woman with an enormous presence that filled a room. At times, Malchus wondered if her husband was actually intimidated by her.

The daughter of Annas, the former high priest and one of the most highly esteemed men in Judea and Galilee, Miriam had been born into wealth and position. She was an impressive figure, and it was rumored that at least one of her granddaughters bore her name, a great honor for a woman. With prematurely gray hair woven into an elaborate Roman style, subtle and skillfully applied cosmetics, and a magnificent wardrobe, the wife of Caiaphas bore her nobility with every proud lift of her head along with every graceful movement. Malchus was quite certain the woman was an iron fist in a delicate velvet glove. Caiaphas did well to tread lightly about her, especially considering the fact that her father's influence had aided his own wealth in securing his coveted position, not to mention maintaining it.

"Malchus."

Instinctively, Malchus stood a bit straighter as Miriam parted the delicate tapestries sheltering the entrance of her elaborate booth. Her dark eyes flashed with impatience.

"My lady?" Malchus managed, uncomfortable in the stately older woman's presence.

"When shall my husband return from his duties at the Temple?"

Malchus' eyes darted toward the glowing western horizon, opposite the Temple compound where the high priest should have long since completed his duties.

"His arrival is imminent, my lady," Malchus responded, hoping his voice sounded calm and controlled.

"The evening meal shall be served upon his arrival?"

"As you have commanded, my lady."

"Very well."

The sound of roughly approaching footsteps echoed upon a marble staircase, and Malchus readied himself for action.

Caiaphas emerged at the mouth of the broad stairway, followed by Hezron and Zadok. Arrayed in dark layers of their finest priestly garments, the men appeared rather like pompous birds with ruffled feathers as they descended upon the terrace, their agitation like a living presence that crackled in the still, dusky air.

Gracefully lifting her elaborately woven head covering, Miriam emerged from the tent, arms open to welcome her husband's colleagues.

"Greetings, my good men. Will you honor us with your presence as we partake of our evening meal?"

"There will be no relaxation until this important matter has been settled," Caiaphas growled, uncharacteristically unaware of his tone toward his wife.

Miriam's sharp brows lifted at her husband's unexpected response. "What troubles you, my husband?"

"What troubles me? The Troubler of Jerusalem, of all of Galilee and Judea!"

"Something must be done," Zadok said, his tone urgent.

Caiaphas paced upon the terrace as Zadok, Hezron, and Miriam studied him with avid intensity.

"The cursed Pharisees and chief priests have taken matters into their own hands. They attempted to arrest the pestilent Rabbi, sending officers to detain Him," Caiaphas explained for Miriam's benefit.

Malchus never ceased to marvel at the influence she possessed. What other politico would reveal such matters to a woman, regardless of her station?

A slight smile tugged at the corners of Miriam's hard mouth. "Ah, rumors abounded as to whether the Man would dare show His face in Jerusalem. He has a high price upon His head, and many enemies."

Malchus wondered why Jesus had revealed Himself now, midway through the feast. Would it not have been wiser to remain in hiding, even if He felt honor-bound to attend the feast in Jerusalem?

"Is He in custody?" Miriam asked coolly, nodding toward a servant girl who scurried away to retrieve refreshments for the hot, dusty Sadducees.

"He is not," Caiaphas responded sharply, his eyes resting upon the Temple compound below, surrounded by makeshift booths. Even the Temple court overflowed with the crude structures. Pilgrims had set up simple tables outside their booths and were now reciting prayers and partaking of the evening meal with their families.

"No?" Miriam's brows lifted in surprise.

"He eluded the guards."

"But how?"

"Cursed if I know!" Caiaphas ground out, his fists clenched at his sides. His gray eyes continued to scan the distant horizon rather like a predator evaluating its prey. "The officers returned to the Pharisees and chief priests without Him."

"Were the officers punished?" Again, from Miriam.

"I should hope to the highest degree!"

"I made inquiries," Hezron said, his cool tone betraying his disgust. "The officers were taken by the self-proclaimed Rabbi's speech. They claimed no one has ever spoken like this Man."

"Fools, all of them!" Caiaphas spat out, turning to rest his bejeweled hands upon the intricate railing as he gazed over a feasting Jerusalem. His gray eyes flashed with black fire. "Something must be done. This is getting out of hand."

"Shall we send our own men to apprehend him?" Hezron dared, eager to punish the offensive perpetrator.

"Are you as foolish as the Pharisees and chief priests?" Caiaphas said under his breath, continuing to present a rigid back to the Sadducees.

Affronted, Hezron said nothing, but his firm jaw twitched in concealed wrath.

"Today, the Pharisees risked our entire institution with one rash act. God knows they are stupid and incompetent. We will not follow suit and risk inciting a riot, which would only serve to provide the Romans with an excuse to crush the rebellion. We will not defile this sacred feast."

"What must be done then?" This from Zadok, an aging Sadducee with leathery skin and sad eyes.

"Nothing. Absolutely nothing –"

Three pairs of stunned eyes turned to Caiaphas in astonished question. Malchus found himself staring at the high priest as well, both startled and relieved by his answer.

"–until the feast has ended."

It was as if Miriam and the Sadducees released a collective breath.

"And then?" Hezron demanded, forgetting his

place in his fierce agitation.

"To ruin Him before the people in the midst of this great feast would only incite rebellion. We cannot risk it. But the moment this feast has ended, the people themselves will end Him. Trust me when I say that they will be crying out for His blood, and they themselves shall take it. Not only will they accomplish our purposes for us – we will not have made ourselves detestable in the sight of the people."

"And if the people fail to meet our expectations?" Hezron dared, his eyes two narrow slits.

"If the people fail to end Him, then He will be playing directly into the hands of the Romans."

Malchus noticed that Miriam asked no questions despite the Sadducees' extreme puzzlement. Rather, a knowing smile played about the corners of her lips. Clearly, she understood her husband well enough to recognize he had formulated a foolproof plan, as impossible as it sounded.

"But, but how?" Zadok asked lamely.

Caiaphas offered no response. Instead he turned to Malchus, his gray eyes afire. "Malchus!"

Malchus was certain his heart had dropped to the pit of his stomach. Of the dozen servants scattered about the terrace awaiting their master's bidding, why must he be the one commanded?

"My lord?" Malchus managed, palms sweating.

Caiaphas' eyes flashed their angry and dangerous fire, silencing further questions or arguments from anyone upon the terrace.

"Summon Lucius."

CHAPTER 22

Alexander

The Feast of Tabernacles was drawing to a close, though a week of feasting, singing, dancing, and storytelling had scarcely whetted the ardor of those crowding Jerusalem's booth-lined streets.

Today was reputed to be a glorious day – the final day of the Feast of Tabernacles, simply known as the great day of the feast.

Alexander leaned against a pillar in Solomon's Court at the Temple, amused by the religious fervor of thousands of Jewish men, women, and children milling about the Temple compound. To him, their religion was cloaked in mystery and odd ritualistic rites. Every moment of the feast appeared to symbolize something that the people clearly accepted. Whether or not they understood the meaning behind each act was beyond him. Whatever symbolism each rite might entail certainly surpassed his own understanding.

The endless sacrifices, haunting chants, and never-ending Scripture recitations ceased to impress him. After spending over a year in Judea, he had long-since wearied of these daily religious practices. It was as if these Jews prayed incessantly to their unseen God. And if they weren't praying to Him, then they were reciting impossibly large, memorized portions of His holy texts.

They lived and breathed the Words of their God. Sometimes, a particular recitation would catch him completely off guard, relating so much to his own situation that the gooseflesh would prickle upon his arms and legs. He could not deny that the words were power-filled, and when spoken with the ardent fervor of one hundred thousand men, it was almost as if the words were alive, living and active, powerful and convicting.

But for the most part, Alexander recognized that the people were simply reciting memorized phrases that had been passed down through the generations. Did they even believe in the words anymore?

Alexander recognized that words possessing such power had the potential to topple empires and reform kingdoms. What if these people were to unite, truly believing the words they recited with such casual boredom? Would anything be impossible for them?

It was a profound and disturbing thought.

Alexander turned his attention back to the chaos and cacophony surrounding him on all sides.

Within the sprawling Court of the Women in the Temple compound, four enormous pillars crowned with massive candelabras burned with the fury and might of a thousand campfires. Alexander had heard legends about these mystical burning lights – that there was not a single courtyard in all of Jerusalem untouched by the far-reaching light.

He hadn't believed it until he saw it for himself the first day of great feast, when nimble Jewish boys climbed the towering pillars and lit the enormous bowls filled with glistening oil. From his position in the Court of the Gentiles, Alexander's heart had sprung into his throat the moment the ensuing flames erupted from the heads of the candelabras. At night, it was as if an entire city encompassed by utter darkness was filled with a marvelous, other-worldly light.

Another ritual associated with the feast interested him as well. Daily, a priest would retrieve a golden ceremonial pitcher and exit the Temple compound with an air of mystery. Along with a procession of priests and a sea of joyous pilgrims traveling to and from the compound, the designated priest would then set foot upon Stepped Street, also known as the Pilgrim Road, which connected the southwestern corner of the Temple Mount to the southern gates of the city. The road was a rather impressive series of stone steps, a unique pattern of two steps at a time followed by a longer landing. This seemingly endless road consisting of hundreds of steps would take the priest directly to the famous Pool of Siloam. There, the priest would kneel, reverently draw water from the cleansing pool, and carry it back up the grueling, layered road all the way back to the Temple Compound, careful not to spill any of the pitcher's precious contents.

Alexander knew this because he had followed and watched with great interest on the first and second day of the feast.

Once the priest reached the Temple compound, three sharp trumpet blasts announced his journey toward the altar. He would then circle the elevated altar of sacrifice located within the Court of the Priests before climbing the marble-stepped ramp that would take him directly to the bronze altar. Frustrated that he was not permitted to pass the Court of the Gentiles, Alexander had inquired about the strange actions of the priest, learning that the water of Siloam was considered by the Jews to be cleansing, living water. The pitcher containing the living water was then emptied upon the altar of sacrifice.

This was performed daily in the exact same manner until the last day of the feast. Then, on the twenty-first day of Tishri, the great day of the feast, the priests were required to circle the altar seven times before pouring the living water upon the altar of sacrifice.

Alexander knew the priests were circling the altar even now. He had considered climbing to the top of the Royal Stoa to observe the ritual from afar, but something even more interesting caught his attention before he had the opportunity to exit the compound.

There, in the midst of an avid and breathless sea of people, stood Jesus Himself! Surrounded by rough-looking Galileans whom Alexander assumed must be Jesus' disciples, Jesus motioned with His hands as He spoke calmly to the vast sea of celebrators.

Leaning casually against the marble pillar, Alexander cocked his head to one side and tried to ignore the fierce urge to rush straight into the crowd of people. He wanted to know what Jesus was talking about, but he certainly didn't want to appear too obvious, too eager. He also knew he must assess the situation. If the people became offended by Jesus' speech, the result could very well be a riot or a stampede, and Alexander had no desire to be trampled.

Despite the uproar His presence had created in Jerusalem, Jesus appeared perfectly calm, at ease. He inclined His head slightly as one of His disciples spoke, listening with great interest before proceeding to answer whatever question had been voiced by His follower.

His curiosity nearly overtaking him, Alexander silently assessed Jesus' closest disciples. He was singularly unimpressed. Most of them possessed the broad, muscled forms of common laborers, their clothing rough and travel-stained. Only a few of them were not bearded with wild, abundant hair. According to popular rumor, most of these men were common laborers and fishermen. One of them was reputed to have been a tax collector.

Inquisitive, Alexander wondered which of the twelve men had possessed the most despised and detested of all Jewish professions. Tax collectors were reviled and spat upon, often ambushed and beaten by their angry brethren. Loyal Jews considered them filthy, good-for-nothing infidels, as tax collectors willingly agreed to extort their brothers for the sake of Roman coin. Tax collectors worked alongside unclean Romans, ruining their own brothers to satiate their greed.

That one, Alexander thought, noting a smaller man bearing a writing tablet. He was better dressed than the others, and his fairer complexion and uncalloused hands indicated he was unaccustomed to manual labor beneath the hot Galilean sun. *He must be the tax collector.*

Why had Jesus selected crude fishermen and traitorous tax collectors to be His closest companions? Why, one of His disciples was even rumored to have been a Zealot! Surely Jesus must know something about them the others did not.

Only one man among the twelve impressed Alexander, and he knew without even having to make a formal inquiry which of the disciples was called Judas Iscariot. The man carried himself with the air of a prince. He was educated and hailed from an extremely wealthy family. Unlike the others, his garments were expensive and elaborate. Alexander suspected that, unlike the other disciples, he was a true Judean.

Now that one has potential, Alexander mused, watching the man with a grudging sense of respect. It was no wonder he had been chosen by Jesus. But the others? They were a complete mystery to him.

It was in that moment that Jesus turned His head, His gaze pinning Alexander's feet in place. Mouth dry and heart pounding, Alexander stared into those fathomless eyes. It was as if Jesus' very presence closed the yawning gap between himself and the famous Teacher.

Attempting to maintain his cool, Alexander swallowed hard and crossed his arms over his chest.

Jesus continued to speak to the crowd, but He didn't look away. There was a smile in His eyes, a clear invitation in His gaze.

Reluctantly, Alexander drew closer, annoyed by his own capitulation.

A soft smile, almost undetectable, transformed the plain features of the Teacher as Alexander drew close enough to hear His words. He continued to speak.

Alexander noticed some unlikely candidates shuffling about the outskirts of the crowd, intently monitoring the Teacher's words. Some were richly dressed Pharisees and severe, dark-robed Sadducees. Alexander relished their obvious fury and discomfort.

Armed officers hovered about the crowd as well, clearly on the alert, weapons at the ready.

One woman in particular snagged Alexander's attention. He had seen her around Jerusalem many times, and he knew about her profession. But as she stood near Jesus, hungrily absorbing His words, she appeared somewhat changed. Her features had softened, and her eyes were wet, desperate. Her immense, inward struggle was so intense it was nearly tangible.

Looking into her eyes, Alexander wondered if her pained expression was mirrored upon his own harsh features.

"The living water has been poured upon the altar of sacrifice!" Someone shouted from one of the outer courts, interrupting Jesus' speech. Excitement rippled through Solomon's Porch.

"It is done!"

"The final oblation!"

"Then we are cleansed!"

Alexander looked to Jesus and detected a hint of sadness in His eyes. But why?

And then Jesus spoke.

"If anyone thirsts," Jesus said, His tone both gently

longing and authoritative, "let him come to Me and drink. He who believes in Me, as the Scripture has said, out of his heart will flow rivers of living water."

Alexander was reminded of a famous conversation this Man was reputed to have shared with a Samaritan woman at the village well...

"Whoever drinks of this water will thirst again, but whoever drinks of the water that I shall give him will never thirst. But the water that I shall give him will become in him a fountain of water springing up into everlasting life."

Word about Jesus' ministry in Samaria had spread like wildfire, for many claimed that no sincere holy man would ever set foot in that despicable place. When traveling, pious Jews opted for the much longer route that circumvented Samaria. But Jesus had not taken the popular route.

Whoever drinks of the water that I shall give him will never thirst... Alexander winced at the recollected words of Jesus. Never thirst? He himself was consumed by his own thirst. Thirst for life. Thirst for pleasure. Thirst for peace and joy and fulfillment.

How could one Man claim to eradicate that fierce, all-consuming thirst?

Alexander considered the "living water" transported over hundreds of steps from the Pool of Siloam, and realized it was symbolic. The ancients had taken great care to preserve this tradition, because they understood it pointed toward the true Living Water that would one day be revealed. Only by that true Living Water could their people be cleansed.

But over time, the ritual had become exactly that – a ritual. The people now exalted the ritual rather than the God who instituted it. And their mistake could very well prove fatal, for if they had forgotten what the symbol represented, how on earth would they recognize the fulfillment of it?

Lost in his brooding thoughts, Alexander suddenly realized with great alarm that the people were growing rowdier. Clearly, they were torn with disagreement about Jesus' controversial claim.

"You, my lord, are a very great prophet!" One woman yelled feverishly, swept away in the excitement.

"A prophet?" Another snorted in disdain. "Have you no eyes in your head, woman? This is the Christ!"

"The Christ?" the crowd erupted in dissension as disagreements broke out among the listeners.

More troubled by his own roiling thoughts than the feverish state of his fellow listeners, Alexander stole away from the crowd, recalling the remainder of the conversation Jesus was reported to have shared with the Samaritan woman...

"*I know that Messiah is coming. When He comes, He will tell us all things,*" the Samaritan woman had said with great feeling.

It was rumored that Jesus had looked into her eyes and spoken with quiet conviction.

"*I who speak to you am He.*"

Heart pounding, Alexander dared a glance over his shoulder in the midst of his retreat. Jesus' eyes were upon him.

Loving.

Compelling.

Beckoning.

Tender.

Compassionate.

For the first time in over a decade, Alexander wanted to weep.

"*I who speak to you am He.*" The Messiah?

Attempting to appear as composed as humanly possible, Alexander fled the scene, the words of a humble Rabbi pounding furiously within his troubled mind.

I who speak to you am He...

CHAPTER 23

Melina

"Julia!" Melina cried the moment her friend emerged from a thick, colorful sea of shoppers at the Upper Market.

Today was their appointed meeting day, and now she was overwhelmingly thankful for it. She was also grateful for the fact that Malchus had left a note that he would be unable to visit them that day. He would certainly not approve of what she was about to do.

Hastening toward her friend, Melina took Julia's hand and prepared to run.

"Melina! Good to see you too," Julia quipped sarcastically. "What has happened?" she added, breathless and confused.

"He is at the Temple, Julia! We must hurry!" Still clutching Julia's hand, Melina's small, sandaled feet flew rather like a bird taking flight.

Digging her heels into the ground, Julia halted, forcing Melina to stop along with her.

Melina looked to her with large, pleading eyes.

"Who is at the Temple, Melina?" Julia demanded, irritated.

Melina's emerald eyes grew large with hope and promise. "Jesus! He is there now, teaching! Chuza informed me before I left the palace. We must see Him, Julia, we must!"

Julia's eyes widened in surprise. The milling crowds were so thick that she wondered if they would reach the Temple before Jesus' departure. It would not be an easy trek.

"Well then, by all means," Julia laughed, taking off and dragging Melina along with her. "We'd best get moving!"

Melina laughed along with her, her heart racing in joyful anticipation.

Would today be the day she met her Messiah?

***

Mara

The morning sun glistened as Mara walked the meandering path leading toward her little home. The brisk autumn breeze was energizing and pleasant.

Despite her troubles, Mara was in rare good spirits. The Feast of Trumpets, followed by the Day of Atonement and then the celebrated Feast of Tabernacles, had certainly prompted her to think.

The God of her fathers had supplied these joyful festivities. Perhaps a God like that could be trusted.

Could He be trusted to change her life, to transform her marriage? She certainly hoped so.

She had begun to pray as Melina had counseled

her to do.

Heal my marriage. Mend my broken heart. Alter these undesirable circumstances.

Perhaps the Lord would indeed listen and intercede on her behalf.

She could only hope.

Mara seldom returned home at this early hour, but she had suddenly feared that perhaps she had failed to put out the fire before leaving in the wee morning hours.

Lucius would probably kill her himself if she burnt their house down.

Mara pushed open the door and gazed about the house. The fireplace was empty and cold. It would appear her concerns were all for naught.

Mara gasped as an unexpected figure rose from the table.

"What are you doing here?" Lucius demanded, his eyes cold.

Mara stared at her husband, her heart pounding from the scare. "What am I doing here?" she repeated, her hackles rising. "I live here, if you recall."

Lucius' eyes were hard and uncompromising as he moved toward the door.

Why wasn't he wearing his uniform?

The chronic knot in Mara's stomach began to recoil and tighten – a familiar feeling that she detested. "Where are you going?" she asked, her eyes narrowing in her suspicion. "Are you not working for Caiaphas today?"

"Another interrogation, I see," Lucius spat bitterly.

"You are never home at this time of day."

"Well, today I am."

"Why?"

"Shouldn't you be going?"

"I could ask the same of you!"

Lucius stared into the face of his wife. His expression was pinched, and his eyes betrayed his guilt.

Mara felt sick. "Lucius, what is going on?"

"That is none of your concern."

"I am so tired of hearing that!"

"And I am tired of your constant complaints, woman!"

Mara gazed up at her husband, her eyes welling with angry tears. Would they ever be happy? Did he even love her?

Did she still love him?

Drawing a shaky breath, Mara gathered her courage and stated bluntly, "I want to know what's going on."

Lucius arched a sardonic brow. "You want a lot, don't you? Well, if it'll keep you off my back, then I'll tell you. It's the day after the great feast. I'm going to patrol the streets to observe the fallout and mayhem as ordered."

"Without your uniform?"

Lucius' eyes shifted in a tell-tale manner. "Caiaphas has asked me to be discreet."

Mara wheeled around to face him as he walked out the door. "Discreet about *what?*"

"This is why I don't bother to talk official business with you. You're far too dense to understand."

"That is not true!" Mara argued, clinging to the doorpost as tears coursed down her cheeks.

"Leave me be, woman! And don't wait up for me tonight. I won't be coming home."

Mara lifted a brow in question. "Let me guess – more official business?"

"Official business that is none of *your* business."

Trembling in anger, Mara watched as Lucius stalked away from her, his shoulders set, his spine rigid.

It was not lost on her that he had bathed, shaved, anointed himself with sweet-smelling oils, and donned his finest garments.

Once, he had taken such pains to impress *her*.

Something wasn't right.

She was sick of being eaten up with suspicion day after day, night after endless, lonely night.

Reaching for her shawl, Mara slipped it over her head and followed the path her husband had taken.

***

Melina

Melina's heart sprang into her throat the moment she saw Him.

There, seated in the midst of a hundred eager onlookers gathered at Solomon's Porch, was Jesus. He smiled graciously as He instructed the people, His eyes filled with hope and promise.

Several simply dressed men flanked Him from all sides, their stances protective. His disciples?

The Temple was packed with Pharisees, Sadducees, religious observers, thrill seekers, and curious passers-by, and Melina had feared she and Julia would never find Jesus in the midst of all the cacophony and chaos.

Even so, the Lord had proven gracious.

Melina's deepest longings were realized the moment she gazed into the face of her Messiah.

Unable to speak, Melina reached for Julia's hand. Julia accepted it with an encouraging squeeze.

"That's Him, Melina. The One we have been waiting for."

Overcome, Melina nodded through her tears, her heart responding to the sound of His voice. "My Savior!"

CHAPTER 24

Mara

Fueled by jealousy and suspicion, Mara carefully picked her way through Jerusalem's litter-strewn streets still lined with abandoned huts and booths. Carefully concealing her face with her shawl, Mara kept a safe distance between herself and her husband. Even so, she doubted Lucius would even consider the fact that she might follow him. She was dutiful and hardworking. It would never even cross his mind that she might shirk her responsibilities in order to follow him, missing several hours of precious work in the kitchen.

Mara's heart pounded steadily in her chest as Lucius approached a makeshift *sukkah*.

Partly concealed behind the opposite *sukkah*, Mara watched tentatively as Lucius looked both ways, squared broad shoulders, then knocked upon one of the crude wooden doorposts.

The crimson curtains obscuring the *sukkah*'s open doorway fluttered before parting.

And in one portentous moment, Mara's entire

world came crashing down around her ears.

The gauzy crimson curtains were parted by a beautiful woman, her sea of black curls cascading down her back, her skin a lovely sun-kissed bronze. Dressed in bright, provocative clothing, the woman's profession was sickeningly evident. Mounds of gold jewelry glittered in the early morning sunlight.

Clenching her fists until her fingernails dug into her own tender flesh, Mara watched in utter horror and betrayal as the brazen woman drew Lucius' head down and kissed him. Then, she took him by the hand and led him into her own private booth. The curtains fluttered shut behind them with an air of terrible finality.

Fury unlike anything she had ever experienced washed over Mara in hot, undulating waves.

Lucius could not have cut her more deeply had he plunged a knife into her aching breast. Laced with pain and bitter anguish unlike anything she had ever known, Mara turned sharply on her heels and pushed past busy pedestrians, her thoughts afire with scarcely contained wrath.

Lucius would suffer for his infidelity and betrayal – she'd make absolutely sure of it! And in that moment, Mara forgot all about her desire to seek God. In fact, she forgot all about God. She forgot about her desperate prayers for help.

Instead, her mind filled with vengeful thoughts, and she relished the pain she hoped to inflict upon her unfaithful husband.

Marching purposefully toward the house of Caiaphas, Mara concocted a plan. She would make Lucius suffer as she had suffered! Perhaps she would give him a taste of his own medicine – after all, she knew of a devastatingly handsome young man who would be more than happy to oblige!

But Mara froze mid-step as another thought collided with the first, and her entire being went cold.

Curse the laws of this wretched, miserable land! She couldn't hurt Lucius as he had wounded her, for a Jewish woman could be stoned for committing adultery! Lucius, a Roman, would not be judged by the rigid, ceremonial laws of her people. But she, a Jewish woman, could very well be stoned to death if she were to indulge in the same sin.

But, wait... Again, Mara paused in the middle of the street, completely oblivious as carts rattled noisily past her and pedestrians passed back and forth.

A plot began to take shape in her tortured mind.

In Jerusalem, a holy city guided by rigid laws of morality, an adulteress would surely be stoned in return for her ugly sin... and that wicked harlot who had stolen her husband was every inch an adulteress!

Mara's mouth tipped slightly in a satisfied smile. She knew exactly what must be done. Having worked for the high priest most of her life, she knew which of Caiaphas' underlings would relish the stoning of that wretched harlot!

With the greatest sense of purpose, Mara hastened her steps, mentally reviewing her brilliant plan. Vengeance was rightfully hers. Justice would prevail. And that miserable wench would suffer for the unspeakable wrongs she had committed against her!

Mara knew she must act quickly. Details fell into place in her mind as the magnificent Temple loomed into view. It was almost as if a dark voice whispered careful instructions into her ear. Fueled by bitter rage and confusion, Mara was all too eager to perform its cruel bidding.

A disturbing smile graced Mara's lips as she reveled in the glory of revenge. She would relish every moment of that wretched woman's agony.

And she herself would cast the first stone.

***

Melina

Mesmerized by Jesus' teachings, Melina's heart nearly broke when she realized her time to return to the palace was drawing near.

How could she bear to depart from the presence of this beloved Teacher?

Despite the fact that people pressed heavily upon Him from all sides, Melina was certain Jesus was aware of her presence. He had looked to her only once, but all the love and joy and peace of the universe had been wrapped up in that one, simple look.

He knew her. He loved her. She was His.

Grasping Julia's arm like a lifeline and holding back tears, Melina's heart swelled within her chest as she soaked up the words of Her Savior. She was certain she could stand here forever, basking in Jesus' calming presence and savoring His every teaching, His every word.

Oh! Why, oh, why, couldn't this blessed moment last forever?

Sudden apprehension rippled through the crowd gathered about Jesus, causing the hairs on the back of Melina's neck to stand on end. The apprehension grew steadily as whispers bred demands coupled with shouts of surprise.

Rocked by the explosive fury of the crowd, Melina grasped at Julia in alarm. "What is happening?"

Julia's dark eyes grew round with fear. "I'm not sure..."

Heart pounding, Melina scanned the crowd, desperately seeking the face of her Master.

Jesus was rising slowly to His feet, His eyes resting solemnly beyond the gathered sea of listeners.

Turning to follow His gaze, Melina saw a procession of scribes, Pharisees, and Sadducees approaching like a flock of hungry carrion birds. Their severe garments fluttered in the morning breezes, the darkness of their showy attire mirroring their stormy countenance.

Julia looked to Melina, frightened. "Religious leaders. They all have a quarrel with Jesus."

Melina's eyes grew wide with fear. "All of them?"

"Well, perhaps not all," Julia amended, her gaze fixed apprehensively upon the approaching men. "My father told me that his friend and colleague, Nicodemus, risked his position with the Sanhedrin to defend Jesus during the Feast of Tabernacles."

"May God protect him."

Gasping, Julia covered her mouth with a trembling hand.

"Julia? What is happening?"

"Melina, we should leave."

"What is it?"

Julia's heart hammered a painful rhythm in her chest as she realized the gravity of the situation upon them. Two of the men dragged a woman through the Temple court toward the crowd.

The religious leaders bore heavy stones in their hands.

"Oh, Melina. You won't want to see this. We must go. Now!"

Melina resisted when Julia took her arm. "Will

they harm her?" she asked, the blood draining from her face.

"Harm her?" Julia hissed, breaking out into a cold sweat. "Melina, they intend to *execute* her!"

The crowd parted as the angry procession of religious leaders dragged a resisting woman along with them.

Flanked by His disciples, Jesus remained rooted in place, His eyes filled with sorrow as He studied the group of enraged men.

"Julia, something must be done!" Melina's voice shook with fierce emotion.

"There is nothing we can do, Melina."

"But this isn't right!"

Melina's heart broke as one of the men wrenched the woman painfully by the shoulder and cast her ruthlessly upon the paved stones at the feet of Jesus.

Bruised, battered, and bleeding, the woman wept in fear and shame.

Melina couldn't bear the sounds of the woman's stifled sobs. It cut her to the very quick.

The crowd drew a collective breath as Jesus raised level eyes toward the Sadducee who had cast the woman at His feet.

***

Malchus

Malchus turned away, repulsed by the behavior of the mob. Sensing a bloody execution, he set his jaw in grim resignation. People were already rushing about, seeking heavy objects to hurl at the guilty offender.

Caiaphas had ordered Malchus to attend him at

the Temple, declaring that important Temple business demanded his attention.

Malchus had been puzzled by the command. Even more unsettling was the fact that Caiaphas had chosen to walk the courts of the Temple today among the common people. He had risked defilement... for what?

For *this?* The murder of one insignificant woman?

Was this the reason Caiaphas had insisted upon Temple business today?

Malchus hadn't the slightest idea. But now, as the crowd gathered around Jesus grew frenzied, Malchus turned to study the face of his own dark master.

Caiaphas' arms were folded solemnly before him. Obscured within the shadows, he observed the mayhem with avaricious calm.

Looking away in disgust, Malchus was thankful Melina was not present to witness such a deplorable scene. He wasn't sure her tender heart could take it.

Shaking his head in disgust, he scanned the bloodthirsty crowd pressing in on all sides.

And then his heart stood still. For there, in the midst of the roiling mob at the opposite side of the court, stood Melina, her face bathed in tears.

Julia stood beside her, her expression bordering near-panic.

Malchus suppressed a groan, his entire being going cold.

For the love of all that is holy and good, what on earth is she doing here?

***

Mara

Pushing her way toward the front of the mob, Mara's heart pounded violently like the steady beat of impending war drums.

There! The worthless wretch was huddled at the feet of an unassuming Man at the center of the fearsome mob. Brooding religious leaders hedged her in from behind even as the onlookers encircled her. Men and women laughed openly at her pathetic form, snickering in derision and lifting brows of contempt.

Fleetingly, she wondered at the fact that both Pharisees and Sadducees were united in the simple undertaking of the execution of one meaningless woman. But just as quickly, she cast the thought aside. She didn't care about the relational status of quarrelling religious sects, as long as her purpose was accomplished.

But who was the Man standing before the hapless woman? Why had the leaders taken her to Him before carrying out her death sentence? Dressed in the simplest of garb, it was clear He was neither a Pharisee nor Sadducee. By all causal appearance, He was unimportant. A nobody.

Who was He?

Her blood afire with lust for revenge, Mara dismissed the insignificant details and centered her entire attention upon this delicious slice of justice. Consumed with rage, the blood coursed through her veins with such ferocity she felt faint.

A malefic smile tipped the corners of her lips as she savored the woman's shame.

The adulteress was huddled on the ground, trembling violently. Her body was torn and bleeding, her face bruised and swollen, wet with tears. She kept her gaze fixed upon the pavement, too humiliated to meet the eyes of her accusers or the Man standing before her.

You deserve it, wretch, Mara thought, somewhat chilled by the dark direction of her own thoughts. Were they even hers?

Another exhilarating wave of vindictiveness swept over Mara, for she realized the woman was wrapped in the scarlet tapestry that had hung from the doorway of her makeshift *sukkah*. The scarlet tapestry was her only covering, and she clutched it desperately about her trembling form, clearly mortified by her lack of dress.

The wretched harlot must have grasped at the curtains in sheer desperation to cover her shame as the officers dragged her away from her *sukkah*, away from her lover...

Away from my husband! My husband! Mara fumed silently, savoring the woman's suffering all the more. *And now you shall pay for your own stupidity! You shall pay with every blow, with every merciless strike of stone!*

Stone... Mara grit her teeth in fury. In her haste, she had neglected to retrieve a stone. And she was unlikely to find one here in the Temple compound. Would the woman's execution occur here, or would the adulteress be dragged outside the city gates? Mara couldn't remember what the Law required. She didn't care, as long as this woman received her just reward.

Mara's eyes grazed an object near her sandaled foot.

There, resting upon a tile near her foot, was a heavy stone. Someone must have dropped it in a frenzied attempt to witness the action.

Stooping down, Mara's fingers curled around the cold stone. Slowly, she drew herself back to her full height, fixing all her hatred upon the woman who had dared to steal her own husband's affection.

The stone felt like a lead weight in her hand.

Even so, Mara's heart continued to pound wildly as she fed off her own rage, hostility and contempt setting her blood afire.

Mara hadn't the slightest idea she was walking a path planned for her long ago. Her battle was not against flesh and blood, though the enemy was skilled at employing useful assistance from willing vessels. She had fallen prey to the tactics of a violent, unseen foe – one who would not only relish the demise of an erring prostitute, but the destruction of Mara's own soul as well.

CHAPTER 25

Julia

Julia drew in a sharp breath as recognition dawned.

Melina looked to her, her spirit heavy. "What is it?" she asked tearfully, wondering why she felt compelled to remain. Wouldn't it be wiser to flee the scene before stones began to fly?

Julia leaned forward, balancing on her tiptoes in her attempt to see over the looming crowd. "Melina," she managed, her voice weak. "I think I know that woman."

"Oh no," Melina's sorrow multiplied. "A friend?"

Julia recalled a brazen woman mocking her upon her own threshold, insinuating shared secrets with Barabbas.

The woman who had purchased her own precious alabaster jar!

"I wouldn't say that," Julia responded tersely. Even so, she wouldn't wish this fate upon anyone – not even a prostitute who planted seeds of doubt about her husband's fidelity.

Julia nearly jumped out of her skin when the man who appeared to be the ringleader raised his voice in fierce accusation, thrusting a threatening finger toward Jesus. "Teacher, this woman was caught in adultery…" he paused, allowing his eyes to scan the crowd of onlookers. "In the very act!" he added, and the crowd erupted with pleasure at this interesting bit of news.

"Harlot!" One woman screamed, as others joined in with searing accusations of their own.

"Adulteress!"

"Worthless wretch!"

"A slow, painful death is too good for the likes of her!"

Julia and Melina exchanged looks of concern. The crowd was becoming more and more agitated.

Another man in the severe garb of a Pharisee joined the first speaker. "Now Moses, in the Law, commanded us that such should be stoned." His eyes swept over the crowd of onlookers before resting his gaze solely upon the quiet Rabbi before him. Adjusting his prayer shawl in a habitual manner, he arched a derisive brow, a predatory smile splitting his stern features. "But what do You say?"

***

Malchus

A trap.

Malchus winced as the Pharisee's loudly spoken words were carried by the wind. It was bizarre to see Pharisees and Sadducees standing together, uniting for a common cause.

That fact alone was enough to prove frightfully concerning!

Malchus' pulse pounded loudly in his own ears, and he realized that he, too, was waiting with bated breath.

It would seem the religious leaders finally had Jesus right where they wanted Him. If He chose to dismiss the woman's sin by extending mercy, then He would most certainly be accused of blaspheming the Law of Moses, a violation worthy of death. But if He upheld the Law and approved the woman's execution, then Caiaphas' underlings would simply report the incident to the Roman authorities who would be all too willing to exterminate one more troublesome Jew. Roman law clearly stated that the Jewish religious leaders no longer possessed the right to capital punishment.

Malchus swallowed hard, recognizing that the famous Teacher was backed into a corner with no possible chance of a positive outcome.

Death by Romans or death by a Jewish mob. Neither option sounded appealing to him.

Malchus turned his head toward Caiaphas, unnerved by the low chuckle that escaped from somewhere deep within the high priest's throat.

Their throat is like an open tomb… Malchus was caught off guard by the ancient Psalm surfacing in his mind. He chanced another glance in Caiaphas' direction. It was as if the psalmist had had Caiaphas and the chief priests in mind the day the literature was penned.

Cloaked in shadow, Caiaphas watched with the sharp eyes of a viper as bystanders awaited Jesus' response. He relished the bloodlust of the crowd, anticipating the final outcome.

Words from the powerful Psalm flooded Malchus' mind, and before he even realized it, he began to offer the words back to God in prayer for the sake of the trapped Teacher at Solomon's Porch – and for Melina's sake. She would be devastated if anything happened to Jesus.

Pronounce them guilty, O God! Let them fall by their own counsels, Malchus prayed silently, grateful that Caiaphas couldn't read his thoughts. *Cast them out in the multitude of their transgressions, for they have rebelled against You...*

***

Julia

The crowd pressed in so tightly Julia feared she would be smothered. Common sense dictated she flee the scene, but it was as if her two sandaled feet were nailed in place.

Melina remained faithfully beside her, her pale face glistening with tears of compassion as the accused young woman wept quietly at Jesus' feet.

Meanwhile, the accusers grew more and more agitated, their severe black garments fluttering in the breeze rather like the dark ruffled feathers of gathering birds of prey.

"Well?" A Pharisee demanded imperiously, his bushy eyebrows lifted in condescension. He crossed his arms in a self-important manner, his face reddening in his outrage.

Surprisingly, Jesus did not acknowledge the overbearing Pharisee.

This infuriated the accusers all the more. Enraged, they raised their voices in protest, talking over each other and even attempting to outshout one another.

Feeding off the bitterness and hatred of the religious leaders, the crowd began to hound Jesus as well, hurling insults and making outrageous demands.

Jesus was completely unaffected.

And then He did something entirely unexpected.

The people watched with bated breath as Jesus knelt before the weeping woman. Then, as if completely alone with His thoughts rather than in the midst of a tumultuous crowd, Jesus began to trace patterns in the fine dust that had collected on the smooth tiles of the Temple compound.

The people erupted with questions, their curiosity deeply aroused, even as the religious leaders grew ominously silent, infuriated by Jesus' peculiar response.

"Can you see what He's doing, Julia?" Melina asked, standing on tiptoes in her attempt to see over the gathering crowd.

"I can't," Julia managed, craning her neck in her attempt to gain a better view. "I think Jesus is writing on the ground."

"Writing on the ground?" Melina repeated, puzzled. "But what is He writing?"

Julia groaned, exasperated. "I can't see a thing. The crowd is too thick!"

***

Mara

"Kill her – the wicked wretch!" The feral cry burst forth from Mara's lips with such ferocity she startled even herself.

Fueled by that one merciless outburst, the crowd and the religious leaders raised another frightful chorus of fury and condemnation.

"That woman deserves death!"

"She is a stink in our nostrils."

"Her very presence has polluted this sacred Temple!"

Breathless and trembling, Mara drew in a ragged breath as Jesus lifted His head to meet the dangerous gazes of the religious leaders. Nearly bursting with impatience, her fingers curled and uncurled about the cool stone she clutched in one hand.

Retribution was rightfully hers. Soon, it would be finished.

Slowly, Jesus lifted Himself to His full height, His eyes boring into those of the gray-bearded Pharisee who had first questioned Him.

Fleetingly, the Pharisee's gaze flitted to the nearly unreadable characters etched into the fine dust on the floor tiles. Paling, he raised startled eyes toward the Teacher.

Full of sadness, Jesus' eyes scanned each and every bloodthirsty face.

Mara clenched her open fist at her side, her fingernails digging into her own tender flesh, her heart pounding its battle cry. In her other hand, the stone grew just a bit heavier.

She lifted the stone, taking careful aim.

And then Jesus spoke.

"He who is without sin among you, let him throw a stone at her first."

The softly spoken words were like a collective punch in the gut, sending an invisible yet tangible shock wave bursting through the entire mob.

And in that instant, the tension ceased. An air of inexplicable sorrow and shame drifted over the crowd.

Pain unlike anything she had ever known pierced Mara's heart to the very core.

And then, Jesus' gentle eyes were upon her.

Shamed beyond imagining, Mara's gaze flitted to the stone in her hand – her weapon for justice now stood as a stark testimony against her own wickedness. Repulsed, her fingers loosened and the heavy stone hit the floor with a resounding *thud*.

Riveted in place, she gazed into the eyes of the Man standing before her worst enemy and saw nothing but compassion reflected in those eyes. Understanding. Forgiveness. Tender mercy.

And it was meant for her.

CHAPTER 26

Melina

Melina grasped Julia's hand, relief flooding her entire being like a warm covering.

Jesus had not condemned the weeping woman. But what of the religious leaders? Had they the power to destroy her?

Julia and Melina watched in wonder as Jesus stooped once more and resumed His mysterious writing upon the ground.

"I wish I could see above the crowd," Julia bemoaned again, her frustration mounting. Her gaze flitted toward the religious leaders, whose eyes were glued to Jesus' finger as He etched a message for their eyes only.

Melina drew in a wondrous breath. "Why does it feel as if we are witnessing that sacred moment when the finger of God etched the everlasting commandments upon tablets of stone?"

"Because, in a way," Julia said, her face awash with reverence and awe, "we are."

"His words are eternal," Melina whispered, her heart full.

Julia chanced a glance toward the religious leaders. Their expressions were drawn, their countenances pale. As one, their eyes were riveted upon the mysterious writing of Jesus.

And then, the aging, gray-bearded Pharisee at the head of the mob drew his prayer shawl about his shoulders. Clearing his throat in discomfort, he lowered his gaze before turning on his heel and walking away, his steps hurried yet ever dignified.

And one by one, the remaining religious leaders did the same.

When it became terribly clear to the mob that no excitement would be taking place, they, too, walked away in disappointment, whispering in hushed tones as they went.

Soon the crowd had dispersed. Only a few curious bystanders remained at a distance, both curious and convicted.

The accused woman dared to lift her head. Gazing about in fear, she realized that she remained alone with her champion.

Trembling violently, she drew herself up to a standing position, clutching the scarlet tapestry about her as if it were a lifeline. Her face, caked in dust, was streaked with trails of tears.

"Julia! Look!"

Startled by Melina's surprising outburst, Julia followed her friend's gaze.

At the opposite end of the court stood Mara, dejected and trembling, her face awash with tears.

She must have sensed the young women's troubled gazes, for she inclined her head toward them.

Melina held out both hands to her.

Mara went to her, weeping in humiliation and repentance as Melina gathered her in her arms.

***

Malchus

"He who is without sin among you, let him throw a stone at her first..."

Malchus was unprepared for Jesus' unexpected response. Chancing a glance at Caiaphas, Malchus' stomach tightened in inexplicable dread.

Never had he seen such an expression on the face of another man. It was terrible, yet hesitant. As if black sins had surfaced in the troubled mind of the high priest... sins he had so carefully concealed, sins he had so easily dismissed...

And then, just as quickly, his expression hardened as his eyes narrowed, forming two dangerously narrow slits.

Repentance rippled through the Temple compound as onlookers and bystanders were convicted by the softly spoken words of the mysterious Rabbi.

Hardening himself against it, Caiaphas turned and stole away, his eyes burning, his jaw clenched, his back and shoulders rigid, his gait uncompromisingly purposeful.

Malchus watched him go, his stomach twisting in the most unpleasant way.

No one dared to thwart the fool-proof plans of his master, Caiaphas.

His gaze flickering back to the Teacher standing before the quickly dispersing crowd, Malchus' lips formed a thin, grim line.

He didn't wish to contemplate the twisted form of justice Caiaphas would inflict upon the only Man ever known to outsmart the capricious high priest of Israel.

***

Mara

Melina draped a protective arm about Mara's shoulders as they watched Jesus in rapt attention.

Most of the onlookers had deserted their posts, but a few curious remained, eager to witness the exchange between Jesus and the exonerated adulteress.

"Who is He?" Mara breathed shakily, her heart pounding dully in her chest.

Julia and Melina exchanged a look of caution but seemed to reach some sort of silent consensus.

"Mara, that Man is Jesus of Nazareth," Melina spoke softly, her eyes alight.

Mara was thankful Melina didn't remind her that His were the followers she had agreed to betray. Her heart constricted in her chest, for she felt the crushing weight of her sins more heavily than she ever had.

There stood the woman she had hoped to destroy, and, astonished, Mara realized that her own sins were no less than the harlot's.

She, Mara, had grown up in the household of the high priest with the Holy Scriptures at her beck and call. The ways of God had not been hidden from her. And yet she had formulated weak and pathetic excuses to avoid obedience to God. She had claimed she wanted nothing to do with the God of the Jews because His high priest was wicked, hypocritical, and capricious.

But for the first time in her life, it dawned on her: Caiaphas was not the head of the Jewish religion.

God was.

Fallible men had placed the high priest on a pedestal, bestowing upon him the rights and reverence belonging to God alone.

Cringing, Mara dashed away angry tears. How could she have been so blind? One by one, her excuses imploded.

Whereas the background of the harlot standing before Jesus was unknown to Mara, she knew her own story. And she had no excuse. Despite her close proximity to the Scriptures, the Temple, and the God of her fathers, Mara had intentionally harbored evil and wickedness in her heart.

Why, she had been ready to participate in the senseless murder of another human being only moments earlier! In fact, she herself had instigated it.

Forcing herself to study the bruised and battered young woman standing before Jesus, Mara was stunned to realize that she envied her. What she wouldn't give to stand before Jesus now.

Jesus spoke, interrupting her tortuous train of thought. "Woman, where are those accusers of yours?"

The young woman raised beautiful, teary eyes to the face of her Maker.

"Has no one condemned you?" Jesus pressed, His face awash with compassion.

Clutching the crimson curtain tightly about her shivering form, the woman answered shakily, "No one… Lord."

It was a declaration. This woman had made up her mind. She had chosen the Lord of her life.

"Neither do I condemn you." Jesus' words were spoken so gently that those gathered about Him instinctively leaned forward. Even His disciples, who remained flanking Him protectively from behind, appeared to lean in a bit closer. They glanced at each other in puzzlement and confusion, clearly restraining themselves from bombarding their Teacher with questions.

Then, Jesus did something entirely unexpected.

Mara looked to Julia and Melina in question, supposing that she should be accustomed to the unexpected when this Man was involved. Already, He had turned her entire world upside down in the most unexpected way.

Unclasping the neck of His white woolen outer garment, Jesus removed His arms from the full sleeves and shrugged out of it. Carefully, He held it before Him.

The young woman studied Him in confusion as He stood before her, the garments He donned beneath simple and travel-worn.

With the faintest hint of a smile, Jesus held His robe open to the woman.

Reluctantly, she slipped her slender arms into the sleeves.

Jesus clasped the robe at her neck, completely covering her shame.

The woman drew in a soft breath, dropping the scarlet curtain she had clutched so protectively only moments earlier. The gauzy scarlet fabric pooled about her bare feet, and yet she was completely covered in the pure white robe of Jesus.

"*My soul shall be joyful in my God,*" Melina whispered softly, drawing Mara's attention. "*For He has clothed me with the garments of salvation...*"

Julia joined in, and her voice mingled beautifully with Melina's as the ancient Scripture came alive before their very eyes. "*He has covered me with the robe of righteousness.*"

Mara looked again to the former harlot now clothed in Jesus' own robe – His robe of righteousness – and her throat tightened with warm tears. "*Though your sins be like scarlet,*" she whispered through her tears, "*they shall be as white as snow. Though they are red like crimson, they shall be as wool. If you are willing and obedient...*"

Willing. Obedient.

"Now go," Jesus said softly, His eyes boring into the young woman's. "And sin no more."

Sin no more.

Jesus turned to look at those gathered nearby. His gaze rested upon Mara for but a moment, and in that one fateful instant, an eternal and never-ending exchange took place.

Neither do I condemn you, Jesus had said, His voice soaked in love and compassion. And as Jesus' tender eyes grazed hers, Mara realized that she, too, was forgiven. Her heart nearly burst at the magnitude of all she was experiencing in the presence of this Man named Jesus.

Mara realized that she now had a starting point, a springboard from which to begin anew.

Sin no more.

By the grace of God alone, she would cling to this commandment of Jesus and begin again. Her sin had bred nothing but sorrow and shame. But the commandments of God were life-giving and pure.

"I am the light of the world." Mara's attention was jerked back to the present by this unexpected declaration from Jesus.

Those milling about the court paused to listen, their heads tilted in confusion.

"He who follows Me shall not walk in darkness but have the light of life."

Instinctively, Mara's eyes traveled above the high walls barring the Court of the Gentiles from the Court of the Women. Towering candelabras stretched heavenward from that magnificent court, and Mara recalled how they had lit the city of Jerusalem during the Feast of Tabernacles, emitting a warm, powerful, and radiant light.

Julia smiled, following Mara's gaze and sensing her train of thought. "It's as if every little detail pointed ahead to Jesus, isn't it?"

"Our people jealously guard each ritual, little knowing that the power lies in the fulfillment – not the ritual itself," Mara mused, amazed.

Mara watched as the forgiven young woman took Jesus' hand, kissed it, and then walked away, tears coursing down her cheeks. Mara felt torn – part of her wished to speak with the young woman, even while another part of her hoped to never see her again.

Another thought assailed her, infringing upon her newfound joy. What on earth was she to do with Lucius now?

Dismissing her troubled thoughts, she fixed her attention instead upon Jesus as He proceeded toward the Court of the Women, His disciples trailing after Him wearing troubled expressions.

And then the impossible happened. Jesus paused before entering the Court of the Women, his gaze resting upon Julia, Melina, and Mara.

The young women collectively held their breath, amazed and overwhelmed.

Jesus smiled, and His love was so big and so evident that they were convinced His outstretched arms could encircle the entire world.

He knew them. They were His.

Then the sacred moment ended. Jesus turned and disappeared through the gate, His disciples close behind Him.

"I will follow Him," Mara declared stoutly, unbending in her resolve.

Melina grasped her hand and gave it a firm squeeze. "How I have prayed for this moment!"

"And I as well," Julia exclaimed, her lovely face alight with joy.

"I have walked in darkness long enough," Mara blinked back tears, her mind made up. She purposed in her heart do exactly as Jesus had bidden: Go, and sin no more. "No matter what may come, I now have the light of life to brighten my path and make the way plain before me."

Even as the two young women rejoiced beside her, Mara sensed there were darker days ahead in which she must cling to Jesus, her Savior.

The light of life.

CHAPTER 27

Caiaphas

Black fury gripped the soul of the high priest.

The plan was perfect. Foolproof. And that fool woman Mara had responded exactly as he knew she would by setting up the wretched harlot and that pestilent Prophet to take the fall.

Caiaphas couldn't explain what had happened in the Temple compound, but he hated it with every ragged breath he drew.

Taking purposeful, measured steps across the Temple court, his brows drew together as he attempted to mask his fury, driven by thoughts so dark his own soul recoiled before he expertly justified his intentions.

It was time to create a more daring plan.

***

Mara

Torn between anticipation and apprehension, Mara entered a cold, dark house. She would quickly wash her face and tidy her hair before walking to Caiaphas' palatial home, where she must resume her work in the kitchen.

How many hours of work had she missed? The servants must be wondering what happened to her.

She herself wasn't entirely sure what had happened. She had reached her lowest moment, felt the stinging pain of betrayal, and determined to exact justice her own way. But then she had discovered the truth, and she was elated... But how was she to conduct herself now? She was married to a cruel and unfaithful husband. Clearly, she had been unable to change his heart.

Only God could change hearts, and she herself was a powerful testament to that truth. Wincing, she realized how foolish she had been to imagine that she could change Lucius by marrying him.

But what to do now? If she were to tell him the truth about Jesus and her desire to follow Him, would Lucius report her to Caiaphas? And even if he spared her – which was doubtful – how would he react when he realized he had lost his most valuable informant?

She cringed at the thought.

Carefully, Mara closed the door behind her, its rusty hinges protesting the entire way. The light streaming in from the few windows did little to ease the darkness in the house.

Mara prayed silently for guidance as she dipped a clean cloth in a basin and gently dabbed at her face. The cool water felt good.

Your will, Lord. I'm done seeking my own way. I want Your will from now on. Please show me what to do.

After washing her hands, she reached for her simple comb and began to detangle her long brown hair. Expertly, her fingers quickly wove the silky strands into a simple braid.

Turning to leave, Mara noticed a roll of parchment resting upon the table.

It hadn't been there when she had left that morning.

Filled with a strange uneasiness and sense of foreboding, Mara crossed the room and picked up the parchment.

Slowly, carefully, she rolled open the parchment scroll.

Blanching as if she had been struck, Mara recoiled and flung the parchment back onto the rough-hewn tabletop.

A certificate of divorce.

CHAPTER 28

Malchus

Stylus flying across his clay tablet, Malchus attempted to chronicle the chaotic interrogation he was unfortunate enough to witness. Later, his recounting would be transferred to a parchment scroll and sealed in Caiaphas' library of records. Then the clay tablet would be wiped clean and readied for further use.

Malchus wished he could just as easily wipe the incident from his memory. Already, the poor man had been interrogated by curious neighbors and the Pharisees. And now Caiaphas and his Sadducees had descended upon the unfortunate man like a sea of ravenous vultures.

Caiaphas had personally demanded Malchus' presence during the interrogation, despite the many scribes at his beck and call. For some reason unbeknownst to Malchus, Caiaphas trusted his ability to accurately record the incident. Perhaps the high priest feared the scribes might embellish the tale depending on their levels of sympathy for the strange Prophet from Nazareth.

Malchus had to admit that it was a fascinating – and unnerving – interrogation. Even so, he would rather be anywhere but here in Caiaphas' palatial mansion witnessing the demise of a fellow countryman.

"Tell us again, from the beginning," Caiaphas ordered tersely, seated upon a throne-like chair on an elevated dais in the enormous marble hall from which he had condemned many a Jew.

Malchus resisted the urge to roll his eyes. Were they really going to go over this again? But he knew his master well. Caiaphas was hoping the man would betray himself with accidental discrepancies if ordered to repeat the story a second time.

One look at the man standing before him, and Malchus knew there would be no discrepancies. This man had been touched by God.

Shifting uncomfortably, Malchus focused on his writing tablet and tried to dismiss the uneasiness swelling in the pit of his stomach. He was already on edge. He had glimpsed Melina at the Temple earlier that week, and the joy reflected in her eyes at the teachings of Jesus was seared into his memory.

Didn't Melina realize that she could be next, standing before a rabid high priest bent on hunting down and destroying every last follower?

"Did you not hear me the first time?"

Drawn back to the present by the man's bold speech, Malchus felt the hairs on the back of his neck stand on end. Huddled about the dais, priests, scribes, and Sadducees whispered to one another in ominous tones.

Malchus had absolutely no desire to witness an execution today.

Caiaphas' fists curled about the claw-shaped armrests of his gilded chair. "You forget to whom you speak, man – the high priest of Israel! I possess the power of life and death, and you would do well to remember that."

Again, Malchus resisted the urge to roll his eyes.

The man remained tall and stoic, unaffected. Dressed in a simple turban and plain, weathered garb, he appeared common and yet magnificent with his shining features and confident bearing.

"Now I will ask again – tell us what happened, from the beginning."

Clasping his hands before him, the man sighed dramatically. "Well, it all began in a dusty little village on the outskirts of Jerusalem. There, I was born to a poor, young couple by the name of –"

"Shut up, you fool!" Caiaphas leaned forward in his chair, his eyes glistening their angry venom. "You know very well what I meant!"

"You told me to start from the beginning." This followed by a smug grin from the man.

"The beginning of the *incident*, you fool. Not the beginning of your pathetic and miserable existence!"

Malchus bit back an amused grin. The mischievous twinkle in the man's eye wasn't lost on him. Clearly, he was enjoying himself. Malchus admired his brass even as he agonized over the possible outcome.

"My name is Anaiah. As you may recall, I was born blind."

"Born in your worthless sins. You deserved your malady."

Malchus glanced in the direction of the hateful speech and was not surprised to see Hezron glaring at Anaiah, his gray eyes dangerous.

Caiaphas held up a hand. Clearly, he did not appreciate the interruption.

"Ah, but there you are wrong," Anaiah stated evenly, his gaze fixed intensely upon Hezron. "The disciples with Him said the same. And can we blame them? Is it not what you were taught when you were small boys learning the Torah at the rabbi's knee? We've been told that illnesses and misfortunes are simply punishments for secret, hidden sin. But not so. This Man speaks differently."

"This Man speaks *blasphemies*," Caiaphas nearly spat. "You were born a sinful wretch, conceived in sin and wallowing in it even now."

"Yes, I am a sinful wretch; but so are you." The fearsome hush that fell upon the few gathered members of the Sanhedrin was awful to behold.

Malchus clenched his eyes tightly shut, loath to witness what was surely to follow. A moment later, Malchus dared to crack open one eye.

Miraculously, Anaiah still stood before Caiaphas, his seeing eyes shining in brilliant intensity. "I meant no disrespect, priest. I am simply stating the truth. Only the truth will set you free."

Caiaphas arched a dangerous brow.

"We're *all* wretched sinners, every last one of us. We are *all* born in sin. And this is why we need a Savior, no?"

"Would *you* dare preach to me?"

"I won't deny my sinfulness. My own sin stood in stark, ugly contrast to the holiness of the Man who restored my sight. But He made it all so *per-

fectly clear, and I speak of more than just my sight."
Another impish grin. "I was not born blind as a
punishment or judgment for some hidden sin. God
allowed the blindness I so despised, that His work
might be revealed in me!"

"The work of God – revealed in *you*?" Caiaphas
sniffed his disdain.

"Let me ask you this, priest: had I been born with
perfect sight, would I be standing before you and
your Sanhedrin now, testifying of the power of
God?"

Chills skittered up and down Malchus' spine at
the awesome proclamation of a man once considered the lowliest of sinners. And Malchus was hit by
the truth of Anaiah's statement like a ton of bricks.
Did the high priest feel the weight as well?

Chancing a glance in Caiaphas' direction, Malchus was sobered by the severity of the high priest's
expression. Clearly, he did not appreciate Anaiah's
frustratingly apparent logic.

"Your opinion is worthless," Caiaphas said slowly,
his tone dangerous. "And I haven't the time nor the
inclination to listen to the careless babblings of an
ignorant fool. Tell me what happened and spare us
your fanciful and blasphemous opinions."

A slow smile spread across Anaiah's face. "Have I
not already told you? First I was blind, then I could
see."

"But how?" Caiaphas demanded vehemently.

"He anointed my eyes with saliva and clay, then
instructed me to wash in the Pool of Siloam."

"Saliva and clay? You disgust me," Caiaphas shook
his head in disdain.

"I would have bathed in the mixture for a week if

it meant my sight would be restored!"

"And what else should we expect?" Caiaphas mused derisively. "Swine will always wallow in the mud."

Anaiah grinned, unperturbed.

"And you say He performed this… this false healing… on the Sabbath Day?"

Anaiah dared a step closer. "Let me ask you, priest: does this healing look false to you?"

Caiaphas' face reddened. "The Man is a false prophet and a deceiver. No holy man would dare break the Sabbath in such a blatant manner. You are every bit as guilty as He for participating in His sins."

"Is not the Sabbath Day set apart for rest, for restoration? Why, then, is a healing unlawful on the Sabbath Day? One can rescue their ox from a ditch, but Heaven help the man who dares rescue a human being on that day!"

"Enough of this!" Caiaphas' eyes flashed their angry fire. "You would do well to hold your tongue, you speaker of foolish blasphemies!"

Hezron stepped forward, looking especially religious with his prayer shawl and multiple phylacteries. "I want to know what this Man did to you. How did He open your eyes?"

"Yes! How?" The chorus of demanding voices was hushed by one look of warning from the high priest.

Shaking his head in disbelief, Anaiah's lips tipped in a knowing half-smile. "I told you already – multiple times – and you did not listen. Why do you want to hear it again?" He paused, lifting a dark brow in sarcastic question. "Do you also want to become His disciples?"

The pandemonium that followed was deafening and somewhat comical. The severe black garments of the religious leaders fluttered haphazardly along with their angry gestures. As he beheld the leaders' agitation, Malchus couldn't help but recall the angry, ruffled hens he had witnessed clucking and squawking within their pens at the open-air market.

"You may be His disciple, but we are disciples of no other than Moses!" Hezron broke from the ranks of religious leaders and circled Anaiah like a hunting panther. "We know that God spoke to Moses; but as for this Man, we do not know where He is from. And you would do well to remember that."

Completely immersed in the riveting drama, Malchus suddenly realized he hadn't been chronicling the last few minutes of dialog. His stylus flew as he attempted to catch up.

Unintimidated and unimpressed, Anaiah drew himself up even straighter and looked Hezron right in the eye. "This indeed is a marvelous thing that you don't know where He is from. You don't know where He is from, and yet He has opened my eyes! Perhaps He would open your eyes as well if you would turn from your stubborn pride and humble yourself before God!"

Hezron drew back his hand and slapped the preaching man's face with a loud *crack* that echoed in the marble hall.

Anaiah never flinched. He stood tall, unblinking, staring down the Sadducee who had struck him.

Malchus saw blood trickling from the corner of Anaiah's mouth and was filled with pity for the courageous man who had dared to stand firm before ruthless members of the Sanhedrin.

"Do you know to whom you speak?" Hezron screamed only inches away from Anaiah's face, his teeth bared like a feral animal. "Do you even know whom you accuse?"

Anaiah offered the faintest hint of a smile as he raised level eyes to Hezron. "Perhaps a more fitting question is this: Do *you?*"

A chill breeze swept through the elegant marble chamber as if in response to Anaiah's penetrating question.

Malchus froze, stylus poised, the question he himself had penned now staring him in the face, piercing his heart.

Do you?

Malchus suspected he already knew who had restored this man's sight, even though He had not revealed His name to Anaiah. Who other than Jesus of Nazareth could have performed such a miracle? Undoubtedly, Caiaphas and the religious leaders suspected it as well or they wouldn't be interrogating Anaiah so relentlessly.

"Some men make a practice of sinning, while others are filled with grief concerning their sins," Anaiah stated quietly, a peace resonating from his eyes that defied human logic. "The latter repent with tears and demonstrate their sincerity by turning from such sins. My good men, perhaps it would be wise to consider which type of man best represents the condition of your hearts."

Heart hammering wildly in his chest, Malchus wondered how much longer Caiaphas would allow this man to speak before ordering his swift, unlawful execution.

"Now we know that God does not hear sinners;

but if anyone is a worshiper of God and does His will, He hears Him," Anaiah continued earnestly. "Since the world began it has been unheard of that anyone opened the eyes of one who was blind."

The room grew strangely, ominously silent.

Anaiah arched a brow, an easy yet challenging smile splitting his radiant features. "One thing I know with absolute certainty: If this Man were not from God, He could do nothing."

The religious leaders erupted with shouts of angry protest. Malchus wished to draw his hands over his ears to drown out the fearsome sound.

"I find it interesting," Anaiah continued, seemingly emboldened by some supernatural force beyond himself, "that you Sadducees despise the Pharisees with a single-minded determination that would be admirable if put to use for something other than hatred, and yet your interrogation has not differed from theirs in the least. Your questions? Identical. Your responses? One and the same. Almost as if you were guided by the same force, reading from the same scroll." Anaiah stood unflinchingly before Caiaphas, awaiting his fate.

Caiaphas stood, towering above the unintimidated man from his elevated dais. His eyes flashed fire as he stated with dangerous calm, "You were completely born in sins, and yet you are teaching us?"

Another mischievous grin. "Ah, the Pharisees said the same."

Cloaked in a dangerous veil of calm, Caiaphas took several careful steps down from his elevated dais and stood before Anaiah, eye to eye. "A pity," he said coolly, "that you are so easily deceived. You are hereby cast out of the presence of Adonai. No longer shall you be permitted to worship or offer sacrifice. If you so much as show your face at a local synagogue -" Caiaphas paused, allowing the threat to dangle in the air.

Caiaphas clapped bejeweled hands, startling Malchus so thoroughly that he nearly dropped his tablet, for the eruption of sound was violent and unexpected in the echoing marble hall.

"Guards!" Caiaphas demanded, his gaze resting threateningly upon Anaiah. "Remove this man from my presence!"

CHAPTER 29

Malchus

Located far below the shadow of the magnificent Temple, on the southern side of the Lower City, the legendary Pool of Siloam was sheltered by ancient walls and marble pillars. Fed by the Gihon Spring and painstakingly diverted through Hezekiah's tunnel, the gently lapping waters of Siloam teased the great stone steps descending into the pool. Measuring over fifty feet long, eighteen feet wide, and nearly 20 feet deep, the pool provided ample space for the many poor to bathe and attend to their weekly laundry, even as the cleansing waters were gathered by the priests to accommodate Temple rituals. Four sets of massive stone steps descended gradually from the street to the sheltered pool, inviting weary travelers to rest beside the cool, soothing waters. The Pool of Siloam was indeed a delicious and shady respite from the hot, dusty streets of Jerusalem.

Quietly, Malchus took the nearest flight of steps and relished the coolness that washed over him as he approached the cleansing pool. Elegant, columned structures provided shade for those seeking refuge near the Pool of Siloam. Malchus paused beneath one such structure, leaning tensely against a marble pillar.

There, kneeling before the Pool of Siloam, was the man he wanted to see. But dare he interrupt the man's anguished, silent reverie?

Alone with his thoughts, Anaiah dipped one bronzed hand into the cool water. After a moment, he thoughtfully withdrew his hand, watching in wide-eyed wonder as glistening silver droplets cascaded from his fingers and back into the cleansing pool.

His dark beard was wet with tears.

Taking a deep breath, Malchus stepped forward and approached the dejected figure.

"Anaiah!"

Startled, Anaiah jerked his head in the direction of the unexpected address. His eyes narrowed in recognition. "Who are you?"

"My name is Malchus. I –"

"You were with the high priest." It was more than an observation. It was an accusation.

Malchus understood his concern. "Not by choice," he responded with a self-deprecating grin.

Anaiah rose to his feet and stood before Malchus. "What do you want? Did your master send you?"

"Caiaphas would probably flog my miserable hide if he knew I was speaking with you," Malchus responded ruefully.

"You followed me after the guards cast me out?"

"I needed to speak with you."

"Didn't you hear enough in that magnificent marble hall? I've heard tales about the lavish lifestyles of priestly families." He paused and shook his head. "If I hadn't seen it with my own eyes – which would have been an impossibility last week – I wouldn't have believed it."

"Believed what?" Malchus asked.

"How well they utilize our faithful tithes."

Malchus bit back a bitter smile. "I admire your boldness."

"If only your master shared that sentiment."

Malchus shrugged in defeat. He couldn't argue that point.

"You know, I never thought I'd see the light of day. But now I see everything – everything! – so clearly. Some things," Anaiah said, his eyes clouding with sadness, "are exactly as I imagined they would be. While others…" his voice quavered slightly, and Malchus' heart went out to him. "Other things are nothing as I imagined they would be."

"Such as?" Malchus asked, brow raised.

Anaiah studied him, clearly uncertain about whether or not Malchus could be trusted. Even so, his frank manner prevailed. "I always thought the high priest would have kind eyes."

The comment hung heavily in the air between them for what seemed an eternity.

"Why have you come?" Anaiah rubbed the back of his neck, weary and heartsick.

"I want to know if the Man named Jesus restored your sight."

"Ah, a man who gets straight to the point," Anaiah chuckled mirthlessly. "Refreshing."

"Was it Him?"

"I wish I knew. I have heard of a Miracle-worker

named Jesus. Perhaps it was Him."

"Don't tell me you don't know," Malchus said coolly. "This Man healed you! Surely you were simply protecting His identity during the interrogation!"

Anaiah grimaced. "When He commanded me to go wash in this pool, I was still as blind as a bat. Do you have any idea how difficult it was to locate this place?"

So you never saw your Healer?" Malchus stifled an impatient groan.

"Never."

"Do you think you'd know Him if you did?"

"Beyond a shadow of doubt."

"How so?" Malchus lifted a skeptical brow.

Anaiah paused, his eyes welling with tears. "His voice. His touch. I would know Him anywhere. Absolutely anywhere."

Anaiah turned from him then, wrapping his arms about his thin frame as if to ward off a fierce chill.

Malchus studied him, a frown splitting his handsome features. Anaiah had proven fearless at the interrogation. Why was he trembling now?

An unfamiliar compassion washed over Malchus, and he suddenly understood Anaiah's trepidation. Reaching out, he clamped a solid hand upon Anaiah's shoulder.

Anaiah turned to face him, a tear slipping into his beard.

"Anaiah," Malchus said with great conviction, "Caiaphas may have cast you out of his presence, but he can't touch your soul."

Anaiah covered his mouth with his hand, weeping.

"You needn't fear. Caiaphas is but a man."

"You don't understand." Anaiah shook his head angrily, swiping at a stubborn tear. "As a child, I loathed the God of Heaven for striking me with blindness. Now, as a young man, I see that He merely *allowed it* to demonstrate His power through me! Before, wild horses could not have dragged me to the Temple. But for the first time in my life, I desire to worship with other believers! And yet, by the authority of the great high priest himself, I am barred from worship. Barred from the synagogues, barred even from the Temple itself! Don't you see? If I am not permitted to offer sacrifices to cover my sins, then I shall perish in them."

Malchus stared at him, strangely moved and unsettled. His soul responded to the fervor of Anaiah's speech.

"For the first time in my life, I found God, Malchus," Anaiah said softly, clenching a fist in pain and deep regret. Weeping, he beat his chest with his fist. "I found God, only to be barred from His presence."

Malchus longed to comfort this man, but he was disturbed by his own vulnerability and lack of wisdom. Who was he to counsel another in such a matter? He thought of Melina and his heart constricted. If she were here now, she would know exactly what to say.

God, grant me wisdom! Malchus prayed silently. After all, that's what Melina would have done. *How can I comfort this man?*

Miraculously, words were supplied.

"You are wrong," Malchus stated with great conviction, his gaze fixed upon a pair of earnest eyes so perfectly restored.

Anaiah looked to him, expectant.

"You say you found God."

"I did! Right here, at this very pool! The moment I washed and opened my eyes to the world for the very first time, I was bathed in the presence of God –"

"You were blind. Now you see. I can't argue that point, Anaiah. You were bathed in God's presence. Even so, you're still wrong."

"Wrong? But why? How?"

"You say you found God, but you didn't, Anaiah."

Anaiah stared at Malchus in disbelief.

"*You* didn't find God – *He* found you. And He will find you again."

Anaiah looked to him, his eyes filling with hope and tears.

"Do you think God needs the help of some pompous windbag like Caiaphas to find you?" Malchus demanded, wondering at the depth of his own thoughts. "Must He confer with a fallible human being to learn the whereabouts of one of His own?"

Covering his face, Anaiah wept softly.

"You can seek the Lord, Anaiah, and you don't need the assistance of some arrogant tyrant donning priestly robes to communicate with the Almighty. Pray. Seek God and then you really will find Him. Is that not what the Scriptures say?"

Lowering his hands, Anaiah stared at Malchus with a look akin to wonder. "God sent you to me this day."

Staggered by that proclamation, Malchus attempted to recover from his initial surprise.

Had God indeed sent him here to speak to Anaiah? Had his own two feet been directed to the Pool of Siloam by a Will far greater than His own? A chill skittered up his spine as he suddenly comprehended the magnitude of his whereabouts – the Pool of Siloam.

Siloam. An ancient word with a powerful meaning.

Sent.

Had he himself been sent to this place by the One who orchestrated the Creation and upheld it by the power of His might? It was a wondrous yet disturbing thought.

Awestruck, Malchus was drawn back to the present when Anaiah placed a steady hand upon his shoulder.

"I fear no man, Malchus," Anaiah stated firmly, his eyes alight.

"That was glaringly evident during the interrogation," Malchus quipped drolly.

"But I must admit – I was shaken to the core when I considered the implications of banishment from the presence of God. But you are right. No man can stand between the God of the universe and His children. I will seek. I will pray." Squeezing Malchus' shoulder, Anaiah smiled broadly through his tears. "My hope is restored."

"I am truly glad, my brother," Malchus said, and he meant it wholeheartedly. "I must leave, but perhaps our paths will cross again."

"If not in this life, then most certainly in the age to come."

In the age to come, Malchus thought drolly. *If I am permitted to gain entrance!* He forced what he hoped appeared to be a genuine smile before he walked away.

Once he reached the shade of the nearest colonnaded structure, he chanced one last glance over his shoulder.

Anaiah knelt reverently beside quiet waters, face lifted heavenward, arms outstretched, lips moving in silent petition to the God he scarcely knew but longed to embrace.

CHAPTER 30

"Well, that was a touching scene."

Beneath a pillared structure overlooking the Pool of Siloam, Malchus spun around and found himself face to face with the last person on earth he desired to see.

"Alexander! What are you doing here?"

"A pleasure to see you as well, dear cousin."

The corners of Malchus' mouth turned down in his disgust. He should have known. Dark alleys and hidden shadows comprised Alexander's natural habitat. "You followed that man! Why?" he demanded angrily.

"You're one to talk," Alexander smirked, his dark eyes glittering like obsidian stones. "You set out before I did."

"If you intend to blackmail that innocent man, Alexander, so help me –"

Alexander drew back further into the shadows, crossing his arms over his chest. "Oh, please. You couldn't harm me if your life depended on it."

Clenching his jaw, Malchus decided not to argue that point. Why bother, anyway? Instead, he challenged yet again, "Why are you here?"

"I happened to be passing by the marble hall when the man was interrogated. Interesting story, that. I want to know if there's any truth behind it."

"Why?" Malchus retorted, his mouth tipped wryly. "Do you think the Miracle-worker might open your eyes as well?"

"A disturbing thought. And one that plagues me at night."

Malchus stared at Alexander, blinking in surprise. "Do you know who is responsible for this healing?"

Alexander arched a sardonic brow. "The One they call Jesus. Who else?"

"How do you know it was Him?"

"Who else works such miracles?"

Malchus' eyes narrowed in suspicion. "You speak with great conviction."

"Ah, yes. I know what I'm about. I wish I could say it ran in the family," Alexander added, lifting an amused and condescending brow.

Malchus felt his fists clenching at his sides. "Some," Malchus shot back, wondering why he even bothered to argue with this despicable cretin, "value caution rather than casting it to the wind and plowing headlong into irreversible trouble."

A harsh laugh. "Tell me, does that flimsy excuse aid your sleep at night?"

Defensive, Malchus prepared his rebuttal.

"Quiet!" Alexander hissed before Malchus could protest. Alexander's fierce brows drew together in complete frustration. "This is precisely why I work alone."

"That, and the fact that no one can stomach your

presence longer than fifteen minutes," Malchus ground out under his breath. But his annoyance evaporated when he followed Alexander's fiery gaze.

There, before Anaiah, stood Jesus.

"Where did He come from?" Malchus demanded, annoyed.

"Heaven, I imagine," Alexander responded drolly.

Malchus turned to Alexander, brows raised. Did Alexander even believe in Heaven? As far as Malchus knew, his Greek cousin stubbornly refused to bend a knee to any god, despite the vast array of deities worshiped in his childhood home in Tiberias. Although Alexander hadn't objected to the many pleasures and amusements offered by the pagan temples lining the elegant streets.

Alexander lifted a finger to his lips, a warning in his eyes. "Not a word."

Malchus clenched his teeth, weary of Alexander's irritating, commanding manner. But as his eyes rested upon Anaiah and the Miracle-worker standing before him, his annoyance evaporated, replaced by intense curiosity. Hadn't he himself assured Anaiah that the Lord needed no assistance in finding His own?

It would seem Anaiah had been found.

But *the Lord*... was Jesus truly Lord as He claimed? As Melina claimed? And what if He was? What did that mean for him? For Melina? For their future together?

Was it possible to accept this Man as Savior without getting too deeply involved? After all, to do so would be intentionally placing his life – and Melina's – at risk. Surely Jesus understood his reservations!

Dismissing his roiling and contrary thoughts, Malchus leaned forward, attempting to catch the softly spoken words of Jesus as pedestrians milled about, laughing and talking in a carefree manner, obstructing his view in the most irritating way.

More and more people were beginning to pour into the surrounding area, some carrying pots and jars, others laden with cloth bags filled with soiled laundry. The excited chatter grated on Malchus' already worn nerves.

Even so, since the pool was set deep within the earth with stone steps rising on all sides, it created a bizarre amphitheater effect that magnified the words spoken between the quiet Rabbi and the newly restored man beside the peaceful waters of Siloam.

Malchus leaned forward, intentionally drowning out the chaos and honing in on the words of Jesus and Anaiah.

He needed to know what was transpiring between the two!

Grimacing in his earnest attempt to eavesdrop, Malchus tensed when several darkly clad Pharisees floated down the stone steps, their severe garments trailing behind them like a peacock's magnificent tail. Their gazes swept the area before landing upon Jesus and the man kneeling at His feet, weeping.

Malchus' stomach clenched. They recognized Him.

The words of Jesus, powerful yet gentle, floated over the marble expanse between them, tugging at Malchus' heart and prying his attention away from the Pharisees standing upon the stone steps.

"Do you believe in the Son of God?"

His words were like a punch in the gut.

The Son of God.

Did he, Malchus, believe? *Could* he believe? What if he did? The consequences would prove disastrous indeed! Possibly even fatal!

Anaiah, on the other hand, did not hesitate. His eyes were wide with hopeful suspicion at the sound of Jesus' voice. Surely, surely his ears had not deceived him... "Who is He, Lord," Anaiah answered cautiously, "that I may believe in Him?"

The hope abounding in Anaiah's eyes nearly brought Malchus to tears. But why? And why was he so moved by the compassionate gaze of the Teacher he longed to escape?

Jesus spoke again. "You have both seen Him and it is He who is talking to you," He said with a tender, knowing smile, and the play on words was not lost on Malchus. Anaiah had indeed *seen* Him – and his ability to see Jesus standing before him was based solely upon the miracle He had performed!

It is He who is talking to you...

The hairs on the back of Malchus' neck stood on end. Yet again, Jesus was claiming to be the Messiah. The Son of God. Savior.

Malchus fought against this revelation with his entire being, for such a fact would surely shatter the quiet, orderly, peaceful life he longed to possess.

His thoughts were interrupted yet again by Anaiah's fervent cry. "Lord, I believe! I believe!" And then Anaiah fell into Jesus' open embrace, weeping uncontrollably as he worshiped.

Troubled to intrude upon such a personal moment, Malchus turned away, his eyes landing upon his brooding cousin. In all the excitement, Malchus had almost forgotten about him, but Alexander was still there, his mouth forming a grim line, his stony gaze fixed upon Anaiah and his new Master.

What was his cousin thinking? Malchus doubted he really wanted to know.

When Malchus turned back toward Jesus and Anaiah, his heart constricted in... what was it? Fear? Dread? For even as Jesus held Anaiah firmly, patting his convulsing back as a loving father might console an injured child, His gaze was fixed beyond Anaiah, toward the covered, colonnaded structure where Malchus and Alexander had taken refuge.

Why did Jesus appear grieved?

"Alexander," Malchus hissed, and his swarthy cousin looked to him with an air of annoyance and long-suffering. "He knows we're here."

Jesus was aware of their presence deep within the shadows! Malchus was sure of it, and it raised the gooseflesh on his arms and legs.

Alexander offered an unusually graceless snort. "That's ridiculous, although the entire region will soon know of our whereabouts if you persist in your worthless babbling and refuse to *shut up!*"

"He looked right at us!" Malchus insisted, strangely unsettled.

"From His vantage point, He cannot see us," Alexander maintained stoutly.

Annoyed, Malchus turned from Alexander and watched as Anaiah drew back from Jesus, his face bathed in tears, his every feature aglow with wonder.

"He knows we're here."

"Impossible."

"So is healing a man," Malchus retorted, "and that

hasn't stopped Him."

Alexander's eyes flickered ever so slightly as the Pharisees began to close in on Jesus. They, too, had overheard His bold proclamations. Clearly, they disagreed.

"Looks like trouble," Alexander stated cryptically. "We'd best be on our way."

"It pains me to agree with you about anything whatsoever," Malchus stated dryly, "but I think you're right."

Malchus fell into step beside his swarthy cousin, wondering at the rigidness of his spine, the firm set to his well-shaped jaw. His smoldering silence was rather unnerving.

Malchus offered a silent prayer for protection for Anaiah as they mounted the wide stone stairs of Stepped Street, hastening toward the Temple compound and the house of Caiaphas. His bold venture to the Pool of Siloam had raised even more questions rather than providing the answers he so desperately sought.

He wondered if Alexander was experiencing the same frustrating sense of defeat.

***

Alexander

Dropping heavily upon a bench in the lavish peristyle, Alexander attempted to process all he had just witnessed at the Pool of Siloam. He also considered the conversation he had overheard between his irritating cousin and Anaiah, the man born blind: *"You didn't find God – He found you. And He will find you again... Must He confer with a fallible human being to learn the whereabouts of one of His own?"*

Alexander couldn't help but acknowledge that Malchus' words were inspired – not that he would ever admit this to his younger cousin. Not in a million years.

Even so, he couldn't argue the power behind those words. Did God truly know those who were His?

Even before they knew Him?

Alexander couldn't deny the fact that He was drawn to the controversial Teacher, and that troubled him. He could only imagine what his dead father would have said had he known his eldest son was mesmerized by the teachings of a poor, unschooled Jewish Rabbi.

What was it about the teachings of Jesus that caused his seething anger to evaporate the moment Jesus began to speak? And why did that anger return full force the moment he walked away?

He needed to know.

Alexander dropped his head in his hands, kneading his forehead in frustration.

It was as if a strange and unfamiliar part of him was drawn to the revolutionary ideas of Jesus even while the rest of him resisted!

He had sought his own pleasure his entire life, and despite his unrelenting pursuit of happiness, he had never once obtained it. Momentary pleasures were easily attained, but never lasting. Why?

He longed for fulfillment, for a sense of *belonging.* He was tired of hiding behind a sardonic mask, wielding a shield of sarcasm and condescension in order to keep others from breaching his walls. He was exhausted. He wanted to rest.

But was he desperate enough to try a route as appalling as the one Jesus taught?

Love your enemies. Pray for those who persecute you. Seek the kingdom of God rather than your own pleasures.

None of it made any sense! And yet... Alexander's own methods, which had made perfect sense to him, had only driven happiness further and further away.

Perhaps it was time to incorporate an entirely different method.

"*You have heard that it was said to those of old, 'You shall not commit adultery.' But I say to you that whoever looks at a woman to lust for her has already committed adultery with her in his heart...*" Alexander groaned aloud, recalling yet another inconvenient teaching of Jesus. Immediately, he thought of Mara. He'd take her from her worthless husband in a heartbeat without the slightest hint of remorse if given the chance!

Whoever looks at a woman to lust for her has already committed adultery with her in his heart... How was any man to conform to such impossible standards?

He couldn't argue that Jesus' teachings were amusing and possibly even groundbreaking. But he, Alexander, was a man, after all. Did Jesus simply expect him to become less male, to somehow abandon the most natural instincts in the world? Certain thoughts were bound to occur to him!

But must you entertain every thought that occurs to you, however base?

Alexander winced at the silent, stinging reprimand. Where had it even come from? What was happening to him?

The truth of the matter was this: he wasn't a saint or an angel. He recalled the pleasures he had enjoyed in Tiberias and was certain he could never forfeit all of them. Some, perhaps. But *all?*

Unfortunately, he had a sneaking suspicion that Jesus would not settle for leftovers. No, Jesus would require his *all.*

But did he possess the discipline to exercise the type of control that Jesus condoned? Did he even want to attempt such a feat?

Temples pounding, Alexander propelled his powerful body to his feet and stalked out of the peristyle, irritated that he was even giving the teachings of this new Rabbi a second thought.

CHAPTER 31

Julia

The month of Cheshvan ushered in the long-awaited season of early autumn.

Enjoying the brisk evening air wafting through the open window, Julia lit the last oil lamp before pausing to survey her work.

A secretive smile tipped the corners of her rosy lips. She was rather pleased with her work. The small home glimmered with the soft light of many lamps as a pleasant breeze filtered through the house. The table was spread with a modest yet sumptuous feast, filling the house with mouthwatering and savory aromas.

Joanna had urged Julia to make tonight an occasion, and Julia had reluctantly accepted her nursemaid's advice. Even so, her stomach twisted in apprehension as she awaited her husband's arrival. How would Barabbas respond to her cherished announcement? Would he take her in his arms and speak to her tenderly? Would he weep with joy or laugh in glorious anticipation?

Or would he be angry?

Julia prayed silently as she went about the last-minute preparations, asking the Lord to grant her favor in the sight of her husband. *May this be a night we will remember, Lord. A night to cherish.*

Still, a disturbing sense of foreboding threatened to settle over her like a dark cloud. With fierce determination and squared shoulders, Julia pushed it away.

The child within her womb was growing steadily by the day, and Julia knew she could no longer keep her secret from her husband. As the baby continued to grow, Barabbas would notice her protruding abdomen. And he would be furious if she did not tell him soon.

Would he be angry she had waited this long?

Joanna knew her secret. Her mother and father knew. And she had shared her joy and apprehension with her dearest friend, Melina, after Joanna had confirmed her niggling suspicion. Despite Julia's own fears and misgivings, her loved ones were rapturous with joy for her.

Only Barabbas, her husband, remained uninformed.

Several days ago, Joanna had taken Julia aside, gently admonishing. "It isn't right, dearest – your husband being the only one in the dark about the baby. He should know, I'm thinking. And he should know soon."

Julia had accepted the reprimand, fully understanding it had been motivated by love for her and concern for her marriage.

Now, Joanna had retired to Deborah's home for

the night, where she continued to house-sit while the couple traveled to hear the teachings of Jesus. Pulse racing, Julia thought of her nursemaid and longed for her calming presence. Soon, Barabbas would return. Soon, she must tell him about the baby.

But why was she so afraid?

After much prayer, Julia had accepted this unexpected child as a gift from God and determined to be a worthy mother. When she was alone, she sang to the child in her womb – songs of the mercy, tenderness, and power of God. Love for the unknown little person within her had gradually gripped her, sneaking up on her unawares, growing steadily by the day.

Still, her sleep was troubled, plagued by nightmares and dread.

Why had God opened her womb? Didn't God know that Barabbas wasn't yet ready to be a father? Perhaps he would never be ready! What if her own husband led their child astray?

Oh, God, help me! Please. I'm so scared.

Be still, and know that I am God.

Yes, Lord, yes. You are God. Please help me remember that. Help me to trust.

Julia started when the door creaked open on protesting hinges. Barabbas stepped into their home, a leather satchel swung carelessly over one powerful shoulder. As always, his fierce presence filled the room with a crackling intensity.

Nervous, Julia drew in a sharp breath. Barabbas was devastatingly handsome, even when covered in sweat and road dust. Once, his fierce charisma and rugged features had captivated her imagination. At the time, she hadn't known about the iron will or the dangerous temper lurking beneath his enticing persona. Instead, she had been completely lost in his deep brown eyes and muscular build.

Carelessly, Barabbas dropped his leather satchel near the door before scanning the room, his dark eyes narrowing in suspicion.

"I am in no mood for company tonight. Whatever it is, call it off."

Julia stared at her husband, striving to maintain control. She was so sick of being dictated to! He hadn't even bothered to ask about the special circumstances before jumping to conclusions and ordering her about!

"We aren't having company, Barabbas."

Barabbas arched a sardonic brow. "No?"

"No."

"Then what's all the fuss about?" he asked, scanning the festive table and cheerily burning lamps with a look akin to disdain.

Pursing her lips, Julia attempted to dismiss her own annoyance. Didn't Barabbas recognize how hard she had worked to create a pleasant and romantic atmosphere for their evening together? And what about the succulent feast she had prepared for him? Did he even care?

Feeling her defenses rising one by one, Julia offered a silent prayer for calm. Rather than preparing for battle and strapping on her invisible armor as she had once been prone to do, she remembered the sound advice Deborah had offered her – advice capable of revolutionizing a marriage, if both parties were willing.

Choose to walk in love.

Julia forced a smile. "I have prepared a special evening for us."

"Why?" Barabbas looked less than interested. In fact, he looked annoyed.

"Because I have something I'd like to share with you, Barabbas, and I'd like this evening to be special."

Barabbas walked over to the table, hungrily scanning the contents. Without ceremony, he reached for a bundle of grapes and began plucking them off and devouring them one by one.

"May we be seated?" Julia asked, striving for calm.

Barabbas helped himself to another piece of succulent fruit. He met her gaze, his eyes glittering in defiance. "What do you need to tell me?"

"If you will allow me to wash your feet, Barabbas, you can change your garments and then we can be seated to enjoy a special supper together. Then I will tell you."

"What's wrong with my garments? Are they not to your liking?" Another challenge.

"Of course there's nothing wrong with them, Barabbas. I just thought you might be more comfortable in a fresh tunic –"

"By the gods, Julia!" Barabbas rolled his eyes in disgust. "Why must you make everything so complicated? I've been working all day. I'm too tired to mess with this."

"You work every day," Julia floundered, her frustration mounting. Even on the Sabbath, she wished to add. Though her father would never expect his men to work on the sacred day of rest, Amraphel – the murderous leader of Barabbas' band – didn't share Simon's sentiment regarding the sanctity of the Sabbath Day.

If I had to marry a Zealot, why couldn't it have been a religious one? Julia thought, peeved. Concerning the Zealots, there were many different brands of men. Some earnestly fought to defend Israel's freedom. Others were zealous for the Law and customs of their land. Still others – like Amraphel and his men – were merely brawlers who vented their wrath upon anything Roman, including Jews who betrayed the slightest sympathy toward Rome.

Frustrated by her own thoughts, Julia forced herself to focus on the present moment. Her husband still stood across the table from her, his gaze challenging. His flashing eyes dared her to defy him.

Why had she even bothered? She shouldn't have wasted the time. "I'm sorry, Barabbas, but I didn't know of a better time to share a special supper," she sighed weakly.

"You didn't even bother to ask," Barabbas cut in sharply. "But then, you never do, do you? You do what you want, then you don't understand why I don't grovel at your feet, fulfilling your every foolish whim."

Hurt by his harsh indifference, Julia's eyes welled with tears. "Barabbas, you would understand if –"

"No, Julia, I don't understand," Barabbas inserted harshly, his stance daring her to defy his speech. "I don't understand you! You are selfish and unthinking. It never even occurred to you that I might be weary after working all day in the hot sun."

"But you weren't traveling today. I thought you might be less weary since –"

"But you wouldn't know, Julia, would you?" Barabbas shot back, coming around the table to face her. "You've never worked a day in your life. You haven't the slightest idea what it's like to labor for your daily bread."

Julia turned away, tears coursing down her cheeks. "This was a bad idea. Forget I even mentioned it."

Barabbas gripped her arm, wheeling her around to face him. "Don't walk away from me!"

"We can do this another time."

"Ah, another time that's convenient for you, I imagine. Don't bother consulting with me. You never do anyway."

Julia looked away. If she spoke, she knew she would say something she'd regret.

"I'm not very hungry, but you may help yourself to anything on the table," Julia managed after a long moment of silent prayer.

"I don't need your permission to enjoy the fruits of my labor."

"No," Julia said softly, feeling sick. "I suppose you don't."

Barabbas' hard gaze rested on her, and she looked away, defeated. She started to turn.

"Where do you think you're going?"

"I'm feeling a bit tired. I think I will say goodnight to the goats before retiring for the night."

"The goats," Barabbas scoffed. "You bestow more affection upon those mangy beasts than you do your own husband."

"If you hadn't noticed," Julia responded before she could stop herself, "you don't make it particularly easy."

Barabbas' chiseled jawline hardened in anger. His eyes glittered dangerously. "You're not going anywhere," he said, reaching for another cluster of grapes. "You said you had something to tell me. What is it?"

Julia gazed into the hardened eyes of her husband, her heart sinking. She couldn't tell him now. "Now isn't the time, Barabbas. Perhaps later –"

"No. You'll tell me now!"

"Barabbas, please –"

"By the gods! Are you deaf? Dumb? Are you too unintelligent to obey a simple command?"

Panic welled up inside Julia. The thought of raising a child with this cruel, insensitive man frightened her.

"Well? Spit it out. I don't have all night."

"Barabbas, please, you don't understand –"

Gripping Julia's arm, Barabbas jerked her toward him, enraged by her resistance. "Enough of this, you stubborn woman! I said enough! Now I suggest you speak, and don't make me ask you again."

Julia's entire body went numb as panic continued to wrap its cold tendrils about her frantically pounding heart. Warm tears coursed down her cheeks.

So much for a night to remember!

Barabbas leaned forward, his cold brown eyes mere inches away from hers. "I said, speak up!"

"Is this the way you intend to speak to our child?" Julia cried out, bursting into violent sobs.

Barabbas froze, his fingers digging into Julia's arm like steel talons in his state of shock. For a moment, he looked as if he had been struck. His sun-tanned face drained of all color. Then his dark eyes narrowed dangerously. Forcefully, he drew Julia closer to him, sweat beading his forehead. "What did you say?" he asked slowly, measuredly.

Julia turned her face away as tears streamed down her cheeks. "I shudder to think of the way you will relate to our child, Barabbas," she gulped between sobs. "Will he live in fear of you? Is that what you wish?"

Gripping her by the shoulders, Barabbas forced Julia to face him. "What are you babbling about, Julia? Tell me!"

Devastated, she avoided his gaze.

"Julia, look at me. Look at me!"

Julia lifted red-rimmed eyes with dangerous calm.

"What are you talking about?" Barabbas demanded officiously. "I won't ask again."

Clenching her jaw at his imperious tone, Julia forced herself to hold her peace. "I am with child."

The ensuing silence was thunderous.

After what felt like an eternity, Barabbas released her shoulders and stepped back. Averting his gaze, he reached for the back of his neck, rubbing it thoughtfully as the color gradually returned to his face.

Julia studied him tentatively, untrusting.

Another seemingly endless eternity passed before Barabbas spoke again. "You're certain?" he avoided her gaze, his face reddening in... anger? Rage? She couldn't tell.

Julia nodded numbly.

"How can you be sure?"

"I confirmed it with both my mother and Joanna. They would know."

"Ah," Barabbas smirked, his expression dark. "I should have known you would run to everyone else in the world to share the news before bothering to tell your husband."

Julia's anger flared. "Women often lose their babies early in the pregnancy, Barabbas. I was afraid I might lose the baby –"

"And is that what you were hoping for?" Barabbas arched a sardonic brow.

Loathing unlike anything Julia had ever experienced reared its ugly head, filling her entire being. "How can you say that?" she cried out fiercely.

"How far along are you?" It sounded like a taunt.

"Three, maybe four months."

"That's how I can say that," he sneered. "I suppose I should be grateful you told me before the child popped out and made a grand entrance!"

"I didn't want you to be disappointed if I lost the baby, Barabbas," Julia hurled back at him, her eyes flashing in angry defense. "I wanted to be absolutely certain before I told you."

"A weak excuse," Barabbas hissed.

"It's true!" Julia looked away, her cheeks stained with color. For deep down in her innermost spirit, Julia recognized her argument was only partially true. That revelation stung. Fear, doubt, and resentment toward her husband had stilled her tongue – not concern for his possible disappointment. In her bitterness toward him, she had intentionally chosen to remain silent.

And she doubted he would ever let her forget it. She had never known another human being with such a long memory. She was certain Barabbas had chronicled every sin she had ever committed, every mistake she had ever made.

The thought infuriated her even more.

"Perhaps now," Julia dared quietly, her eyes downcast, "you understand why I tried to make this evening special."

Barabbas turned from her, his broad shoulders as rigid as the set of his firm jaw. "Save it, Julia."

Julia stared at her husband in disbelief. "Aren't you going to say something? Anything?"

Barabbas turned to face her, raising cold, level eyes to hers. "About what?"

"About the *baby!*" Julia exclaimed, incredulous.

"Why should I?" Barabbas shot back, lifting his leather satchel and slinging it over his shoulder. "You didn't say anything about it for four months." Satisfied he had cut her deeply, Barabbas slipped out the door and disappeared into the night.

CHAPTER 32

Mara

"It is a lovely evening, is it not?" Mara noticed Malchus' shoulders stiffen at her approach, but she knew she must accomplish what she had set out to do – despite her misgivings. She had done enough arguing with the Lord to last a lifetime. Now, she was determined to obey.

Malchus studied her from the marble bench upon which he sat, a rueful smile playing about the corners of his lips. "May I ask why I am honored by your presence this evening?" His tone was light, but Mara knew Malchus well enough to know he was presenting a façade. There was no light in his eyes, no joy in his tone. He was simply suffering her presence – his flimsy attempt at keeping the peace.

Once, Mara would have faulted him for his stubborn obstinance regarding the friendship they had lost. Now, her role in the destruction of their friendship was painfully, glaringly evident to her. Though it pained her to admit it, she realized that she was, in fact, at fault. She had betrayed his trust in order to gain the favor of a wicked man.

And now she must confess.

Oh, Lord, please don't let him gloat, she groaned silently as she considered abandoning ship and forfeiting her mission.

But the quiet, persistent voice within would not allow her that luxury.

Sitting gently beside Malchus on his curved marble bench, she offered a pacifying smile. "I'm going to get straight to the point."

"No subterfuge?" Feigning surprise, Malchus arched a brow. "That's a first."

Mara bit back a snide comment. He wasn't going to make this easy! Striving for calm, Mara reminded herself that she had earned his disdain. "I owe you an apology."

A harsh laugh escaped Malchus' lips. Rising from the bench, he rubbed the back of his neck in agitation before allowing his dark brown eyes to rest upon her in disbelief. "You're serious?"

"Completely serious."

Malchus studied her skeptically.

"I should have come to you long before now," Mara admitted, forcing herself to maintain eye contact. "But I was full of hurt and pride. I wasn't willing to admit that I was wrong."

"About?"

Mara's brown eyes studied Malchus intently. Was he genuinely interested in her apology or was he mocking her? *I suppose it matters not,* she sighed inwardly, dismissing her irritation. *I must apologize for my actions either way.*

Folding her hands delicately in her lap, Mara

sought Malchus' gaze. "I have come seeking your forgiveness."

Malchus' eyes darted about the peaceful surroundings within the peristyle. He appeared exceedingly uncomfortable. "Why are you making an issue of this now?"

"I was wrong," Mara managed, drawing on the Lord for boldness. "I betrayed my own people in order to gain the favor of a ruthless soldier. I betrayed your trust, Malchus. I regret that more than you know."

Malchus studied her features, strangely touched and unsettled. Her tone of voice, her mannerisms, her very eyes were different. "What happened, Mara? Something has changed."

"I hope I have changed," Mara spoke with great conviction. "The life I led dishonored God. I rejected Him because He hadn't granted my heart's desires – beauty, security, freedom, a husband, children. But now I see that God works in mysterious ways. I thought I knew what I wanted, Malchus, but what I needed was His mercy and forgiveness. Now I have it. And I can no longer live the way I once did."

Malchus stared at the humble maidservant, aghast. Despite the gentle stirrings deep within his heart urging him to forgive, common sense demanded he remain wary, on guard. "Trust has to be earned, so I'm sure you understand why I cannot simply dismiss all that's happened and hand my heart over to you on a silver platter, Mara."

"I understand."

Malchus did a doubletake, unprepared for her calm, quiet response. He almost wished she had lashed out at him instead. Then perhaps he could more easily dismiss the unwanted waves of guilt nearly choking him.

"Does Lucius know you're here? I can't imagine he's pleased about losing his key informant – that is, if your apology implies you intend to change your ways."

"By the grace of God, I fully intend to turn from my sins. And my whereabouts are no longer Lucius' concern."

Malchus lifted a skeptical brow. "He's your husband."

"Not anymore."

"What?" Malchus gaped, eyebrows raised in suspicion.

Mara's soft eyes filled with tears.

Malchus couldn't help but recognize that she looked very much like her old self – calm, composed, compassionate. For some reason unbeknownst to him, he found himself fighting against the urge to weep. Mara's miraculous transformation touched a chord deep within his heart. He remembered how tenderly she had mothered him after he lost his family. He remembered the camaraderie they once shared.

"You were right, Malchus," Mara was saying, a tear tracing a slender line down her pale cheek. "Lucius was using me for his own gain, to further his own agenda."

"So you left him?" Malchus questioned in disbelief, his admiration for her rising.

"No," Mara responded sadly, lowering her gaze. "He signed a certificate of divorce and sent me away."

"Ah. And I suppose now isn't the time to say *I told you so?*" Malchus couldn't help himself.

Shockingly, Mara did not retaliate. "You were right all along, Malchus. I should have listened to you – and to God."

Troubled by Mara's humility and refusal to retaliate, Malchus became defensive. "So you find yourself alone again, and now you come crawling back to me seeking friendship. Is that it?"

Tears spilled over Mara's cheeks. "My apology is genuine, Malchus. Even if you no longer wish to continue our friendship, I still must confess my sin to you. It is the right thing to do."

"Forgive my skepticism, Mara, but since when do you care about doing the right thing?"

"Since I met Jesus and He set me free."

Her soft reply was like a physical punch in the gut. Malchus stared at her, his insides churning. "You too?"

"If you are asking if I have become a follower of Jesus, the answer is a resounding yes. He has opened my eyes, Malchus. For the first time, I saw my own sin, my desperate need for cleansing. And when His eyes met mine, it was as if my sins were instantly forgiven – as if Jesus lifted them from my shoulders and bore them Himself somehow."

Chills pricked at Malchus' cool skin, raising the hairs on the back of his neck. Even so, his cautious nature argued against his instinct. "Only God can forgive sins, Mara."

Mara met his gaze, her soft eyes filled with wonder and the peace he craved. "Exactly."

Malchus' entire body went cold.

Reaching out to touch his arm, Mara smiled with all the warmth and affection she had ever possessed for him, despite the fact that he stiffened at her touch. "May He open your eyes as well, that we may walk together and be agreed once again."

With an ache in his throat, Malchus watched as Mara departed gracefully, stopping to touch a delicate blossom before passing beneath a pillared portico.

It would seem he had lost yet another loved one to the teachings of a wanted Man.

CHAPTER 33

Melina

Backing up against the heavy, gilded double doors which opened into Salome's abandoned yet opulent chambers, Melina pushed with all her might, grinning with satisfaction when the heavy doors bowed inward with groans of protest. She had long since learned to enter the chambers this way when her arms were burdened with a tall pile of freshly laundered sheets and bedding.

Satisfied, she smiled as brisk winter breezes wafted through arched, elegantly tiled windows. She had intentionally left the windows open to dismiss the mustiness of disuse hanging heavily in the air.

Despite the fact that Salome no longer resided within this impressive suite, Melina still received strict orders to maintain the chambers in case the newlywed princess chose to visit her mother and stepfather.

"By the gods, I thought you'd never show up!"

Her vision hindered by an enormous stack of

folded bedding, Melina froze, her stomach churning. *Surely, surely not...* Cautiously depositing the laundry on the enormous canopy bed, Melina turned tensely and found herself face to face with the very last person she expected to see.

"Salome?"

Propped casually against a marble pillar, her stance as arrogant and daring as ever, Salome tipped her head to one side, a cascade of luxuriant black waves sweeping over her shoulder. "Surprised?"

"I... I..." Melina stammered dumbly. Pausing to catch her breath, she started over, her forehead beaded with perspiration at the amused, catlike grin playing about the corners of Salome's richly painted lips. "Salome – I mean, my lady – I didn't expect to see you here."

"Why ever not? After all, it is *my* room."

"Yes," Melina agreed, releasing a shaky breath. "Yes, it is."

Salome arched a carefully preened brow. "Don't tell me you've gotten a bit too comfortable in my own private chambers in my brief absence."

Stung by the insinuation, Melina drew back. "I have simply maintained your quarters to the best of my ability, my lady."

Salome released a skeptical *harrumph*.

Straightening and folding her hands before her in the expected, subservient stance, Melina offered lamely, "I do apologize, my lady, but I was not alerted about your arrival –"

"Neither was anyone else," Salome stated vehemently, lifting her chin in a proud manner. "I am a married woman now, and I needn't seek anyone's permission or approval – not even Philip's."

Salome's angry outburst was loaded with venom, and Melina suspected the princess' unexpected arrival may have been instigated by a marital spat. "Does Philip know you are here, my lady?" Melina dared softly.

"He'll figure it out, soon enough," Salome snapped with a careless toss of her head.

"But will he be angry?"

Salome's emerald eyes filled with black fury. "Who are you to question me, slave? I needn't answer to Philip nor to anyone else! I am absolutely sick of being ordered about. I am capable of making my own decisions!"

The statement hung in the air far longer than was comfortable. Unsure about what to say next, Melina cleared her throat uncomfortably. "How may I best serve you, my lady? How long will you stay?"

"As long as I wish, and I don't need anyone's permission to do so either."

Carefully, Melina studied her young mistress. Much to her dismay, Salome appeared to be her same old self – spoiled, selfish, and entitled. Melina had hoped that marriage to a decent man might improve Salome's willful disposition. But such hopes had proven vain. Salome was just as obstinate as the day she had left to be joined to Philip.

A disturbing thought occurred to Melina, and though she risked inciting her mistress's wrath, she decided she must voice her concern anyway. "Will there be any dangerous repercussions, my lady, for leaving your husband's estate without his permission or consent?"

Salome's stony countenance paled momentarily, but she quickly gathered her wits about her. "I don't care if there are! Let the old goat worry and stew! He doesn't get to control my life! I'm sick and tired of being locked up behind those dreary palace walls!" Pacing like an angry tiger, Salome ran slender fingers through her luxuriant hair. "You wouldn't understand, Melina," she whined, her tone petulant. "Sometimes I'm so bored I think I'll just die!"

"Surely," Melina dared hopefully, "there are many interesting tasks to tend to as the wife of a respected and noble ruler."

Salome dropped heavily upon her unmade canopy bed, carelessly toppling over the pile of neatly folded bedding. "I'm far too young and full of life to be bothering with appearances and politics!"

"But I imagine you are capable of becoming a worthy consort for your husband. You maintain a very influential position, my lady, and perhaps you might make a difference –"

"I don't care!" Salome sat up violently, her eyes flashing their angry fire. "Why would I bother trying to make a difference in this wretched province? All I want is to be free of it – free from Philip!" Salome rose from the bed, whirling about like a young girl. "I want to go somewhere exciting, like Rome or Ephesus or Alexandria! That's where I belong – not rotting away in a miserable stone fortress surrounded by dust and peasants."

Melina was filled with sadness. Salome hadn't the slightest idea how blessed she was. "I wish you could be happy, my lady."

"I'll never be happy as long as I'm with Philip!" Salome spat angrily. "I hate him! He's a disgusting old man obsessed with governing a wretched, miserable region! He should be aspiring for bigger and better things! But no, he's perfectly satisfied fraternizing with commoners and furthering his reputation as *a friend of the people*," Salome snorted sarcastically, rolling her eyes in disgust. "If Philip wants to waste his own life, that's fine! But it's completely unfair for him to force me to waste mine as well."

Stooping to gather the bedding Salome had carelessly upturned, Melina offered a soothing smile. "Perhaps God led you there for a purpose, my lady."

"I don't need some mysterious, faraway deity to govern my life. I know what I want for myself and I know how to get it."

Melina considered asking Salome how that had worked out so far but thought better of it. Salome had never been one to accept reason. Her raging emotions triumphed in every situation.

"Aristobulus understands me," Salome whined as she watched Melina meticulously making the bed. "His visits are the only thing keeping me sane."

Melina straightened from her work, vaguely disquieted by Salome's statement. "Who is Aristobulus?"

Salome turned and offered a wicked grin. "A relative, which is why Philip permits his frequent visits. Ah, my husband is such a fool."

Melina's stomach clenched in disgust.

"Aristobulus is so very interesting, and handsome too. He sets my blood afire and fills me with excitement!"

Disturbed by Salome's infatuation with another man, Melina deftly changed the subject. "You must be hungry after your long trip, my lady. Shall I have a tray sent up to you?"

"Oh, I'm hungry, but not for food," Salome mused,

prowling about the room like a restless predator. Pausing before her gilded vanity mirror, Salome studied her reflection with great interest. "It will be challenging, I know, but I want you to make me look like a commoner."

Fluffing the pillows, Melina glanced up in surprise. "My lady?"

"You heard me. I'm positively desperate for a diversion, Melina. I want an adventure, and you are going to make it happen!"

Apprehension washed over Melina as her knees weakened. "What would Herod and your mother say—"

"Haven't you heard a word I've said? I don't care what they say!"

"If that's the case, then why do you wish to leave disguised as a commoner?"

Salome's face reddened in rage. "You have no right to question me! Now do as you are commanded, or I shall have you flogged!"

Despite Salome's threat, Melina held back a small smile. She supposed she shouldn't be surprised by Salome's angry threats and imperious demands. It was just like old times.

"What adventure are you seeking, my lady?"

Sensing her handmaiden's capitulation, Salome relaxed. "I want to gain entrance to the Temple of the Jewish God. I wish to see Jesus of Nazareth."

Melina nearly fainted. "The Jewish Temple, my lady?"

"Isn't the Court of the Gentiles open to pilgrims of any race? Surely you can get me in there, even if you are Greek. That Jesus of Nazareth is rumored to speak often at Solomon's Porch, which is accessible to Jews and Gentiles alike."

"But, my lady—"

"Now go get one of your ugly little gowns for me to wear," Salome ordered imperiously. "Oh, and a cloak too – one with a large hood."

"My lady," Melina stammered, her heart pounding furiously in her chest. "Why do you wish to see a Jewish Teacher?"

"Do I need your permission to do so?" Salome challenged dangerously. "The Man is a rebel-rouser who has the entire Jewish Sanhedrin in a complete state of frenzy! I've heard He even performs miracles and healings. I'm desperate for a distraction, and this gutsy magician interests me."

Melina stared at her mistress, uncertain.

"Now, go!" Salome commanded, her tone laced with annoyance. "The Man is rumored to be speaking at the Temple now."

"But my lady," Melina ventured rather shakily, "Jerusalem is in the midst of the Feast of Dedication. The entire city is in a state of utter chaos –"

"Which makes this so much more exciting!" Salome exclaimed, rubbing her manicured hands together gleefully. "Now hurry up – go gather some garments and help me look ugly and plain like you."

Thanks a lot, Melina thought, amused. As she hastened toward the servants' quarters, she uttered a silent prayer of desperation. She was in a rather tenuous position, for Salome could easily punish Melina for disobeying her orders, and Herodias could end Melina's life for jeopardizing her daughter's safety.

Melina was likely to suffer punishment either way.

Oh Lord God, what should I do?

An unmistakable peace settled over Melina, calming her fears and soothing her spirit. In that instant, she knew. This might be Salome's only opportunity to meet Jesus, the Son of God, Savior of the world. And Melina knew that Jesus was about the salvation of souls – *all* souls. Even a soul as dark as Salome's.

Holding back an expectant smile, Melina hastened her steps and resumed her mission with confidence.

CHAPTER 34

Despite the ominous black clouds darkening the entire city and threatening an unpleasant and potentially dangerous downpour, the streets were thick and bloated with a swelling sea of rowdy celebrators and observers of the politically charged Feast of Dedication.

"Tell me, Melina, are all Jews so hopelessly zealous?"

Melina turned to her mistress, her heart pounding in her trepidation. What if Salome was recognized on Jerusalem's streets? Even with her face scrubbed clean of cosmetics, Salome's vibrant green eyes, luxurious mane of raven black tresses, and exotic features caused her to stand out like a striking lily among thorns. Despite Melina's greatest efforts, the faded, hooded robe she had selected did very little to mask Salome's voluptuous form. And the girl carried herself with the air of a Roman goddess, head held high and chin lifted proudly. She didn't walk at a brisk, harried pace like the women about her – she glided with the grace and poise of a queen.

Salome's "adventure" might prove far more difficult and dangerous than Melina had anticipated.

"Hello? Is there anything inside that head of yours apart from empty space?" Salome goaded a bit too loudly, miffed that Melina had ignored her rude inquiry.

"I do apologize, my lady," Melina quickly amended. "I was lost in thought."

"I don't like that word – lost – when roaming about a dangerous city, alone."

Melina held back an amused smile. "I know my way about Jerusalem, my lady. You needn't fear getting lost." *Other things like getting trampled, robbed, abducted, or worse – yes, she added silently. But getting lost, no.*

"You still have not answered my question!" Salome pointed out imperiously.

"I'm afraid I didn't hear you above the din." Melina winced, for she realized her statement was only partially true. Yes, the chaotic streets of Jerusalem were deafening, but her own frantic thoughts nearly drowned out the frenzy. *Lord God, protect us. Don't let me depart from Your will in this.*

"I asked if all Jews are so hopelessly zealous," Salome repeated, observing the mayhem with an air of disdain as she strode proudly alongside her handmaiden.

"The Jewish people are very careful to observe their laws and feast days. The Feast of Dedication is no exception."

"What *ever* is it about, to create such uncivilized mayhem?" Salome demanded in annoyance. "And why so many lights and burning lamps? Surely these people sense the rain is coming. They wasted their time lighting all of their lamps when the rains will simply put them out."

"The Feast of Dedication is also called the Feast of Lights," Melina explained, somewhat relieved to divert her attention from her own concerns in order to answer Salome's questions. "It commemorates the cleansing and rededication of the Temple after a man named Judas Maccabaeus drove out the Syrians about 200 years ago."

"What a bore," Salome declared. "So, these people sing and shout and light lamps and wave branches about like madmen and dance around like fools – just to celebrate ancient history?"

Melina hid another smile. "It isn't terribly ancient, and I suppose the events grant them hope."

"Hope for what?" Salome snorted. "Despite their ridiculous antics, they are still a conquered people. And they will die in their bondage if Rome has its way – which she will. Rome always has her way."

"There is a bondage far worse than political oppression," Melina said quietly.

Salome paused mid-step and cast her servant a suspicious glance. "You are terribly philosophical for a dumb serving wench. What does that even mean?"

Melina hoped she hadn't overstepped her bounds. She prayed silently as she replied, "Only the truth can set us free, my lady. We are all enslaved to something."

"Like you, for example," Salome said haughtily, resuming her steps. "You are enslaved to me."

Melina looked to her young mistress sadly. Salome might never realize that she was far more enslaved to herself than Melina would ever be. She offered a warm smile. "In spirit, I am free."

"You don't look very free to me."

"Not according to this world's standards."

"You have dwelt among the Jews too long. You sound like them – speaking in riddles," Salome retorted in annoyance.

"This life is temporal, my lady. But what comes after – that is eternal."

"As most religions grandly proclaim. Who is to know which is true, if any at all?"

"If you seek it," Melina answered slowly as the magnificent Temple loomed into view, its golden peaks gleaming despite the dark clouds overhead, "you will find it, if you search for it with all your heart."

"And I suppose you – a pitiful servant without a shekel to your name – possess the answers to the mysteries of the universe?" Salome nearly taunted.

"Absolutely not," Melina responded, refusing to be offended by Salome's cruelty. After all, today's encounter with Jesus might be Salome's only hope. "But I have met the One who does."

Salome arched a provocative brow. "Who?"

Fear coursed through Melina unlike anything she had ever experienced. If she dared to speak the truth to Salome, would she be punished for it? Taking a deep breath, she mustered the strength her Lord provided and calmly replied, "The Man you wish to see."

Salome laughed loudly enough for several pass-ers-by to stop and stare.

"Please, my lady," Melina begged quietly, "try not to draw undue attention. I wish to keep you safe."

"I'm sorry," Salome laughed, covering her mouth with one manicured hand. When Melina failed to join in her merriment, Salome froze and pinned Melina in place with her look of utter shock. "Wait, you're serious?"

"I am."

"Melina, that Man is a magician from Nazareth! He is probably crooked to the very core!"

Melina refused to be insulted. She knew that Salome was about to encounter the only Truth that could set her free, and the enemy of her soul would do everything in his power to prevent that from happening. Offense was one of Satan's most effective and destructive tools. "Don't take my word for it," Melina smiled, reveling in the peace steadily descending upon her despite her precarious position with Salome. "Wait and see for yourself."

Salome shook her head, her lips curved in a mocking smile. "Well," she pronounced, resuming her graceful gait among the thronging pedestrians, "this just got a lot more interesting."

CHAPTER 35

It was rumored that Jesus once said it was easier for a camel to go through the eye of a needle – a ridiculously low, narrow, and inconvenient entrance – than for a rich man to enter the kingdom of Heaven.

Now, Melina felt rather like that poor camel in the object lesson as she attempted to gain entrance to the Temple compound with Salome. The holy site was absolutely swollen with worshipers. Noisy, overly excited revelers filled both the inner and outer courts. Talented Temple musicians accompanied the haunting and soulful lyrics of the *Hallel*, sung by professionally trained Temple singers. The melody drifted upon the wind, raising the hairs on the back of Melina's neck as she considered the significance of the ancient words of Scripture.

"I hate to admit it, but this place is magnificent," Salome shouted above the din, adjusting her hood in order to obscure more of her face.

Wishing that Salome would have consented to wearing a veil as she had suggested, Melina nodded her agreement, warily eyeing their boisterous surroundings. If anyone appeared too curious about Salome, they would make a prompt exit and return to the palace.

"I never knew a Jewish Temple could be so grand," Salome mused, her eyes wide with wonder. "Practicing Jews are always so boring and prudish."

Dismissing the insult, Melina forced a smile. "Shouldn't it be grand? Your grandfather built it."

"Herod the Great had many projects," Salome harrumphed in disinterest. "His dreams of turning Jerusalem into some great metropolis rivaling Roman cities died along with him."

Solomon's Porch was overflowing with eager listeners, and Melina's heart skipped a beat when she saw the crowds pressing in on all sides. Only one Man in all of Jerusalem garnered crowds like that – Jesus was close at hand.

"My lady," Melina instructed gently, taking her mistress's arm and guiding her beneath the beautifully columned structure. "This way."

"Where is He?" Salome demanded, standing on tiptoes to see above the vast ocean of men and women.

Melina's observant eyes scanned the entire length of the impressive hall. There, near the front and shielded by several protective disciples, stood Jesus. Despite the tense stances of His men, Jesus appeared completely at ease, relaxed even.

"That Man near the front – that's Him," Melina stated, her heart swelling with warmth for her Savior.

Salome craned her neck to see above the crowd, then smirked in derision. *"Him?"*

"Is something wrong?"

"You say *He* has the answers to life's mysteries? Look at Him! He doesn't even own a decent garment. He's a peasant."

"He is a humble Man with a very important mission."

"And what mission is that?" Salome sneered.

"Saving souls."

Salome did a double take. "A high and lofty response," she replied sarcastically, attempting to mask her mounting curiosity. "How exactly does He intend to do that?"

"We are all enslaved to sin. Jesus sets us free."

"Sin?" Salome laughed, shaking her head. "And by *sin*, I suppose you mean any activity that's the least bit enjoyable? Jews obey rigid laws of morality and deny themselves life's simplest pleasures."

"There is no lasting pleasure in sin, my lady," Melina said quietly.

"Spoken like someone who has done what was asked of her from the day she was born. You haven't the slightest idea what it is to really *live!*"

"But do you?" Melina dared softly, her gentle eyes sympathetic rather than condemning. "Are you truly happy, my lady?"

Salome's eyes filled with rage. "If you weren't my only hope of returning to the palace in one piece, I'd have you beaten and flogged right here for your insolent speech."

"I speak frankly because I care about you, my lady," Melina spoke gently, disarming her. "I desire only your good, your peace and ultimate fulfillment."

Salome rolled her eyes and tossed her hair carelessly over one shoulder. "You are such an odd little maid," she smirked, shaking her head. "Sometimes I don't know what to do with you."

"You could try listening," Melina offered with a shy little smile. "What if Jesus is right?"

Salome huffed in annoyance. "Remember your place, Melina. I don't take advice from cheap slaves."

Or anyone else, Melina thought, annoyed. Even so, she knew she mustn't show it. There was too much at stake.

"There is absolutely nothing commendable about Him," Salome remarked critically. "He is plain, simply dressed. Although," she added with a hint of mischief, "a few of His disciples are rather rugged. Not bad-looking at all!"

With great effort, Melina suppressed her annoyance and held her tongue.

"Come, Melina," Salome commanded, already on the move. "Let's get as close as we can. Maybe He'll perform a healing or do something interesting!"

Sighing, Melina followed after her excitable mistress.

As they drew closer to the front of the crowd, Melina noticed that Jesus appeared to be retreating. Her heart sank. Had they missed His sermon? Had they arrived too late?

Attempting to reach the front of the crowd, Melina felt her panic rising as men and women continued to press in around them with alarming violence. The crowd was closing in on Jesus, blocking any means of His escape. Men began to shout, and women cried out shrilly. They were all asking the same questions.

"Who are You?"

"How long do you intend to keep us in doubt, shrouded in mystery?"

"Are You the Messiah?"

"If You are the Christ, tell us plainly!"

A frightening realization struck Melina like a ton of bricks. In the midst of the Feast of Dedication, amidst frenzied political and religious fervor, these people intended to goad Jesus into action. They wanted a Messiah like Judas Maccabeus – a revolutionary to destroy their oppressors and unleash a new era of political freedom.

They wanted Jesus to be their Judas Maccabaeus.

Salome gripped Melina's arm, her own excitement escalating. "The crowd is getting restless," she nearly squealed. "Isn't this exciting? We might even witness a revolt!"

That is exactly what I'm afraid of, Melina thought, pursing her lips in concern. She wondered if she and Salome should vacate the compound before the situation spun out of control.

Calmly, Jesus turned and addressed the crowd. But His words were nearly smothered by the angry mob of observers.

"I can't hear a thing!" Salome whined, her long fingernails digging painfully into Melina's arm. "Let's get closer!"

"My lady –"

Salome jerked Melina toward her and pulled her further through the crowd, angering those gathered with them as she shoved past them.

"The works that I do in My Father's name, they bear witness of Me," Jesus was saying as His gentle eyes swept across the crowd of impatient men and women. "But you do not believe, because you are not of My sheep, as I said to you."

Quivering with joy at the sound of her Savior's voice, Melina forgot about the pressing crowd and hungrily absorbed the words of Jesus. Cautiously, she chanced a glance at Salome, who appeared mesmerized by the Teacher's words.

"My sheep hear My voice, and I know them, and they follow Me," Jesus continued patiently. "And I give them eternal life, and they shall never perish; neither shall anyone snatch them out of My hand."

Tears sprang to Melina's eyes. Her position was a precarious one indeed, but she was secure in the arms of her heavenly Father. Jesus Himself had said that no one could snatch her from His hand. What a precious assurance!

"My Father, who has given them to Me, is greater than all," Jesus explained, His expression far gentler than the fierce countenances of His wary disciples, "and no one is able to snatch them out of My Father's hand. I and My Father are one."

Nearly melting beneath the warm glow of the Messiah's powerful testimony, Melina was jerked back to reality when a man near the front of the crowd lifted a fist and screamed violently, "Blasphemer!"

The crowd erupted with shouts of fury and accusation.

"He says He is equal to the Father!"

"Blasphemy! Blasphemy!"

A look of sadness crept into Jesus' tender eyes. Quietly, He turned and prepared to leave.

"He must die!" An older woman shrieked shrilly, raising her fist in defiance.

"Stone him!" Another shouted, and the crowd exploded with shouts of agreement. "Stone Him, stone Him, stone Him!"

Jesus paused, turning to face the crowd once more. "Many good works I have shown you from My Father. For which of those works do you stone Me?"

Salome laughed merrily, catching Melina off guard. "He's funny," she remarked, her eyes alight with interest.

Melina stared at her mistress in awe. Didn't

Salome realize this was no laughing matter? They were caught up in the midst of a murderous mob! "My lady, we must leave."

"But it's just beginning to get exciting!"

"Please trust me," Melina pleaded, taking Salome's arm. "These mobs become dangerously violent in an instant. We must go. Now. It is my responsibility to see you safely back to the palace."

"What a bore you are!" Salome shouted above the din, shaking her head in disgust. "Don't you ever have any fun?"

Ignoring Salome's protests, Melina led the young woman away from the mob with great difficulty. Casting a concerned look over her shoulder, she saw that Jesus had already disappeared. Several of His disciples remained behind, barring the way of the dangerous crowd with little success.

Thank You, God, Melina prayed silently, relief flooding her entire being. *Thank You for protecting Him. By Your grace, He has evaded death yet again.*

Neither woman spoke again until they reached the paved streets of Jerusalem, palace bound. Overhead, the roiling clouds grew more and more ominous.

"That Man is certainly fascinating," Salome remarked, cringing as a gentle rumble of thunder resonated off the heavy black clouds. "It's as if the gods are angry the people attempted to stone Him. Just look at that sky!"

"The gods have no power over Him or anyone else," Melina replied, her patience growing thin. "God is His Father, and there is but one God."

Salome gave her a sideways glance. "You've been in this dusty province far too long. You're actually starting to believe the fanatical religious views of this godforsaken land."

"Didn't you sense the power of Jesus' words?" Melina asked, disappointed.

"What power? He just rambled on and on about sheep, of all things! Sheep are the dumbest, smelliest, most stubborn and miserable beasts on earth! God knows what He sees in them."

Yes, He certainly does, Melina thought with a small smile. "It was an analogy," she explained patiently, trying to ignore the chill breezes swirling about them. Instinctively, she pulled her shawl tighter about her shoulders. "Those who believe on Him are the sheep of His pasture."

"He compares His followers to sheep? How utterly insulting!" Salome cried, dismayed.

"You said sheep are dumb and stubborn – how are we any different?" Melina teased.

"I don't appreciate His analogy," Salome huffed, annoyed. "But perhaps those crazy enough to follow Him are dumber than sheep, after all. Anyone who pledges allegiance to that Man has a death wish."

Sighing, Melina wondered if their risky trip to the Temple had proven totally fruitless. How could Salome possibly seek answers when she was convinced she already possessed them? *Lord God, she prayed silently, in earnest. You promise that Your Word shall not return to You void. Today, Salome heard Your Word, Father, spoken by Your precious Son. May Your words be within her a fountain that springs forth to everlasting life. May they not return to You void.*

"The Jews think He's their Messiah, don't they?"

Shaken by Salome's frank inquiry, Melina scrambled for a satisfactory response. What if Salome were to report such to her stepfather, Herod Antipas? The man jealously guarded his position, and he would share it with no man. The results would prove disastrous indeed if Salome planted a seed of doubt in the wicked heart of the tetrarch.

"Well? Stop making me repeat myself, for Heaven's sake!" Salome complained, petulant.

"The Jews are eager for a radical Messiah to sever their Roman bonds," Melina answered truthfully. "But Jesus Himself has said that His kingdom is not of this world. He has come to give the people what they *need* – not necessarily what they *want*."

"Ah, more riddles," Salome smirked. "How very scholastic, not to mention obnoxious."

"Jesus is not a revolutionary, and the Jews believe their Messiah will be a valiant warrior like king David of old."

"He all but claimed to be the Messiah when the people asked Him."

"Jesus has indeed come to release us from captivity, Salome, but not from Roman bonds. Jesus has come to free us from ourselves, from the sin that so easily ensnares us. Once we are no longer enslaved to our own sinful passions, we are free to serve God."

"They say He works miracles – real miracles," Salome mused, her eyes brightening, "Perhaps He could free me from Philip!"

"I think it's more likely He would help you learn to serve your husband in love and sincerity," Melina said gently, praying that Salome's heart would be opened to the truth.

"I serve no one," Salome responded tersely. "Why would I wish to relinquish my freedom only to serve another master?"

"Jesus' yoke is easy, Salome, and His burden is

light."

"I have enough burdens to shoulder without having to worry about another one, however light."

At that moment, a fearsome crack of thunder nearly shook the ground beneath them, illuminating the area with a magnificent flash of lightning. As if in response, the heavens opened, sending a pounding, merciless rain upon the dusty city below.

Laughing, Salome lifted her face heavenward and raised her arms. "Isn't this divine?" she exclaimed. "Philip would hyperventilate if he knew I was splashing about the streets right now!"

Melina sobered. "We must hurry, my lady. Your garments are already soaked, and you might catch a cold."

"Always the mother hen," Salome teased. "Let's run like the wind!"

Both women were drenched and chilled to the bone when they finally reached the palace grounds. As they hastened toward Salome's warm, dry chambers, Salome continued to giggle and whisper about their adventure.

"Wouldn't it be something?" Salome mused, pausing long enough to order several hovering maidservants to fetch warmed, fresh towels from the baths.

"My lady?" Melina asked, confused.

"If that Man – Jesus, yes? – turned out to be the Messiah after all!"

Melina watched her mistress, cautious. She hoped there was safety in silence.

"My grandfather did everything in his power to annihilate every male child that might possibly grow up to become the Messiah. Herod the Great would relinquish his throne to no one, and certainly not to a squalling infant. No, Herod did what was necessary to protect his rule."

Saddened, Melina lowered her gaze.

"Herod was thorough. Nothing escaped him, absolutely nothing. As whimsical as the idea of a Messiah may be, I guarantee you the promised One was wiped off the face of the earth that night when Herod slaughtered all the male babies in that nasty little town."

Accepting the warm towels the maids had brought, Melina hid a knowing smile. Herod the Great had indeed been a brilliant and calculating ruler. But he had been foolish to imagine he could thwart the plans of Almighty God.

"Wouldn't it be funny, though?" Salome exclaimed, chuckling in amusement as Melina gently towel-dried her luxuriant hair.

"Wouldn't what be funny, my lady?" Melina asked, setting aside the towel in order to select a dry gown for her mistress.

Salome's large green eyes gleamed with mischief. "Wouldn't it be funny if Herod had driven himself absolutely mad wiping out all those babies," she grinned, "only to miss the One that truly mattered?"

Melina offered a genuine smiled, overwhelmingly grateful that the will of God always prevailed.

CHAPTER 36

"I suppose I should be happy to see you."

Standing behind Salome, who was seated at her vanity while her maidservant twisted her hair into an elegant Roman style, Melina's fingers froze mid-twist, tightening about the thick strands of raven black hair. An unwelcome shiver skittered up and down her spine. She knew without bothering to turn around exactly who it was standing poised in the doorway, her dark presence filling the entire chamber like a malevolent being.

Salome remained seated at her gilded vanity, her back ramrod straight. Melina could sense the girl's tension almost tangibly.

"I might ask," Herodias said, her tone dangerously controlled, "why I was not alerted as to your arrival?"

Salome's spine straightened even further in her rigid stance. She didn't even bother looking in her mother's direction. "Have you forgotten, Mother?" Salome purred with acid sweetness. "I am a grown, married woman now, after you and Herod pawned me off to that miserable old goat in Galilee. I come and go as I please."

Melina didn't dare turn to witness the fierce anger kindling in the eyes of the older woman. She prayed silently, her hands trembling.

"That may be so," Herodias replied, her anger seething just below the surface. "Even so, that does not give you the right to completely disregard appropriate social graces – such as alerting your host about an upcoming visit."

"My, my," Salome responded, clicking her tongue chidingly. "When did we become so formal, Mother?"

Herodias' fury was like a tangible presence filling the entire chamber.

"Melina, do finish my hair," Salome ordered airily, intentionally ignoring her mother. "I must look presentable when I join my *host* and *hostess* for supper this evening – that is, if I am welcome."

Herodias took a careful step into Salome's chambers, her every move performed with calculated grace. "Don't be ridiculous, Salome. You know you are always welcome here."

"Well!" Salome exclaimed, studying her own reflection in the mirror with obvious approval. "You certainly could have fooled me, Mother."

Helplessly, Melina attempted to fix her eyes upon the back of her mistress's head as she continued to style her hair. She felt trapped in the midst of a violent dogfight with no means of escape.

"I am curious, daughter," Herodias continued, momentarily dismissing Salome's blatant disrespect, "as to when you planned to make your presence known to me. Tonight? Tomorrow perhaps? Surely you would have graced me with your serene, lovely presence before returning to your beloved husband?"

Salome wheeled around in her chair, catching Melina off guard. "I've only just arrived, Mother, and I was covered in filth and road dust! Surely you would permit me a few paltry minutes to freshen up, or is that simply too much to ask?"

"A few paltry minutes, you say?" Herodias replied, arching a dark, slender brow. "Don't take me for a fool, you stupid girl. You arrived hours ago, then marched about the city unchaperoned, returning dripping wet after getting caught in a dangerous storm! By the gods, Salome, what were you thinking? Where did you go?"

Melina expected Salome to repeat her favorite speech about her own independence and her refusal to submit to any form of authority. Instead, Salome offered a pacifying smile and said in her most innocent tone, "I wasn't unchaperoned, Mother, though I do appreciate your concern. Melina accompanied me, and —"

"A naïve, ignorant bondwoman does not constitute a worthy chaperone, daughter!"

"I simply asked Melina to tend to my needs as I meandered about the palace gardens, Mother. We did not expect to get caught up in a downpour, but we returned to the palace promptly and —"

"The palace gardens?" Herodias repeated dully, her tone laden with suspicion. "You never left the premises?"

"Unchaperoned? I would never do such a thing and stain the family name, Mother. Why, Philip would be positively horrified!"

Melina stared at her own sandaled feet, her face

flushing with discomfort. She suddenly understood why Salome had insisted they exit and return by means of the lush palace gardens. She didn't like being drawn into Salome's intricate web of deceit. And what if Herodias discovered that Melina had known of Salome's duplicity, yet remained silent? The punishment would prove even more severe!

Cautiously, Melina lifted gentle eyes toward Herodias, chancing a quick glance in her direction before swiftly returning her gaze to the floor. Whether or not Herodias believed Salome's unlikely story, she chose not to pursue it further.

Despite her averted gaze, Melina could sense Herodias' stony glare pinning her to the floor.

"Melina, step outside and wait for us in the hall. I will summon you if your service is required."

"Yes, my lady," Melina responded quickly, grateful to escape Herodias' fearsome presence.

"No, Melina. Stay," Salome ordered tersely, lifting challenging eyes toward her mother. "You must finish my hair, and you are my maid, after all. You will take your orders from *me*."

"Melina, go," Herodias cut in, her tone bidding no argument. "Unless you wish to be thrashed within an inch of your miserable life."

Hastily, Melina hurried toward the large double doors, her heart dropping into the pit of her stomach. She wouldn't dare challenge Herodias. Herodias' threats were never made in vain.

Salome looked to her mother in disbelief. "Melina is my maidservant, Mother—"

"Melina is no longer your property, Salome. That changed the day you married Philip, and you acquired his entire staff to wait on you hand and foot."

Even as she retreated, Melina could imagine the look of sheer defiance Salome must be wearing. Melina heard the sound of gently rustling fabric as Herodias sat gracefully upon the edge of the bed, then patted the empty space beside her, inviting her daughter to join her.

"Come. You've been away for months and I want to hear all about your new life – without a nosy serving wench absorbing every word…"

Herodias' voice faded as Melina slipped out the massive double doors and closed them behind her, her heart pounding loudly in her own ears. Relieved she had escaped Herodias' ire, Melina bowed her head, silently asking God to work the day's unlikely circumstances for the salvation of Salome – the most stubborn and unhappy young woman she had ever met.

CHAPTER 37

Julia

"Your father sends his fondest regards and deepest regrets that he cannot join us this evening," Iskah stated sincerely, elegantly attired like the impeccable hostess that she was. "Unfortunately, he had to call upon a business associate."

The early evening air was pleasantly brisk, and the magnificent marble fountain created soothing splashing sounds which rested lightly upon Julia's senses as her mother ushered her toward a comfortable settee in the lush garden courtyard. Grateful, Julia allowed her mother to ease her upon the low settee. The walk from her Lower City abode to her father's magnificent villa in the Upper City was becoming more challenging as her child grew heavier in her womb.

Rubbing her lower back with a rueful grin, Julia noticed the concerned gleam in her mother's eyes. "I'm fine, Mother, really. Thank you so much for opening your home to us."

"I do wish I could send a litter for you, my daughter. But I do understand that would create quite a stir in your little neighborhood."

"We wouldn't want to be making ourselves a target, now," Joanna stated practically, looking a bit uncomfortable as Iskah urged her toward her own plush settee. "In those neighborhoods, it's best to blend in." Joanna, terribly aware of the social protocols of a ridiculously wealthy household, had stoutly refused to recline at the table the first few times she and Julia had visited Simon and Iskah. Eventually, she had conceded after Iskah beseeched her with tears in her eyes. "You have stood by my precious Julia from the moment she was born," Iskah had insisted. "You are family, Joanna. Please, sit with us."

Still, Joanna refused to recline. She sat rather rigidly upon her own settee, appearing vaguely disquieted as servants she had once worked alongside served the bread, meats, cheeses, and fresh fruit.

Julia held back a smile, amused by Joanna's angst. Scanning the lovely courtyard with its towering palms, marble benches, and meandering mosaic pathways, her entire body relaxed as she breathed in the fresh scent of garden flora and listened to the gentle splashing of the fountain. These delightful garden respites in the presence of her beloved family were precious to her, and Barabbas permitted her to visit her loved ones when he was absent.

"Next time, you must bring your husband with you," Iskah said lightly as she settled gracefully upon her own settee. The furniture had been arranged in the courtyard triclinium-style, with three large settees forming a semi-circle about a long, rectangular table heavy-laden with rich delicacies. "Surely he has a bit more free time now, considering the state of Simon's caravans."

Julia and Joanna exchanged blank stares. This was news to them.

"Is Father having trouble with his caravans?" Julia asked innocently, her stomach clenching in dread.

Iskah looked surprised. "Haven't you asked Barabbas about his time at home?"

What time at home? Julia wished to snort. Her husband had been absent even more than usual. But she had no desire to alert Joanna about her husband's questionable activities. Already, she feared her practical nursemaid might be a bit suspicious after Iskah's casual statement.

"Simon has allowed the caravan guards a few weeks off while he hires additional forces to accompany the caravans and buckles down on security protocol," Iskah explained. "I'm surprised Barabbas hasn't mentioned this to you."

"I doubt he wanted Julia worrying about him in her present condition," Joanna said, always the gracious one. She looked to her young charge and offered a cheerful wink.

"She needn't worry," Iskah assured them both as she took a slow sip from her goblet. "Barabbas is an extremely capable guard. His caravan is one of the few that hasn't been ambushed."

"I imagine Barabbas would be a mighty scary fellow to reckon with," Joanna laughed, completely ignorant about Julia's inner struggle. "If I were a Zealot, I'd stay away from him too."

Julia felt the sweat beading her delicate brow. "But the other caravans – they have been ambushed?"

Iskah nodded solemnly, setting her goblet down. "By Zealots. We've lost several men and much merchandise. Simon is worried sick over it. He is going to do everything in his power to protect his men, and of course, the merchandise as well."

Sitting a bit straighter, Julia battled the waves of nausea sweeping over her. Her father's caravans were being ambushed, and men were dying. Yet Barabbas' caravan remained unaffected. It was too suspicious, too perfect.

As if to confirm her worst fears, Iskah spoke again. "Simon fears this may be an inside job. The attackers always know which caravans protect the most expensive and valuable goods. They seem to know the routes as well. Their timing is always impeccable."

Attempting to appear natural, Julia reached for her goblet and took a slow sip. Her head swam as she digested the information her mother unwittingly presented against Barabbas.

"I do hope Simon is wrong about that," Joanna interjected, shaking her head sadly. "About it being an inside job, that is. Simon is an honorable man and a wonderful employer. It breaks my heart to think of one of his own betraying him in such a way."

"Mine as well," Iskah agreed sadly. "And Simon fears for his men and their families." Iskah's eyes softened as she studied Julia's faithful nursemaid. Reaching forward, Iskah squeezed Joanna's plump hand. "You understand far better than any of us how serious this is."

Joanna nodded grievously, her eyes distant. Was she remembering her devoted young husband who had fallen prey to a Zealot's dagger so many years ago? "We must all pray fervently that the matter will be resolved. Hopefully Simon will get to the bottom of this right away. It can't be good for business to put his caravans on hold, I'm thinking."

"It certainly isn't," Iskah agreed thoughtfully. "But, at the moment, Simon is far more concerned about the safety of his men than what's good for business. Please do pray that we get to the bottom of this."

Oh, Lord God, what if it's Barabbas? Julia prayed frantically. What if he is the man on the inside, tipping off the Zealots about when and where to ambush? Oh God, may it not be so...

"Simon has hired a private investigator," Iskah continued, her food remaining untouched before her. "The man is ex-military and seems very capable."

A private investigator? Julia had heard about such men. How exactly did they execute justice when the perpetrator was apprehended? She doubted she wanted to know.

Iskah turned to her daughter, her dark eyes sympathetic. "You are terribly quiet, dear one. I do hope I haven't worried you." Iskah bit her lower lip, clearly regretting her frankness.

Julia forced a smile, though she doubted it was an impressive one. She was indeed worried, but not for the reasons her mother suspected. Julia wasn't the least bit concerned about her husband's safety – clearly, he could handle himself. But she was nearly petrified when she considered his integrity, or lack thereof. Surely Barabbas wouldn't stoop that low! Surely, surely not!

"Julia?" Iskah repeated, her eyes filling with concern. "Are you all right?"

"I'm fine," Julia managed, hoping she sounded far

more confident than she felt. "I am simply saddened by this report regarding Father's caravans." Longingly, Julia wished she could bare her soul to these two trusted women, sharing her fears, doubts, and concerns. But if she did, her husband could be in grave danger. His life might even be in jeopardy. And one thing she knew for certain: Barabbas was not ready to meet his Maker. She was thankful the caravans had been halted. Perhaps she could reach Barabbas now, without fearing for the lives of innocent men in the process.

"Enough talk of caravans and thefts and Zealots," Iskah stated firmly, sensing Julia's apprehension. Reaching for a large cluster of grapes, she proclaimed merrily, "Let us now enjoy this blessed evening and break bread together!"

Try as she might, Julia failed to enjoy the remainder of the grand supper. Her mind was filled with tragic images of the form of a much younger Joanna, her shoulders heaving in despair as she wept over her dead husband – a brave young caravan guard ambushed by a pack of murderous Zealots.

Surely Barabbas would not condone an ambush upon a clearly Jewish caravan, resulting in the loss of Jewish husbands and fathers!

Barabbas was going to have some serious explaining to do if he ever decided to come home and take advantage of the "free time" he was supposed to be enjoying with her.

***

Later that evening, Julia sat at her own rickety table, her eyes glued to the gently smoldering oil lamp before her.

Joanna sat across from her, piecing together a small baby garment, humming lightheartedly as she worked. Aware of Julia's pensive mood, she was clearly attempting to brighten the atmosphere with her cheerful presence.

"Won't be long before your little one will be wearing these adorable little garments," Joanna stated in her knowing way, her eyes gleaming with anticipation.

"M-hmm," Julia murmured tensely, scarcely aware of her own response. Her lovely hazel eyes followed the lamp's gently writhing flame, her own eyes reflecting the same burning intensity.

"I just can't wait to find out if it's a little boy or a little girl we'll be welcoming into this home," Joanna added, turning the small garment in her hands for careful inspection.

Julia didn't respond. She couldn't stop thinking about her mother's hushed words in the garden courtyard. They swirled around and around in her mind, troubling and taunting her. *Simon fears this may be an inside job...*

Why was it that just when one thought their situation couldn't possibly get any worse, it invariably and unmistakably did? Barabbas' association with the Zealots was bad enough. But to betray his own faithful employer, putting the lives of his fellow associates at risk for selfish gain? It was unthinkable!

She thought of Amraphel, the ruthless leader of Barabbas' faction, and her anger deepened. Surely he was responsible for this! It would be just like the lazy oaf to sit on his fat rump and order her husband to take advantage of his position with Simon's caravan, in turn accumulating more wealth for himself at another's expense!

"Julia?"

The concern in Joanna's voice drew Julia's from her seething reverie. Sighing, she clenched her hands in her lap to still their trembling.

"Is everything all right, dearest?"

Before she could respond, the door slammed open violently, banging into the wall with the force of a battering ram.

Both women sprang to their feet, somehow stifling shrieks of surprise.

"Barabbas!" Julia gasped, her eyes widening in horror. "What have you done?"

Slamming and bolting the door behind him, Barabbas' presence filled the room as he surveyed the quiet house, his broad shoulders heaving as he attempted to catch his breath. Though his torn, dirty garments were concerning, it was the blood covering his chest and dripping down one bare arm that disturbed her most. His brow was bruised and quickly swelling, as if he had taken an unexpectedly hard hit. Dried blood had crusted over a nasty-looking gash on his lower lip.

Julia had never seen him look so fierce, and yet so vulnerable. Anger welled inside her unlike anything she had ever faced. Was Barabbas trying to reveal his true identity to Joanna? If the poor woman had harbored any suspicions at all about Barabbas before now, those suspicions would certainly be confirmed after tonight! And what then? Surely Joanna wouldn't stay and serve a man who aided the murderers who had stolen the life of her husband! Her very nature would cry out against it.

Oh, God, Julia pleaded silently, guilty tears stinging her eyes. *I can't bear to lose Joanna and have this baby alone! I can't!*

Barabbas' hard eyes flashed toward Joanna. When he spoke, his voice was low and challenging. "Why is she still here?"

Julia was in no state of mind to deal with this. "She is still here because it's *late,* Barabbas, and you weren't home."

"She is supposed to be next door at Deborah's by now. The evenings are ours."

"Since when?" Julia shot back, her emotions raw. "Since when have you spent evenings here with me, Barabbas?"

Barabbas' glare was dangerous.

"I wasn't feeling well," Julia nearly spat out, struggling to contain her fury. "That's why she stayed. She stayed to take care of me, since you clearly weren't going to."

Barabbas pursed his lips, visibly forcing himself to tame his rage. "I'm here. She can go now."

Julia cringed at his tone. He acted as if Joanna was an annoying object only to be used when absolutely necessary! Didn't he see how much the woman meant to her? Barabbas certainly wasn't going to take her to the market, to visit her parents, or to attend the local synagogue every Sabbath Day. Didn't he at least appreciate Joanna for relieving him of the responsibilities he sorely detested?

Julia cast an apologetic look toward her nursemaid. The woman smiled, and Julia knew what she was thinking. *Hold your peace, child.*

Gathering up her things, Joanna prepared to leave.

Amazed by her calmness, Julia stared at her

nursemaid as she swung a cloth bag over her shoulder. Barabbas had just burst into the house like a soldier fresh off the battlefield, wounded and bleeding! And yet Joanna had not bombarded him with questions or demanded an explanation. She simply prepared to retire for the evening!

Joanna paused near the door, her kind eyes traveling toward Barabbas. "If you need any help tending those wounds, son, you know where to find me." Then she calmly unbolted the door and stepped outside, gently closing it behind her.

Barabbas stared after her, stunned to silence. After taking a moment to gather his wits, he turned accusing eyes toward his wife. "I suppose I shouldn't be surprised that you haven't even bothered to ask if I'm all right."

"I can see you are not all right," she snapped. "What exactly are you trying to do, Barabbas? Scare Joanna away so that she never comes back?"

"Ah, I should have known you'd be more concerned for that old maid than for your own husband. It's not as if I'm wounded and bleeding –"

"By your own choice!" Julia nearly shouted, forgetting everything she had learned in her state of fierce agitation. "And how did you come by those wounds, Barabbas? Was it by doing something honorable? Something noble?"

A muscle in Barabbas' jaw twitched as he clenched his fists at his sides, his rage dangerously close to the surface.

"I thought not," Julia declared, placing her hands protectively over her protruding abdomen. "So please forgive me if I fail to throw myself at your feet, weeping over your self-inflicted wounds. I imagine your pain cannot compare to that of the widows' who lost their husbands at the hands of your own men! Tell me, Barabbas, how long have you been betraying my father for selfish gain?"

Barabbas paled momentarily, but very quickly gained his composure. "I don't know what you're babbling about now, but you sound like a mad woman. Now pull yourself together and tend to these wounds before I bleed out."

Trembling in her fury, Julia gathered the supplies she would need to clean her husband's wounds. It wouldn't be pleasant for him, and she was glad about it. He deserved the discomfort!

"You're going to need to stitch me up in a few places."

Julia froze in horror. "You know I'm not qualified to do that!"

"You can't do a lot of things. But you're going to need to figure this out tonight."

"Barabbas, you need to see a physician!"

"You know I can't go to a physician!" Barabbas snarled, sitting on the splintered bench before the table. "The first thing he would do is ask about how I got these wounds. And then he'd go straight to the authorities if he had any suspicions."

"You can't even see a physician, Barabbas. Perhaps that should tell you something about your line of work."

"Just get over here and figure it out. I've sewn men up before, but I can't sew my own upper arm with one hand. I'll talk you through it."

Trembling, Julia gathered the remaining supplies she would need and went to her husband. "I'm going to say this once, Barabbas, and then I will not speak about it again," she said quietly. "Father believes a man on the inside is tipping off the Zealots about his caravans. He doesn't suspect you, but I do."

Barabbas' mouth tipped in sardonic amusement. "Why doesn't that surprise me?"

"You should know that he's hired a private investigator who will get to the bottom of this. Barabbas, for the sake of our child, stop what you are doing before it's too late."

Barabbas' mouth formed a thin, grim line. Though he didn't respond, Julia sensed that her warning had taken root. Even if he was at fault as she suspected, Barabbas had no desire to be apprehended by Roman authorities, and she doubted that even Amraphel – as despicable and greedy as he was – wished to lose one of his very best men.

Forcing the issue from her mind and steeling herself for the task at hand, Julia bit her lower lip in concentration and tended her husband's ugly wounds.

She imagined the state of his battered body was a mere shadow of the state of his darkened, wounded soul.

CHAPTER 38

Alexander

It was the most disturbing dream he'd ever had, and Alexander couldn't get it out of his mind. It plagued him by night and haunted him by day. He felt like an athlete trapped within Herod's spectacular Hippodrome near the Synagogue of Freedmen – as if he was racing in a frantic pattern of ceaseless circles while powerful horses and chariots bore down on him, threatening to crush and overtake him.

But it was the dream that pursued him, not the horses and chariots. And there was no escaping it.

Still troubled by his nightmares, Alexander now stood upon Caiaphas' elegant terrace overlooking the breathtaking Temple compound below. The Temple was magnificent, resplendent. Bathed in silver moonlight and awesomely lit by thousands of fiery torches, it slumbered like a crowned, powerful beast, and it struck fear in his heart. He couldn't gaze upon the Temple without remembering the dream.

He hadn't the slightest idea why the Temple should trigger such dread or remind him of his recurring nightmares. But it did. Perhaps the fact that the famous Teacher who frequented the Temple always appeared in his dream.

The silver moonlight slanted across Alexander's chiseled profile as he gazed upon the Temple compound, chin resting lightly in his poised hand, his stance both thoughtful and powerful. Though it pained him, he closed his eyes and forced himself to consider the vivid vision of his dreams the previous night...

The smell of death hung heavily in the air. Instinctively, Alexander had known he was about to die. Weighed down with heavy burdens, his knees had buckled beneath the weight of them. As he dropped painfully to his knees, one of the burdens upon his back was jarred, and a sea of golden coins spilled out, clinking and bouncing as they hit the ground. In horror, he recognized the coins. He had obtained them through bribery, blackmail, dishonest gain. Suddenly, the golden coins weighed even heavier upon his conscience than they had upon his back. Darkness pressed in all around him, choking him, crushing him. The darkness was about to destroy him. He could feel it, smell it, taste it. Hot puffs of sulfurous heat filled his senses, burning his throat and stinging his eyes. Fear clutched at his heart as the sound of diabolical laughter filled his ears. He was about to die, and someone – or something – was rejoicing over his demise. But who? Why?

And then his entire field of vision was filled with the face of one Man. Alexander's heart soared, for he saw the love in Jesus' eyes. He had come to rescue him! His entire being filled with hope.

But, instantly, Alexander's joy evaporated, for his Rescuer was covered in blood. His head. His hands. His feet. Alexander had never seen anything so gruesome. How could Jesus possibly save him in that condition? They were both doomed to destruction. Filled with pain and revulsion, Alexander blanched and doubled over.

The darkness continued to close in. The devilish laughter deepened in triumph.

But Jesus reached for him. Repulsed, Alexander squeezed his eyes shut as Jesus placed bloody palms upon his head. Stunned, he realized he was covered in the blood of Jesus.

And instantly, the darkness fled. The diabolical laughter turned to screeches of horror and then ceased as the sound of desperately flapping wings rather like those of frantically retreating bats faded into oblivion.

The blood was like a cleansing, healing balm. His guilt-ridden burdens disintegrated into fine dust, carried away upon the wings of the wind as far as the East is from the West. A bright light burst forth, shining upon him, welcoming him, blessing him.

He was free! He was saved. Joy unlike anything he had ever experienced filled his entire being, and he nearly burst with the wonder of it.

But then he remembered Jesus. The Jesus who had banished the darkness. The Jesus who had conquered death. The Jesus who had scattered unseen forces of evil – the very forces seeking to destroy him.

But Jesus was gone.

Night after terrible night, Alexander awakened to

that awful realization: Jesus was gone. He had been covered in blood. Was He mortally wounded? Had he rescued Alexander, only to perish in the process?

And was he, Alexander, somehow responsible for Jesus' demise? The thought sent shafts of fear coursing through his heart, a fear so terrible that he no longer remembered the ecstasy he had experienced upon the lifting of his burdens.

One thing Alexander knew for sure: the dream meant something, and he would not rest until he discovered the truth.

***

Mary

In a small, poverty-stricken village skirting the Mount of Olives, a striking young woman pressed her back against the wall near the open door of a house near her brother's home. This house belonged to a man named Simon, a man whose oozing, leprous sores had rendered him unclean… until the day Jesus had touched him. Like herself, Simon had been cleansed by the great Teacher.

Nervously, she twisted the ends of her long, trailing veil, marveling at the softness of the light blue fabric. It was a strange new sensation – the weight of a veil resting upon her head, covering her abundant sea of black curls. But the weight was far from burdensome – if anything, it was freeing. She felt safe, sheltered from the stares of bold men and disapproving women.

Laughter should have filled the air about the house, for Jesus dined with His disciples within.

Instead, the air fairly crackled with tension. Mary had long since learned to detect disdain, and it hung heavily in the air.

Something wasn't right. Despite the food and the festive environment, she sensed the subterfuge, the danger. The conversation inside the house was stilted, strained. Jesus remained unusually quiet, as did her brother, Lazarus.

The familiar sound of a man's voice met her ears, causing the gooseflesh to prickle upon her clammy skin. She recognized the voice. It belonged to one of the Lord's disciples, a man by the name of Judas. The man was the only disciple among the twelve who didn't seem to garner immense disapproval. He was handsome, polished, successful, accomplished.

But something about the sound of his voice caused her heart to beat just a bit faster. His disapproving scowl had not been lost on her the day they met. He studied her with smoldering, scornful eyes, as if she was an unclean vessel to be trampled underfoot. Judas hadn't even attempted to mask his contempt in her presence.

Knowing that Judas Iscariot dined at the table with Jesus gave her pause as she contemplated her daring plan.

Releasing a shaky sigh, the young woman drew a breathtaking alabaster jar from the inside folds of her garment. Tears filled her eyes as she turned the jar carefully in her hands. Typically, a bride would anoint her husband on the eve of their vows with this fragrant oil. Reverently, she would place the oil upon his head, his hands, and his feet. The custom symbolized a woman's love, loyalty, and unwavering commitment to her bridegroom.

Mary had never known a man worthy of such a gift... until now. Unlike most women, she hadn't a husband to love and to serve. But she could offer herself to the God of the universe, the Creator of all mankind. She now understood that He desired her love and service. She was a willing vessel, and she longed to pour herself out as an offering to Him.

Steeling herself for the daunting act of worship she was about to perform, Mary drew her shawl to her chin and entered the house of Simon.

Tonight, she would demonstrate her unwavering devotion to the Savior of the world.

CHAPTER 39

Malchus

The night air was fresh and tantalizing, carrying the aroma of new spring blossoms upon gentle, caressing breezes.

Once again, Malchus enjoyed traveling the meandering garden paths beneath a sea of twinkling stars as he no longer worried about stumbling upon Mara and Lucius in these sacred groves. Their moonlit trysts had ended long before their marriage had, and the gardens were his at twilight once more.

Despite the idyllic, utopian setting in the lush garden enclave, Malchus' mind buzzed with distressing and portentous thoughts.

Earlier that day, Caiaphas had arranged an urgent, secret meeting of the Council, and certain members of the Sanhedrin had been intentionally omitted from the guest list. Malchus had watched in horror as Pharisees and Sadducees alike united against Jesus of Nazareth, unashamedly plotting His demise. Very few of the powerful men present had possessed even the slightest of qualms about the dark plans of the wicked chief priests, and even they had been quickly persuaded by Caiaphas' derisive speech.

"Blundering fools," Caiaphas had nearly spat, his dangerous gray eyes scanning the severely dressed men in the marble hall. "You know nothing at all."

"But an arrest – would it not encourage an uprising among His loyal followers, which are many?" one man had dared to question. "The Romans will not tolerate revolt, and they will strip us of our power."

Caiaphas had shaken his head in grim displeasure. "As I previously stated, you know nothing at all, nor do you consider that it is expedient for us that one Man should die for the people, and not that the whole nation should perish."

The hairs on the back of Malchus' neck had stood on end at Caiaphas' bold declaration, and he had nearly dropped his tablet and stylus.

"But how will one man's death prevent the dissolution of our nation?" another dared to ask.

"The Romans fear Him, you fool. The death of one troublesome Jew will not concern them. But the feverish multitudes that grow larger and larger by the day, gathering all over the province to hear Him speak? Rome will crush any potential threat. I suggest we extinguish the flame – a mere Man – before He sets our entire nation ablaze, destroying all that we hold dear."

The Council had erupted in shouts of consent, and Caiaphas had simply stroked his neatly manicured beard as his sharp gray eyes scanned each and every face within the room. Malchus had known Caiaphas was carefully gauging each man's reaction, ever ready to detect the slightest hint of resistance. With the assistance of loyal henchmen like Lucius, any further resistance would be crushed, swiftly and without a shred of mercy.

"My, my. Your expression tells me you carry the weight of the world upon your shoulders."

Drawn out of his brooding reverie by the unwelcome interruption, Malchus froze beneath the shelter of a towering palm, instantly annoyed by the sound of his cousin's voice. Did Alexander consider it his duty to intrude upon his every sacred moment?

"Tell me," Alexander mused, stepping into the moonlight, "what troubles you on this paradisal evening, Cousin?"

Malchus studied his older cousin's striking features, troubled by what he saw there. Alexander's guarded expression was impossible to read, which placed Malchus at an extreme disadvantage. He had barely survived his childhood by remaining one step ahead of this miserable cretin. His survival rate decreased dramatically along with his inability to interpret his cousin's brooding thoughts.

Alexander clicked his tongue chidingly, shaking his head in annoyance. "Your lack of trust is rather astounding, my dear cousin. We are, after all, relatives. Will you refuse to share your sorrow with one who cares?"

Anger welled up inside Malchus. "Since when have you cared about anyone but yourself?"

Alexander laughed, a low, self-deprecating chuckle. "You know, I've asked myself the same question."

Malchus raised a skeptical brow, wondering what cruel tricks Alexander had up his sleeve.

"I noticed you were privileged to attend an exclusive meeting of the Council today."

So, there it was. Alexander sought information about the meeting.

"Is that what troubles your spirit, Cousin?"

Malchus looked away, his insides clenching in frustration. Alexander sounded almost sincere.

"Ah, I thought so," Alexander mused, his chiseled features bathed in moonlight. "What dark portents transpired between the most honorable religious leaders to render your countenance so?"

Malchus shook his head, torn by his desire to dismiss his prying cousin and his need to air his roiling thoughts. "They've initiated a plot to murder the Teacher from Nazareth." Even as he spoke, Malchus wondered if he would regret it.

Alexander's expression was enigmatic. "I thought as much, considering those selected to attend. But many attempts have been made on the Man's life, none of which have proven successful. I imagine they will only further frustrate themselves."

Malchus considered the intensity by which the men of the Council had spoken and doubted his cousin's words. "They are gaining momentum and support. It's only a matter of time for the Man called Jesus… and for His followers."

"His followers needn't fear," Alexander said with confidence. "Your venerable high priest seeks the life of the Man, not His followers."

"Not anymore," Malchus responded tersely, wondering why he was still talking to this atrocious relative. "They have already arranged for the death of one of His followers."

Alexander arched a sharp brow. "Ah, I see the plot has thickened. And who is this unfortunate follower doomed to certain death?"

"A man by the name of Lazarus. Apparently, his testimony regarding Jesus of Nazareth is a bit too persuasive for the chief priests' liking."

"It sounds interesting indeed. And what does this exciting new testimony entail?"

Malchus hesitated, realizing just how ridiculous it sounded. "Jesus raised Lazarus from the dead."

A series of unreadable expressions crossed Alexander's face, but he quickly regained his composure. "This *is* interesting. Do you believe the man's testimony possesses any merit?"

"I'd say definitely not, except for the fact that Caiaphas is determined to wipe him off the face of the earth."

"Oh, why bother, Caiaphas, you stupid priest? Jesus of Nazareth will only raise him again. And wouldn't it be rather tiresome to continue killing the poor man, only to find him resurrected again and again?"

Malchus stared at his cousin, surprised by his careless words. "Surely *you* don't believe it actually occurred?"

"Why else would Caiaphas risk it all to exterminate one unimportant, poverty-stricken Jew?"

Alexander's cool assessment gave Malchus pause. "Perhaps it was a misunderstanding."

"Come, now. You've served the priest far longer than I have. Surely you know him better than that."

Malchus wasn't sure how to respond.

"Caiaphas' sources are rock-solid. Trust me, I've checked them out thoroughly."

"Why doesn't that surprise me?"

"Well, blackmail must be accurate in order to

prove effective."

Malchus stared at his cousin, loathing filling his being. "Why are you still here?" he demanded, gritting his teeth in disgust.

"Because we are in the middle of a conversation, and I am far too polite to walk away before it's finished."

"You know what I mean, Alexander! Why are you still here serving Caiaphas in a city you detest? You've amassed more than enough wealth through blackmail, bribery, trickery, and who knows what else to disappear for good!"

"Well, that was uncalled for."

"Uncalled for perhaps, but completely accurate!"

"Quite frankly," Alexander said coolly, tilting his head to one side and studying his cousin with contempt, "my personal decisions are none of your business and do not concern you in the least."

"If only your decisions did not concern me!"

"I had hoped you would have outgrown your childish tendency toward piteous whining by now."

Malchus bit back a sharp retort and forced himself to focus on the matter at hand. "Look, Alexander, you knew far before setting foot in this place that you would vanish into the night the moment you got what you came for! So, I'll ask again, why are you still here?"

There was a long pause as both men stood opposite each other, tense, measuring. The moment stretched on for what seemed an eternity.

Then Alexander released a low, harsh laugh. "Perhaps, my dear cousin, I simply have not obtained what I came for."

"Oh?" Malchus cocked his head to one side, certain he knew what was keeping Alexander. "And what, pray tell, is that?"

"If you suppose it's a woman I have in mind, you would be only partially correct in your assessment," Alexander responded coolly. "But then again, as previously mentioned, my affairs do not concern you."

Malchus watched in sheer frustration as Alexander turned on his heel and left the garden with powerful strides, leaving him standing alone beneath the whispering palm fronds. Malchus was certain he had never known a more frustrating human being in his entire life!

Attempting to dismiss his annoyance, Malchus dropped heavily upon a curved marble bench, nervously raking his hands through his abundant, wavy brown hair. Today, the Sanhedrin had taken yet another step toward the fulfillment of their depraved plans regarding Jesus, the humble Carpenter from Nazareth. And it was now glaringly evident that even His followers were unsafe. Caiaphas would hunt them down one by one, and their demise would be sure and swift.

Stomach lurching, Malchus thought of Melina and her unwavering commitment to the Man she believed to be the Son of God.

He didn't like it one bit, but he was going to have to confront her. Melina hadn't the slightest idea what she was up against, and Malchus was completely unwilling to lose the only woman he had ever loved. Heart pounding and palms sweating, he realized that his gentle Melina was no match against a man like Caiaphas and his ruthless mercenaries.

He would simply demand that she see reason. After all, her life was in very real danger! Didn't she desire to marry him, to bear his children, to dwell in peace and safety?

Why, oh why, did she insist upon clinging to her stubborn beliefs about a wanted Man? Somehow, he must convince her that her faith was misguided. It was their only hope for a secure and happy future.

Surely she would understand his concern.

CHAPTER 40

Barabbas

Despite the fact that the Passover was nearly two weeks away, the city of Jerusalem fairly buzzed with frantic activity as pilgrims and proselytes poured into her ancient borders. Merchants set up shop along every available street, taking full advantage of the festive season and hawking their wares with enthusiasm and zeal. Infants shrieked in protest as shopping mothers balanced them on their hips, typically with a string of laughing, teasing children in tow. Slaves and servants rushed about the city in a tense state of anxiety, desperately hoping to attain whatever their masters had sent them to purchase.

Barabbas loathed crowds along with the feast days that attracted them, but what rankled far more than the utter chaos of the city was the tripled presence of Roman soldiers monitoring Jerusalem with wary eyes and rigid stances. Their armor clanked as they tramped about the city, their hands ever resting upon the hilts of their gladiuses. Some rode upon magnificent steeds, their crimson-plumed helmets glistening in the sunlight and reminding Barabbas of the blood they had shed.

Barabbas despised them with his entire being. He hated them so entirely that the bile rose in his throat the moment he heard the tell-tale tapping of their hobnailed sandals upon the stones. He could literally taste the bitterness in his mouth as red-hot anger coursed through his veins, threatening to become his undoing. He would not rest until every last one of them had been vanquished. One day, the Romans would be destroyed, utterly defeated. And he would be part of it.

For the umpteenth time, he vowed inwardly that he would not rest until he had avenged the blood of his family.

Barabbas had not intended to get lost in the maze of weary travelers and eager shoppers passing through Small Market Street. Lost in his own hatred and silent brooding, his own two feet had carried him unawares into the very heart of the chaotic scene.

Muttering a few fierce words under his breath, Barabbas instinctively placed a battle-worn hand upon the hilt of the dagger strapped at his belt, hidden just beneath his outer covering. He would steal away from this madness, preferably unscathed, before the sun set, bathing the city in darkness. Perhaps if he hastened, he wouldn't be terribly late for supper. Julia had become increasingly understanding and no longer bickered with him when he failed to arrive in time for supper. Perhaps that bothersome nursemaid provided a calming influence for her, or perhaps Julia had simply recognized the futility of arguing with him.

He refused to allow anyone to dictate to him

within his own house – not even the lovely young woman who carried his child.

A sharp pang struck Barabbas' heart every time he considered his wife's condition. Her belly grew rounder by the day, and he knew the child would be arriving soon. He still wasn't sure how he felt about it. Why bring a child into this wretched world, anyway? Perhaps they should have been more careful. Was his flighty little Julia even prepared to mother a squalling infant?

But Barabbas' harried thoughts disintegrated in an instant as full-bodied rage gripped his entire being. His knuckles whitened as he clenched the hilt of his dagger, his eyes narrowing until they were little more than two dark, dangerous slits. For there, mounted upon a magnificent Roman steed not twenty paces away, glowered the young soldier who had stolen the life of his dearest friend.

The filthy Roman dog! Barabbas' entire being rebelled, for the soldier now donned a helmet bearing the distinctive and highly esteemed *crista transversa*. Why, the wretch had been promoted and now bore the prestigious title of centurion! Clenching his fists at his sides, Barabbas struggled against helpless rage. Perhaps the soldier's promotion accounted for his unexpected journey to Rome. While a centurion often achieved rank by election, it was also possible for a man displaying unrivaled courage in battle or remarkable leadership skills to be appointed by the Roman Senate.

Closing his eyes, Barabbas steadied his own rapid breathing and forced himself to think. It took all the might of his will to keep his black rage at bay long enough to formulate a cohesive plan. Barabbas considered murdering the man in cold blood right then and there, but immediately thought better of it. In the midst of this chaos, innocent people would likely get hurt. And that aside, the vast number of witnesses hindered his ability to act now. He had no desire to exact justice only to suffer an agonizing death upon a Roman cross hours later.

No, he would have to formulate a foolproof plan, and he already knew the man who would be more than willing to aid him in the destruction of a pompous Roman dog like this. But Barabbas knew he must act quickly – who knew when the wretched centurion would board another ship and set sail for Rome again? No, he had waited far too long for this moment, and he refused to allow the wretch to slip through his fingers once again.

Drawing his dark hood over his head to obscure his own striking features, Barabbas forced himself to keep walking, despite the fact that he would like nothing more than to slit the centurion's throat.

As he stole into the shadows of a dim, seedy alley, he hoped his little wife wouldn't mind sharing another lonely dinner with that odd nursemaid of hers, because he now had pressing business to attend to – business that would render him unable to dine with his expecting wife tonight. And perhaps for many nights to come.

***

Melina

Melina was strangely disquieted. She couldn't quite place it, but something wasn't right. She could feel it, sense the tension crackling in the air.

It was more than just the typical unrest that was

to be expected when the Jewish Passover drew near. She sensed the still, small voice within urging her to be strong, to wait, to pray.

Apprehensive, Melina's lips moved in silent prayer as she skillfully rolled fresh towels for the palace's luxuriant baths. Herod Antipas was expecting guests for the Passover season – Governor Pontius Pilate and his regal wife, Claudia Procula, among them – and the staff scurried about in an attempt to ready the palace for their imminent arrival.

"Melina."

Melina turned, not at all surprised by the deep, direct address. She had been expecting something to happen all day.

Chuza stood beneath an enormous, tiled archway leading into the pristine baths. His barrel arms were crossed over his broad chest, and he did not look happy.

"My lord?"

Chuza's lips tipped ever so slightly at Melina's deferential reply. He was her brother in the Lord, yet she still regarded him with the utmost respect. "A young man has arrived under the pretense of delivering a message from his master."

Melina waited, wondering what this casual disclosure had to do with her.

"He requested an audience with my wife."

"But Joanna is with Jesus," Melina reminded him with an envious smile.

"As you can imagine, I was curious when I received word that a handsome young man had demanded a private audience with my wife in the palace gardens," Chuza stated rather dryly. His deep voice boomed and echoed within the austere marble baths. "When I met him, I discovered that he simply requested an audience with my wife because he believed she could be trusted."

Melina's heart began beating rapidly in her chest as she sensed the direction in which Chuza's message was headed.

"Quite frankly, the man has risked much to speak with you, Melina. He asked for Joanna because he knew she is of high station and a friend of yours. Joanna and I are permitted to receive visitors. Obviously, it would have raised a few red flags had he asked to speak with you."

Melina swallowed nervously. In nearly three years of friendship, not once had Malchus risked meeting her at the palace! Surely his message was desperately urgent.

"Did you send him away?" Melina asked faintly, her heart fluttering like a trapped bird.

Sensing her distress, Chuza softened despite his protective nature. "First, I'd like to know if he has any legitimate business setting foot upon palace grounds under false pretenses. Do you know a man by the name of Malchus, a manservant of Joseph Caiaphas, the high priest?"

Melina drew in a shaky breath. "I do."

"Are you involved with this man?"

Melina's color deepened, and she wasn't entirely sure how to answer Chuza's direct question. "He is a dear friend."

Chuza studied her skeptically, his arms still crossed. "Yet he risked everything to see you? A bold move... for a friend."

Melina understood his skepticism. Setting aside the remaining towels, she closed the distance between herself and Chuza, placing a gentle hand upon his muscled forearm. She knew she could trust him with her life, much less the secret longings of her heart. "Malchus has asked for my hand in marriage, but I have not yet consented. I do care for him very much. He has behaved honorably toward me in every way."

Chuza studied her for a long moment, then released a short sigh. "It would be inappropriate for you to visit a man alone in the palace gardens at this late hour."

"I agree," Melina said, smiling rather mischievously. "Do you happen to know where one might find a worthy chaperone?"

"Come along," Chuza sighed in grim resignation.

CHAPTER 41

Malchus

Nervously wringing his hands, Malchus stood sheltered within a lush garden enclave on the premises of Antipas' palace. A frighteningly imposing man called Chuza had invited him to be seated within a lovely, circular pillared structure that resembled a marble shrine of sorts. It was a cozy little spot lined with graceful marble benches, but he was far too anxious to sit and wait placidly. Instead, he paced about the small structure, silently, rehearsing the speech he planned to present to his beloved. Fleetingly, he wondered if he would be punished for begging God to ensure Melina's capitulation. *God, let her see reason!* Surely God didn't wish to place one of His most devoted followers directly in the line of fire!

Even as he mentally justified his motives, Malchus was frustrated by the apprehension that gripped his spirit.

"Hello, stranger."

Malchus' stomach tightened at the sound of his beloved's silvery voice. That lovely voice had gone straight to his head the moment they had met, and Melina still couldn't possibly understand how deeply she affected him. Slowly lifting his head, Malchus' heart pounded as Melina gingerly stepped through the garden, approaching him rather shyly.

He forced a casual smile. "Hello, beautiful."

Even in the dim moonlight, Malchus saw Melina's face flush with embarrassment. His jaw clenched in frustration, for Chuza stood several paces behind them, still as a statue, his strong arms folded across his barrel chest. He looked rather like one of those imposing, chiseled statues of a Roman deity, and Malchus had to admit the steward was intimidating.

Gritting his teeth, Malchus strove for calm. He had hoped for a bit of privacy! He wondered if the stubborn man was within earshot. He certainly hoped not.

Oblivious about Malchus' raging emotions, Melina went to him, hands outstretched. Malchus took them and squeezed them gently, resisting the urge to stoop and kiss her forehead. He didn't wish to invoke the wrath of her giant-like chaperone. "I've missed you," he said huskily, reluctantly releasing her hands.

"Not as much as I have missed you, Malchus."

Malchus hoped she would feel the same way after their conversation. "I'd hoped to share a private discussion with you," he said under his breath, his eyes resting pointedly upon Chuza.

Unblinking, Chuza returned his gaze from across the garden.

Melina grinned. "You needn't fear. Chuza is our

brother in Christ."

Malchus winced. His impossible task just became even more challenging.

"Chuza is Joanna's husband," Melina added, as if to set his mind at ease.

Malchus resisted the urge to clench his fists. He should have known this man would be some relation to Melina's austere, self-appointed chaperone! Had Chuza also influenced her decision to follow Jesus? The thought rankled.

"What is going on, Malchus?" Melina asked gently, concern softening her features. "Has something happened? Surely it must be urgent for you to risk so much to come here."

Taking a deep breath, Malchus forced himself to meet her innocent gaze. "I've come to warn you, Melina. Your life might be in danger."

Melina stared up at him, her lips parting in surprise.

"Caiaphas called a secret meeting – a puppet council, if you ask me."

Melina studied him, confused. "But what have I to do with the high priest's council?"

"They are going to kill Jesus, Melina. A plan is in motion, and they think it's foolproof."

Melina smiled warmly. "Malchus, they have attempted to kill Jesus many times. God has always protected Him."

"This time it's different," Malchus insisted, running a hand nervously through his dark hair. "I can feel it, Melina. Trouble unlike anything we've ever seen is coming."

Melina held his gaze, undisturbed. Peace radiated from her entire being.

Annoyed by her unprecedented calm, Malchus plunged ahead. "They are going to kill His followers, too. They've already arranged the death of a man named Lazarus, a follower. Don't you see, Melina? Your life is in danger." Impulsively, he cupped her cheek with one strong hand. "I love you, Melina. I am afraid for you."

Melina did not shy away from his touch, but her eyes burned with intensity. "Malchus, all of their attempts to silence Jesus have proven futile."

"Not this time, Melina. They want to kill Him, and they will succeed. First, they will murder the Teacher. Then His followers will be tracked down like dogs and slaughtered, one by one. Caiaphas will not rest until he has uprooted this threat. He won't allow anything to sabotage his position."

Undisturbed, Melina touched his arm. "Throughout history, God has used even wicked men to accomplish His purposes. Caiaphas may not be aware of it, but he is still under authority. Nothing can happen without God's permission, Malchus. We must trust that He is in control, even now."

"Don't think that this Jesus is untouchable simply because He has evaded a few half-hearted attempts to end His life," Malchus argued, desperate for her to see his point. "I was at the meeting, Melina. The religious leaders plan to take Him to the Roman authorities this time. The priests have been unable to touch Him, but they know Rome always has her way."

"Jesus has done nothing worthy of execution, Malchus. What can the Romans do?"

"Don't underestimate the enemy, Melina. Caiaphas is shrewd. He plans to wait for the arrival of Pontius Pilate – that man detests Jews. He's famous for it. Pilate has slaughtered hundreds of innocent Jews without a second thought. The priests are grooming false witnesses even as we speak. They'll present their testimony to the procurator, who will be thrilled to witness the demise of another Jew. He'll order the execution himself."

Melina shook her head. "I disagree, Malchus. Have you forgotten? Pontius Pilate was reprimanded by the emperor for his cruelty toward the Jews. Pilate is stubborn and vindictive, but surely he fears the emperor! I cannot imagine he would disregard a direct order from Emperor Tiberius."

"Don't forget who it is we are up against. This is *Caiaphas*, Melina. How do you think he's maintained his power so long? All the other high priests were displaced from power, one by one. Caiaphas is calculating, shrewd. He will find a flaw, a weakness, in Pontius Pilate and use it to his own advantage. I've seen him do it hundreds of times before."

"Then I suppose we must pray earnestly for God's will, despite the schemes of wicked men," Melina said with a gentle smile. "We can trust God, Malchus. It pains me to see you troubled so."

Malchus dared a glance toward Chuza, wondering if this was the moment to present his case. Based on the steward's impatient stance, he hadn't much time. "Melina, please listen to what I am about to say. It's important."

Melina raised knowing eyes to his. Dismissing the concern he saw reflected in those lovely emerald pools, Malchus plunged ahead. "I want you to disentangle yourself from this Jesus and His sect. It's not safe, and I'm just not willing to lose you."

Tears sprang to Melina's eyes, but she held them back. "Malchus, you know I cannot do that."

"I need you to, at least until all this blows over."

"And what if it never does, Malchus? The enemy will always come against the truth."

"Marry me, Melina."

Stunned, Melina drew in a sharp breath.

"I will take you back to the mansion of Caiaphas as my bride. You can abide with me, and I will protect you."

"And do you suppose," Melina asked with tear-filled eyes, "I would be any safer there? Do you intend to take me directly to the dragon's lair?"

Caught off guard by the anger that coursed through him, Malchus attempted to regain control. "Caiaphas would never suspect a thing about you, Melina. You are Greek, not Jewish. He would never assume you were a convert. You would be safe with me."

"Oh, Malchus. How would I be safer in the house of a devil than in the hands of a loving God?"

Malchus' jaw clenched. "It sounds poetic enough, Melina, but it isn't practical."

"*For My thoughts are not your thoughts,*" Melina said softly, a tear trickling down her cheek. "*'Nor are your ways My ways,' says the Lord.* Malchus, will you place your faith in your earthly master and turn from your Heavenly One?"

"I haven't turned from Him."

"But you have," Melina whispered, her tone sorrowful rather than accusing. "You refuse to trust Him with our lives, and you have denied His Son."

Her soft rebuke was like a dash of cold water, and Malchus' defenses rose. "For Heaven's sake,

Melina! I haven't turned from God! I believe in the God of our ancestors. But this Jesus shows up, and suddenly we're all supposed to worship Him, too? Well, Abraham didn't. Moses didn't. David didn't. All your great heroes of old didn't even know about Him, and yet you claim salvation does not exist apart from Him?" Somewhat embarrassed by his outburst, Malchus looked away. When he finally forced his gaze back to his beloved, he was amazed by her remarkable sense of calm.

"They may not have known Jesus by name, Malchus," she said quietly, "but they knew Him, and they waited expectantly for His coming. Abraham knew Him as the Traveler who visited him outside his tent, promising the birth of his son. And Moses said, '*The Lord your God will raise up for you a Prophet like me from your midst, from your brethren. Him you shall hear.*' David knew Jesus as the One who was to come, the One to whom the Lord would say, '*Sit at My right hand, till I make Your enemies Your footstool.*' Jesus has always been there, Malchus, waiting for the day of redemption. He was there in the beginning, when God said, '*Let Us make man in Our image, according to Our likeness.*' He has always been, Malchus, and He will forever be. Please, do not deny Him."

Resisting the urge to sling her over his shoulder and carry her back to Caiaphas' house, Malchus clenched his fists at his sides. "I love your passion, Melina, but I fear it may be your undoing. You've chosen to embrace this radical faith, and I understand that. But I need you to keep it to yourself now. I need you to promise me this, Melina. I'll go crazy worrying about you otherwise."

"Keep it to myself?" Melina repeated, stunned by his words. "How can I keep silent when others are perishing without the knowledge of the truth?"

"Quite frankly, I'm far more concerned about the prospect of you perishing!"

"*Whoever confesses Me before men, him I will also confess before My Father who is in Heaven. But whoever denies Me before men, him I will also deny before My Father in Heaven.* These are the words of Jesus, Malchus, and we must heed them."

"Fine, then. Don't *deny* Him. Just don't say anything at all!"

"I can't do that."

"I need you to do that."

Melina looked away, her eyes clouded with tears of sadness.

Regretting his harshness, Malchus reached for her. "Melina, if I didn't love you, I wouldn't even be asking this of you."

Melina looked at him then with clear green eyes. "If you loved me, Malchus, you would never ask this of me."

"You would doubt my love for you?" Malchus asked in disbelief. His hackles rose in self-defense. "All I want is to protect you! I can't bear the thought of losing you. Don't you understand? If you choose to publicly embrace this message, then we will be hunted our entire lives. Our children's lives will be in jeopardy. We will live in sheer panic and constant upheaval. That's not the life I want for us. I desire peace, Melina, peace above all else! And this is the only way."

"No," Melina said with great conviction. "Jesus is the way."

"For the love of all that is holy and good! What can I do to make you see reason?" Malchus groaned, turning away from her in sheer frustration.

Melina watched him with wet eyes and an aching heart. "Do you refuse to accept Jesus as the Savior and Messiah?"

Malchus turned to her then, his expression drawn and his shoulders drooping in defeat. "I've already lost so much, Melina. I can't bear to lose you, too."

"*For whoever desires to save his life will lose it, but whoever loses his life for My sake and the gospel's will save it,*" Melina reminded him gently.

"Will you stop flinging that Man's words at me every time I turn around? I know what Jesus said, Melina!"

"But you refuse to accept it."

"Yes, I refuse. I can't go there, Melina. I just can't, and I won't."

Melina's eyes filled with tears, and this time, she couldn't hold them back. They spilled over her cheeks like a sorrowful flood. For the very first time, she understood why the Lord had not granted her peace about a union with this man whom she loved so desperately, and the knowledge hurt far more than she had ever thought possible. "Then I am afraid I must ask you not to see me again, Malchus."

Malchus' head came up in shock. He stared at her, stunned into absolute silence.

"The Lord forbids a believer to marry one who does not share the faith."

"You can't be serious!"

"Oh, Malchus, I wish I wasn't."

Malchus went to her, but she took several steps back, distancing herself from him. If he took her in his arms, she might not have the strength to retreat. "I must go, Malchus. But please know that I love you, and I always will." She stepped out of the covered marble shrine, away from him.

"Melina, don't do this to us!"

"Goodbye, Malchus."

"I believe in *God*, Melina! Isn't that enough?"

Melina paused in the midst of her desperate retreat, turning to face him once more. *"He who does not honor the Son does not honor the Father who sent Him."*

"I can't believe you are doing this!" Malchus exclaimed, his entire world reeling. "I am simply worried for you! Can't you understand that?"

With one last tearful glance over her shoulder, Melina said quietly, "Oh, Malchus. I am even more worried for you."

Malchus stared after her, wondering what had happened, for in a few short moments, his entire world had come crashing down around his ears. His heart constricted as he watched her turn softly on her heels, stealing past the surprised steward standing guard. Malchus could scarcely believe it as she walked out of the garden – and out of his life.

Possibly forever.

CHAPTER 42

Julia

The darkness was heavy, too heavy. Oppressive. Despite the flickering oil lamps Joanna had placed routinely about the house, the gloomy blackness seemed determined to close in, to swallow the light.

Julia was on edge. Barabbas had left far too early that morning, and something was wrong. She had sensed it in the rigid set of his broad shoulders, the tenseness of his square jaw, the way he had refused to look her in the eye. He would have slipped out of their home completely unnoticed had something not awakened her. Perhaps it was her own intuition, or – even more likely – the Spirit of the living God, that had urged her from her bed.

Rising from her sleeping pallet, Julia had placed a protective hand over her swollen belly and reached for her husband. "Barabbas, what it is?" she had asked pensively.

"I have to go."

"So early?"

"Stay out of this, Julia."

Julia had spent the next ten minutes pleading with him, asking him what he intended to do. She knew something was terribly amiss, and fear had closed its cold, unrelenting fingers around her heart as Barabbas had fastened his dagger to his belt and reached for the latch on the door.

"Barabbas, please don't go," she had pled, fearful.

"Leave it alone, Julia."

"But something is wrong!"

"I said leave it alone!"

"What are you going to do?" she had dared to ask, almost fearful that he might actually tell her. Did she really want to know? His fiery countenance was fearsome to behold.

"I need to do this, Julia. Now stay out of it."

"Barabbas, please. Consider our child. Please."

Something had flickered slightly in her husband's gaze. Then, he had turned, unlatched the door, and walked out, disappearing into the hazy, pre-dawn mist.

Now, after a seemingly endless day, Julia was nearly consumed with anxiety. She couldn't imagine what horrors her husband might be practicing. Of one thing she was certain: people would get hurt. And it was entirely outside of her power to prevent it. She felt cornered, helpless, defeated.

Lord God, help me! She pleaded silently, wishing with all her heart that she could confide her dreadful fears to Joanna. But the baby was due within a matter of weeks, and Julia needed her. She couldn't risk telling the awful truth now.

"Well, that's that," Joanna stated pleasantly, stacking the last of the clean supper dishes on the shelf near the hearth. "Everything is in order. I suppose I should be getting myself on over to Deborah's house before your husband returns!"

Before your husband returns... But would he return? Why did she have this sinking feeling that he wouldn't? She remembered watching him disappear into the early morning fog, her heart pounding wildly in her chest. Her apprehension was growing steadily by the moment.

Somewhat frightened, Julia wished to ask Joanna to stay, but she didn't want to be selfish. The woman had been working hard all day. She deserved a peaceful night's rest. "Thank you so much for everything, Joanna. I couldn't do this without you."

Joanna offered Julia her warmest smile. "I doubt that. God always supplies the strength we need. And you can count on that."

With great difficulty, Julia rose from the table to see Joanna to the door.

"Now how often do I need to be telling you to stay put?" Joanna huffed, leading Julia back to the table. "You need to be resting. It's good for you and for the baby!"

Julia resisted slightly. "I've been resting all day." The last thing she wanted to do was rest. She had far too much on her mind to rest. Besides, every time she allowed herself to be still, a disturbing dream of many nights past resurfaced in her troubled mind... a dream in which she had gone through the deep waters and hot fires. Yes, the Lord had been with her, leading her through the raging waters and the searing heat. But it was still terrifying nonetheless. Why couldn't she stop thinking about it? Was it simply the haunting premonition she had experienced as she watched her husband's swiftly retreating back that morning?

No, she certainly did not want to rest. She needed to keep her mind and hands busy – even if it meant re-washing the gleaming dishes Joanna had just stacked neatly on the shelf. She'd certainly find *something* to do!

Julia nearly jumped out of her skin when someone pounded a heavy fist against the bolted door. Joanna looked to her in question.

"Barabbas!" Julia gasped breathlessly. Flustered, she rushed to the door without pausing to consider the fact that her husband would not knock on his own front door.

"Julia, wait–" Joanna exclaimed, but it was too late. Julia had already swung open the heavy door.

And there, standing upon the threshold, was the most hateful looking man Julia had ever seen. Cold black eyes bore into her as vile lips twisted into a vulgar sneer. "Hello, gorgeous."

Julia recognized the man in one terrible instant. Amraphel.

***

Despite Julia's frantic effort to slam the door in Amraphel's face, the wicked Zealot had reached for it with an iron grip and pushed his way into her home. Another fierce-looking Zealot had followed closely behind him, cautiously closing and bolting the front door.

Now, Julia stood trembling as Amraphel held her from behind, one filthy, calloused hand wrapped around her throat. She didn't dare squirm for the sake of the child within her womb. She doubted this ruthless man would hesitate to choke the life right out of her, regardless of the little life she nurtured inside.

Attempting to stifle her panic, Julia's eyes traveled toward Joanna. The second Zealot angled a knife toward the older woman's ribcage, gripping her by one arm and daring her to attempt escape.

Oh, Joanna, Julia thought, her heart breaking. *What have I done? How did you get caught up in all this?*

"Well, well," Amraphel purred, a low chuckle escaping his foul lips. "Our Barabbas did indeed possess secrets of his own."

Sweat began to bead Julia's brow as her heartbeat picked up speed. Why was Amraphel speaking of her husband in the past tense? "Where is my husband?" Julia demanded, rage emboldening her tongue. "What have you done to him?"

Amraphel turned her slowly about to face him. She could barely stomach the smug grin peeking out from his dirty, unkempt beard. "Let's just say we had a little altercation. We landed ourselves in a bit of trouble, and Barabbas didn't approve of the only obvious way out."

"Where is he?" Julia ground out, meeting Amraphel's glittering gaze head on.

"Lying in a ditch somewhere in a pool of his own blood, I imagine" Amraphel responded, relishing every word.

"No!" Julia screamed, writhing in fierce anger and sorrow. She attempted to wrench away, but Amraphel gripped her throat again.

"Shut up before I make you," he hissed, his foul

breath puffing against her hot, tear-streaked face.

"Julia," Joanna said calmly, her own eyes wet with tears of sorrow, "be still. Remember your child."

"Ah, yes. Your child," Amraphel cooed, his narrow eyes traveling over her swollen belly. "Barabbas, that clever dog. He kept you secret for a time, but I have my sources. Even so, the pregnancy is a bit of a surprise. I knew Barabbas worked for the richest merchant in the entire region. Barabbas simply failed to mention he had married the nitwit's daughter. That bit of information would have proven rather advantageous, don't you think?"

Clenching her teeth, Julia averted her gaze, trembling in unfamiliar rage.

"Amraphel, there is little time." This spoken by the Zealot guarding Joanna.

Amraphel's eyes flashed. Roughly taking Julia's elbow, he pushed her toward the door. "Let's go. You're coming with me."

"No!"

"What about this one?" the other Zealot asked nervously as he gestured toward Joanna.

"Now what on earth would I want with that one?" Amraphel spat out cruelly. "Kill her."

"No!" Julia screamed until she thought her lungs would burst, only to be silenced by a stunning blow to the face.

"What did I tell you?" Amraphel jeered, shaking her. "Shut up, and I mean it this time. Now let's go."

"What will you do to her?" Joanna demanded, her voice husky.

Amraphel arched a despotic brow. "Oh, I have several ideas," he taunted, brushing his hand lightly over Julia's hair.

Infuriated, Julia jerked away, only to be shaken violently again.

"But don't you worry about your pretty little charge," Amraphel continued, his face contorting into a menacing sneer. "I do plan to release her, after her ridiculously rich and influential father pays the ransom and convinces the Roman brutes not to press any charges. Simon has friends in high places – the kind of friends capable of erasing a criminal's record, if you know what I mean. You see, this pretty little thing is my key to freedom. So, I'll be taking real good care of her."

Joanna raised bold, clear eyes toward Amraphel. "Son, I suggest you consider your actions carefully before you proceed. Not only will you have to reckon with the Roman authorities you just mentioned, but you will also stand before God. And He is a righteous Judge."

"Lem, you imbecile!" Amraphel shouted, his face contorted in rage. "Why is that old woman still breathing? Finish her!"

Amazingly, the young man – Lem, Amraphel had called him – hesitated.

"Do it!" Amraphel screamed, his teeth bared like a rabid beast.

"I'm thinking of the young woman," Lem dared, his voice tremorous. "She is great with child–"

"Ah, an excellent observation! Yes, indeed," Amraphel sneered violently.

"And the nursemaid might be of some help should her time to deliver arrive before her father–"

"Do you think I'm the least bit concerned about a smooth delivery?" Amraphel cried out, enraged.

Oh dear God, intervene. Julia couldn't imagine

bearing a child while captive to this vulgar man. *Lord God, save me. Save Joanna. Save my baby.*

"Get rid of the old maid and do it quick," Amraphel ordered tersely. "We're running out of time."

Lem hesitated once again, his knuckles whitening upon the hilt of his dagger. And then Joanna's voice rang out like a battle cry, raising the hairs on the back of the men's necks and stunning them to utter silence.

"In the name of Jesus Christ, the Son of the Living God, I command you to release her!"

No one moved. No one breathed. It was as if an invisible shock wave had exploded within the small, dimly lit house, threatening to drown the criminals in its fierce wake.

For the briefest moment, Amraphel – the great ringleader himself – faltered.

And then the front door splintered and caved in with a mighty *crash* as uniformed Roman soldiers spilled into the tiny home, spears lifted and weapons raised.

Amraphel reached for his dagger, prepared to take Julia hostage. Instinctively, Julia ducked as the hilt of a Roman gladius exploded on the side of Amraphel's head, knocking him out cold.

Lem immediately dropped his knife and lifted his hands in surrender as several soldiers surrounded him.

Pushing herself to her feet, Julia rushed to Joanna and threw her arms around her, trembling violently. Joanna held her close, stroking her hair back from her face and whispering words of comfort.

In the midst of the unexpected chaos, a tall centurion of regal bearing approached them, removing his elegantly plumed helmet and cradling it in one arm as his men hauled away an unconscious Amraphel and his pale companion.

"Pardon the intrusion, my dear ladies," the soldier said with a chivalrous bow and the slightest hint of humor. "My name is Cornelius, and I am at your service."

Clinging to Joanna, Julia dared a glance at the dashing soldier. He was indeed an impressive figure.

"Now how did you know we were in trouble?" Joanna asked, shaking her head in disbelief.

"We received a tip after making an arrest – a tip from another Zealot. He insisted those two would be here, likely taking hostages."

Julia pulled away from Joanna, her heart pounding so fiercely she was certain it would explode. "This Zealot – what was his name?" she gasped, praying unlike she ever had before. Did she even dare to hope?

Cornelius pursed his lips grimly. "A fellow by the name of Barabbas."

Barabbas was alive! Julia's heart soared, for she realized her husband had a fighting chance. Had he perished in the fray, his soul would have been lost forever. *Oh, dear God, thank You for preserving him,* her heart sang.

"We've been after him for some time," the centurion continued solemnly. "Unfortunately, by the time we discovered him he'd been severely beaten, probably by this cruel lot. We found him in a ditch near the scene of an ambush. Surprisingly, he was coherent and directed us to this very place."

Pressing the heels of her hands against her eyes, Julia wept as if her heart would break.

Joanna drew a trembling Julia close, her own heart aching for the young woman. "But he is still alive?" Joanna dared to ask.

"Alive and awaiting his trial," Cornelius replied matter-of-factly.

"His trial?" Joanna repeated in dismay.

"That's right," the centurion said grimly. "If he's any relation of yours, I'd start beseeching any and all available gods on his behalf."

Joanna held her peace for Julia's sake. "And why do you say that?"

Cornelius' gaze was surprisingly apologetic. "If convicted, Barabbas will be sentenced to death by crucifixion. He will die upon a Roman cross."

CHAPTER 43

The kindly centurion had generously offered to escort Joanna and her trembling young charge to any place of safety they so desired, and without hesitation, Joanna had accepted his offer and requested that they be taken to the house of Simon.

The soldier's brows had risen in surprise. He surely had not expected two modestly clad women residing in a pitiful residence within the poorest district of the Lower City to be associated with the wealthiest merchant in the region.

Now, Julia sat upon the lovely marble bench encircling her favorite fountain in the midst of her father's peaceful garden enclave, trembling hands protectively sheltering her protruding belly. It had been odd to spend a sleepless night in her own opulent quarters within her father's palatial villa. Little had been altered in the room since she had left, although the lovely suite was now used to house guests and relatives when they were in residence.

It was now evening, and delicate silver stars splashed across the dusky sky like so many glittering gems. The sound of the gently splashing fountain was soothing, and Julia could hardly believe she had nearly been taken hostage the previous night. One would have never known observing her now, clothed in fine garments and surrounded by every imaginable comfort.

Despite her idyllic surroundings, Julia's heart ached.

The house should have been abuzz with frantic activity as the servants rushed about making preparations for the Passover. Instead, a reverent hush had fallen over the elegant residence, as if the entire household held its collective breath, waiting for something to happen. Julia knew her mother must have cautioned the staff to tread lightly, encouraging the peaceful environment that Julia so desperately needed in her time of grief. Her parents had asked very few questions. Surely Joanna had shared the necessary details after their arrival, long after Julia had drifted into a tormented sleep.

"Mind if I be joining you?"

Julia glanced up, surprised but not dismayed by her faithful nursemaid's presence. She managed a weak smile and nodded gently.

Joanna sat rather heavily beside her, wiping floury hands upon her apron. Despite Iskah's constant protests, Joanna still insisted upon making herself useful while in residence.

The two women remained in companionable silence for some time. Julia couldn't help but recall another time she had shared this bench with Joanna. At the time, she had been filled with bitterness and resentment. She had loathed the woman's very presence as Joanna had kindly attempted to ready her for her approaching wedding night. Julia had resented the fact that Joanna had been sent to delve into this sensitive topic with her.

Now, Julia welcomed Joanna's presence and wondered at her own selfishness of years past. She couldn't imagine a life without this pleasant, cheerful soul in it! Her own rebellion had blinded her to the wisdom of her father, her mother, and yes, this kind, aging nursemaid.

"How are you holding up?" Joanna finally asked, her kind eyes threatening to unleash the fountain of tears Julia was so desperately restraining.

Julia released a tremorous sigh. "I feel... numb."

Joanna nodded her understanding, placing a motherly hand upon Julia's knee. "I understand. You've been through quite a shock."

Julia allowed the words to linger in the air. It took great effort to formulate a sentence at this point, so she took her time in doing so. "I'm so scared, Joanna. And so confused."

"Also understandable."

Julia turned and looked at Joanna, her eyes brimming with tears of sorrow and confusion. "Barabbas will die in agony. And I didn't even get to say goodbye. His child will never know him."

Joanna gave a slow, sorrowful nod.

"I should have done something. I should have done more."

"And what could you be doing about this, dear one? I imagine you did all you knew to do."

"But what if I could have done more? I should have found a way to stop him, to intervene. I was just so afraid that he would be sentenced to death if anyone found out. And Barabbas isn't ready to die." At this, the tears trickled down her cheeks. Her husband would perish in his sins and rebellion. There was no hope for him.

"Julia, this is not your fault. Remember, the devil

– the enemy of your soul – is the great accuser, and he will hold this over your head every single day if you let him. You did all you knew to do without jeopardizing your husband's soul."

"I considered going to Father so many times, but I just couldn't put him in that position. Father would feel honor-bound to intervene knowing that men's lives were at stake. And then, even if Barabbas was somehow spared, many Zealots would likely perish – without hope for salvation."

"I know."

"But, Joanna, I prayed so fiercely! Every minute, every day, I was praying for Barabbas."

"I know."

"Joanna, I should have told you about Barabbas. It was so wrong to put you in that position. But I was just so afraid! I was so afraid you would leave if you knew," Julia confessed, dissolving in tears.

Joanna tilted her head and studied the weeping young woman, her eyes penetrating. "If I knew what, Julia?"

"If you knew that Barabbas belonged to the murderous order that stole the life of your husband."

Taking Julia's hands in her own, Joanna met her gaze. "Julia, look at me. Look at me, child!"

Julia did, tears coursing down both cheeks.

"My dear, dear girl, I knew your husband was a Zealot within a week of setting foot in that house."

Julia stared at her, openmouthed and stunned. "Then why didn't you leave?"

"Because love never fails, Julia. And neither can my love for you, my love for Barabbas, and most importantly, my love for God. When God sends one to minister to another, he or she had best obey. And God sent me to minister not only to you, Julia, but to Barabbas as well."

"But you were so patient, so kind to him!"

"Isn't that what love is? Barabbas already understood hatred, bitterness, revenge. He didn't need any more of that. No, what your husband needed was to witness a bit of love in action."

Lowering her head, Julia wept, touched and overwhelmed.

***

Barabbas

He hadn't meant to kill an innocent man.

Barabbas winced as he leaned his bruised forehead against the cool, unrelenting iron bars of his prison cell. He had never felt so helpless, so defeated, so full of blasted, futile rage in his entire life.

He had hated the forces of Rome for so long that his burning hatred was simply a part of him. He had turned to the Zealots seeking a capable and worthy ally.

And now, that very ally had turned against him, stabbing him in the back. Even now, his beautiful young wife was probably within the possession of that wicked dog, Amraphel. What had he done to her? To her unborn child?

When their ambush had gone south, Amraphel had become far more desperate than the plight of their mission. The daring attempt was supposed to be Dan's vindication. Amraphel had insisted that the dogged centurion who had stolen Dan's life would be part of the envoy guarding a prominent Roman politico vacating Jerusalem before the festivities began. The unfortunate politician had slighted

Amraphel in some small way, and Amraphel had decided the pompous man would pay with his life.

Barabbas had hated the idea of murdering the man in cold blood before the watching eyes of his horror-stricken family. But it was the only way. Amraphel had agreed to help Barabbas kill the centurion only by those terms. "I never give to anyone without the promise of something in return," Amraphel had spat the day they had drawn up the plans. "You put that pompous old goat out of his misery and you can have your soldier too. The boys'll be right there with you to overpower the guards, and I'll have your back. After all, I want to be there to watch the life drain from his eyes after you slit his worthless throat."

Barabbas' unease had only increased the day he had lain in wait for the envoy accompanying the politician's family. And the moment the signal had been given and the Zealots exploded into action, Barabbas' entire world had unraveled before his very eyes.

The centurion wasn't there. Barabbas' angst and rage had risen within him the moment he'd realized Amraphel had simply used him to accomplish his own purposes. Perhaps that's simply what he had been doing all along.

In the midst of the fray, people died. Guards and soldiers had sprung into action, and most of the Zealots were arrested or killed.

But it was his own actions that haunted him, for Barabbas had unintentionally taken the life of an innocent man – a boy, really – that day. The loyal young son of the politician had sprung into action, coming at Barabbas with weapon in hand.

It had all happened in a flash, the blink of an eye.

Barabbas hadn't meant to kill him, only to incapacitate him. But in the end the boy lay lifeless upon the dust as the haunting screams of his mother tore at Barabbas' heart.

And now Barabbas was sick. Completely, utterly sick. For he realized he was no better than the Roman centurion who had unwittingly ended Dan's life in his attempt to reach Barabbas. He, Barabbas, had unintentionally ended the life of a young boy whose eyes had borne the same impossible combination of fire and peace as Dan's.

And now, Barabbas' wife and unborn child were in danger and there was absolutely nothing he could do about it. When he had fled the scene along with Amraphel and Lem, a new recruit, a contingent of Roman soldiers had been close on their heels and certain to find them. Amraphel had insisted that taking Julia hostage was the only way to ensure their escape. How had the filthy dog even known about her?

For the first time in their comradeship, Barabbas had defied Amraphel's wishes – and nearly lost his life as a result. Now, Julia would probably lose hers as well. Their innocent, unborn child would never see of the light of day.

Ignoring the ghostly old man hovering in the corner of his prison cell – another victim of beastly Rome – Barabbas gripped the iron bars and bellowed out his rage.

CHAPTER 44

Melina

"Is it something I said?"

Forcing a weak smile through her tears, Melina lifted her head. Gently swiping the tears away from her pale cheeks, she forced a very weak smile. "Elias? What brings you to the palace gardens, so very far from your kitchen?"

The crusty old cook arched a knowing brow. "Despite your stellar performance for the staff, I've known you long enough to know when something is wrong."

Melina was touched that Elias had taken the time to seek her out. He was certainly not an emotional creature, and she knew he must feel entirely out of his element now.

"So?" he prompted. "Do I need to belt someone for you?"

"Heavens, no! I'm alright, but thanks all the same, Elias."

"Hogwash."

"Really, I'll be fine."

"Is it that boy you've been seeing? Did he hurt you?"

Melina couldn't help but smile at Elias' protectiveness. "I asked Malchus not to see me again. It was a difficult decision, and it still hurts," she admitted, surprised at how painful it was to say it aloud.

"What did he do to you?"

"It's not anything he did, but rather what he refuses to do."

"Ah. Another one of the 'not-marrying' kind, I imagine?"

Melina hid another smile. "Quite the opposite, actually. He asked me to marry him, but I couldn't. He doesn't believe in Jesus, Elias."

Elias stared at her blankly. "Is that all?"

"It's a serious thing."

"People can agree to disagree, Melina. Look at our friendship."

Melina was warmed by his reference to their friendship. And what an unlikely friendship it was! "Yes," she responded with a soft smile. "But I'm not married to you, Elias, and the Lord forbids a believer to marry an unbeliever."

"An unbeliever? He serves the high priest, for heaven's sake!"

"He has rejected Jesus as the Messiah."

Elias scratched his head in confusion. "Your man worships the God of the Jews, but rejects the Man you believe to be the Jewish Messiah?"

"Jesus, Son of God, Savior," Melina whispered, her eyes filling with tears. "*He who does not honor the Son does not honor the Father who sent Him.*"

"Maybe he'll come around."

"I do hope so, Elias."

Elias sobered, his heavy brows knit closely together. "Melina," he said, his deep voice serious, "are you sure you know what you're doing?"

Melina looked to him tentatively. "What do you mean?"

"You are but a maidservant trapped within the walls of this godforsaken fortress. And if I know you at all, I know you love this man. I'll admit I'd hate to see you go, but this might be your only chance at happiness."

"There is no happiness apart from the will of God," Melina whispered, praying that the Lord would strengthen her resolve.

"But this man has so much to offer you – his love, his life, his children. I mean no disrespect, Melina, but what can your God give you? Cold, stone walls? A life of servitude? Loneliness? Tears?"

Rising from her marble bench, Melina took Elias' calloused hands in her own. Willing away her tears, she responded quietly, "The promise of salvation. Eternal life. Truth. A purpose on this earth. A future and a hope." Squeezing his rough hands, Melina forced a smile that she hoped would reach the closed heart of this good-willed man. "This is what my God can give me, Elias. And the most beautiful part is that He already has."

***

Malchus

The tenth day of Nisan exploded with frantic activity, for this was the day each family was required to choose a lamb to be slain for the Passover. On this day, the innocent creatures would be embraced by the people, loved, accepted, and taken into their homes. The lambs would then be slaughtered by the same adoring, Jewish families four days later on the fourteenth day of Nisan.

Crushed and angry, Malchus pushed through the obnoxious crowd as he neared the Golden Gate, the impressive eastern gate of the Temple Mount. The influx of people pouring into the city by the Golden Gate was like a mighty outpouring of raging water. Typically, Malchus would have avoided the chaos at all costs. But today, the seething madness matched his mood. Today, he found himself curious about the uproar rather than apprehensive. Something was happening, and he was going to find out what it was.

Malchus was hard-pressed to see above the heads of the immense throngs of people lining the streets. People were laughing and shouting as they waved palm branches in the air. The cacophony was both distracting and deafening.

Strangely enough, the road began to open up as people respectfully lined the streets, palm branches waving madly. Beneath the shelter of a merchant's canopy, Malchus crossed his arms and watched with veiled interest as men began removing their outer garments and placing them reverently upon the paved street.

"Hosanna!" Women shrieked, frantically waving their branches, and surprisingly, even the men joined in the frenzied shouting. "Blessed is He who comes in the name of the Lord! The King of Israel!"

Malchus turned toward the small, balding man standing near his elbow. "What is all this?"

"The people are welcoming a mighty revolutionary. This multitude has followed Him all the way from Bethphage and Bethany, and as you can see, many more are joining the welcoming committee."

A mighty revolutionary? Malchus craned his neck, now even more interested.

And then Jesus broke through the crowd, confidently astride a strong young donkey. Another placid beast, most likely the donkey's mother, trailed alongside her colt. The multitude shrieked its delight as Jesus' striking, snow white donkey placed tentative hooves upon the garments that had been spread out like a thick carpet.

A stab of rebellion pierced Malchus' heart, and his dark eyes narrowed as Jesus drew nearer, for this Man – Jesus of Nazareth, Melina's Messiah – stood between him and the ultimate peace and happiness he craved. If not for this one Man, Melina would be his bride.

Malchus didn't appreciate the feelings coursing through him with such ferocity. In fact, they greatly disturbed him. Deep inside, he recognized the fact that Jesus had not forced Melina to reject his earnest proposal. Still, the sight of Jesus so completely accepted and embraced by this adoring multitude rankled.

Why was Jesus even here? Was He completely unaware of the fate that awaited Him in Jerusalem? *Perhaps if the chief priests are successful, Melina will see that this Man is, in fact, fallible,* Malchus thought, surprised by the course of his own dark thoughts. If Jesus was assassinated as planned, would Melina finally admit that she had been deceived?

Changing the course of his thoughts with great

effort, Malchus pondered the true purpose of Jesus' arrival in Jerusalem. Was He simply tempting fate? Did He enjoy taunting the powerful religious leaders with His presence? Perhaps He had simply come to select a Passover lamb. It was, in fact, the day the people were commanded to welcome their sacrificial lamb into their homes.

Despite the fact that there were far too many frenzied people piled in front of Malchus for him to gain a clear view of the Rabbi upon His timid mount, Malchus' skin tingled as Jesus' colt passed by on the street.

Behold, your King is coming to you, lowly, and sitting on a donkey, a colt, the foal of a donkey...

The hairs prickled on the back of Malchus' neck as the ancient Messianic prophecy whispered its way, unbidden, into his tortured mind. Why did this Man have to fulfill practically every prophecy he'd ever read?

Even after Jesus had passed, men and women continued to cry out, even their children joining in: "Hosanna! Blessed is He who comes in the name of the Lord! Blessed is the kingdom of our father David that comes in the name of the Lord! Hosanna in the highest!"

Malchus wished to clamp his hands firmly over both ears to drown out the ear-splitting madness. Instead, he remained tall, unbending. Arms folded across his chest, he watched grimly as thousands of verdant green palm branches were waved wildly in the air like a raging sea of fresh green.

Malchus knew what these people wanted, and he winced at the very thought of it. As they waved their branches above their heads, Malchus knew that each man, woman, and child was privately nurturing visions of another ruler, another conqueror: Judas Maccabeus. In ages past, the people had greeted the victor in this very way, waving palm branches and singing praises.

But surely this Jesus had not come to banish the Romans with an iron fist? Melina would say the captivity Jesus had come to destroy was far more powerful than any tyranny Rome might inflict. His heart constricted at the thought of the woman he loved, the woman who now refused to see him.

Still, these people were stupid and foolish, Malchus thought grimly, for they tempted power-hungry Romans to crush their spirit of rebellion. Clearly, they desired one thing above all else: revolution.

The grimness of Malchus' features intensified as he shook his head in disgust and prepared to return to the house of Caiaphas.

An uprising could mean only one thing: certain death for everyone. Even the innocent.

CHAPTER 45

Melina

It was proving rather challenging to appear calm and natural, for Melina struggled against the temptation to stare wide-eyed at her incredibly lavish surroundings. Having resided within Herod's garish Jerusalem palace for many years, Melina was no stranger to opulence. But this was the first time she had walked through the grand halls of a Roman-style villa in the Upper City, and frankly, her surroundings took her breath away. The swirling marble mosaics gracing the tile floors, vivid, colorful frescoes splashed across towering walls, magnificently arched entryways, endless rows of staid marble pillars, richly upholstered furniture gilded in gold, silver, and bronze, sheer Babylonian tapestries that fluttered in the gentle morning breezes...

"My lady." Having reached the grand entrance of an elegant courtyard, the well-dressed manservant escorting her offered a slight bow before turning sharply on his heels and disappearing around a bend.

"Oh, Melina! I'm overjoyed to see you, my dearest friend! Thank you for coming!"

Melina had scarcely set foot upon the tiled floor of the most elegant central garden courtyard she had ever seen before Julia had rushed her, throwing both arms around her neck. When Julia pulled away, tears were tracing slender lines down both cheeks.

"Julia! I was rather surprised to find your father's servant waiting for me beneath the colonnades. I must admit, it gave me quite a scare since we were supposed to meet today. I was so afraid something might have happened to you." Her eyes traveled to Julia's bulging belly. "I have been praying ceaselessly for a smooth, safe delivery."

"I appreciate that more than you know," Julia said with great feeling. "I do apologize for sending someone to escort you here, but the baby is due very soon, and Mother is rather adamant that I stay off my feet."

"In that case," Melina said with a teasing smile, "let's sit you down, then!"

Julia allowed Melina to escort her to a nearby marble bench. Melina bent to assist her friend before seating herself beside her.

Melina then looked to Julia with questioning eyes. "Considering the fact that you are staying at your father's villa, I imagine much has transpired since last we met? Did you and Barabbas have words?"

Julia's eyes filled with tears. Biting her lower lip to still its trembling, she said quietly, "Oh, Melina, it's so much worse than that."

Melina touched her arm. "I'm here for you, friend."

"I know. You have always been here for me, Melina."

Melina offered a warm smile. "What has happened?"

Julia took a deep breath, then plunged straight into the topic at hand. "Barabbas has been arrested for treason, theft... and murder."

Melina stifled a gasp.

"Quite frankly, Melina, I'm stunned. And sickened. I can hardly wrap my head around this."

"Oh, Julia. I'm so very, very sorry."

"Father – he is such a gracious man – went to make some inquiries and attempted to put in a good word for Barabbas with the Roman authorities. He insisted that Barabbas had served him faithfully for many years. Father learned that the murder was most likely an accident – a young man was killed in the midst of the Zealots' ambush. But accident or not, the young man is dead. And nothing can bring him back. Father is an influential man, but he was mocked for defending Barabbas. He was told that Barabbas is a notorious criminal deserving of death." At this, Julia's eyes filled with tears. "Melina, he's not ready to face eternity."

Taking Julia's hand, Melina squeezed it gently. "Is there nothing we can do?"

"Not unless you know someone capable of breaking him out," Julia half-teased. She sighed, her eyes downcast. "But even if Barabbas was rescued, I imagine he would revert right back to theft and revolution, only to be arrested *again* at a later date. What he needs is a change of heart, Melina."

"Then that's what we'll pray for, Julia, without ceasing! There is still time. Even if Barabbas' life is forfeit, he has an eternity to gain or to lose. We must pray that God will do whatever it takes to reach him."

"Our marriage is so far from perfect, Melina. But

it hurts to lose him all the same. I had such high hopes for us. I was certain that the Lord would eventually reach him."

"But you're forgetting that there's still time."

"For his salvation, yes. And I pray for that with all my heart. But our chance to grow strong in our marriage, to love each other and to walk with the Lord together, is lost forever."

Ever so gently, Melina reached out and touched Julia's protruding baby bump. "But the Lord has blessed you, Julia, with this precious little one by which to remember him."

"Oh, Melina, what will I tell this sweet child when she asks about her father?"

"*She?*" Melina asked with a warm smile. "It sounds like you have your heart set on a baby girl."

"I will love whatever God sees fit to give me, but I just can't imagine raising a son without a father... But if this child asks about her father, what will I tell her? That her father was a murderer crucified by the Romans... just like *his* father? My baby comes from a long line of... of rebels!"

"But don't we all?" Melina offered gently. "We are all rebels, Julia, in one way or another. God's grace is what changes us, and that grace is available to every single one of us."

"If only Barabbas would accept it! What really gets me is the fact that I'll never know, Melina. Barabbas might receive the grace of God, but I will spend the rest of my life so afraid that he didn't."

"You can't do that, Julia. It will eat you alive. Instead, you must pray without ceasing. And trust."

"I do find great solace knowing so many are praying for my husband's salvation. You, Father, Mother, Joanna... Oh! Will you be seeing Malchus soon, Melina? It would mean the world to me if he'd be praying for Barabbas too–" At Melina's ashen expression, Julia halted mid-sentence, her eyes narrowing in suspicion. "What is it?"

Melina's soft eyes were strangely downcast. Wringing her hands in her lap, she managed with an odd little catch in her voice, "Much has transpired for me, as well, since last we met."

"Meaning?"

"I won't be seeing him anymore, Julia."

"What?" Julia nearly croaked in her incredulity. "But why not? You two are perfect for each other!"

"Not by God's standards," Melina answered softly. "Malchus has rejected Jesus as the Messiah, and God is very clear that His children are not to be unequally yoked."

"Oh, Melina! How you must be hurting! I can be so dense – I should have sensed that you were in pain."

Melina placed a reassuring hand upon Julia's arm. "I'll be fine, Julia. The Lord is my Shepherd, and He will lead me through this. I fear most for Malchus. Like Barabbas, he must make a decision that will impact his eternal soul. Please pray for him, Julia."

"You know I will."

"My greatest fear for Malchus is that he will ultimately lose his life in his own desperate attempt to preserve it." Both women remained in silence for what seemed like a very long time, each one thoughtful, pondering.

Releasing a troubled sigh, Melina was the first to break the silence. "I must be going now, Julia, but I want you to know that I will be praying for Barabbas without ceasing."

"And I will be praying for Malchus as well. And

for you, Melina."

"Thank you, friend. Before I return to the palace, may we pray together?"

Julia's smile was sincere. "I would like nothing more."

Taking each other's hands, the two young women bowed their heads, pouring out their souls to the God who created them, the only One capable of setting things right.

Long after the women had tearfully embraced and Melina's soft footsteps had retreated from the lush garden escape, part of Melina's prayer resounded in Julia's mind, and as she went about her day she continuously offered it back to the God who possessed the power to lead her safely through the deepest waters and the hottest fires.

Our dear Barabbas, meaning son of the father, may have been fitly named, for his own father taught him to hate, not to love. But You, most gracious, merciful God, are our loving heavenly Father. May you transform our brother, Barabbas, into Your own image, that when we dwell in perfection with You for all eternity with our dear brother – and by faith we believe that we shall – we may grandly proclaim him to be fitly named: Barabbas, son of the Father, our heavenly Father, conformed to Your image, and bearing Your likeness! Stagger him by Your great power, Lord, and bring him to his knees. Demonstrate to him beyond any argument or doubt that YOU ARE GOD, and that You will stop at absolutely nothing to redeem him from himself.

CHAPTER 46

Malchus

Malchus supposed he shouldn't have been surprised when Caiaphas ordered yet another secret meeting of the Council. Again, select members were intentionally uninformed about the clandestine affair. In fact, only the high priest's most trusted associates were in attendance tonight.

With Passover a mere two days away, Malchus wondered at the high priest's priorities. Hadn't he far more important things to worry about as one of the most crucial festivals of the entire year loomed just ahead?

Standing at the ready with tablet and stylus in hand, Malchus wrestled with his own pain and frustration. He wasn't quite sure about where to direct his wrath. First, there was Melina. She had rejected him when he rejected her Messiah. Second, there was Jesus Himself. The Man insisted upon wreaking havoc wherever He went! If He would have been a bit more cautious around the religious leaders, then this entire issue could have been avoided! And then there was Caiaphas and his ever-zealous band of Pharisees, Sadducees, priests, and scribes. What was their problem, anyway? Perhaps they were the worst of all, for they were the ones jeopardizing the lives of everyone else.

Malchus had paid little heed to the goings-on within the dim, candlelit chamber housing several men wearing severe garments and even more severe expressions. Frankly, he was tired of all of it.

As the men awaited the meeting's commencement, arguing quietly about the futility of their mission, Caiaphas rose from his regal chair and allowed his dangerous gray eyes to scan those seated within the dark chamber.

The room grew eerily silent as the powerful presence of the high priest demanded the attention of everyone within the sequestered chamber.

"Until recently, our quest did indeed prove futile," Caiaphas admitted with such calm control that Malchus knew something bad was about to happen. "But no more. Gentlemen, I'd like you to meet the man who has agreed to make it all possible. Lucius!"

It was a command, and the soldier emerged from a dark corridor a moment later, bearing a kindling torch that cast writhing shadows over his stony features.

Beside Lucius strode another man – tall, confident, commanding, even. For some reason unbeknownst to him, Malchus recoiled at the mere sight of him, for it was as if a dark, sinister presence had settled over him. Malchus wondered if he was merely imagining the malignant evil emanating from the man's powerful form. Warily, Malchus watched the well-dressed, self-assured man as he crossed the room and took his place near the high priest. Unable to tear his eyes from the riveting scene, Malchus felt the heavy sense of foreboding in the air threatening to choke him.

"Gentlemen," Caiaphas stated, spreading his hands before him with the flair of a thespian villain upon the stage, "please welcome the man we have all been waiting for: Judas Iscariot."

***

Barabbas

"My God, my God, why have You forsaken me?"

Clenching his fists, Barabbas grit his teeth and attempted to drown out the eerie, soulful dirge of the ghostly wraith sharing his small prison cell. The grimy elderly man was propped rather casually against the stone wall of their holding cell, shouting out Psalms at the top of his lungs.

Barabbas could have gleefully strangled him.

"Why are You so far from helping me, and from the words of my groaning?"

Barabbas considered giving him something to groan about.

"O my God, I cry in the daytime, but You do not hear…"

Barabbas was certain the entire province could hear, even if God could not.

"…and in the night season, and am not silent!"

That was no exaggeration. Attempting to shut his ears, Barabbas paced about the small stone cell like a prowling animal, restless, filled with fury.

"But You are *holy*," the old man's song took an entirely different turn, sending chills up and down Barabbas' rigid spine. The wonder in the old prisoner's soulful tone was unnerving. "Enthroned in the praises of Israel! Our fathers trusted in You, and were not ashamed..."

Again, Barabbas clenched his fists. His father had trusted in the God of Israel to free them of their captivity. A lot of good it had done for him.

"...But You are He who took Me out of the womb; You made me trust while on my mother's breasts. I was cast upon You from birth. From my mother's womb You have been my God. Be not far from Me, for trouble is near; for there is none to help—"

"Enough!" Turning sharply on his heel, Barabbas faced the old man head-on. He couldn't stomach another moment of that dreadful Psalm nor the gravelly voice that proclaimed it.

The older man stared back at him, unblinking, unperturbed. Then, he opened his mouth and began to sing again in a low, mournful tone, "They gape at Me with their mouths, like a raging and roaring lion. I am poured out like water, and all My bones are out of joint—"

"Stop." Barabbas' tone was low and threatening.

"My heart is like wax; it has melted within Me. My strength is dried up like potsherd, and my tongue clings to my jaws—"

"Didn't you hear me, old man?"

"You have brought Me to the dust of death. For dogs have surrounded Me; the congregation of the wicked has enclosed Me. They pierced My hands and My feet..."

"By the gods—"

"They look and stare at Me. They divide My garments among them, and for My clothing they cast lots—"

Consumed with fury and grief, Barabbas exploded into action. Before he even knew what he was about, he had pinned the old man to the cold stone wall. "I said enough!" Barabbas growled fiercely, his face only inches away from the old man's.

The old man raised feathery gray brows in amusement, completely unperturbed. "The Psalm – it strikes a chord deep within you, it does."

Strangely unsettled, Barabbas loosened his grip. Even so, the prisoner made no attempt to escape his grasp.

"I've heard the priests proclaiming this very Psalm over the Passover sacrifice. Mighty words, they are. Full of power."

Barabbas took several awkward steps back, eyeing the old man warily. Was he sharing this small cell with a man who had gone completely insane? It wasn't a pleasant thought. "Who are you?"

"You may call me Azarel."

"Why are you in my cell?"

"My, aren't we possessive. If you want this dank little cell, you can have it."

Barabbas' ire rose in response to Azarel's amusement. "You're rather glib for one sentenced to die, old man."

"I am not sentenced to die."

Barabbas' brows lifted in derision. "No? Then why are you in this cell?"

"For the same reason you are."

Barabbas laughed out loud. "You are a Zealot?"

"Zealous, yes. A Zealot, no."

"Look, I'm in no mood for stupid games. So, I'd appreciate it if you'd leave me be."

"May I remind you that *you* assaulted *me?* I was minding my own business."

"And screaming at the top of your lungs. Can't a man enjoy some peace before he is crucified?"

"Crucified? Crucifixion is a ghastly practice."

Barabbas turned away. He needn't be reminded. He had witnessed his father and brothers die slow, torturous deaths upon Roman crosses. And now he was to share their fate. He couldn't allow himself to think about it, or else he would go mad. His only hope was a chance at escape when he was escorted to the cross. He could only pray he wouldn't be as heavily guarded as he had been for the trial. He had knocked out two prison guards before he had been subdued. But the narrow stone passageways and slews of Roman guards had prevented any possible chance at escape then.

"When is the crucifixion to take place?" Azarel interrupted the course of his troubled thoughts.

"Friday morning." Barabbas' entire body broke out in a cold sweat just thinking about it. Perhaps his only mercy was the fact that he would be nailed to a cross on a Friday. If he was still alive near sunset, then he would be dispatched and no longer required to suffer upon the cross. It would be an excruciating death, for soldiers would break both his legs, rendering him unable to prop himself up to drag air into his burning lungs. But some criminals suffered and agonized for days before finally succumbing to death. Since Jewish law forbade a man to remain upon his cross on the Sabbath Day, perhaps he would be spared multiple days of harrowing pain.

Since this would be a High Sabbath ushering in the Passover, Barabbas was fairly certain he could count on the observance of that law.

"You don't have much time."

Barabbas clenched his jaw, hardened and angry.

"When will you repent?"

Barabbas looked to Azarel, shocked. "Why would I cry out to a God who has clearly forsaken me? What can I expect from Him? More pain? More misery?" he sneered with scathing bitterness.

Settling himself upon a narrow slab of stone, Azarel crossed his legs at the ankles, appearing to ready himself for a nice, long chat.

Barabbas was in no mood to oblige.

"Let me ask you this, young man: had you chosen to walk in God's way rather than your own, would you be facing these dire consequences? Perhaps God is not to blame."

"What are you implying?" Barabbas ground out. "That *I'm* to blame?"

"You catch on rather quickly, don't you?"

"*I* did not crucify my father and my brothers! *I* did not murder my kind mother! God could have saved them, but He did nothing!"

"God gives all men free will, Barabbas, just as He gave you the free will to participate in an ambush that stole the life of an innocent young man – not to mention many others. When your family was put to death, it was the result of another man's free will. But the penalty for sin is death. Those who live in sin will not gain the ultimate victory. Instead, they will perish. God's justice will prevail."

Fleetingly, Barabbas wondered how this irritating prisoner knew so much about his circumstances.

The prison guards spoke too freely.

"By refusing God's mercy, you deny yourself the peace you crave. And ultimately, you deny yourself the joy of being united with God and reunited with the loved ones you have lost."

Barabbas turned and gripped unyielding iron bars, his spirit troubled.

"The enemy is a wily one," Azarel continued, despite Barabbas' angst. "The devil wreaks evil, havoc, and devastation upon this earth – and then he convinces weak human beings that God is responsible for the pain, suffering, and death that he – the enemy – inflicts. Men and women then turn against God, the only One who can straighten out this mess and banish evil once and for all! Can't you see it?"

Leaning his head against the cool iron bars, Barabbas closed his eyes, wishing he could close his ears just as easily. He surely wouldn't admit it, but the words spoken by this odd little man named Azarel made sense, resonating deep within his innermost being.

"Perhaps if God Himself were suffering as we are, then He would act a bit faster," Barabbas drawled, his words bathed in sarcasm. "But He sits enthroned above the circle of the earth, safe and sound, indifferently watching this entire story unfold."

"But what if God became flesh and dwelt among us?"

Barabbas stared at Azarel, annoyed that his heart was responding to his mystical hogwash.

"And what if we beheld His glory, full of grace and truth?" Azarel continued, his eyes bright with wonder. "What if God took the sins of the entire world upon Himself? What if He took our place, and our suffering became His? Then would you suppose He truly cared about His creation?"

"That will never happen. I've learned a dark little secret, my friend: *God doesn't care.*"

"Oh, but He does. And only God knows why He continues to reach for the most stubborn, ungrateful creatures on this earth, assuring them of this very fact!"

Barabbas' lips tipped ruefully. "Why do I get the impression that you consider me as one of those stubborn, ungrateful creatures?"

"Such a bright young man! How you can be so dense regarding spiritual matters is beyond me."

Barabbas supposed he should be insulted. Instead, he was amused. "You speak strangely for a criminal in a prison cell."

"I am not a criminal."

"Ah, another falsely accused, I imagine?" Barabbas drawled sarcastically.

Azarel simply grinned before launching into yet another refrain of his beloved Psalm: "I will declare Your name to My brethren; in the midst of the assembly I will praise You! You who fear the Lord, *praise Him!*"

CHAPTER 47

Malchus

Malchus felt as if he were being sucked into a deep, dark slough of sheer desperation and despondency. Caiaphas must have sensed his irritation with this whole blasted affair. Perhaps the cunning high priest even suspected that Malchus sympathized with Jesus of Nazareth. Why else would the malevolent priest order Malchus to accompany Lucius, Judas Iscariot, and a ridiculously large troop of officers to detain Jesus?

It was a test, and Malchus was terrified.

"You look like you've just seen a ghost."

Malchus paused beside one of the marble columns upholding the four-sided structure enclosing the elegant peristyle, somewhat relieved to see Mara stepping gracefully into the lush garden enclave. In recent months, Mara had changed drastically. Not only had her former compassion and cheerfulness returned full force – there was something more to it than that. She fairly glowed with warmth, a quiet, inner strength, and a calm contentment that defied her circumstances. Despite the fact that Malchus would never, ever admit it aloud, he trusted her again. Implicitly.

In fact, she reminded him more and more of Melina with every passing day.

At the thought of his beloved, Malchus sat heavily upon a curved marble bench, his heart constricting in pain. Part of him was convinced that this was only a season, that he would surely win Melina back. Another part of him feared that he might never see her again. Anger and confusion swirled about his tortured mind, threatening to suffocate him.

Mara seated herself on the bench beside him, her motherly expression filled with concern. "Do you wish to talk about it?"

Malchus stared awkwardly at his own large hands. Where should he even begin?

"What's on your heart, Malchus?"

Her gentle inquiry was almost his undoing. Steeling himself, Malchus said rather sarcastically, "I'm suddenly beginning to understand why Romans commit suicide just to end it all."

Mara's expression sobered. "Don't even jest about that, Malchus. What has happened?"

"What has happened? My entire life – along with my hopes, dreams, and aspirations – has gone up in smoke. Other than that, very little has happened, I suppose."

Mara offered a comforting smile. "I understand. I've been there, too."

"I doubt you've ever been where I'm going tonight."

"And where is that?"

"To a lovely little place called Gethsemane at the foot of the Mount of Olives. There, I shall assist in the betrayal of a perfectly innocent – however controversial – Man named Jesus of Nazareth. Have you ever stooped so low?"

Though the color had drained from Mara's face, she drew upon the inner strength her Lord supplied and said very slowly, "Actually, Malchus, I'm surprised you would even ask, given the history of our friendship. I, too, have betrayed Jesus. Thankfully, He has forgiven me and accepted me as His own."

This was not the response Malchus had expected. "What do you mean?"

"When I aided Lucius in his quest to hunt down the followers of Jesus, I was indeed betraying Him. Jesus said, 'Inasmuch as you did it to one of the least of these My brethren, you did it to Me.'"

Malchus winced. That was not a comforting thought.

Gently, Mara laid a hand upon his wrist. "You don't have to do this, Malchus."

"Caiaphas made it perfectly clear that I am to remain at the very front of the mob in order to accurately report every detail. He also mentioned that I will have the remainder of my wretched, miserable life to regret my ineptitude should I fail in this assignment. You know the high priest, Mara. He wouldn't think twice about selling me off to mind the oars in the stinking belly of a ship or to be buried within the bowels of the earth toiling in the mines for the rest of my miserable days."

Mara studied Malchus with clear brown eyes, her features appearing softer in the early morning sunshine. "I believe the real question, Malchus, is this: Whom do you fear – God or man?"

"Both, quite frankly," Malchus admitted, annoyed.

"And therein lies the problem," Mara said, chuckling softly. "Malchus, when will you begin to trust God?"

"I do trust Him."

"If you did, would we be having this conversation?"

Malchus' hackles began to rise. He felt as if he were being interrogated by Melina all over again. "Why does everyone doubt my faith?"

"Perhaps you should ask yourself that question," Mara said, very gently.

Malchus rose from the bench, pacing before Mara in fierce agitation.

"Malchus, it's obvious that you believe God exists. But you doubt His watchful care and provision. You shy away from the Savior our God has sent to us because you are worried about possible repercussions. When will you recognize that the only safe place for us is in the palm of His hand, in the center of His will?"

Malchus turned away, unwanted visions from his past taunting him. "My father and my mother trusted God implicitly, Mara, and yet they were burned alive – helpless victims of men like Caiaphas and his lackeys. I don't desire the same fate."

Mara rose from the bench and went to him, her eyes full of compassion. "Malchus, your parents need never worry or fear again – they are in God's hands. Don't you wish to see them again? When God sets things right, He will create a new heaven and a new earth. There, we will dwell in perfection with our heavenly Father and our loved ones for all eternity. There will be no more pain, suffering, or death, which means we will never fear! Don't you long to be part of that?"

Malchus studied her solemnly, attempting to curb his frustration.

"Tell me, Malchus, what would Melina say if she knew you planned to assist Caiaphas in his wicked act?"

"It doesn't matter anymore, Mara. She doesn't want to see me again!"

This gave Mara pause.

"That's right. She walked right out of my life, simply because I refused to place our lives in jeopardy by groveling at the feet of her beloved Rabbi!" Malchus' voice rose, and he realized he was in grave danger of losing control. Taking a deep breath, he said dryly, "I suppose she must love Him far more than she ever loved me."

Mara's features filled with pity. "Oh, Malchus, isn't that as it should be? We are to love God first, above all else. If anything in our lives takes precedence before God, then it has become an idol. You cannot ask Melina to forsake her faith."

"I cannot bear to lose another loved one, Mara!"

Mara raised level eyes to his, her expression enigmatic. "And yet, you already have. By your own choice."

For whoever desires to save his life will lose it, but whoever loses his life for My sake and the gospel's will save it, whispered its way through Malchus' anxious mind. Perhaps the phrase applied to the things one held dear, as well. Annoyed, Malchus shoved the unwanted proverb out of his mind.

"Are you still an avid follower of this Jesus?" Malchus demanded, intentionally changing the subject.

"I am."

"Then I'll tell you what I told Melina: you may want to reconsider."

"And I'll tell you what Melina surely said to you: I cannot."

Malchus grit his teeth in frustration. He was surrounded by stubborn women, and he didn't like it!

"What does Caiaphas' plan for tonight entail?" Mara's tone was so calm that it grated on Malchus' worn nerves.

"Let's see: betrayal and arrest, followed by swift and certain execution," Malchus said snidely.

"The chief priests have made many attempts on Jesus' life."

"This one is different, Mara. Caiaphas will succeed."

"How can you be certain?"

"Caiaphas has taken ridiculous measures to ensure his success tonight. Listen to me, Mara. In the past, Caiaphas has simply employed his own Temple guards to make an arrest. This time, he has appealed to Pontius Pilate to supply a cohort of Roman soldiers under a tribune from Antonia Fortress."

Mara raised a brow in question. "An entire cohort to arrest one Man? That's over four hundred trained soldiers, Malchus."

"Exactly. With a ratio like that, your Man doesn't stand a chance."

"Pilate will never grant a cohort of Roman soldiers to a Jewish priest."

"Think again, Mara. He already has."

Mara stared at him, openmouthed. "You can't be

serious!"

"Caiaphas is sly. Pilate thinks the soldiers are required to keep the peace during the Passover week, which obviously commences this evening. The governor has been in enough hot water lately with both the emperor and the tetrarch. He'll do whatever it takes to keep the peace."

"People are still speculating about whether or not Jesus will even return to Jerusalem for Passover. He was here, but I think He may have returned to Bethany," Mara said hopefully. "How does Caiaphas intend to find Him?"

"One of His disciples has agreed to betray Him," Malchus said, and shame settled over him as he realized that he, too, was participating in Jesus' betrayal. "Judas Iscariot will lead the band of soldiers to Jesus tonight. According to this disciple, Jesus plans to visit the Garden of Gethsemane after partaking of the Passover meal with the Twelve. By arresting Him in the dark of night outside the city limits, Caiaphas hopes to prevent a riot. Everyone will be at home partaking of their Passover feasts, too busy to notice the demise of one Man."

Mara lowered her eyes sadly, and Malchus sensed that she was also praying. Uncomfortable, he plunged ahead rather dumbly, "Since it will be dark, the soldiers will carry torches and Judas will identify Jesus with a kiss on the cheek. Caiaphas feared the soldiers might arrest the wrong man, as His disciples will likely be with Him. This Judas seems eager to hand over the good Teacher, despite the loyalty of the remaining eleven."

Mara gasped. "No! But why?"

"It seemed to me that Judas harbored some type

of grudge against Jesus. He agreed to betray Him for thirty pieces of silver."

Mara's eyes filled with tears. "The Son of God, sold for the price of a slave. It isn't right."

"It's the way of the world, Mara. We can't change it."

"No," Mara said, looking steadily at him. "We can only change ourselves, by the grace of God."

Sensing her unspoken reprimand, Malchus looked away in agitation.

"Malchus, you cannot participate in this. It is evil and pure wickedness."

"What would you have me do, Mara?"

"The right thing!"

"Well, then, it was nice knowing you."

"Have you so little faith?"

"Have you so much? What has God truly done for you, Mara? You are a maidservant, little more than a slave! You have no husband, no children. You will spend the remainder of your days toiling in the hot kitchen of a sadistic man. And yet you have such faith?"

Mara looked to him then, her soft eyes wet with unshed tears. "Our ancestors wandered through the wilderness for decades, bitter and angry about their circumstances. They were so focused on the dust, the rocks, the serpents, and their unfulfilled desires that they completely missed the Promised Land. You speak truth, Malchus, when you say I have no husband, no children, no place to call home. I may be a servant under the yoke of a cruel master, but none of that matters to me anymore. Do you know why?"

Malchus stared at her, mesmerized.

"Because my eyes are fixed upon the Promised

Land," Mara finished with great conviction, her eyes burning with intensity. "Like our fathers, I might not like what I see here in the desert. But the Promised Land looms beautiful and golden upon the horizon, and I absolutely refuse to miss it."

Applause erupted behind them, and both Mara and Malchus spun around to see Alexander emerging from a sheltered portico.

Malchus' insides twisted in contempt. How long had that despicable cretin been eavesdropping? He now regretted baring his soul to Mara. He should have known his good-for-nothing cousin would be hiding in the shadows somewhere, taking notes.

"That," Alexander stated grandly, offering Mara an overly dramatic bow, "was a lovely little speech."

Mara flushed as she looked away, flustered by Alexander's powerful presence. His advances had been far too bold after he had discovered her husband's defection, and yet, somehow, he had eventually respected her desperate pleas and ceased to plague her. Part of her had been relieved, even while another part of her – the carnal, fleshly side, she realized – had been disappointed. Regardless, she was grateful that Alexander possessed the decency to give her space, respecting her convictions. If marrying Lucius had proven disastrous, a union with this man would surely prove even more so! She imagined Alexander possessed the power to utterly devastate her heart in a way that Lucius never had.

"I can't help but admire your great faith, my dear," Alexander stated, watching Mara with unsettling intensity. "Personally, I'd love to claim such a faith for myself, but I fear, like my poor wavering cousin, I am unwilling to make the ultimate sacrifice."

"Then I shall continue to pray that you will have a change of heart," Mara said quietly.

Alexander's sharp brows lifted in amusement. "You pray for me, my sweet?"

"Leave her alone, Alexander," Malchus threatened.

Alexander ignored him. "I'm touched."

"What do you want, Alexander, apart from intruding upon yet another personal conversation?" Malchus demanded, his patience already stretched to its limit.

"Ah, yes, it was rather personal, wasn't it?" Alexander mused, stroking his chin with great interest. "I'm absolutely crushed knowing that any woman would have the audacity to break my cousin's heart."

"Yes, I'm sure you are," Malchus ground out in annoyance.

"Tell me, what was it about this girl that so drew you?"

Malchus wondered if Alexander was simply trying to prolong his pain. "She is sweet, kind, compassionate, and full of tender mercies. Melina is the embodiment of peace."

"A thought to consider—" Alexander mused, and his manner irritated Malchus more than he cared to admit, "perhaps you fell so head-over-heels in love with this girl because she possesses a light within – the peace that you crave."

Malchus stared at his cousin, disturbed that he was so easily read by someone like Alexander.

"In asking her to relinquish that light, would you not be asking her to forsake the very thing that makes her so exceptional?" Alexander concluded with annoying logic.

Malchus couldn't help but wonder at his cousin's astute assessment. Without Melina in his life, he felt nothing but darkness, despair, and gloom. The future dragged on before him like a dark, hopeless abyss. It had never occurred to him that it was not Melina but rather the light burning brightly within her that had drawn him to her. What was the source of that light, that all-encompassing peace?

"Jesus is the source of that Light," Mara whispered, as if reading Malchus' thoughts. Her uncanny timing gave him chills.

"*I am the Light of the world...*" Alexander mused, crossing his arms thoughtfully. "I heard Jesus speak those words at the Temple. A rather bold proclamation, is it not?"

"It is not merely a bold proclamation, Alexander," Mara said. "It is truth."

Malchus' mind was so muddled with frustration and anxiety that he was having trouble following the course of their conversation. But before he could further expound upon his own disturbing contemplations, Alexander interrupted yet again, "I am intrigued by Caiaphas' elaborate plan to trap the good Teacher."

"Intrigued?" Mara said, disgusted. "I am sickened by it."

"I don't think you should shirk this assignment, Cousin," Alexander said with great feeling, his eyes glittering with... something.

"And why not?" Malchus demanded, unsettled by his cousin's encouragement. If Alexander was urging him on, then perhaps he should run the other way as fast as his legs could carry him.

"You've just been given a front row seat to an epic

drama, possibly one of the greatest in history," Alexander supplied, his striking features consumed with interest. "This Jesus has evaded arrest every single time because the hand of His God is upon Him. Even I cannot deny the power of this God. Just imagine the display when hundreds of armed soldiers come against His Anointed!"

Malchus began to feel a sickening knot tightening in the pit of his stomach.

"All I can say is that I certainly wouldn't pass up an opportunity like that," Alexander continued, his dark eyes glittering. "In fact," he added, a slow smile splitting his handsome features, "I won't be passing it up, because I'm going with you."

"What?" Malchus and Mara gasped in unison.

"I'm flattered by your enthusiasm." Alexander's mouth tipped ruefully.

"Just when I thought it couldn't possibly get any worse," Malchus grumbled under his breath.

Mara looked back and forth between the two relatives, her expression troubled.

And for the first time since he had found himself bound to the house of Caiaphas, Malchus began to question his own philosophy. Despite his desperate efforts to maintain peace and avoid conflict at all costs, his life was completely consumed with turmoil. It was as if his entire world was spinning out of control, and Malchus hated it with his entire being. The violence he had so vigilantly avoided was now crashing down upon him from all sides, threatening to crush him, to utterly destroy him. How on earth had he become so hopelessly tangled in this vile web? How had he – a peace-loving, easy-going man by nature – become an accomplice to the bloody schemes of a sadistic high priest?

Even as he mulled over his own intractable thoughts, raising silent objections, Malchus realized that he would never stand up to Caiaphas. And he couldn't help but wonder if he was making the biggest mistake of his entire life. Turning away, he left the peristyle without another word, leaving Mara and Alexander to puzzle over his silent retreat.

As he walked pillared walkways, traveling down elegant, frescoed halls, Malchus was haunted by the silent refrain that had become his constant companion: *For whoever desires to save his life will lose it, but whoever loses his life for My sake and the gospel's will save it...*

Setting his jaw, Malchus hastened his steps, his frustration continuing to boil just below the surface. This time, it was clearly directed at the Teacher who had stolen the love of his life and shattered the peaceful existence he had struggled, clawed, and grasped to maintain.

Whoever desires to save his life will lose it...

Pausing halfway down a lonely corridor, Malchus determinedly squared his shoulders, his anger rising steadily.

So be it.

CHAPTER 48

Melina

"Melina, a word."

"My lord?" Straightening with broom in hand, Melina turned to face her solemn overseer.

Chuza stood beneath an enormous arched entryway, arms folded across his broad chest, expression grim. "You have another visitor."

Melina's heart sprang into her throat. Malchus? Had he possibly experienced a change of heart? Had he come to tell her? She looked expectantly to Chuza, and he seemed to read her thoughts.

He shook his head, extinguishing her small flicker of hope.

Attempting to dismiss her keen disappointment, Melina forced a smile. "Who could have possibly come to see me?"

"Do you know a woman named Mara?"

"Oh, yes! May I see her?"

Cautiously, Chuza surveyed their surroundings. "I will permit it, but you'd best stop making a habit of this before we both get into trouble."

Melina clasped her hands together in gratitude.

"Oh, thank you!" What a comfort it would be to share her heart with a friend who could truly understand her grief. Mara had also lost the man she loved.

"In recent weeks, you have welcomed more guests than the tetrarch himself," Chuza remarked, leading her toward the palace gardens.

Melina held back a smile.

Mara sat anxiously upon an elegant marble bench, nervously wringing her hands. When she saw Melina entering the exotic gardens, she stood and waved rather shyly.

Melina hurried toward her, filled with joy at her presence. "Mara! What an unexpected and welcome surprise! What brings you here, dear friend?"

Mara lowered her gaze, and Melina knew something was wrong.

"Mara?"

"Perhaps we should sit down," Mara suggested, gesturing toward the bench.

Once the women had settled themselves upon the bench, Mara took a deep breath. "Malchus told me about what happened."

Melina's eyes filled with tears. "I didn't want it to be this way, Mara. I love him so much."

"Oh, I know you do," Mara assured her, taking her hand. "I am praying for that stubborn man. Perhaps he shall come to his senses."

The women shared a sad chuckle.

Mara's expression sobered. "I have come to warn you, Melina. Caiaphas has hired a cohort of soldiers to arrest Jesus tonight. I learned that my former husband, Lucius, will be among the arresting officers. It breaks my heart." She paused, collecting her thoughts, before plunging ahead. "Melina, you need to know that Caiaphas has ordered Malchus to attend them."

Melina's eyes widened in shock. She covered her mouth, horror-stricken.

"We need to pray for him, Melina," Mara said with quiet conviction. "God is at work in his heart, I have no doubt about that. But whatever transpires within the next few hours might very well determine our brother's eternal fate. He has a decision to make, and I fear the battle for his soul is already raging."

Melina nodded slowly, unable to withhold her tears.

"We haven't much time," Mara said, her eyes darting nervously about the peaceful gardens. "If Caiaphas knew I was here..." she shuddered, unable to complete the thought. "May we pray for Malchus together before I must depart?"

"Oh, yes," Melina managed, attempting to slow her pounding heart. "Yes, please."

Clasping each other's hands, Mara and Melina presented their beloved brother before the very Throne Room of God.

From his post at the front of the garden, Chuza watched the two dark heads bent closely together, tears falling as their lips moved in fervent prayer. Observing his alert stance, one would have never known that the fearsome man had silently joined his sisters in their prayerful petition.

Hear their prayer, Almighty God, and grant their request at any cost.

***

Julia

Barabbas will die tomorrow.

Shuddering at the never-ending refrain assaulting

her mind, Julia stood within her father's magnificent triclinium-style banquet hall, wrapping her hands protectively about her unborn child and gazing up at the lintel of the beautifully tiled entryway.

The scarlet paint still remained upon the lentil and doorposts – a reminder of the final Passover she had celebrated at home with her family prior to her union with Barabbas. She still vividly remembered her shock and horror when Simon had taken the dripping hyssop branch and slashed it violently across the pristine doorposts. She also remembered the strange thought that had occurred to her at the time: the blood manifested itself both vertically and horizontally. It was as if that blood reached up and down and side to side – North, South, East, and West – to embrace the entire world.

...When He sees the blood on the lintel and the two doorposts, the Lord will pass over the door and not allow the destroyer to come into your houses and strike you... That night, her father's booming voice had recited the story of the Exodus, retelling God's command to sacrifice the Passover lamb and spread its shed blood upon the lintels and doorposts of the Israelites' homes. Only those covered by the blood of the lamb were saved, spared by the destroyer.

Julia sighed, defeated. Barabbas had not accepted the blood of the sacrifice, and the destroyer had surely come for him. How easily the enemy deceived! Without the covering of God, all were susceptible to the devil's cruel snares, leading to ultimate destruction.

With a bit of effort, Julia settled herself upon one of the plush settees near the gleaming banquet table. She was thankful the servants had not yet begun to ready the chamber for the Passover feast, but she supposed they would begin their preparations very soon.

Gazing upon the blood at the entrance, Julia attempted to recall the words her father had spoken that evening so long ago. The Lord had been tugging at her heart then, but she had refused to listen. Her thoughts had been entirely consumed with Barabbas. What if she had known how terribly it would end? What if she had known that the man she loved would perish without hope? Again, her thoughts drifted back to that fateful night when she had closed her ears to the still, small voice within.

So you see the significance of the blood of the lamb, Simon had explained that night. Without the covering of the blood of that perfect, spotless lamb, the people would perish and grant the destroyer access into their homes and their hearts. We, like our forefathers, have a decision to make...

Oh, Barabbas, why did you turn from God? Julia's heart cried. *Why did you choose wickedness? Why did you leave me?* Covering her eyes, Julia resisted the urge to weep. She had shed more tears than she had ever thought humanly possible. She knew she must be strong for the sake of the child she carried. She had lost her husband; she refused to relinquish his child. Squaring her shoulders, Julia lifted her head and gazed squarely upon that scarlet stain. It was so very significant, and yet she couldn't quite decide *why.* It was a symbol, her father had said. But a symbol of *what?*

This command to keep and remember the Passover was the very first command ever to be given to our people, Simon had explained after expounding upon the miraculous tale of the Exodus. *The command was given before the Law, even before the Ten*

Commandments. Very literally translated, this law commands us to take the lamb, to receive and accept the lamb.

Julia wondered if Barabbas had ever offered a sacrifice. Surely, he would not be permitted to do so now, trapped within a merciless stone cell. Even if – by some miracle – he chose to repent, would his sins be covered if he were unable to offer the blood of a perfect, spotless lamb? Julia knew the Law by heart – all things were purified with blood, and without the shedding of blood there was no remission of sin. Her father had taught her about that first sin committed in a garden so very long ago – the man and the woman had fallen prey to the lies of the serpent, blatantly rebelling against their loving God. God then sacrificed a sinless lamb in their place, covering their nakedness by its own skin. Thus, blood sacrifice was required to cover the sins of another.

Julia's shoulders slumped. She was too tired to think, too weary even to pray. She felt as if her mind was under attack, as if a merciless accuser was assailing her thoughts. Clasping her hands, she mustered the strength to beg her God to intervene. Still, hateful thoughts continued to assail her, pounding at her heart like angry waves upon the battered shore, threatening to drown her in a sea of fear, tension, and anxiety.

Surely there was no hope for Barabbas.

CHAPTER 49

Malchus

The silver moon bathed the Kidron Valley in an eerie, otherworldly light. Malchus imagined dark spirits darting about the arid plain, feeding the bloodlust of the feverish mob traveling steadily toward the tranquil olive grove gracing the base of the Mount of Olives. Despite the soft light of the storybook moon, darkness unlike anything Malchus had ever experienced cloaked the entire contingent. The darkness was so heavy, so oppressive, he could *feel* it.

This graveyard is aptly named, Malchus thought in revulsion. *Kidron – gloomy, to make black, to make sad.* His soul responded to the gloom, filling his entire being with dread. Was it the valley itself, or the errand on which he had been sent? The endless stretch of land made his skin crawl, and he imagined that the valley's dark legends contributed to his aversion. Here, the mighty David had fled from his betrayer, his son Absalom, ultimately resulting in the prince's gruesome death and the king's wretched heartbreak. Here, idols had been crushed and burned by righteous kings and priests, their ashes carried away by the waters of the Brook Kidron. Here, thousands of bodies had turned to dust in the days of Josiah, when the forlorn region became the house of many tombs.

Indeed, this was a place of death. Even now, blood flowed freely through the Brook Kidron as Passover lambs were slain in preparation for the great feast. The sacrificial blood was swept down a drain at the base of the Temple's altar, to be carried into the waters of the Brook Kidron and eventually emptied into the Dead Sea. Repulsed, Malchus averted his eyes from the gruesome sight, for blood flowed freely beneath the lonely bridge they must cross to reach their destination. The waters were cast in an ethereal crimson glow beneath the light of hundreds of burning torches carried by a mob hungry for the blood of one Man.

With a steely hand, Lucius gripped Malchus' shoulder and pushed him over the bridge. Alexander drew up beside him, his countenance troubled, and crossed the bridge with his cousin. The nature of their assignment demanded silence, and Malchus was glad for that. He had no desire to entertain Alexander's overly dramatic musings. Alexander was a foolish thrill-seeker, in Malchus' opinion, chasing after the supernatural to satisfy his own morbid curiosity. Alexander was there by choice, but he, Malchus had not been given the luxury of choice.

Or had he? Malchus closed his eyes briefly, nearly stumbling as he reached the other side of the bridge. He remembered Mara's heartfelt plea as she had beseeched him to do the right thing. What was the right thing, anyway? Fleetingly, he saw Melina's graceful form the day she had approached him in Herod's gardens. The gentle breeze had caressed the silky, raven-black hair about her face. She had smiled at him then, a smile so pure, so tender. She would be absolutely crushed if she knew that he was participating in this death trap.

Shaking his head as if to dispel the aching memory from his mind, Malchus forced himself to focus on placing one sandaled foot directly in front of the other. If he could just get through this night, then he could return to the house of Caiaphas and his crazy life would settle right back to normal again.

And yet, Malchus possessed a niggling suspicion that his life would never be normal again.

Crossing the bridge was a bothersome task, for it hindered the progress of the ridiculously enormous troop. Only a few men could take the bridge at a time. Lucius and the cohort's battle-hardened tribune glowered and stewed as they waited for the remainder of the troop to cross over to the other side.

It was certainly a bizarre entourage, and Malchus despised his position at the front of the multitude near Lucius, the cohort's tribune, and Judas Iscariot. The tribune was a solidly built officer touting battle scars. His glowering countenance signaled that he clearly detested his assignment, loathe to get tangled up in the religious quibbles of overly zealous Jews. And yet the expressions upon the faces of Lucius and Judas Iscariot were truly fearsome to behold. Lucius marched ahead with great purpose, always ready to inflict pain. But one look at Judas Iscariot caused

Malchus' blood to run cold. The man's expression was uncompromising, and his entire being resonated with a dark, malevolent, and powerful presence. Malchus imagined the eyes of a demon peering out from the depths of Judas' own dark eyes.

The writhing shadows cast by hundreds of lanterns and torches illuminated the stony faces of silent, battle-trained men as they crossed the Brook Kidron, their hobnailed sandals clank-clank-clanking a fearsome rhythm, every single one of them armed to the hilt. Malchus had never seen so many swords, clubs, and daggers. He couldn't possibly fathom the need for such a mighty arsenal. Were these battle-hardened warriors truly so terrified of one Man boasting only eleven followers?

The knot in the pit of Malchus' stomach grew steadily tighter. Perhaps the soldiers' fear was not entirely unfounded. They had battled the enemies of Rome with great success, and yet, Malchus realized that Jesus posed a far greater threat to the pleasure-seeking, blood-lusting Roman Empire than warring nations or feral tribal wars ever could.

These trained mercenaries were experts in the art of war, Malchus thought as he marched grimly onward, and yet all the training in the world could not have prepared them for the spiritual battle they were about to face.

***

Alexander

Malchus' tension was like a tangible force between them. Alexander hated to admit it, but his own apprehension was growing steadily with every passing moment. Dark forces were at work, and he couldn't deny it. Alexander could sense the corruption in the night air. A chill breeze swept through the rugged valley, raising the hairs on the back of his neck.

Perhaps he had made a terrible mistake.

For the first time in his entire life, Alexander had spoken to the God of Israel before slipping casually into the ranks alongside his nervous cousin. For months now, Alexander had faced a raging battle within. He was weary of fighting it. The God of Israel was a powerful Being. He had come to terms with that. But was he, Alexander, destined to serve Him?

Tonight would determine his fate. Alexander couldn't deny that he hoped to elude this omniscient, miracle-working God. In the past, he had served no one but himself, and he wasn't entirely sure he was ready to change that.

It's in Your hands, mighty God of the Jews. If I'm meant to be Yours, then prove it. If Jesus is Your Son, show me.

Shoving troubling thoughts aside, Alexander set his jaw solemnly, terribly aware of his surroundings. This was certainly the last place on earth he had ever expected to be. When he had left Tiberias to start over in Judea, he never could have imagined that his journey would have taken him here. Oh, how his pleasure-seeking brothers would laugh if they could see him now – groveling at the feet of a righteous Jewish God, contemplating the possibility of forsaking his own pleasures for something bigger, something more.

He could scarcely believe it himself, but he had witnessed a purity in Jesus of Nazareth that had halted his mad quest for pleasure. Firsthand, he had seen the way Jesus transformed the lives of His followers. Their circumstances did not necessarily change, but their perspectives certainly did. With an odd little pang in his chest, he thought of Mara. Despite the hurt she had suffered, her character had blossomed as she sought to obey the Teacher's instruction. Her features had softened. Her words were now sweet, her actions pure and selfless. Alexander still desired her fiercely, but a quiet voice he scarcely recognized cautioned him against seducing her. Once, he would have demanded favors from a woman as proof of her love. Now, he restrained himself because he sensed that – dare he say it? – his love for Mara demanded it. If he truly loved her, would he compromise the convictions she held so dear?

Alexander chanced a sideways glance toward Malchus and was satisfied to see that he appeared equally troubled. At least they were in this together.

It was a motley crew that traveled steadily toward the base of the mount. Pharisees, Sadducees, Temple officers, and Roman soldiers had united to perform the bidding of a wicked priest. Caiaphas had not utilized the entire cohort to execute the arrest. Instead, he had sent a multitude toward Gethsemane, stationing the remaining men at critical locations between the mount, the city, and his own home, where he intended to question Jesus along with his powerful father-in-law, the former high priest. Alexander supposed Caiaphas was taking every possible measure to thwart any heroic attempt at rescue. Once he had Jesus in his custody, the crafty priest intended to keep it that way. How many times had the troublesome Teacher slipped through his hands in the past? Caiaphas must have supposed his success was guaranteed with hundreds of trained soldiers at his beck and call.

While the experienced tribune led the multitude with Lucius and Judas Iscariot, the Temple officers were placed strategically at the head of the contingent while the Roman soldiers provided reinforcement. Alexander had been surprised at the shocking number of torch-carrying elders, scribes, and chief priests gathered near the front with the Temple officers. Weren't they supposed to be ushering in the sacred Passover? Alexander's lips curved in sardonic amusement. Apparently, they were far more interested in trapping an innocent Man than reciting prayers to their God.

CHAPTER 50

Malchus

The twisted, gnarled trunks of ancient olive trees stood like dark sentries in the night, bathed in the eerie light of the silver moon. The Garden of Gethsemane boasted a veritable sea of the age-old trees, which provided a bounty of olives for an enormous olive press that typically hummed with frenetic activity. Now, in the dead of night, all was quiet. Even had the sun risen above the eastern horizon, the press would have remained eerily silent, for it would not be in operation this time of the year.

Malchus' senses were filled with a subtle woody fragrance as he entered the haunting grove of magnificent trees. He could not shake the feeling that he was standing upon holy ground. Here, at Gethsemane, the sacred anointing oil to be used in Temple rituals and sacrifices was pressed. It was a very special grove, and the operation even boasted a stunning array of ritual baths to guarantee purity and ritual cleanliness. Perhaps that accounted for his strange premonition.

Clutching his clay tablet and stylus as if it were a lifeline, Malchus trailed closely behind Lucius, Judas Iscariot, and the tribune, Alexander still by his side. Almost instantly, the garden appeared ablaze beneath the flickering light of hundreds of burning torches, casting dark, writhing shadows that danced upon the treetops as guards and foot soldiers poured into the sheltered respite. Their armor clanked so loudly within the peaceful surroundings that it assaulted the senses, the sound nearly profane, even as the rhythm pounded by hundreds of hobnailed sandals was muffled within the soft grass.

Malchus forced himself to stand tall, assuming a confident stance, although he would have preferred to make himself small and disappear within the sea of silent trees. A fear unlike anything he had ever known closed its cold fingers around his heart, and Malchus marveled at his own cowardice.

Why was he so afraid?

"Rabbi, Rabbi!"

Malchus nearly jumped out of his skin as the abrasive greeting ripped through the serenity of the peaceful garden. Mere steps ahead of him, Judas approached a tight cluster of men with outstretched arms.

"Greetings, Rabbi!" Judas persisted, the voice as cold as the man.

Malchus was faintly aware of the fact that Alexander had gripped his arm, holding him back.

Lucius waited, one hand resting upon the hilt of a deadly looking sword as an entire army drew up behind him, torches ablaze, weapons drawn. The tribune's scarred face crinkled in surprise and confusion.

There, only a few feet away, stood Jesus with His eleven remaining disciples, their faces strangely illuminated in the flickering orange glow of the torchlight. The panic seizing the disciples attested to the fact that they had been caught completely off guard. Jesus, on the other hand, stood quietly, hands folded before Him, calm resignation emanating from His still form.

Malchus caught his breath at the sight of Jesus, taken aback by what he saw. Though Jesus stood before the entire mob, unshaken, at peace, His entire garment was drenched in sweat and... blood? His dark hair was slick with sweat, curling slightly and clinging to his forehead, and His face and neck was smeared with a thin sheen of sweat and blood.

Had He been injured? Malchus studied Him closely, his stomach turning. But no, the blood appeared to be oozing from the Man's very pores.

With the bearing and shamelessness of a harlot, Judas closed the gap between himself and his former Rabbi. Taking Jesus by the shoulders, he raised cold eyes to his Maker.

That one look conveyed all the hatred and bitterness that had been eating Judas alive for many, many months. Jesus had not met his expectations, had even dared to criticize his own judgment. Jesus had failed to institute a glorious kingdom in which he, Judas, would take his rightful place. He had failed to banish their enemies and failed to make His devoted followers rich. He had failed to grasp the power that was rightfully His. He had failed to dispel the Romans, and now the Romans would dispel Him.

"Friend," Jesus spoke for the first time, His tone exceedingly sorrowful. "Why have you come?"

Judas' eyes gleamed with bitter vengeance as he leaned forward and boldly kissed Jesus' cheek, now wet with tears.

Malchus had never seen a look akin to the one Jesus offered Judas in that moment – a look so full of pain, so full of heartbreak, betrayal, and sorrowful resignation, and yet so filled with love. Stunned, Malchus stared at the pair so diametrically opposed, his writing tablet completely forgotten.

"Are you betraying the Son of Man with a kiss?" Jesus asked, His voice so faint and heavy laden with sorrow that Malchus and Alexander had to lean forward to catch the quiet words.

For one brief moment, Judas' gaze fell as his face flushed in shame. But when he lifted his gaze, the eyes of a demon bore into the eyes of the One who commanded the hosts of Heaven's armies. "You're the Son of God," Judas sneered, his voice unnaturally deep. "You tell me."

Chills scurried up and down Malchus' rigid spine as his entire body broke out in a cold sweat. He chanced a glance toward Alexander and was surprised to see the fury contorting his swarthy features as his dark eyes bore holes into the back of Judas Iscariot.

Malchus was drawn back to the present when several Temple guards broke rank and approached the disciples, who stood like frightened deer ready to spring into the depths of the black forest. Jesus held up a hand.

Amazingly, the guards froze.

"Whom are you seeking?" Jesus demanded with

great authority as He addressed the guards.

The solemn-faced tribune's eyes scanned his cohort in disbelief as Lucius' lip curled in derision. Surely the entire mob did not answer to this one Man?

Lucius stepped forward then, next to Judas Iscariot. "We seek Jesus of Nazareth, as You very well know."

"I AM HE."

When Jesus spoke, an invisible shock wave burst through the entire garden with the force of a mighty whirlwind, knocking trained soldiers off their feet and sending them sprawling upon the ground. A powerful wind tore through the garden, upsetting the crimson plumes of soldiers' helmets and tearing at their bright red capes. Shouts of fear and awe radiated through the ferocious mob as countless torches were extinguished. Those bearing covered lanterns scrambled to their feet and lifted them high in a desperate attempt to dispel the rising darkness.

It took a moment for Malchus to realize that he was on the ground. The sharp smell of fresh, moist dirt and damp grass assaulted his senses, and immediately he lifted his head and looked around. Pushing himself up on one elbow, he attempted to slow his rapid breathing and racing heart. What had just happened? Power unlike anything he had ever seen had erupted from the humble form of the sweat-stained, blood-streaked Teacher. And yet, there Jesus stood, gazing with compassion upon the faces of those sent to capture Him.

"He *is* the Son of God," Alexander breathed in wonder.

Gathering up his tablet and stylus, Malchus

turned to glimpse his cousin kneeling beside him, his handsome features transformed.

The Son of God.

I AM HE, Jesus had said.

Instantly, Malchus was carried away to an ancient time and place. In his vision, a floundering Moses stood upon holy ground, arguing with the Almighty God about the plan the Lord presented to him. Moses had resisted God at every turn, presenting every possible argument to dissuade the Creator of the universe from carrying out His plans.

What had God said to Moses? *"I AM the God of your father – the God of Abraham, the God of Isaac, and the God of Jacob..."*

Moses had argued like a scared, obstinate child. Exasperated, he had finally demanded to know the name of God. How else would the stubborn Hebrews believe he had been sent?

"I AM WHO I AM," God had proclaimed, and Malchus imagined that Moses had quaked in awe and reverence and fear.

I AM the God of Abraham, the God of Isaac, the God of Jacob...

I AM WHO I AM.

I AM HE.

Shakily pushing himself to his feet, Malchus stared at Jesus as if it was the very first time he had ever laid eyes upon the humble Teacher. Jesus – the One God had promised to send.

"Thus you shall say to the children of Israel, 'I AM has sent me to you...'" The Lord had spoken to Moses from the mysterious burning bush.

I AM has sent Me to you...

Years later, Moses had proclaimed by faith, *"The*

*Lord your God will raise up for you a Prophet like
me from your midst... Him you shall hear..."*

Shaking his head, Malchus stared into the face
of the One they had longed for, prayed for, waited
for... for centuries. The One the great I AM had sent.

The Son of God.

Shame washed over Malchus as he stood amongst
the godless throng of viperous priests and elders,
Temple guards, and hardened soldiers.

He suddenly understood Mara's admonition. He,
too, was a partaker of their sins, an accomplice in the
betrayal of God's beloved Son. Sensing the presence
of a holy God, Malchus resisted the urge to cower in
fear, for he realized that he himself was unworthy
to stand in His presence. Like the timid shepherd
shrinking before the burning bush, Malchus had
resisted God's will for far too long. Malchus' gaze
traveled to his own sandaled feet. He was indeed
standing upon holy ground.

Holy ground.

But was there hope of forgiveness for a transgres-
sor like him? Moses had argued for but a moment.
He, Malchus, had resisted God's will for years.
Turning his face away, he bit back a cry of agony and
shame. It was as if the entire world had halted to slow
motion, and Malchus was completely alone with his
anguished thoughts. The soldiers and mercenaries
faded into the background. The flickering lamplight
eluded him. The shouts of rage and defiance failed
to reach his ears.

But then, Malchus was drawn from his anguished
reverie as the amazingly calm voice of Jesus sliced
through the night. Raising His eyes toward Lucius,
Jesus repeated quietly, "Whom are you seeking?"

Nodding to several armed soldiers, Lucius turned to face Jesus once more. The Roman's cold eyes kindled with hatred as he sneered, "Perhaps You did not hear me, Jew. We seek Jesus of Nazareth."

Taking their cue, the armed soldiers began to close in on the disciples, clearly planning to bind them. Several disciples instinctively reached for their daggers, even as their eyes frantically traveled toward their Teacher, waiting for permission to engage.

"Lord, shall we strike with the sword?" one of the disciples called frantically, his white-knuckled hand clutching the hilt of his weapon. Malchus recognized him as a fisherman from Galilee, the one Jesus called Simon Peter.

Jesus did not respond. Instead, He turned to Lucius and said with great authority, "I have told you that I am He. Therefore, if you seek Me, let these go their way."

The moment that followed fairly crackled with tension as Lucius considered Jesus' command. Clearly, he did not appreciate the instruction.

Exchanging a nervous glance with Alexander, Malchus craned his neck to see over the shoulder of Judas Iscariot. After his kiss of betrayal, he had withdrawn and now obscured Malchus' view as Lucius drew daringly closer to Jesus. Malchus was nearly smothering in his own anxiety as his logical mind pondered the possible outcomes. One look toward Alexander confirmed that he was fighting to restrain his fury.

And then the disciple called Simon Peter exploded into action, drawing his sword from its sheath with a metallic clang that reverberated throughout the entire grove. With a vicious, downward slice, he lunged at Judas Iscariot, his teeth bared as he screamed his rage.

Before Malchus even knew what was happening, Judas had twisted and plunged aside, landing heavily at the tribune's feet.

Malchus tried to duck as a savage blade filled his entire field of vision, but it was too late.

He knew he was about to die.

"God, forgive me!" he cried out as his entire world exploded in searing pain. And then he hit the ground, writhing, reaching for the wound. Whirling in a sea of agony unlike anything he had ever experienced or even thought possible, Malchus reached for the place where his right ear should have been...

At his appalling discovery, Malchus withdrew his bloodied hand and nearly fainted, his entire body quaking violently as shock threatened to overtake him.

CHAPTER 51

Alexander

"Cousin!" Alexander threw himself on the ground beside Malchus, reaching for him. "Stay with me."

Malchus' dark eyes were distant, cloudy. He was going into shock.

Revulsion unlike anything Alexander had ever known filled his being. He was certain he had never seen so much blood. Had Malchus already lost too much to survive? He didn't know. Tearing off the sleeve of his own expensive garment, he pressed it against the wound. Malchus groaned in response as Alexander desperately applied pressure to the wound. His own rising fury was even more difficult to suppress than the blood of his injured cousin.

That wretched disciple would pay for this!

Ignoring the whispered murmurs of the crowd, Alexander forced himself to assess the damage. There, on the grass, lay his cousin's severed ear. Alexander struggled against nausea as continued to apply pressure to the side of Malchus' head. He attempted to draw Malchus up, without success.

The guilty disciple stared down at them in open-mouthed horror, his blood-stained blade clutched tightly in a trembling hand. Clearly, Judas Iscariot had been his intended target, not some insignificant servant of the high priest.

"God, help me," Alexander gasped under his breath. His eyes traveled imploringly to Jesus. For the first time in his life, Alexander did not resent being at the mercy of another Man. Jesus Christ was mercy wrapped in human flesh.

Gentle compassion swept over Jesus' features, transforming His face so fully Alexander was convinced that light radiated from His countenance. Amazed, Alexander wondered at the fact that the soldiers had not already dispatched the rebellious, sword-wielding disciple. Clearly, they were as spellbound by the scene as he was.

Reaching out to touch Peter's glistening sword, Jesus slowly lowered the blade, His gentle eyes holding Peter's gaze. "Put your sword in its place, Simon Peter," He said quietly, and Peter's eyes filled at the understanding he saw mirrored in the eyes of his Master. "For all who take the sword will perish by the sword," Jesus reminded him, His gaze slowly sweeping across the brutal Roman forces sent to apprehend Him.

When one of the disciples started to protest, Jesus interrupted him. "Do you think that I cannot now pray to My Father, and He will provide Me with more than twelve legions of angels?"

The disciples looked to one another sheepishly, lowering their heads in shame.

"Shall I not drink the cup which My Father has

given Me?" Jesus asked them, a gentle reminder in His tone. Had they known this was coming? Had Jesus Himself known? Surely God would not allow His only Son to be executed!

Alexander watched, curiously transfixed by the interaction of Jesus with His dearly beloved disciples. His heart ached and even grew desperate as his cousin continued to slip away before his very eyes. Malchus was pale as death. Clearly, those intent on making an arrest felt no compulsion to help an injured man. Again, Alexander raised pleading eyes to the Savior.

"How then could the Scriptures be fulfilled, that it must happen thus?" Jesus finished gently. Turning, he motioned toward the blood-thirsty crowd. "Permit even this."

Then, Jesus did the unthinkable. Kneeling before the unimportant, insignificant servant lying in a sticky pool of his own blood, Jesus turned and looked directly at Alexander. Jesus smiled softly, all the compassion and tenderness in the world harnessed in that one unexpected smile.

Alexander stared at Him, heart racing.

Jesus reached for the bloodied ear and picked it up, ignoring the gasps of revulsion that followed His shocking action. Then, He placed the severed ear upon Malchus' gaping wound as simply and gingerly as a child might place the final piece of a complicated puzzle in its proper location.

Swiftly, soldiers and religious leaders alike drew back in fear, for the flow of blood was stanched instantly.

Jesus' countenance was glorious as another joyful smile graced His features. He delighted in the healing of one child, the answered prayer of another.

Malchus' ear was restored, completely whole.

A mere touch from Jesus had healed him!

With one sharp breath, Malchus shot up like a lightning bolt and found himself gazing directly into the face of *love...*

***

Malchus

His father's long-forgotten prophecy tore through his mind with such dizzying clarity that Malchus clutched his head to still his rapid thoughts.

You yourself shall gaze into the face of love...

As Malchus stared into the radiant face of Jesus Christ, the Savior of the world, he realized that his father's prophecy had been fulfilled. Tears stung his eyes as he awkwardly pushed himself up and knelt before Jesus.

The time of the Savior draws near, his father had proclaimed boldly, years before his violent death. *It shall happen in your lifetime, Malchus.*

And so it had. Not only had Malchus discovered the truth about Jesus, he had also learned the truth about his father, and he was amazed at the sweet relief flooding his entire being. His father had not been a raving lunatic as everyone claimed. No, his father had simply seen what others refused to recognize: the truth within the Word of God.

"Cousin?" Alexander breathed, overcome. He, too, had been gazing intently at the face of His Maker. "You are healed," he declared in disbelief.

Overwhelmed by grief and riddled with guilt,

Malchus lifted his head and gazed once more into the kind eyes of his loving Savior. "Forgive me," he whispered brokenly.

But the compassion in the eyes of Jesus affirmed that He already had.

And then the wonder of the moment shattered as Lucius' rabid cry rent the air. "Bind His followers and seize Him!"

As the Temple guards stood at a distance, quaking at the miracle they had just witnessed, Roman soldiers rushed forth to perform Lucius' command. One soldier snatched the arm of a young disciple, but the terror-stricken man slipped out of his mantle and fled in his undergarments, leaving the Roman soldier to stare, thunderstruck, at the torn garment still in his hand.

"Enough!" The tribune roared as several other disciples followed suit and fled after their undignified brother. "Leave them. Our orders are clear: it's Jesus of Nazareth we want."

Lucius stepped forward then as Judas brushed himself off, his eyes burning like fiery coals after the tribune so casually dismissed the man who had attempted to slay him.

Gripping Jesus roughly by the arms, Lucius jerked Him away from Malchus, binding His wrists behind His back before the crowd of cheering soldiers and eager spectators.

Stumbling to his feet with Alexander's shaky assistance, Malchus watched in horror, for the religious leaders stood calmly by as Lucius brazenly breached Jewish Law and disregarded protocol. It was unlawful to bind a man before he had been tried and condemned, unless the offender resisted with violence. Yet Lucius relished his task as he tightened the ropes about Jesus' wrists, even as Jesus made no attempt to stop him. Instinctively, Malchus knew that Jesus would not be granted a fair trial when the sea of Jewish witnesses made no protest regarding Lucius' blatant breach of the Law. In fact, many erupted in cheers as Lucius roughly spun his unresisting prisoner around to face the crowd once again.

Jesus then addressed the Temple guards, elders, and chief priests as the few disciples that remained blanched in horror at the sight of their beloved Master, bound. "Have you come out, as against a robber, with swords and clubs to take Me?" He asked, His eyes penetrating, searching. "I sat daily with you, teaching in the Temple, and you did not seize Me."

Malchus wondered at the fact that Jesus had not addressed the Romans, but rather the Jews present. Was this because most of the Romans were simply obeying orders, acting in ignorance? The elders, the chief priests, and the Temple guards had no such excuse. They had witnessed Jesus perform miracles with their very eyes. They had sensed the power and authority of His teaching. And yet, consumed with resentment and jealousy, they had preyed upon Him like a flock of hungry carrion birds, eager to rip flesh from bone.

Jesus interrupted Malchus' rapid-fire train of thought with a final declaration, "But all this was done that the Scriptures of the prophets might be fulfilled." His statement was filled with sorrow, determination, and, yes, acceptance of His fate.

Lucius' lip curled in derision as he spat on the ground near Jesus' feet. "Didn't those same Scriptures predict the Jewish Messiah would overthrow us unworthy Roman swine and restore your nation unto lasting peace?" he looked to the laughing crowd. "Well, this is it. Now's Your chance, O holy One. Go ahead. Destroy us! Wipe us off the face of the earth with one almighty command!"

Malchus' insides twisted as religious leaders and soldiers alike howled at Lucius' cruel taunts. Had Lucius not the slightest hint of fear? Had he simply missed it when power resonated from Jesus' form, sending an entire army sprawling to the ground? Didn't Lucius recognize that he now taunted the One who had spoken the earth into existence, tempting Him to crush his own Roman countrymen by the word of His mouth? Didn't he recognize that Jesus possessed the power to do so?

When Jesus remained silent, eyes downcast, Lucius pushed Him roughly. "Well?" he demanded, his face mere inches from the Savior's. "Where's Your power, O mighty One? Now is Your moment, Your time to prove Yourself once for all. Don't tell me You haven't the guts to perform! Is this not Your hour?"

At this, Jesus raised knowing eyes to his.

Lucius shifted uneasily in spite of himself.

"This is your hour," Jesus said, His features clouded with both sorrow and deep resolve. "And the power of darkness."

As if in response to Jesus' statement, a chill breeze swept through the garden, rustling low hanging branches and eliciting frightened whispers from the mob.

There was no doubt in Malchus' mind that the powers of darkness now reigned. If he had ever doubted the presence of evil, any misgivings were permanently laid to rest tonight. But for some reason unbeknownst to him, Jesus had not resisted the sinister forces sweeping in to crush Him. And Malchus had a sinking feeling that the terrible forces of darkness were about to unleash their fury upon this Man and those who loved Him.

With a sharp intake of breath, Malchus realized he could now be counted among them.

"Take Him away!" Lucius shouted, furiously shoving the bound Savior headlong into the mob. The few disciples who had dared to remain – including the man who had attempted to rob Malchus of his ear – fled the garden like so many frightened rabbits. The hurt that passed over Jesus' face stabbed Malchus' heart, consuming him with grief.

Malchus knew he could no longer participate in this insanity. He would not assist these wicked men in their attempt to snuff out the Light of the world, even if it cost him his life.

Alexander must have sensed the direction of his cousin's thoughts. Gripping Malchus' arm, he held him back. "You can't leave now."

"I won't be part of this," Malchus hissed.

"He needs us now," Alexander argued, his gaze fierce. "Would you desert Him in His hour of need?"

"And would you assist this bloodthirsty mob in their attempt to kill Him?"

"I won't leave Him," Alexander vowed, unbending.

"And I will not stay and aid their madness!"

"Cousin–" Alexander argued, exasperated. Only moments earlier, he had nearly lost his cousin. Was he to lose him again so soon? Alexander was blown away by the stunning realization that he even cared.

Jerking his arm away, Malchus left his blood-spattered tablet and stylus lying in the damp grass and crashed into the black grove of olive trees, blinded by tears of deep regret. He heard Alexander calling after him, but he didn't turn back.

He utterly refused to perform the bidding of his dark master a moment longer. Despite his smooth, priestly façade, Caiaphas was governed by the same diabolical forces possessing Lucius, Judas Iscariot, and the blood-lusting mob. Had he, Malchus, been serving those same dark powers all along while offering his unremitting, blind obedience to the high priest?

That would all change tonight, he thought. No more. Surely there was something he could do to intervene. He had remained passive long enough. Surely now was the time for action!

But what kind of action was required?

As he plunged through the haunting olive grove, blindly stumbling over roots and stones, Malchus could not shake the feeling that he was being pursued. And it was not flesh and blood that sought to claim his soul.

Little did he know, the battle had only just begun.

CHAPTER 52

Mara

"We must do something!"

Startled, Mara spun around, wooden spoon in hand. Delicately wiping her brow with the back of her sleeve, her heart sprang into her throat the moment Alexander approached her in the kitchen, his eyes burning with intensity.

"You have returned," Mara managed weakly, lowering her spoon. Her forehead was beaded with perspiration, and she knew it had little to do with the warm cooking pot she had been tending to. She had been praying fervently for hours, beseeching her heavenly Father to protect the two men she cared about so deeply.

Alexander closed the distance between them with purposeful strides. Taking her shoulders, his dark eyes bored into hers. "You were right all along."

Mara opened her mouth in question, but he plunged ahead before she could voice her confusion.

"Jesus is the Son of God, Mara."

Tears sprang to Mara's eyes. "I knew you would come around," she whispered, managing a wobbly smile.

Tenderly, Alexander tucked a silky brown strand of stray hair behind Mara's ear. "We need to talk about this, but not now."

Aware of his closeness, Mara's heart hammered rapidly in her chest. "What happened?"

"They have Him, Mara."

Mara's eyes widened in disbelief. "But... but how?"

"He's here now, in the courtyard. Awaiting trial. They want to kill Him."

"But they can't begin a capital trial at night – it isn't lawful!"

"I don't think they're concerned about whether it's lawful or not," Alexander said, his tone acrid. "They've been after Him for months. They'll do whatever it takes to eliminate Him now that He's within their grasp."

"I don't understand. They tried to apprehend Him before, but God always protected Him. What has changed?"

"Jesus said it was happening to fulfill the Scriptures of the prophets. You've studied Torah. What did the prophets say?"

Mara's eyes filled with regret. "I've only just begun studying with Melina. I cannot read, so I am making very slow progress. I wish I had cared enough to learn the Scriptures before now."

"I've never seen anything like it," Alexander admitted. "Power burst forth from that Man unlike anything I've ever seen, and yet He allowed Himself to be taken."

"But why?"

"The only thing I know for certain about this, Mara, is that I know nothing at all," Alexander groaned, reaching for the back of his neck in agitation. "But we must do something. And fast."

"What can we do?"

Alexander gazed into her eyes, attempting to curb his longing for her. His entire life had been turned inside out in an instant. Now was not the time to act on fierce emotion. Sighing, he shook his head in frustration. "I wish I knew."

Peeking tentatively over Alexander's shoulder, Mara's stomach tightened in apprehension. "Alexander?"

"Hmm?" Clearly, he was lost in thought.

"Where is Malchus?"

Alexander winced.

Oh no. Mara's insides twisted in fear. "Alexander? Where is he?"

"About that..."

"Tell me he is alright!"

"It's a long story, and you wouldn't believe it even if I told you."

"Try me!"

Alexander released another frustrated sigh. "Listen, come with me to the outer court. Jesus is there. I'll tell you what happened on the way."

Reaching for her shawl, Mara slipped it over her dark hair and wasted no time hastening after him.

***

The outer courtyard was an impressive affair. Designed for the sole purpose of ushering guests into the magnificent priestly villa, the ornate, gated entrance was guarded by vigilant doorkeepers as well as guards. The palatial villa towered several stories above the sprawling open-air courtyard, where the high priest maintained a birds-eye view of anyone entering or leaving the mansion. Lush, enclosed gardens flourished on either side of the lavish courtyard. One must simply unlatch the breathtaking wrought-iron gates framed by lovely marble archways to enter the peaceful garden respites gracing either side of the great reception area.

Mara caught her breath the moment she and Alexander reached the outer court. Despite its enormity, there was scarcely room to set foot within. The crude, guttural voices of hundreds of soldiers filled the air, demolishing any remaining semblance of tranquility. Red-caped, armor-clad soldiers filled the elegant space, appearing extremely out of place as throngs of nervous servants scurried about. Menservants were busily aiding several officers as they coaxed a bonfire to life in the massive fire pit at the center of the courtyard. Mara was shocked by the appalling number of guards and Roman legionnaires surrounding the entire premises. A sea of crimson-plumed helmets formed an uncompromising border around the impressive estate.

Shivering in the cold night air, Mara drew her shawl tightly about her shoulders and allowed Alexander to guide her toward the raging bonfire. An enormous stone bench encircled the fire pit, but Mara was far too restless to be seated. Amused, she watched as servants and officers alike gathered around the warmth of the steadily rising flames like a sea of buzzing insects swarming about the light.

Attempting to still her own fierce trembling,

Mara clutched her shawl tightly about herself, her eyes scanning the overly crowded space for any sign of her Master.

"There He is," Alexander whispered grimly, gently turning her in the right direction.

Mara's heart dropped the moment she saw Him at the far end of the outer court, intentionally removed from the comfort of the fire's warmth. Jesus' wrists were tightly bound, His face and beard crusty with dried blood. His forehead was slick with perspiration despite the night's chill. Flanked on all sides by grim-looking Roman soldiers, He waited meekly with head bowed, offering no resistance.

Mara sensed that He was praying. Tears slipped down her pale cheeks, unbidden. Jesus had rescued her from her own pit of despair, and yet she must stand idly by, unable to comfort Him in His own hour of need. Heart constricting in sorrow, she glanced up at the dark, strikingly handsome man beside her and realized that he, too, was struggling with his own raw emotions.

An argument erupted on the other side of the bonfire, drawing Mara from her silent thoughts. Both men and women argued vehemently, but it was the guttural cursing of a Galilean that rose above the din, drowning out the rest.

Alexander tensed, drawing a protective arm about Mara. Surrounded by hundreds of Roman soldiers, a simple dispute could prove fatal to everyone within reach. Several soldiers turned their heads in the direction of the disturbance, their hands resting almost causally upon the hilts of their gladiuses. Sensing danger, those involved in the dispute lowered their voices, while several servants shuffled away.

A broad-shouldered, simply dressed man stalked away from the fire, his fists clenched. Watching his retreating back as he took purposeful strides toward the garden gate, Mara imagined the man was one to be reckoned with. She wondered if perhaps it had been his deep voice rising above the din moments earlier.

Somewhere in the inky darkness, a rooster crowed its lonely dirge.

Interestingly enough, several servants left their coveted stations near the fire's warmth and flocked toward the dark stranger pacing at the gate.

Mara's curiosity grew. Who was he, and why were the servants so interested in harassing him? He did look vaguely familiar. Where had she seen him before?

She looked to Alexander and saw that he, too, was watching the mysterious man.

"By the gods," Alexander declared under his breath. His color deepened when Mara looked at him disapprovingly. He realized he possessed several choice habits he must now break. His speech was certainly going to require serious revision.

"I know that man," Alexander hissed as he turned on his heel to approach the newcomer.

"Alexander, wait," Mara pleaded, grabbing his sleeve. She recognized the determined look on Alexander's face. He was not interested in pursuing a friendly conversation with the Galilean.

Fiercely agitated, the person of interest had stepped onto the porch leading into the privately enclosed garden with a glistening fountain at the center, but Caiaphas' servants surrounded him, hemming him in.

"He's the man who tried to kill Malchus!" Alexander ground out, his dark eyes fierce. "He will pay for his rash act!"

"But, Alexander, Malchus was healed!"

"Does that excuse his repulsive behavior?"

"Remember whom you now follow," Mara reminded him gently.

Just then, the disciple erupted in anger, drawing the attention of several stoic guards. Shaking his head vehemently, the disciple pushed past the servants of Caiaphas and stalked toward the fire... and directly toward Alexander.

Several nosy servants scurried after him like baby chicks pursuing the mother hen. They talked over each other in their excitement as the disciple drew alongside Alexander and Mara, presenting a rigid back to them as he warmed his calloused hands by the fire.

"Surely you are one of them; for you are a Galilean, and your speech betrays you!"

"Yes, surely this fellow was with Him!"

"Is he not a Galilean?"

Alexander raised cold eyes toward him then, his tone filled with icy calm. "Are you not the one they call Simon Peter? The sword-wielding coward?"

Peter's face contorted in both fear and fury the moment he recognized Alexander.

"Ah, I thought so."

"Alexander," Mara begged quietly, tugging at his sleeve. "Leave it alone. Please."

Instead, Alexander took a step closer, crowding him. "Did I not see you in the garden with Him?" he dared. "You spineless coward!"

Mara cringed, instinctively covering her ears when the Galilean fisherman released a string of angry profanity, his blazing eyes shifting about like a wanted man's.

"I swear, I don't know this Man!" Peter cried out fiercely, his guttural accent bespeaking his nationality. "I told you, I don't know this Man of whom you speak!"

"Then who are you and why are you here?" another servant demanded.

The angry exchange was cut short by yet another lonely cry from a rooster, cutting through the nighttime sounds and the hiss of the crackling fire like a sharpened knife.

Peter's eyes snapped open, realization and horror washing over his frantic features bathed in flickering orange firelight. Following Peter's desperate gaze, Mara realized that his eyes were fixed upon his bound, beloved Teacher.

And Jesus' tender gaze was upon him, His soft eyes wet with tears that slipped down his bloodied cheeks and fell into His beard. Something passed between them that Mara could not understand.

Releasing a guttural cry of horror, Simon Peter grasped his face with filthy hands and fled the courtyard, crashing into the darkness of night.

CHAPTER 53

Alexander

The night trial was a screaming farce.

Somehow, Alexander had convinced Mara to retire to the gardens to pray. Emotions were running on overdrive and the stakes were just too high tonight. Disaster lurked just below the surface, and he didn't want Mara anywhere near it.

Lurking just beyond the great marble hall, Alexander listened intently as the former high priest, Annas, interrogated Jesus while the Sanhedrin noisily assembled themselves, preparing themselves for the trial. Not only had Annas once possessed the prestigious priestly title, he was also the father of Caiaphas' sophisticated wife, Miriam.

Disturbed by what he was hearing, Alexander couldn't help but wonder about his cousin's whereabouts, not to mention his fate. Was Caiaphas even aware of Malchus' absence? Had Lucius already gleefully reported his glaring failure? If he'd harbored any doubts before, Alexander was now convinced that Caiaphas possessed not a shred of mercy... or integrity.

Shaking his head in disgust, Alexander decided to worry about his cousin later. Right now, he needed to stay informed about the trial.

It galled him every time he considered the blatant hypocrisy of these religious ignoramuses. In the first place, this night trial was completely illegal. As Mara had stated, no capital trial could lawfully commence at night.

And yet, Jesus was bound and presented before the Sanhedrin with one clear goal in mind: His execution.

To add insult to injury, Caiaphas had conjured up a puppet jury. Many of the elders and chief priests responsible for plotting Jesus' arrest were now to be His "impartial" judges. And certain members of the Sanhedrin known to be sympathetic toward Jesus' cause were intentionally uninvited and uninformed.

In a cool, controlled tone, Caiaphas ordered Jesus to state His case before the Sanhedrin.

Alexander's heart jumped at the sound of the Creator's voice, and with it came the sharp and bittersweet recognition: *My sheep hear My voice, and I know them, and they follow Me...*

Alexander thanked God that he now recognized the voice of his Shepherd. *God, help me follow You. I don't know what I'm doing!*

"I spoke openly to the world," Jesus responded quietly, in answer to Caiaphas' cool demand. "I always taught in the synagogues and in the Temple, where the Jews always meet, and in secret I have said nothing. Why do you ask Me? Ask those who have heard Me what I said to them. Indeed they know what I said."

Alexander's insides twisted in dread at the bold admonishment.

A sharp blow echoed through the marble hall, and Alexander knew that Jesus had been struck. Clenching his teeth along with his fists, he struggled to keep his cool.

"Do you answer the high priest like that?" Lucius' dark tone echoed through the vast hall, laced with bitterness and disdain.

Expectantly, Alexander waited for Lucius to be reprimanded for striking a Man not yet proven guilty. And yet, the reprimand never came.

Outrageous! Alexander trembled in his fury and mentally calculated where he might next discover Lucius alone in a dark alley.

Then Jesus' voice broke through the proceedings as He addressed the Roman soldier, clear and strong. "If I have spoken evil, bear witness of the evil; but if well, why do you strike Me?"

Alexander wondered if Lucius' insides quaked at a reprimand given by the God of the universe.

Probably not. Lucius was too dense to recognize His own Creator standing right in front of him!

The works that I do in My Father's name, they bear witness of Me. But you do not believe, because you are not of My sheep...

Perhaps Annas was growing uncomfortable with the proceedings, for Alexander heard the soft rustling of rich fabric as the former high priest rose to his feet and murmured something to Caiaphas.

Annas had spoken alone with Jesus before any of the rest. What had Jesus said to him?

Caiaphas was clearly frustrated by his relative's

sudden departure, but Alexander couldn't discern the heated words passing between father and son-in-law.

Alexander listened closely to be sure Annas would not exit via the massive archway by which he eavesdropped. To his great satisfaction, Roman guards escorted Annas from the marble hall by means of another entry point.

Holding back a smirk, Alexander imagined that Annas had good reason to avoid any further participation in this sham. After all, he had been deposed and stripped of his coveted position by the fearsome Valerius Gratus after disregarding the Roman law governing capital punishment.

The Roman government was surprisingly generous in her willingness to allow conquered nations to abide by their own ancient laws, as long as those laws did not violate or contradict Roman policy. However, if the emperor suspected that his kindness was being abused, he didn't hesitate to strip away the privileges of such a nation.

And by Roman law, the Jewish high priest maintained most of his priestly privileges. But the right to capital punishment had been stripped from him, to be determined and executed instead by the Roman procurator. Annas had sampled a taste of Rome's strict discipline after violating this law when the procurator was absent.

Alexander doubted that Annas had any interest in tempting fate again.

Coward, he thought, annoyed.

After Annas' rather hasty departure, Caiaphas now presided over the secret meeting. A slew of "witnesses" came forth to testify against Jesus, and yet their testimonies sorely contradicted each other's.

Alexander bit back a grin of amusement. Perhaps these fools wouldn't be successful in their endeavor, after all.

Even with a cloud of witnesses testifying against Him, Jesus remained completely silent. He spoke not a word of defense on His behalf, nor did He lash out at His accusers.

There was an awkward pause as an unsuccessful witness shuffled away in defeat, and Alexander realized that Caiaphas had run out of witnesses.

Crossing his arms over his chest, Alexander leaned against the cool stonework just beyond the marble hall, relief washing over him.

Did this mean it was over?

The voice of Caiaphas broke through the silence, harsh and condemning. "Well?" he demanded, his sarcasm echoing and reverberating off the stone walls. "Do You answer nothing?" he challenged scathingly. "What is it these men testify against You?"

Nothing but worthless, fabricated nonsense, Alexander wanted to shout.

Caiaphas' challenge was followed by glaring silence.

Then Caiaphas' voice rang out, and Alexander nearly shuddered at the dark presence seeping from the marble hall, emanating from the form of a devil in priestly robes. "I put You under oath by the living God," Caiaphas stormed, and a fearsome hush fell over the entire Sanhedrin.

How dare you, Alexander thought, his heart pounding like a war drum. *You know nothing of the living God! You serve your father, the devil. You are a great deceiver, sweeping in to scatter the very sheep you were called to shepherd!*

I am the good Shepherd, Jesus had said. *The good shepherd gives His life for the sheep. But a hireling, he who is not the shepherd, one who does not own the sheep, sees the wolf coming and leaves the sheep and flees; and the wolf catches the sheep and scatters them…*

Did Caiaphas even recognize whom he was serving? Was he intentionally feeding his sheep to the wolves? Didn't he realize that the wolf would eventually come for him, too?

"Tell us if You are the Christ, the Son of God!" Caiaphas demanded stridently.

Alexander drew in a sharp breath, breaking out in a cold sweat. Caiaphas was crafty indeed. His witnesses had utterly failed, and now Caiaphas attempted to draw a confession from Jesus' own mouth!

Despite the fact that a tried individual could not be lawfully convicted by the words of his own mouth, Alexander doubted that would matter to the high priest. Caiaphas stood before Jesus upon an elevated dais, condemning Him for breaking the very law he himself so shamelessly manipulated.

"Are You the Christ," Caiaphas persisted, "the Son of the Blessed?"

"I am."

Had Alexander simply imagined the raw power resonating behind those two simple words? Drawing as close as he dared toward the elegantly tiled entryway, Alexander craned his neck and listened carefully.

"Nevertheless," Jesus continued steadily, His voice flooding Alexander with hope and warmth, "I say to you, hereafter you will see the Son of Man sitting at the right hand of the Power and coming on the clouds of Heaven."

One could have easily heard a pin drop at the stunned silence that followed. An intense dread had swept over the entire assembly, and for a moment, Alexander imagined a trembling Caiaphas standing before the throne of a just God.

His thoughts were interrupted by the sharp rending of fabric followed by the shocked gasps of the assembly.

Unable to resist, Alexander chanced a peek around the corner. Red-faced with fury, Caiaphas was tearing at his robes, ripping the delicate fabric in two.

Swiftly, Alexander withdrew, his breathing labored. Surely his eyes had deceived him! Even he – an unreligious Greek – knew that God Himself forbade the Jewish high priest to tear his priestly robes! Alexander couldn't help but wonder if the Almighty would tear Caiaphas' priestly position from his hands just as easily as Caiaphas had rent his own garments.

"What further need do we have of witnesses?" Caiaphas thundered as the Sanhedrin erupted in mad applause.

How convenient, seeing as you don't have any at all! Alexander fumed silently.

"You have heard the blasphemy!"

Loudly, the Sanhedrin voiced their agreement.

"He has spoken blasphemy!" Caiaphas spat out again, fanning the flames of hatred within each heart. "What do you think? What say you?"

"Death!" grown men screamed, near hysteria. "He is worthy of death!"

Pressing himself against the cool stone wall, Alexander shut his eyes and prayed fiercely as Caiaphas neatly ended the illegal session, dismissing the Sanhedrin.

A sea of severely clad men poured past him, but Alexander scarcely noticed them and no longer cared if his presence was known. So be it. Let one of them accuse him if they dared!

Once the marble hall was emptied of its foul occupants, Caiaphas was left alone with Jesus and a slew of Roman soldiers.

Alexander knew that Caiaphas addressed Lucius when he stated with devilish calm, "Have your way with Him."

Crumpling, Alexander's back slid against the cool stone until he was sitting on the cold floor, knees drawn up, his face in his hands. Cruel soldiers descended upon the gentle Savior like filthy carrion birds hungry for human flesh.

"Blindfold Him!" Lucius commanded, and hobnailed sandals rushed to perform the soldier's cruel bidding.

The sounds that followed were too dreadful to bear as the soldiers attacked their Maker, spitting upon Him and mocking Him as they did so.

Lucius' acrid tone rang out above the rest. "Prophesy to us, Christ!" He sneered. A disabling blow echoed and resounded through the staid marble hall as the high priest stood by, observing coolly. "Who is the one who struck You?"

The good Shepherd gives His life for the sheep...

Therefore My Father loves Me because I lay down My life that I may take it again. No one takes it from Me, but I lay it down of Myself. I have power to lay it down, and I have power to take it again.

The good Shepherd gives His life for the sheep...
Burying his face in his knees, Alexander wept.

CHAPTER 54

Malchus

Hundreds of brightly burning torches formed an ominous barrier around the palatial house of Caiaphas. Even from Malchus' distant vantage point, the house shone brightly from its hilltop perch. Malchus imagined hundreds upon hundreds of Roman sentries standing guard, weapons belted at their sides and deadly spears glistening in the eerie firelight.

Pacing nervously about a broad, stone avenue near Caiaphas' estate, Malchus agonized over the still small voice bidding him to return.

Return? To the dragon's lair? How could he possibly do something so foolish? And yet, the still small voice persisted, urging him straight toward the lion's den.

Groaning, Malchus dropped heavily upon a bench cut into the intricate stonework lining the Upper City's fashionable streets. A torch sputtered quietly above his head. Cloaked in darkness, the streets remained ghostly silent.

Touching his ear, he marveled anew at the miracle he had experienced. If not for the fresh blood staining his tunic, he would have sworn it had been a dream. But no, it had really happened. Jesus had restored him, despite his faithlessness, doubt, and cynicism. He had sought to preserve his own life and nearly lost it in the process.

In that moment, he had resolved never to make that mistake again.

But now this... was God truly calling him back to Caiaphas' estate? Would he ever fully understand the concept of losing his own life for the sake of Christ? Would it always be this dreadful, this mind-numbingly terrifying?

The haunting sound of a grown man weeping floated upon the still night air, interrupting his silent musings.

Malchus straightened upon the bench, instantly alert. Muffled at first, the sounds grew louder until great, heaving sobs shattered the silent night. A broad-shouldered, shabbily dressed man stumbled toward him, weeping like an inconsolable child.

Malchus stiffened. Was this man mad? Drunk? Possessed?

Was his own life in danger?

Insides churning, Malchus watched warily while the man stumbled toward him like a drunkard. Too close for comfort, the stranger paused in the middle of the quiet street, bending at the waist and planting his hands on his knees as he attempted to catch his breath. His chest and shoulders heaved with the effort as nervous sweat soaked his ragged garments. Entirely unexpectedly, the stranger clenched his fists before straightening to his full height. Throwing his head back violently, he released an anguished scream that nearly curdled Malchus' gut.

Perhaps, Malchus thought, suppressing his own panic, if he remained very quiet, very still, the madman would stumble past him and he would remain unseen.

Removing shaking hands from his dirt and tear-stained face, the stranger lifted tired red eyes toward Malchus.

Malchus winced in fearful expectation. Was it acceptable to pray to become invisible?

The madman looked Malchus straight in the eye and both men instantly stiffened in recognition.

"You!" they gasped in unison.

Malchus sprang to his feet, fists clenched. "You tried to kill me!"

"You got in the way."

Malchus' eyes widened in shock at Simon Peter's arrogance. "You have got to be kidding me!"

"The blow wasn't meant for you," the Galilean said through clenched teeth.

"Is your aim always so bad?"

"My fists have proven more effective than my sword."

"Well, that wouldn't take much," Malchus snorted in disdain.

"Perhaps you'd like a demonstration," Peter snarled, his fists tightening at his sides.

Malchus released his breath in frustration. "Just save it. We serve the same Master now."

At that, Peter's eyes filled anew and he looked away, his color deepening in shame. Rubbing the back of his neck, he shook his head. "I'm sorry about that, man."

Malchus sensed that he truly meant it. Peter stood before him, a broken man. It seemed petty to argue now, with their beloved Teacher in chains. Peter had reacted in panic and blind rage. Could Malchus fault him for that?

Shifting uncomfortably, Malchus rubbed the back of his neck. "Think no more of it." Another thought occurred to Malchus, one too terrible to consider. "Please tell me they have not executed Him without a trial."

Peter ran a nervous hand through his dark hair. "They have Him in custody. That's all I know."

"Were you there?"

"I left."

"What happened?"

Peter released a shaky sigh, his very presence conveying the deepest kind of sorrow. "I betrayed Him."

Malchus' eyes narrowed in confusion. "*Judas* betrayed Him."

"They were asking me about Him, right there in the courtyard," Peter said vehemently, shaking his head in fierce agitation. "I was afraid. What if they arrested me, too? I said I did not know Him."

Malchus understood Peter's grief. "I denied Him, too. For years. Surely He will pardon one moment of weakness on your part."

"I denied Him *three times*," Peter nearly shouted, his fists clenching angrily at His sides. "How could I do it, man? How could I betray Him?" Sitting heavily upon the stone bench, Peter buried his face in his hands, shoulders shaking as sobs racked his body again.

Malchus didn't know what to say.

"He told me it would happen," Peter managed shakily. "I didn't believe Him."

"How did He know?"

"He knows everything – everything! But we were too stubborn and arrogant to believe Him. He said He would be betrayed and arrested. He asked us to pray for Him, but we couldn't even do that small thing." Peter shook his head in agony.

"Wait," Malchus interrupted, staring at Peter's desolate form upon the bench beneath the flickering torchlight. "He knew He was about to be arrested?"

Peter looked at him bleakly. "He said He must go to Jerusalem and suffer many things from the elders and chief priests and scribes. But those vultures have been after Him for years. They've never succeeded in capturing Him! Why should we have believed it would be any different now?"

"But it was," Malchus mused, wishing he had paid far more attention to the scrolls he had shared with Melina. Hadn't they read about the Messiah?

"Yes, it was," Peter wept brokenly. "In every way."

"How did He know?"

"He knows all things. We should have listened to Him."

"What else did He say?"

Peter looked at him then, his red-rimmed eyes hopeless and empty. "He said He would be crucified."

"Crucified?" Malchus drew back, repulsed. The Roman method of criminal execution was the most degrading, humiliating, shameful, and excruciating death imaginable. "We cannot let this happen!"

"Careful," Peter said from somewhere deep in his throat. "I said the same thing, and He rebuked me for it."

"You defended Him, and He rebuked you?"

"I couldn't bear to hear Him prophesy His own destruction. When He said He would be killed, I said, 'Far be it from You, Lord; this shall not happen to You!' and He turned to me and said almost fiercely, 'Get behind Me, Satan! You are an offense to Me, for you are not mindful of the things of God, but the things of men.'"

Malchus stared at Peter incredulously. "He called you Satan?"

"I am ashamed, so ashamed," Peter groaned, his head in his hands. "He addressed Satan because I was allowing the enemy to speak through me."

"Can the devil do that?"

"If you'd been walking with us, seeing what we've seen these past few years, you wouldn't even ask that question," Peter said, his eyes haunted. "Just as the Spirit of God can guide a man, the enemy also uses willing vessels as his chosen instruments of destruction. In that moment of weakness, I allowed him to use me to discourage Jesus in His mission."

Malchus contemplated Jesus' response to Peter. *You are not mindful of the things of God, but the things of men.* Malchus realized that he, too, was worthy of Peter's reprimand. He had run from God for years, seeking to preserve his own life by his own practical logic – man's way – rather than God's.

"I see it all so clearly now," Peter groaned. "Before His arrest, we had our supper with Him in an upper room. He wanted it to be meaningful, but we were all so busy vying for recognition and attempting to attain the places of honor that we scarcely paid Him any mind. We thought He was about to establish His kingdom. James and John even had the nerve to ask for the places of honor at His right and left hand. The rest of us were furious, and we weren't about to let the Sons of Thunder upstage us. John managed to sit at Jesus' right hand, while Judas snagged the seat on His left. I was just relieved that James didn't get it."

Malchus wondered where Peter was going with this. Having dwelt in the house of Caiaphas for over a decade, Malchus understood the politics behind seating arrangements and places of honor. It would seem Jesus' disciples did, too.

"We had thrown the supper together in such haste that we hadn't thought to hire anyone to serve us," Peter continued shakily. "Not that we could have afforded to hire anyone even if we'd thought of it. So, there we were in the upper room, arguing about who was to perform the menial tasks and spouting off about who was the greatest and worthy of the highest role. I am ashamed to admit that we had forgotten all about Jesus by that point. We had just taken our seats when we realized we had failed to wash the dust from our feet." At this, Peter lowered his head, tears dropping into his lap. "We knew supper could not commence until our feet had been washed, but there was no servant available to do the job. We'd just spent the last half hour arguing, contesting for the highest positions. The large basin loomed before us, beckoning someone to stoop to the task. I must admit, I considered doing it myself. But then I realized that if I did, my fate would be sealed forever – I'd be the one washing their dirty feet for the rest of my miserable existence and performing whatever menial tasks the others scorned. And I wasn't about to do that. Nor was anyone else willing to set that precedent for himself. The Sons of Thunder were staring at me, just daring me to do it. And I wasn't about to give in." Shaking his head, Peter wept again brokenly, his words nearly incoherent. "Jesus had just been speaking to us about servanthood. 'The kings of the Gentiles exercise lordship over them,' He had said. 'But not so among you; on the contrary, he who is greatest among you, let him be as the younger, and he who governs as he who serves.' But we were too deaf to hear His message. Instead, we harbored selfish ambition and pride. Every single one of us knew what needed to be done, but no one took the towel. While we sat there staring at each other, refusing to be branded the slave, Jesus rose from the table. Without a word, He removed His outer garment, took a towel, and girded Himself. I'll never forget the look on His face in the soft lamplight. There were tears in His eyes. Then He just lifted the basin and knelt before each of us."

"He washed your feet?" Malchus asked incredulously.

"He washed *all* our feet – even Judas'. I've never been more ashamed in my entire life – until that moment when I denied Him in the garden." Peter's shoulders shook with tremendous, gut-wrenching sobs. "All along, He's been trying to teach us, but we've been so blind! He was honest with us from the very beginning, and yet we all had our own ideas about what we wanted Him to do for us."

"And He knew you would deny Him in the courtyard, too?" Malchus asked, captivated by Peter's sorrowful recollection.

"He did. And He said that Satan had asked for me, to sift me as wheat."

Chills skittered up and down the back of Malchus' spine at the thought of the devil asking for anyone, let alone the broken man before him.

"But Jesus said He had prayed for me so my faith wouldn't fail. But it did," Peter cried out in shame. "My faith *did* fail."

"Simon Peter, it isn't over yet." Malchus wondered where the words had come from even as he spoke them.

Peter met his gaze and something flickered within those fierce, dark eyes.

"What else did Jesus say?"

"He said…" Peter's voice trailed off as he struggled to recall one of the last conversations he had shared with his Savior. "He commanded me to strengthen my brethren after I had returned to Him," he finished, his eyes widening in hope.

"Jesus said you would return to Him?"

"But how can I?" Peter mourned. "They are going to kill Him."

"I'm new to all of this," Malchus said quietly. "But perhaps faith has something to do with it."

Peter looked at him then, his expression thoughtful. "You remind me of someone I heard long ago – a prophet speaking in Jerusalem. I was scarcely a man at the time. The prophet said the Messiah would come soon. His proclamation resonated deep within me despite the jesting crowd. I have thought of him many times since. In fact, I saw his face as clear as a bell the day Jesus called me. I knew his words had come true. That man stood firm, despite great opposition. He looked somewhat like you."

Malchus' stomach tightened as his throat nearly closed. "Was he preaching at Solomon's Porch?"

"He was. They called him Daniel, I believe. He was murdered shortly after that. Why? Do you know him?"

"Know him?" Malchus looked away, overcome. "He was my father."

"He said the Messiah would make atonement for our sins," Peter said cryptically. "And here we are, ushering in the Passover week. In the past, the blood of the sacrificial lamb covered our sins. But at supper, Jesus instituted a new system. He said His body would be broken and His blood would be shed for the remission of sins."

Malchus studied Peter, the pieces beginning to fall into place for him.

"I believe Jesus is about to sacrifice Himself in our stead," Peter said hoarsely, rising slowly from the bench. "He will become the ultimate sacrificial Lamb. His blood will cover our sins."

Everything Malchus had learned as a child at his mother's knee came rushing back to him in that instant. The sacrificial system, the blood of the covenant, the need for atonement.

Melina had once said that the Messiah wouldn't save them from the Romans – instead, He would save them from themselves! It was beginning to make sense, and that new knowledge presented a stunning blow as well.

"Jesus is going to die," Malchus managed, his voice sounding strained in his own ears. "They're going to kill Him. This is what the prophets have foretold all along." Even his father had known.

"Oh, God, my God." Peter's eyes filled with all the desperation in the world. "We should have seen this coming."

CHAPTER 55

Mara

"Did you sleep at all?"

At the sound of his voice, Mara went to meet Alexander as he closed the distance between them with long, powerful strides. When he paused before her, she gazed up at him bleakly.

"I thought not. Neither did I," Alexander muttered, looking more agitated than she had ever seen him.

The gardens were cool and peaceful at this early hour. Overhead, the pastel colors of dawn still streaked across the morning sky like the delicate brushstrokes of a skillful artist. Mara wondered how the sky could possibly reflect such breathtaking beauty when its Creator had been committed into the hands of wicked men.

"Was there another trial?" Mara asked, her eyes filled with expectation.

Alexander hated to crush her high hopes, but he couldn't lie. "The trial commenced at dawn, but it was merely a repeat of the illegal gathering they hosted last night."

Mara's eyes clouded with tears of disappointment.

"When I consider the arrogance of those men..." Alexander's voice trailed off. With his anger boiling just below the surface, he didn't want to say anything he would regret in front of Mara. "This is a joke, Mara. No man could possibly be condemned under such circumstances!"

Mara shook her head in frustration. "Caiaphas is manipulating the very law he falsely condemns Jesus for breaking."

"That's a monumental understatement," Alexander muttered. "Caiaphas illegally tried a capital offense. On top of that, the former high priest, Annas, examined Jesus last night before the trial even commenced, which of course, is also unlawful. The witnesses were clearly bribed, and the incriminating verdict was obtained by the words of Jesus' own mouth. They have no evidence of a crime, no proof. Only the testimony of one Man, despite the fact that their law clearly states they must have at least two or three witnesses."

"There's even more than that," Mara added quietly. "Caiaphas knows he cannot try a man on a feast day. And yet, that's exactly what he has done."

"And the judges who condemned Him were anything but impartial," Alexander groaned, raking a hand through his jet black hair. "Many of the judges even participated in His arrest. This is unbelievable."

"Surely Caiaphas has no grounds to condemn Jesus under these outrageous circumstances," Mara said hopefully.

"Well, we may have just gained a leg to stand on."

"There is hope?" Mara asked, her tone pleading.

"Annas has counseled against carrying out an execution without the approval of the Roman procurator. They are taking Jesus to Pontius Pilate as we speak. Right now, they're hoping that Pilate will accept the Sanhedrin's guilty verdict and order a crucifixion. But if anything I've heard about the governor is true, he won't accept the word of any Jew, high priest or not."

"Pilate detests Jews," Mara affirmed sadly. "But wouldn't that make him all the more eager to exterminate one?"

"Perhaps Pilate will exact his rage on Caiaphas instead," Alexander said ruefully. "Wouldn't that be thrilling?"

"Thrilling, yes. But it won't happen that way."

Both Mara and Alexander turned in surprise at the unexpected voice behind them.

"Malchus!" Mara cried, running to meet him. She halted midway and blanched at the sight of his bloodied tunic.

"I'm fine," Malchus assured her, crossing the garden to meet them. "Did Alexander fill you in?"

"He did, but you still look frightful!"

"I'll change in a minute. First, something must be said." Malchus met Alexander's gaze. "Cousin, you were there for me when I needed you."

Alexander's eyes flickered in surprise. "This doesn't mean I have to like you now," he said, jabbing Malchus' shoulder.

"I must ask your forgiveness for –"

"Nonsense," Alexander interrupted, a bit uncomfortable with the unfamiliar warmth and joy spreading through him. "I must ask for your forgiveness a thousand times over."

"All is forgiven," Malchus said with great conviction. "Mara?"

Mara looked at him with soft eyes.

"I must ask for your forgiveness as well."

"Oh, Malchus, you already have it," Mara assured him, squeezing his arm.

"Unfortunately, we're going to have to continue these touching sentiments at a more opportune time," Alexander inserted with a wry grin. "For now, we must focus on the matter at hand. Malchus, you think you know how this is going to end?"

"When I spoke with one of His disciples, it became startingly clear," Malchus explained in a rush. "But if Jesus is being taken to Pilate, there's little time to explain now if we want to stand by Him until the end. Allow me to slip into a fresh tunic and I'll fill you both in on the way to the Praetorium."

***

Julia

Barabbas will die today.

Bleary-eyed and heartsick, Julia set aside her plush covers and lifted herself slowly from her canopy bed. She was certain the precious child within her had grown heavier overnight, and yet even that could not compare with the heaviness of her aching heart. With one hand resting on the small of her sore back, she managed to swing her bare feet over the side of the bed.

The glorious, golden sunlight pouring through

an open window did little to ease her sorrow or dismiss her impending sense of doom.

Resisting the overwhelming exhaustion threatening to claim her entire being, Julia forced herself to rise slowly from her bed. She had tossed and turned half the night, alternating between muffled sobs and silent, stinging tears.

Crossing the room upon trembling legs, Julia rested her forearms upon the windowsill, remembering a night long ago when Barabbas had met her here. She had found it terribly romantic at the time, until he had lost his temper with her. That night, she had responded in alarm after he had revealed his decision to join the Zealots.

How different their lives might have been had Barabbas made a different choice.

Julia knew very little about criminal justice – especially the brutal Roman version of it. But she was certain that her husband would suffer dreadful torment before drawing his final breath. The thought was nearly unbearable. But the knowledge that most plagued her was the fact that he would die alone.

I could go. I could stand at the base of his cross, comforting him until he dies. Julia was alarmed by the train of her own thoughts. Why, it was absurd! Crucifixions were gruesome, bloody ordeals. Did she even have the stomach to witness the sordid execution?

If I were sentenced to die today, I would want someone there to stand beside me. It was settled. Despite her doubts and gnawing fears, Julia squared her shoulders and prayed for strength. She was still married to Barabbas, despite his many sins. He had failed her, but God's love never failed. Perhaps God had granted her this opportunity to demonstrate His unfailing love toward her husband one last time.

Blinking back tears, Julia swept open her closet doors and selected one of the plain garments she had brought from her home in the Lower City. After dressing, she combed and braided her hair, washed her face, donned a simple head covering, and left a hastily scrawled note for her parents upon her gilded vanity. She would not disturb them, for their villa was practically overflowing with guests – family members staying for Passover. Besides, she knew her compassionate father would feel obligated to accompany her if she informed him about her daring and possibly reckless venture. His tender heart would break at the sight of tortured men, regardless of their violent criminal records.

Slipping quietly out of the sleeping, palatial villa, Julia hastened toward the imposing fortress of Herod Antipas. Since it was the Passover week, the governor should be residing there. She could only hope that her husband would be presented at the Praetorium before being forced to shoulder his cross.

**

"Julia!"

Surprised by the unexpected address, Julia turned and saw Mara approaching her at a near gallop, parting through thick crowds of people like Moses and the Red Sea. Relief flooded Julia's entire being. Just moments before, she had been filled with alarm, for the city was in a state of turmoil unlike anything she had ever seen. The sound of the swelling crowds was deafening, and she had been pushed, shoved, and jostled by harried travelers more times than she cared to recount. Sheltering her unborn child with protective hands, Julia hurried to cross the distance between herself and her welcome friend.

Gripping Julia's shoulders, Mara pulled her into a full embrace, laughing when Julia's bulging belly got in the way. "Look at you!" Mara exclaimed, her eyes shining with joy. "You will be cradling a little one in your arms before you know it."

"If I am not trampled first!" Julia laughed, noticing as Malchus and a strikingly handsome young man drew up alongside them. "Malchus!" she exclaimed, sadly remembering her last conversation with Melina. Had circumstances improved between them? "It is good to see you."

"Julia, it's good to see you too. There's much more of you than I remember seeing last time," Malchus remarked dryly with a meaningful glance at her round belly.

A bit embarrassed, Julia looked toward the young man next to Malchus in question.

"Ah, this is my cousin," Malchus hurried to explain. "Alexander."

Alexander offered an overly dramatic bow. He was a bit darker than Malchus, with smooth olive skin, jet black hair, dark flashing eyes, and a clean-shaven chiseled jawline. Even so, he did remind her quite a bit of his younger relative.

Julia arched a brow in question. This was the famous Alexander she had heard so much about?

Sensing the direction of her thoughts, Malchus chuckled in amusement. "I'll have to fill you in."

"Apparently!" Julia agreed, her lovely eyes alight

with curiosity.

"Are you going to the Praetorium?" Mara asked, her eyes clouding with sadness.

Julia was shocked. "How did you know?"

"Everyone in the city knows," Alexander remarked, amused by Julia's reaction.

"About Barabbas?" Julia asked, puzzled.

"Your husband?" Clearly, Mara was not following.

"That's why I'm trying to get to the Praetorium. Barabbas will be crucified today."

"Oh, Julia." Mara reached for her, drawing her close.

Malchus and Alexander exchanged uncomfortable glances. There were no words to comfort a woman in Julia's situation. Malchus supposed he should have seen it coming. Barabbas was a dangerous criminal. Still, he ached for Julia. How she must be suffering! And a little one on the way, too.

"Julia," Mara said very gently, "I'm afraid you must not have heard about Jesus' arrest."

Julia's heart constricted. "Oh, no. When?"

"Last night. He was tried before the Sanhedrin late last night and this morning, but Caiaphas is determined to see Him crucified. He's being tried before the governor at the Praetorium now," Mara explained.

Julia lowered her gaze, unwilling to display the tears filling her eyes. Would she lose her husband and her Savior today? Good heavens, were they to be crucified side by side? Was it even possible for the Savior to die? She didn't know.

"God was gracious to arrange this meeting," Julia managed after a long, silent struggle. "I'm not sure I could bear this alone."

"You won't have to," Mara put in stoutly, taking her hand. "We'll be right here beside you, Julia, until the end."

Holding back tears, Julia nodded her deepest thanks.

"I do hate to be insensitive," Alexander cut in, his expression strained, "but we should really hurry."

"It's alright; I understand," Julia assured him. "You're right. We should hurry."

"Malchus, you must tell Julia about your encounter with Peter last night," Mara said as they resumed their hurried trek toward the palace, mindful of Julia's hindered pace. "Julia needs to know everything before we arrive."

With a solemn nod, Malchus launched into a succinct recount of recent events. He had a lot of ground to cover before they reached the palace, and there wasn't time to mince or waste words.

With a heavy heart, Julia listened to the tragic tale of Jesus' late-night arrest, the miraculous conversions of both Malchus and Alexander, and the unexpected encounter with Simon Peter.

Malchus seemed convinced that Jesus was about to sacrifice Himself for the sins of the entire world. Frightened and confused, she couldn't bear to even consider her newfound Savior suffering upon a Roman cross. She couldn't imagine a world without the sweet presence of Jesus dispelling the rising darkness.

Oh, dear God, please give me strength.

CHAPTER 56

Julia was certain she was about to faint with expectation when the notorious Roman procurator, Pontius Pilate, finally emerged from a magnificently arched, heavily curtained entryway upon the low-hanging balcony overlooking Gabbatha, the marble pavement where hundreds of screaming and shouting Pharisees, Sadducees, scribes, elders, soldiers, and commoners had gathered. The Jewish accusers had refused to set foot within the Roman Praetorium, or judgment hall, within Herod's palace, vehemently stating that they would be defiled and therefore rendered unclean and deemed unfit to participate in the Passover festivities that stretched before them.

Julia could scarcely believe her own ears. These pompous, self-important religious leaders were certain they would be defiled by stepping into a secular building, and yet they possessed absolutely no qualms whatsoever about killing an innocent Man!

"Start praying," Mara whispered, reaching for Julia's hand.

"I haven't stopped," Julia replied, squeezing her hand in response.

"Then keep it up," Alexander said grimly. "This isn't looking good."

Scanning the vast crowd assembled at The Pavement, Julia had to admit that Alexander was right. Never had she witnessed such bitter hatred upon the faces of human beings. It was as if a dark presence had settled over the crowd, fanning their flames of hatred and deepening their animosity. Heavily drifting clouds obscured the brightly burning sun overhead, casting dark, slanting shadows upon the people gathered below.

Shuddering, Julia wondered if she was simply imaging the dark forces at work swirling all around her, raising the gooseflesh upon her skin and sending unwelcome chills skittering up and down her spine.

"I'm not even sure if I'm praying correctly," Julia admitted as Pilate crossed the large balcony and planted two steely fists upon the marble railing. This was her very first glimpse of their governor, and it wasn't promising. He was a lean, muscular man of military bearing, his glowering countenance colder than stone. He looked terribly Roman, donning richly embroidered garments that bespoke his high station, and yet his fashionable princely apparel did little to soften the man. Strong, bronzed arms peeked out from beneath the white linen sleeves, and his muscled calves appeared too large for his carefully tied sandal straps.

"What do you mean you don't know if you're praying right?" Malchus asked, his eyes never straying from Pilate. "Is there a wrong way to pray?"

"You say that Jesus will die either way," Julia said shakily. "What, then, should I pray for?"

"Pray that my cousin is wrong," Alexander put in dryly. "It wouldn't be the first time."

"No," Mara said gently, always a peacemaker between the two cousins. "Remember how Jesus taught His disciples to pray?"

A lump formed in Julia's throat. Her dearly missed neighbor, Deborah, had told her all about the Lord's famous prayer before departing on another journey. Perhaps Deborah was here even now, hidden amongst the crowd. "Thy kingdom come," she whispered softly. "Thy will be done."

"Thy will be done, Lord. Not mine," Mara repeated fervently, her eyes swimming with tears. "His will is always right, even when we can't see it."

"What accusation do you bring against this Man?" Pilate's voice rang out over the crowd, deep, threatening, and ominous.

Julia marveled at the way his voice boomed over the vast expanse of The Pavement, but she supposed Herod the Great, an architectural genius, had built this magnificent section of his palace with acoustics in mind. Surely the quality of sound here rivaled even that of his grand theatre!

"Well?" Pilate growled, leaning over the low-lying balcony. A sea of heads covered in plumed helmets or prayer shawls stretched out a few feet beneath him. The alarming number of religious leaders coupled with Roman soldiers presented startling evidence that both church and state had united to destroy Jesus and everything that He stood for. "Your accusation?"

The crowd erupted in mad fury, screaming over each other and shouting out accusations.

"I will address the high priest," Pilate roared, and

the crowd grew silent with alarming speed.

They must truly fear this man, Julia thought, her stomach turning in fear.

"Your charge?" Pilate repeated, a muscle twitching in his firm jaw.

Joseph Caiaphas stood front and center, just below the glowering Pilate. Unlike his associates, Caiaphas was not intimidated by Pilate's fearsome scowl. "If He were not an evildoer, we would not have delivered Him up to you," he said coldly, his gray eyes challenging.

Julia glanced at Malchus and noticed that his fists were clenched by his sides. She wondered how he must feel, knowing that this man possessed the power to ruin him... or worse.

Pilate laughed harshly, derisively. "And I'm to simply take your word for it, Priest?"

"Why ever not, our dear Pontius Pilate?" Alexander mused sardonically, his arms crossed in amusement.

Caiaphas' face turned scarlet with fury.

"Your petty and frivolous religious qualms are none of my concern," Pilate continued harshly, and Julia breathed a sigh of relief even as the crowd tensed in fury. "You take Him and judge Him according to your own Law."

Caiaphas' jaw twitched in bridled rage even as he answered pointedly, "It is not lawful for us to put anyone to death."

A hush of anticipation fell over the sea of onlookers as they awaited Pilate's response.

Pilate's brow arched. "You seek a death sentence?"

Caiaphas' curt response was cold as ice. "Crucifixion."

The crowd erupted in delirious shouts of approval and Julia was nearly rocked by the force of it. The mob of angry men and women was like one massive, living beast, breathing and spewing putrid fire, eager to devour the innocent. They moved and breathed as one, pumping balled fists into the air, rocking to and fro, shouting and screaming.

"You have yet to present your accusations against Him!" Pilate nearly snarled, his knuckles turning white as he gripped the marble ledge and towered over the crowd.

At that moment, several armed soldiers escorted Jesus onto the balcony.

Julia's heart constricted in sorrow. Bound, bruised, and bleeding, Jesus spoke not a word in His defense. Her heart broke at the sight of Him.

The appearance of Jesus had the completely opposite effect on most gathered on The Pavement. Religious men in severe garb broke rank, drawing alongside Caiaphas and shouting out accusations against Jesus.

Pilate looked to Jesus then, ignoring the feverish mob. "Do You answer nothing? Do you not hear how many things they testify against You?"

Jesus stood quietly upon the balcony, His hands bound before Him, His eyes downcast.

"Well?" Pilate snarled, irritated by the jarring silence. "See how many things they testify against you! Will you say nothing?"

Even then, Jesus held His peace.

Pilate shook his head, clearly marveling at Jesus' restraint.

The crowd exploded with further accusations, hungry for the death of the innocent Man on the balcony.

Annoyed, Pilate raised his hands and the mob quieted, though it was obvious it took a monumental effort on their part. "As you are incapable of speaking plainly, I will again address your priest," Pilate barked, an unsightly vein bulging in his forehead. His face continued to redden in suppressed fury. Clearly, his Friday morning was not proceeding as planned. "Priest, what is your charge?"

Caiaphas drew himself a bit taller, his hands clasped religiously before him. "We found this Man perverting the entire nation."

Pilate rolled his eyes at Caiaphas' dramatic charge.

Julia's attention was drawn from the riveting scene when Malchus shook his head in disgust. "This is unbelievable. Caiaphas knows Pilate couldn't care less about Jewish law, so he's trying to turn Jesus into some political revolutionary. What a joke."

"Surely Pilate has better sense than that," Mara exclaimed passionately. "Not once has Jesus instigated revolt or political unrest!"

Fueled by Pilate's sarcasm, Caiaphas' eyes darkened as he said coldly, "I should have hoped you would have been more concerned about such charges, Governor."

Pilate's dark eyes bored into the priest's, cold, challenging.

"Not only has this Man forbidden us to pay taxes to Caesar, He says that He Himself is Christ, a *King*." Caiaphas' eyes narrowed as he waited for the magnitude of that charge to sink in. According to Roman law, anyone claiming kingship directly opposed their revered emperor.

Pilate paled, his eyes flickering slightly at the final accusation. Emperor Tiberius was extremely jealous of his title. Not only that, but Sejanus, a ridiculously cruel and powerful confidant of Tiberius, was particularly zealous in guarding the sacred title. Sejanus would not hesitate to stamp out one minor politician like Pilate to make an example of him.

Julia's heart sank.

"Outrageous!" Alexander ground out, his eyes flashing. "Caiaphas is a vile snake."

"You're just figuring that out?" Malchus snapped, clearly agitated.

"Caiaphas knows that Pilate would be a fool not to examine that last charge," Alexander groaned. "It's treason."

"Treason," Malchus repeated in disbelief, "punishable by death. In the Roman mind, it's the worst crime a citizen could commit."

"How else was Caiaphas to convince Pilate to convict Him?" Alexander said, shaking his head in disgust. "That wicked priest knows what he's doing."

"If Pilate chose to ignore a charge like that and word reached the emperor, Pilate would be executed instantly," Malchus said grimly. "This just got a lot more interesting."

"Is it true that Pilate has fallen out of the emperor's good graces?" Mara asked, a bit embarrassed to repeat the ugly gossip of the day.

"It is," Malchus responded grimly.

"Then I'm afraid Pilate is going to be even more careful not to upset the emperor in any way," Mara acknowledged sadly. "And he would be taking a huge risk by dismissing Caiaphas' charge."

Julia scarcely heard her friend's worried dialogue. She was far too heartbroken at the sight of her Savior and the thought of her condemned husband. She couldn't help but wonder if Barabbas' execution would be delayed as a result of the madness and mayhem. Perhaps that would allow him more time to repent. Attempting to focus on the present conflict, Julia lifted her gaze toward the obstinate governor and the pernicious high priest.

A slow, predatory smile crept over Caiaphas' face as Pilate sternly contemplated the accusation against Jesus of Nazareth. Julia was sickened by it. She would have loved to ask one of the nearby soldiers to wipe the smugness right off the priest's pompous face.

Without another word, Pilate turned and disappeared through the elegantly curtained entryway by which he had come. One of the soldiers roughly grabbed Jesus' shoulder and shoved Him headlong through the opening as several more soldiers trailed behind them.

Julia was amazed that Jesus offered not the slightest bit of resistance. Quietly, willingly, He accompanied the stern-faced soldiers.

"What is happening?" Julia asked, her heart pounding so rapidly she feared it might harm the baby. Forcing herself to take slow, measured breaths, she placed a hand over her abdomen, seeking solace from her unborn child.

"It looks like Pilate has decided to question Him privately," Malchus muttered, his eyes scanning the vacant balcony. He couldn't help but hope to catch a glimpse of Melina. He ached to see her again, to tell her about his newfound faith. How was she taking this? If only there was some way to comfort and shield her.

"It's a smart move on Pilate's part," Alexander asserted. "No man could possibly think straight with all these filthy hyenas screaming for his attention."

"What do we do now?" Julia asked weakly, accepting Mara's comforting squeeze.

"We wait." Malchus' expression was exceedingly grim.

"We wait?" Julia repeated bleakly, her eyes wet with tears. "I've never been very good at that."

"I've yet to meet someone who is. I've never been one to wait either," Alexander replied ruefully, exchanging a knowing look with Mara that made her blush. "But I'm learning, despite my own cursed stubbornness."

The look that passed between Mara and Malchus' former nemesis was not lost on Julia.

"We can do more than simply wait," Mara said, her eyes shining with hope and unshed tears. "We can pray."

Bowing their heads, the four unlikely friends offered their earnest prayer to the God of the universe even as the entire world reeled beneath their feet. "Our Father which art in Heaven, hallowed be Thy name…"

Despite her roiling fears and doubts, Julia knew one thing with absolute certainty: God's Kingdom would, in fact, come. And His will alone would be done. The kingdom and the power and the glory were His forever.

And she believed.

CHAPTER 57

Melina

Melina went about her chores woodenly, her heart quaking as raucous shouts and violent cheers erupted from The Pavement from the opposing palace wing. Melina knew it must be an enormous crowd to create such frightful mayhem. She could scarcely believe that her beloved Master stood on trial before Pontius Pilate. How she longed to stand beside Him, to speak on His behalf! But what could she – an insignificant handmaiden – possibly do to influence the hands of powerful, dangerous men?

"Melina?"

Turning at Chuza's address, Melina wasn't surprised to see the tall overseer standing with arms crossed at the doorway of Salome's vacant chamber. "Please tell me you have good news, my brother."

Chuza's eyes darkened, his righteous anger lurking just beneath the surface. He offered one curt shake of his head.

Melina's eyes filled with disappointment.

"It is the Lady Procula," Chuza said, his tone betraying his own great caution.

Melina's slender brows rose in surprised question. "The governor's wife?"

Chuza nodded, his expression enigmatic. "Claudia Procula has summoned you."

***

Melina entered the grandiose chambers of the governor's wife with the caution of one stumbling across a dragon's lair. Of what possible interest could *she* possibly be to an aristocratic woman like the Lady Procula? She was absolutely astounded that the powerful woman even remembered her!

After being unceremoniously ushered into the large room by a very solemn-looking manservant, massive gilded double doors were shut behind her with a creaking *thud* of finality.

Watchfully, Melina allowed her eyes to scan the perimeter of the impressive suite. Several nervous handmaidens fluttered about, attending to various chores. Sheer sunlight poured in from arched, oversized windows, the lush Babylonian tapestries drawn aside and tied back with luxuriant golden cords. The room was breathtakingly furnished, slightly less opulent than Salome's former suite.

But it was the elegant woman seated in a straight-backed gilded chair, her slender arms resting calmly upon the bronze armrests, that completely stole Melina's attention. The grandeur of the great room paled in comparison with the burning intensity of this woman's dark eyes, the urgency of her rigid stance. Claudia Procula still possessed the grace and poise of a queen even in her agitated state, and one wouldn't think to question the royal blood flowing through her veins. Her legs were crossed gracefully, and lovely folds of rich, exquisitely embroidered garments draped her slender figure, pooling about her elegantly sandaled feet.

At Melina's hesitant entrance, the woman turned her head, her delicate amphora earrings tinkling slightly with the graceful movement. Her abundant brown hair was arranged atop her head in a simple yet sophisticated Roman style that bespoke her desirable status and position.

Feeling slightly choked, Melina offered a respectful curtsy and said rather shakily, "It is a pleasure to see you again, my lady. How may I serve you?"

Claudia Procula's dark eyes studied her with great perception. It was unnerving. Melina sensed the woman could see into her very soul. When Procula finally spoke, Melina was completely unprepared for the question that issued forth from Procula's fair lips.

"Melina," Procula said, her eyes pinning Melina in place, "are you a follower of Jesus?"

Her softly spoken inquiry was a like a punch in the gut. Melina was certain that the breath had left her lungs. Trembling, she realized that Malchus' admonitions had likely come to fruition. Her life was about to end.

Oh, it was a very simple question, requiring a mere *yes* or *no*. But Melina understood that her life now hung in the balance. Whether she lived or died was entirely dependent upon the answer she chose to give. But even as fear closed its cold, ugly talons about her rapidly beating heart, Melina knew she could not deny her Lord. She had been privileged to live for Him. It would seem she was now granted the privilege of dying for Him as well.

In that dreadful moment of silence that seemingly stretched into eternity, Melina's throat closed as she thought of Malchus, the man she loved so fiercely. Would he turn his face against God forever if she perished? She thought of her dear friend Julia and her swollen belly, the precious newborn child she would never meet. Her mind was filled with the memory of a faithful prophet chained in a prison cell, awaiting certain death. Some of his final words to her rang in her mind now with the clarity of a crashing cymbal: *Though He slay me, yet will I trust in Him. He has never failed me in life. He will not fail me in death.*

Yes, it was indeed a struggle, for her flesh urged her to cling stubbornly to life. But her struggle was only momentary. *Whoever desires to save his life will lose it, but whoever loses his life for My sake and the gospel's will save it...*

"Melina?" Procula's smooth, cultured voice drew the handmaiden from her private struggle. "I must ask again: Are you a follower of Jesus?"

Melina raised clear eyes to the Lady Procula, bathed in a peace she could not comprehend. "Yes, I am."

Procula rose to her feet then, her long gown trailing behind her with a soft rustle of fabric as she drew one hand to her pale forehead. "Oh, I am so relieved."

Melina stared at Lady Procula, stunned.

"I suspected," Procula continued, shaking her head in disbelief, "but I couldn't be sure until I asked you directly."

"M-my lady?" Melina managed through trembling lips.

"Oh my! I see I have given you a terrible fright," Procula exclaimed, dismayed. Taking Melina's hand, she drew her toward the gilded chair and helped her sit down. "You are pale as death."

"I thought perhaps I would soon be facing it," Melina chuckled a bit shakily.

"I can see why you might think so," Procula agreed, feeling Melina's clammy forehead with the back of her smooth hand the way a caring mother would. "I should not have been so direct. I'm afraid I can be terribly frank at times."

"I admire your honesty, my lady," Melina said, and she meant it. It was a rare trait in a woman of Procula's class. "Are you a follower as well?"

"I'm not sure," Procula admitted, her regal features troubled. "But after today, perhaps I should be."

With great effort, Melina held her tongue and her peace. How she longed to persuade this kindly woman to make a decision for Christ!

"I am afraid for my husband," Procula continued, kneading her temples with slender, tapered fingers as she paced before Melina. "Jesus of Nazareth is a just Man, and the people are hungry for His blood."

Melina waited, perched nervously on Procula's impressive, throne-like chair. She felt ridiculously out of place.

"This is a dreadfully precarious position for my husband to find himself in," Procula explained, a beam of fresh sunlight slanting across her queenly form. "I cannot imagine the outcome will prove favorable for him regardless of the decision he makes."

Melina agreed with Procula's assessment.

"Melina, I need to know what is happening, but my husband has forbidden me to observe the trial. He fears for my safety, and I can understand why – the roar of that unruly mob makes me quake inside. But how can I sensibly advise him when I am tucked away in this comfortable suite?"

A worthy question.

Melina drew in a sharp breath when, unexpectedly, Procula bent gracefully before her, taking both her hands. Procula's dark eyes burned like fire as her lovely face fairly glowed with earnest intensity. Melina met her gaze, her own luminous green eyes filled with questions.

"Melina," Procula said, her tone urgent, "I believe I can trust you, and I need your help."

CHAPTER 58

This assignment was unlike any she had ever received.

Suppressing a shudder, Melina stole quietly past rows and rows of imposing marble pillars, her stomach churning and her insides quivering in fear. Procula's urgently spoken words still rang loudly in her ears: *I must know what is happening. Simply tarry near the Praetorium, gleaning whatever information you can.*

Alarmed by the overwhelming number of Roman guards flanking the Praetorium, Melina averted her eyes from their wolfish grins and glistening spears. Attempting to appear as casual as possible, she slipped beneath a low-hanging archway and entered the enormous Judgment Hall. She was completely unprepared for the bruised and bloodied form of her Savior, and her heart nearly broke at the sight of Him.

Jesus stood before Pilate with His head bowed, His bound hands clasped patiently before Him. Despite Pilate's glowering countenance and the vast host of armed guards spilling out of the Praetorium and filling the surrounding area, Jesus displayed not a hint of fear. Melina marveled at the calm acceptance and quiet resolve that radiated from His very being.

Slipping nonchalantly amongst the curious bystanders gathered within the sprawling marble hall, Melina wondered fleetingly if these were observers from the streets of Jerusalem or simply members of Pilate's staff. They were obviously Gentiles – most likely Greeks or Romans – since the Jews refused to set foot within the Judgment Hall during Passover week. Were commoners even permitted to enter the Praetorium to observe ongoing trials? She didn't know. If discovered, would she be punished?

Attempting to combat her rising distress, Melina's gaze traveled toward the front of the room where Pilate stood questioning Jesus before an elegantly curtained entry point leading out to the overhanging balcony. The ominous clamoring and tumult of the murderous mob below drifted through the entryway, raising the hairs on the back of her neck. Unsettled, she nearly jumped out of her skin when Pilate's hard voice rang out unexpectedly.

"Are You the King of the Jews?" Pilate demanded impatiently, his countenance truly fearsome to behold.

Jesus raised calm, knowing eyes to meet Pilate's steely gaze. "It is as you say."

Stunned gasps along with snickers of derision swept through those assembled in the Praetorium, drawing a sharp stare from the agitated procurator. The crowd quieted instantly, and Pilate returned his scowling attention upon the accused.

Much to the surprise of everyone in the room, Jesus addressed Pilate again. "Are you speaking for yourself about this," He asked quietly, "or did others tell you this concerning Me?"

Melina's heart nearly melted. Did the governor realize that Jesus was offering him the chance to accept Him as king of his own heart as well? *Please, God, Melina prayed, for the sake of Lady Procula as well as his own, open Pilate's eyes to Your truth.*

But Pilate's countenance only darkened as the lines around his steely eyes hardened. "Am I a Jew?" he spat out incredulously, his infamous hatred for the chosen race evident in his very stance. "Your own nation and the chief priests have delivered You to me! What have You done?"

Surprised, Melina realized she was not the only one in the crowd leaning forward, tensely awaiting Jesus' response with bated breath.

"My kingdom is not of this world," Jesus explained patiently, His eyes never leaving Pilate's cynical face. "If My kingdom were of this world, My servants would fight, so that I should not be delivered to the Jews; but now My kingdom is not from here."

Pilate frowned, clearly pondering the gravity of Jesus' confession. His expression was so telling that Melina could nearly read the thoughts barreling through his sharp mind: Jesus had said His kingdom was not of this world *now*. But would that change someday? Would He, in fact, rule the world? Or was He simply a deranged lunatic who had somehow succeeded in accumulating a rather impressive following?

"Are You a king, then?" Pilate demanded, and Melina noticed that his tone was slightly less skeptical this time.

"You rightly say that I am a king," Jesus replied,

and Melina was amazed by the humility that some-how resonated from that remarkable statement. "For this cause I was born, and for this cause I have come into the world, that I should bear witness to the truth," Jesus said, His eyes shining with power. "Everyone who is of the truth hears My voice."

"*The truth*," Pilate scoffed, shaking his head in derision. "Tell me, what *is* truth?"

What is truth? Melina's heart cried, anguished to witness the hardening of yet another heart. *Oh, Pontius Pilate, can't you see? You are looking into the very face of Truth! Jesus is truth!*

Annoyed by what seemed to him a mystical and lofty statement, Pontius Pilate turned on his heel and vanished onto the balcony.

***

Julia

The mob erupted in frenzied, defiant shouts the mo-ment Pontius Pilate emerged from the Praetorium and stalked across the balcony. Waving their fists and screaming defiantly, they rocked back and forth like the unrelenting waves of the sea, their voices nearly as thunderous.

"The governor has returned," Mara announced pensively, taking Julia's arm and leaning in close.

Malchus and Alexander straightened, their dark eyes narrowed, their expressions cautious and drawn.

Tensely, they watched as Pilate gripped the mar-ble railing, his muscled forearms taut. Setting his jaw, Pilate allowed his dark eyes to scan the mob below before stating harshly, "My verdict shall be pronounced upon my judgment seat on The Pavement. I advise you to consider the heavily armed guards surrounding the perimeter as I state my case."

Without another word, Pilate vanished into the Praetorium once more.

Feeling faint, Julia dabbed at her perspiring brow with her shawl. "Why must he keep us waiting?"

"The verdict must be rendered from the judgment seat," Malchus explained, having to raise his voice to be heard above the din. "I suppose it will be brought out to The Pavement since the Jews refuse to enter the Praetorium."

Observing the wild behavior of the crowd, Julia grew nervous. "Do you suppose Pilate will instruct the soldiers to engage? Was he threatening us when he mentioned the armed guards?"

More than once, Pilate had commanded Roman soldiers to dispatch rowdy Jews swiftly and violently in the midst of revolt. His great cruelty had been formally reprimanded by the emperor himself.

"That depends," Alexander mused, arching a dark brow. His eyes traveled to Julia's bulging belly. "Mara, perhaps we should help Julia home. This could become dangerous fast."

"I won't leave," Julia said uncompromisingly. "The Shepherd knows His sheep, and Jesus is aware of the followers standing with Him. I will be here for Him, not matter what happens."

Malchus and Alexander exchanged looks of deep concern.

"God will protect me," Julia insisted. "And what of my husband? I still don't know when he will be executed. I need to know. I need to be here."

"Very well," Alexander stated resignedly, his lips forming a thin, grim line. "Soon Pontius Pilate should arrive with his armed guard for protection. We can make a more informed decision once he has stated his verdict."

***

Mindful of Pilate's warning, the crowd remained tensely, terribly silent as the monumental judgment seat was mounted upon The Pavement. Even so, the tension in the air was paralyzing, suffocating. It was as if a dark cloud of fearsome animosity had settled over the crowd, relentlessly fanning the flames of violence harbored within their hearts. The thundering silence was almost worse than the raucous fury, for Julia was tormented by her own harrowing thoughts in the stillness. Rather than dwelling on them, she prayed silently, beseeching God to perform His will. *Give me the strength to bear this, whatever happens,* she prayed desperately.

Tensely, Julia watched as Pilate climbed several stone steps and seated himself upon the judgment seat. He grasped the gilded arms of the chair with such strength that Julia wondered if they would snap. Still bound, Jesus was led onto The Pavement by a band of wary soldiers, their eyes nervously scouring the agitated mob. Hobnailed sandals pounded against stone as military reinforcements poured onto The Pavement from every direction, their armor catching the bright morning sun.

A strange hush settled over the crowd like a puff of hot wind on a summer day. It was uncomfortable, unsettling.

Pilate's steely gaze scanned the sea of accusers with contempt. His lip curled slightly as he stated in a booming voice that bode no argument, "I find no fault in this Man."

Julia nearly fainted in relief, but her consolation was immediately cut short. Instantly, the silence was shattered by a deafening uproar capable of awakening the dead. Men and women screamed with reckless abandon, shouting out their protests as their faces contorted grotesquely in hideous rage.

Julia had never seen nor heard anything like it. The unholy cacophony echoed and reverberated off the stone walls, chilling her to the very core.

Enraged, Pontius Pilate threw himself into action, rising from his seat and raising an implacable hand. His color deepened in fierce anger as he towered above the people. "I find no fault in Him at all," he reiterated, his booming voice echoing out over The Pavement.

The menacing roar of the mob was chilling. In the midst of the hair-raising frenzy, Caiaphas drew as close as he dared to the judgment seat, his priestly garments resplendent in the bright morning sun. "Would you be so foolish, Governor? So naïve?"

Pilate's countenance hardened into a chilling scowl.

"Would you so easily pardon this Man?" Caiaphas dared, his gray eyes challenging. "He stirs up the people, teaching throughout all Judea, beginning in Galilee to this place."

Pilate raised a thick brow in question, his expression shrewd, calculating. "Did you just say *Galilee?*"

***

Melina

"Please tell me that my husband acquitted that just Man," Procula said the moment Melina was ushered into her suite.

Lowering her gaze, Melina clasped nervous hands before her.

Rising from her gilded chair, Procula began to pace gracefully before the row of arched windows. "Tell me what happened."

Melina drew a nervous breath and said quickly, "You will be relieved to know that the matter is now out of her your husband's hands, my lady."

"Out of his hands?"

"Yes, my lady. He has delivered Jesus to Herod Antipas."

Procula stood very still. "But why? Jesus of Nazareth should have been acquitted. He is innocent of all wrongdoing."

Surprised by Procula's declaration, Melina replied, "Your husband discovered that Jesus' ministry began in Galilee, which is Herod's jurisdiction."

Sighing quietly, Procula paused before an open window, her expression troubled. Melina knew what she was thinking: Pontius Pilate had taken the cowardly way out.

"Your husband did proclaim Jesus' innocence, my lady," Melina tried to assure her. "But the people refused to accept his verdict."

"I suppose I should be relieved that my husband is no longer caught in the middle of this," Procula said softly, crossing the room and seating herself in the gilded chair. "Thank you for keeping me informed, dear one."

Melina was touched by the warmth in this woman's address. "It is truly an honor to serve you, my lady."

"May I ask one more thing, Melina?"

Melina was stunned to be asked anything. As a maidservant, she was expected to perform instantly. Whether or not she wished to perform a task was not even taken into consideration. "Of course, my lady."

"I want to know the verdict of Herod Antipas."

Surprised by the uncompromising tone of this gentle woman, Melina nodded her understanding. "As soon as the verdict is pronounced, I shall return to you, my lady."

***

Julia

Pontius Pilate returned to the Praetorium and Jesus was led across the compound to the opposing wing of the palace where Herod Antipas resided. Those waiting on The Pavement grew increasingly agitated and violent as they awaited Herod's verdict.

With all her heart, Julia wished they had been permitted to follow the procession of soldiers escorting Jesus toward the notorious tetrarch. Her heart had ached as they led Him away. She felt as if He was slipping away from her, and she couldn't bear it.

"I'm confused," Mara said, perplexed. "Pilate clearly pronounced Jesus' innocence from the judgment seat on The Pavement – not once, but twice! Why, then, is He being sent to Herod?"

Malchus and Alexander exchanged knowing looks.

"This trial has been a farce from the very beginning," Malchus said gruffly, running a nervous hand through his dark, wavy hair. "According to Roman law, Pilate's verdict of acquittal was officially rendered from the judgment seat. The trial should have ended and Jesus should have been released."

"But He wasn't," Mara mused sadly.

"Of course not! Why would they bother with legality now?" Alexander scoffed.

"But why was He sent to Herod Antipas?" Julia asked, wondering if Melina would be privileged to glimpse her Savior one last time. She certainly hoped so.

Malchus' mouth tipped in amusement. "It's no secret that Pontius Pilate and Herod Antipas detest each other. Herod is constantly harping about Pilate stepping on his toes and meddling in his own jurisdiction in Galilee."

"So Pilate was all too willing to oblige Herod by sending him an inconvenient prisoner from Galilee," Alexander added. "After getting caught in the middle of this, I doubt Herod will be so quick to gripe about Pilate stepping on his toes in the future."

"Didn't Herod Antipas murder Jesus' cousin, John the Baptizer?" Mara asked uneasily.

"He did," Julia replied sadly, remembering the gruesome details Melina had recounted.

"Then I am afraid he won't possess any qualms about executing Jesus, either," Mara said, grieved. "Herod Antipas has no fear of God."

"It's certainly looking worse rather than better," Alexander agreed, his dark eyes flashing at the injustice of it all.

"Meaning?" Malchus asked grimly, the two women at his elbow looking toward Alexander with questioning eyes.

Crossing his arms over his broad chest, Alexander turned and studied the towering walls of Herod's palatial compound with glittering eyes. Massive walls and parapets shimmered radiantly, gloriously golden in the early morning sunlight. "If we thought Pontius Pilate was cruel, then Herod Antipas is the devil himself."

CHAPTER 59

Melina

Rows of stern-faced Roman soldiers lined the exterior of Herod's colossal Great Room where he often sat upon his throne on an elevated dais, rendering judgment. It was blatantly obvious that the doors were now closed to curious visitors as the trial was in session.

Heart dropping, Melina turned and nearly collided into her dear friend, Joanna.

"Joanna! How glad I am to see you," she cried, wrapping her in a warm embrace. "It's been so long!"

Joanna drew back, her luminous eyes filled with grief. "I returned after the arrest."

"Does Chuza know?"

"Of course. My husband was the first to know about my return. He is in the Great Room now. He was permitted to observe the trial."

Melina was relieved to know that someone she could trust was on the inside. "Was anyone else permitted to gain entrance?"

"Very few," Joanna replied quietly.

"Melina! By the gods, where have you been, woman?"

Melina and Joanna turned to see Elias, the cook, approaching them, his thick brows furrowed in frustration. Drawing up to them, Elias noticed the sophisticated, elegant Joanna standing beside Melina. He colored slightly, embarrassed. "My lady," the irascible cook amended before turning his attention to Melina. "I've been looking for you!"

Melina considered teasingly asking if he had been *worried* about her, but she knew he would deny it with his dying breath. Instead, she offered a pacifying smile. "Lady Procula summoned me early this morning," Melina explained, gently touching his arm in apology. "I am still under her orders."

"The *governor's wife* summoned you?"

"She did. I have served her on several occasions. She is a kind, lovely woman."

"She's certainly *lovely*," he muttered, blushing slightly when Joanna lifted a slender brow in reprimand. "Melina, I thought you should know. They've arrested your Messiah."

"I know. He can be your Messiah, too, Elias," Melina reminded him gently.

"Some Messiah – He got Himself arrested and now they want to crucify Him. And you forget, I'm more Greek than Jew," Elias muttered distractedly. "Besides, the Jews have been trumping that horn for millennia. If there really was a Messiah, He would've shown up long before now. The Messiah is a myth, the wishful thinking of a conquered nation."

Melina was surprised when Joanna spoke in her smooth, silky voice. "The prophets predicted that the Messiah would come."

"Well, He hasn't," Elias responded testily. "And I wouldn't hold your breath."

"But what of the ancient prophecies?" Joanna pressed. "Do you so easily dismiss them?"

"Quite easily. They are fanciful writings penned by equally fanciful dreamers."

"But what if the words of the prophets came to pass?" Joanna asked, her soft eyes glowing with intensity. "Even then, would you dismiss them?"

Elias shifted uncomfortably. "They won't."

"But if they did?"

Melina looked between her two friends, praying silently for her beloved Elias. She had never seen this side of Joanna before, and she had to admit that the woman had become quite the evangelist.

"If they did," Elias admitted grudgingly, "it would be rather difficult to dismiss them."

"*Surely He has borne our griefs and carried our sorrows; yet we esteemed Him stricken, smitten by God, and afflicted...*"

Melina recognized the ancient words of the prophet Isaiah the moment Joanna began to speak, and her heart sprang into her throat at a revelation so glorious she could scarcely contain herself! How could she have possibly forgotten about this passage?

"*But He was wounded for our transgressions, He was bruised for our iniquities; the chastisement for our peace was upon Him, and by His stripes we are healed.*"

"The prophet Isaiah," Elias affirmed gruffly, clearly dismissive. "What of it?"

Joanna was not to be deterred from her mission. She spoke softly, distinctly, directly to Elias' stubborn heart. "*All we like sheep have gone astray; we have turned, every one, to his own way; and the Lord has laid on Him the iniquity of us all. He was oppressed and He was afflicted, yet He opened not His mouth; He was led as a lamb to the slaughter, and as a sheep before its shearers is silent, so He opened not His mouth. He was taken from prison and from judgment, and who will declare His generation? For He was cut off from the land of the living; for the transgressions of My people He was stricken. And they made His grave with the wicked – but with the rich at His death, because He had done no violence, nor was any deceit in His mouth.*"

"I should get back to the kitchen–"

Joanna wasn't finished. "*When You make His soul an offering for sin, He shall see His seed, He shall prolong His days, and the pleasure of the Lord shall prosper in His hand. He shall see the labor of His soul and be satisfied.*"

"Might be rather challenging to be satisfied with His labor if He's dead," Elias grumbled. "Killed with the wicked and buried with the rich, remember?"

"*By His knowledge,*" Joanna finished with a graceful sweep of her hand, "*My righteous Servant shall justify many, for He shall bear their iniquities... He poured out His soul unto death, and He was numbered with the transgressors, and He bore the sin of many, and made intercession for the transgressors.*"

Chills scurried up and down Melina's spine as she considered the wonder of this passage. Why, Isaiah had predicted everything that would happen! How had she forgotten such inspired words?

"I fail to see your point," Elias said, his tone challenging.

"All these things are coming to pass. We are witnesses of the Messiah's atonement."

"Oh, Joanna, how could I have been so blind?" Melina cried, shaking her head in disbelief. "God laid everything out for us – He told us exactly what would happen!"

"I wouldn't get too excited about that," Elias cautioned her. "According to your passage, the Messiah is going to die an ugly death."

"He will," Joanna said solemnly, her eyes moist. "And He will be killed with evildoers and buried with the rich."

"A happy ending, eh?" Elias scoffed.

"Yes," Joanna said, her voice strong. "Because Jesus will rise from the dead. In the weeks before His arrest, He warned us multiple times that He would be arrested, tried, and crucified. His words are coming to pass."

"He's read the ancient scrolls just like we have," Elias argued, crossing his arms over his barrel chest. "Perhaps He's simply trying to make it seem as if the prophecies are being fulfilled."

"If that's all there is to it, it shall prove rather challenging to raise Himself from the dead then, won't it?"

Joanna had his attention now. "What do you mean, raise Himself from the dead?" Elias demanded, his dark eyes narrowed.

"Jesus said He would die, but He also said He would rise again on the third day, and this passage supports that as well. The Messiah is clearly put to death in Isaiah's passage, but in the end, He is alive. He is our atonement."

Elias shook his head, clearly critical. "I'll believe

it when I see it."

"You will see it," Joanna responded without missing a beat. "Sooner than you think."

Melina grasped his hand then, her eyes pleading. "It's true, Elias. I wouldn't lie to you."

"Not intentionally," Elias murmured, softening at her touch. "But you are naïve, Melina. You see the best in everyone and everything. Don't be so easily deceived." With that, Elias turned and stalked away, the rigid set of his broad shoulders displaying his displeasure.

"Oh, dear God," Melina prayed softly, "open his eyes. May he clearly see that he is the one deceived – deceived by a cunning adversary."

Joanna touched her shoulder sympathetically. "I stand in agreement with Melina, dear Father. May Your will be done."

***

"I have never seen anything like it," Chuza said, his voice low. "The tetrarch and his soldiers tortured Him mercilessly. They taunted, jeered, and beat Him, and yet He spoke not a word in His defense."

Melina had never seen such haunted eyes. Chuza had witnessed the unthinkable, and she ached for him.

Reaching for her husband, Joanna placed a gentle hand on her husband's strong back. "*He was oppressed and He was afflicted, yet He opened not His mouth,*" she whispered tenderly, tears sparkling in her lovely eyes. "Jesus is truly our Messiah, my husband."

Staunch as ever, Chuza nodded and squared his

broad shoulders. "We must brace ourselves," he said in his deep, strong voice. "The worst is yet to come."

"And the best is yet to be," Joanna reminded him. "God will see us through this. We must have faith."

Sequestered in the palace gardens with Joanna and Chuza, Melina wondered how much she should report to Claudia Procula. Should she divulge the ancient prophecies coming to pass before their very eyes, or should she simply state the facts? At this point, she hadn't much to share. Clearly, Chuza was not eager to discuss the trial.

As if reading Melina's troubled thoughts, Joanna said quietly, "Melina has been commanded by Lady Procula to report the verdict of Herod's trial. What can you tell us, Chuza?"

Chuza's eyes grew vague, distant. "There was no trial."

"No trial?" Joanna asked, puzzled.

"Herod Antipas is sly as a fox, crafty as a serpent. He is far too shrewd to involve himself in a trial involving treason against Tiberius. Furthermore, it's no secret that Pontius Pilate clearly acquitted Jesus of Nazareth. Herod knows he cannot legally conduct a retrial."

"Then what happened in the Great Room?" Joanna prompted gently.

"Herod has long desired to see Him. First, I believe he wished to confirm with his own eyes that Jesus is not the reincarnation of His dead cousin, John."

"How could He be?" Melina asked incredulously. "The two men were involved in ministry at the same time."

"I won't even begin to try to understand the inner

workings of the twisted mind of Herod Antipas," Chuza said coldly, his body taut. It was the first time Melina had ever heard him say anything negative about his superior. "Herod also wished to see Jesus perform a miracle. He loves a good show. He taunted and goaded Him mercilessly, pestering Him with many questions. But Herod's great interest turned deadly when Jesus refused to take his bait."

"Oh no," Joanna breathed, well aware of Herod's cruelty.

"Herod ordered a royal robe to be brought in. The robe was placed on Jesus, then the soldiers mocked Him and beat Him until He struggled to stand on His own two feet."

A small sob caught in Melina's throat, and Joanna reached for her hand. Helpless against the waves of sorrow sweeping over her, Melina blinked back hot tears. Oh, Jesus. Sweet Jesus. To think that her own selfish sins had brought all of this upon Him – it was unbearable.

"If you intend to follow this through to the end," Chuza said slowly, clearly struggling to keep his composure, "then you must brace yourselves now. You will not recognize Him when you see Him. He is swollen and disfigured. He took a fierce beating, and it isn't over yet."

Joanna went to her husband and he took her in his strong arms, a grim expression on his somber face. "You may tell Lady Procula that Jesus is being sent back to her husband without the guilty verdict the people demand," Chuza said after his wife reluctantly released him.

Melina's slender brows rose in surprise. Claudia Procula was not going to like this.

"Pilate's cowardly attempt to sidestep the issue failed miserably," Chuza stated without sympathy. "And now he must make a decision – for the Christ, or for the crowd."

CHAPTER 60

Claudia Procula rose regally from her gilded chair the moment Melina was ushered into her chambers. "Has Jesus been released?"

Melina lifted a tearstained face toward the dignified woman.

"No," Procula breathed, her voice low and sorrowful. "Herod has condemned Him?"

Struggling to harness her emotions, Melina shook her head. "I am afraid it is worse than that, my lady."

Procula paused before an open window as the crowd gathered nearby released a new wave of rabid shouts and jeers. The sound floated eerily upon the air, wafting through the open window. "Has He been killed?" she inquired, clearly striving for calm. Her typically poised expression had morphed into a strange combination of fear and incredulity.

"Not yet, my lady."

"What is it, then?"

"Herod Antipas dismissed the case," Melina stated simply.

"Herod released Him?"

"He sent Jesus back to your husband, my lady," Melina managed nervously, "without a guilty verdict."

Procula's lovely features paled as full realization sank in. The woman became so quiet, so still, that Melina grew concerned. "My lady?"

"His life is in my husband's hands," Procula murmured, her eyes filled with dread and torment.

"No, my lady." The words had escaped Melina's lips before she was scarcely aware of them.

Procula lifted one slender brow in question. "No?"

Swallowing nervously, Melina uttered a silent prayer before plunging ahead. "Your husband has no power over Him, my lady, except for what has been granted him by the one true God."

Troubled, Procula crossed the room and lowered herself wearily into her elaborate chair. "Do you speak of the God of the Jews?"

"I speak of the God of the *universe,* my lady. He is the Creator God, and Jesus is His beloved Son."

Procula stared at her, wide-eyed and clearly confused.

Breathless, Melina rushed ahead with her explanation, determined to finish before Procula summoned the guards to remove her by force. Melina knew she must sound half-mad to this refined, learned woman. "Long ago, the prophets foretold His coming. By their writings, we know that Jesus will be condemned and crucified. He will take the sins of the entire world upon Himself and become our atonement. He will do this to restore our broken relationship with His Father."

Procula tilted her head to one side, soft curly

tendrils of dark hair framing her exquisite face. "His Father?"

"God the Father, the great I Am. The one who was, and is, and is to come."

Procula's hands tightened ever so slightly upon the arms of her chair. She leaned her head back, soul weary. "I'm afraid I do not understand."

"Jesus said it this way," Melina explained, desperate for Procula to understand. "*For God so loved the world that He gave His only begotten Son, that whoever believes in Him should not perish but have everlasting life.*"

"How can this be?" Procula asked, her eyes betraying her doubt. "Has He come to judge the wicked? To condemn us?"

"*For God did not send His Son into the world to condemn the world,*" Melina continued softly, "*but that the world through Him might be saved. He who believes in Him is not condemned; but he who does not believe is condemned already, because He has not believed in the name of the only begotten Son of God.*"

"But of what use is a Jewish God to a Roman citizen like myself or my husband?" Procula asked rather sheepishly. "Surely He has no interest in saving the enemies of His people."

"We are all His people," Melina responded with great feeling. "Even I, Lady Procula. I am not Jewish, but Greek. But God sent His Son into the world to save it – *all* of it."

"But how can the death of one Man result in redemption for the entire world?"

Melina prayed silently, wishing she was far more eloquent. "My lady, it is the week of the Passover. Do you know what that means?"

"I know very little about these Jewish customs," Procula admitted. "But I know the Jewish people slaughter an innocent little lamb, believing the blood of that sacrifice covers their sins. A Passover lamb, yes?"

"God instituted the Passover long ago to point us toward this very moment in history, my lady," Melina explained, her eyes burning with fervor. "Year after year, for centuries, God patiently reminded us of what was to come. God knew that He would send His Son at Passover to cleanse us, to redeem us. You see, the blood of animals could not bring permanent cleansing. This is why sacrifices have been performed year after year. But now Jesus is our ultimate Passover Lamb. The prophets explained that He would die, bearing the burden of sin for us all. The penalty of sin is death and eternal separation from a holy God. But Jesus loves us so much that He is willingly taking our punishment upon Himself. If we accept His sacrifice and His cleansing, we will be purified. Eternal life will be ours."

"But how can He accomplish such a feat?"

"Because He is God."

"Many claim the gods of their lands and their fathers to be true. But how is one to know the truth?"

Melina drew closer, willing Procula to believe. "The proof of His Lordship, my lady, is this: He will rise again."

"But it is impossible!"

"The prophet Isaiah said He will be killed with the wicked and buried with the rich. Then He will rise from the dead. My lady, I pray that you will believe when all of these things come to pass."

The fair Claudia Procula shook her head in utter disbelief. "How could I not, if a dead Man rises from His grave?"

Warmed to the very core, Melina smiled and bowed her head respectfully. "I hope I have not spoken too freely, my lady."

"Your words both comfort and trouble me," Procula confessed, massaging her temples as if she suffered a pounding headache. "Melina, I summoned you this morning because I believe your God spoke to me by a dream, a vision, if you will."

"What did He say, my lady?" Melina dared to ask, her skin tingling.

"My soul is so troubled I cannot speak of it."

Melina lowered her head in disappointment, but she would not pry.

"But I know this Jesus is a just Man," Procula continued. "And if He is a god as you say —"

"Not *a* god, my lady," Melina dared, her heart pounding steadily in her chest. "*The* one true God."

Procula was too polite to argue, even with a subordinate maidservant. "If my husband orders Jesus' execution, his soul will be in jeopardy," she said, her voice thick with anxiety. "When I awakened from my dream, I realized that my husband is being manipulated by a powerful force. He must resist, Melina, or he will be destroyed."

"You are very wise, my lady," Melina said, praying she would not further trouble the woman. "The force you speak about is the enemy of God, the devil. He is called the destroyer because he delights in the destruction of souls."

Procula covered her face with her hands, trembling. "I believe you, because I sense his presence here." When Procula raised her head again, her eyes were filled with torment unlike anything Melina had ever seen. "And he wants my husband."

Chills wracked Melina's spine. She longed to set Procula's mind at ease, but how could she? Everything the woman had stated was true. The great deceiver had set his heart upon the destruction of Pontius Pilate and many others.

"I must warn my husband," Procula whispered, her voice thick with concern. "But how?"

"A messenger, my lady?" Melina suggested, hoping to set the woman's mind at ease. "Would you like me to locate a palace courier to deliver your message?"

"No, this is too important," Procula said decidedly, reaching for some parchment and hastily scrawling a message in large, bold print. With deft fingers, she rolled the parchment into a cylinder-shaped scroll and held it out to Melina.

Melina recoiled at the proffered scroll. "My lady?"

"You must take this to my husband," Procula said breathlessly, her cheeks flushed with concern. "You understand what is at stake. I would not trust this message with anyone else."

Melina supposed she should be flattered. Instead, she was terrified.

Rising from her chair, Procula closed the short distance between them, placing a comforting hand on Melina's shoulder. "Melina, will you do this for me? For my husband? He has no idea what he is up against."

Accepting the scroll with trembling hands, Melina imagined the same could be said about herself. Pontius Pilate often proved deadly when crossed, and the devilish mob had been rattling his cage for hours. She would be walking straight into the lion's den.

Her heart thudded with great trepidation as a frightful thought assailed her: Was she prepared to confront the king of beasts?

***

Barabbas

"For the kingdom is the Lord's, and He rules over the nations. All the prosperous of the earth shall eat and worship..."

Weary of Azarel's endless songs and nauseated by the thought of his impending execution, Barabbas gripped iron bars and clenched his teeth as sweat appeared upon his bruised brow. Hadn't this strange little man the slightest hint of sympathy?

"A posterity shall serve Him," Azarel continued, *his raspy voice somehow majestic. "It will be recounted of the Lord to the next generation –"*

"Enough!" Barabbas shouted, turning sharply on his heel to face Azarel head-on.

The bearded man in rags stood looking at him as if he had lost his mind.

"Must you continue singing your songs to one with a heavy heart?"

"They are more than simple songs."

"I don't care what they are," Barabbas hissed. "What does it matter now?"

"It matters now more than ever."

"I'm about to *die!* I have no use whatsoever for stupid songs."

"Times like these are when the inspired words

become most useful. They are truth."

Clenching his fists at his sides, Barabbas fought for composure. He would already die with a black conscience. Did he truly wish to attack this half-crazed old man, simply adding one more regret to his lengthy list?

"Who are you, Azarel?"

Rather than answering his question directly, Azarel responded with yet another ancient Scripture. "*'Now therefore,' says the Lord, 'Turn to Me with all your heart, with fasting, with weeping, and with mourning.'*"

Barabbas stared at Azarel, the hairs pricking on the back of his neck as a hollow ache began to fill the pit of his stomach. Recognition flashed across his conscience like an unexpected lightning bolt, and along with the recognition swept in great awe and trepidation.

"*Return to the Lord your God, for He is gracious and merciful, slow to anger, and of great kindness,*" Azarel reminded him gently, "*and He relents from doing harm. Who knows if He will turn and relent, and leave a blessing behind Him.*"

"You have spoken these words to me before," Barabbas said in awe. "You stood behind a row of freshly dug graves, urging me to repent."

"There is still time."

"Who are you *really*?"

Azarel smiled, a wealth of mysteries concealed behind that one simple gesture.

And then he was gone.

"Wait!" Barabbas shouted, half-crazed with hope, dread, and trepidation. "Azarel! Azarel!"

"Who in the name of the gods is Azarel?" A crude

voice snorted in the midst of Barabbas' distress. Two uniformed soldiers drew up to Barabbas' cell, their hobnailed sandals echoing off the stone floor and bouncing off the cavernous walls of the dank prison.

"Maybe he calls his conscience Azarel," the second soldier jeered.

"I doubt this one has a conscience."

"Unlikely. An imaginary friend, perhaps?"

Ignoring the soldiers' flagrant mockery, Barabbas clutched the iron bars, his face etched with confusion. "The other prisoner – the one sharing this cell – did you take him?"

The Roman soldiers snickered, exchanging knowing glances. "What other prisoner?" the first soldier sneered.

"The prisoner who was just in this cell!"

"This might come as a shock to you," the second soldier taunted, "but you're the only one behind those bars."

"I've been the only prisoner in here? The entire time?"

Both soldiers snickered derisively before the first one responded as if addressing a slow child: "The entire time."

Drawing a ring of heavy keys from his belt, the first soldier selected an ancient-looking key and turned it in the lock. There was a loud, resounding *clank* as the iron bolt was thrown back, then the prison door was opened as it creaked upon protesting hinges.

Barabbas was far too stunned to put up a fight as the soldiers pinned his arms behind his back, clamping iron shackles upon his wrists.

CHAPTER 61

Julia

"According to popular rumor, Herod Antipas has sent Jesus back to Pilate," Alexander divulged, returning after questioning several chief priests at the front of the crowd. "He did not pronounce a verdict. Apparently, he is generously allowing Pilate the privilege."

Julia touched her forehead, surprised by the heat of her own skin. She wasn't sure how much more of this she could take.

Sensing Julia's distress, Mara put a comforting arm around her. "What happens next?" she asked Alexander, her large brown eyes filled with concern.

"Pilate will be forced to pronounce a verdict," Alexander said grimly.

Malchus shook his head in frustration. "This is getting ridiculous. The people won't put up with this much longer."

As if in response to Malchus' observation, Pontius Pilate appeared with his entourage, flanked by bodyguards as he descended a massive stone staircase and approached the judgment seat on The Pavement.

"Oh God, Thy will be done," Mara continued to pray quietly, her voice quavering. "Thy will be done, Father."

As Pilate took his rightful place on the judgment seat, Julia noticed armed guards escorting not one but two prisoners toward The Pavement. The sight of the first tore at her heart. She clasped her round belly, attempting to curb her own nausea.

Bloodied and bruised, Jesus of Nazareth was escorted onto The Pavement. He stumbled on the stone steps as soldiers roughly led Him to the elevated dais upon which sat Pontius Pilate on his judgment seat. It was as if Jesus was cruelly, intentionally placed on display for all to see.

As shouts and insults rained down upon the disfigured Savior, Julia buried her face in her shawl, weeping softly. She could hear Mara crying beside her.

Oh, God, why? Julia's heart cried. *Malchus says Jesus is the Passover Lamb, that He must suffer to remove the sins of the world. But why? Why must He suffer, God? He has done nothing wrong!* Praying frantically, Julia begged the Lord to intervene. She couldn't bear this. And to think there was more sorrow yet to come! Her husband would be executed next.

Julia wiped her eyes with the corner of her shawl as the second group of soldiers escorted yet another prisoner to The Pavement. Flanked by Roman soldiers, the second prisoner mounted the stone steps and was placed on the dais. Jesus stood at Pilate's right hand, the second prisoner at his left.

Determined to see this through to the end, Julia blinked back tears and forced herself to lift bleary eyes toward the elevated dais and the judgment seat. Yes, there stood Jesus at Pilate's right hand. And on his left, a powerfully built man stood with broad shoulders thrown back, his hands bound behind him. He raised his head, his fierce eyes scanning the sea of angry men and women beneath him—

And Julia's heart nearly stopped as a sharp gasp escaped her lips. She felt Mara's gaze upon her, but she was completely unable to formulate a sentence of explanation. Her tongue felt like lead in her mouth as her heart pounded relentlessly within her chest. For there, amidst the chaos and tumult of the shrieking, devil-driven mob, Julia found herself gazing directly upon the bruised and beaten face of her husband, the Zealot.

***

Melina

Sickness washed over Melina as she mounted the stone steps, guided by Pilate's aide onto the elevated dais where she would face the governor. Pale and trembling, she clutched Procula's parchment scroll as the aide approached Pilate upon his judgment seat.

There stood Jesus at Pilate's right hand, His battered form nearly unrecognizable. A Roman soldier clutched His shoulder tightly, forcing Him to stand upright before the crowd. Trembling at His nearness, Melina allowed her tears to fall without shame.

Her heart broke for her Savior, her Messiah.

She did not recognize the prisoner on Pilate's left, but he exuded a brutal force, a restlessness, that disturbed her spirit. Judging by his split lip, black eye, and various gashes and bruises upon his person, she suspected he had taken a brutal beating either prior to or during his arrest. She couldn't help but wonder why a violent prisoner now shared the platform with Jesus.

Pilate's aide hovered nervously at the governor's elbow, for Pilate had stood and was now addressing the crowd, his deep voice carrying over the avaricious mob gathered below the dais. "You have brought this Man to me," Pilate boomed, gesturing toward Jesus with one strong arm. "Indeed, having examined Him in your presence, I have found no fault in this Man concerning those things of which you accuse Him—"

At this, the mob bellowed its rage, their shouts and jeers chilling Melina to the very core. Wrapping her arms about her slender frame, she attempted to ward off the chill settling over her.

"Neither did Herod," Pilate shouted above the din, clearly seeking an ally by which to align himself. His next few words were lost, drowned by the tumult of the murderous crowd of accusers.

"Nothing deserving of death has been done by Him," Pilate insisted, clearly at his wit's end.

Melina longed to breathe a sigh of relief, for it was obvious that Pilate was hard-pressed to prove Jesus' alleged guilt. Clearly, he had rendered his verdict, professing Jesus to be innocent. According to every law in the book – both Jewish and Roman – Jesus was officially acquitted; therefore, He must be set free.

But Melina's heart squeezed within her, for she knew the Word of God never failed. Jesus would be tormented. He would be put to death.

But He would also rise again.

She clung to that blessed hope as Pilate once more addressed the mob: "I will therefore chastise Him and release Him."

Chastise Him? Melina looked toward the piteous form of her Savior. Hadn't he been chastised enough? What more could they possibly do to Him?

***

Julia

The crowd erupted in violent fury when Pilate announced his intent to release Jesus. Jostled about like a tiny fish trapped in the currents of the raging sea, Julia reached for Mara's arm, her panic rising.

Malchus and Alexander drew closer to the women, attempting to shield them from the violence of the mob. "Julia, look," Malchus breathed, his eyes glued on the small, trembling form of his beloved on the platform. Timidly, Melina had mounted the stone steps, guided by a very important-looking person now waiting at the governor's elbow. His heart ached at the sight of her.

"I see her," Julia murmured softly, her eyes filling with tears at the sight of her husband and her dearest friend. "The other prisoner–" A small catch in her throat forced Julia to take a breath.

Malchus, Alexander, and Mara turned questioning eyes toward her.

"My husband," Julia managed through her tears.

Understanding, Mara took her hand and squeezed it. "We are here for you, dear sister."

Julia's heart skipped a beat as Pilate's voice boomed out over the vast expanse of The Pavement, now nearly bursting at the seams with rowdy occupants. "You have a custom," Pilate shouted above the din, "that I should release someone to you at the Passover."

The crowd grew ominously suspicious, guessing the direction of their governor's thoughts.

"Do you therefore want me to release to you the King of the Jews?"

"Ah, the Paschal Pardon," Alexander mused, disgusted. "It would seem our recreant governor is grasping at yet another easy way out."

"The Paschal Pardon?" Julia repeated faintly. "Is that the custom allowing the governor to release a prisoner in honor of the festival?"

"Exactly," Malchus confirmed. "Pilate knows Jesus must be released, but he also knows the people will revolt unless His release is their decision."

"Surely he knows the people will demand another's release," Mara spoke up, incredulous. "They are bent on Jesus' destruction."

"And that is why Julia's husband has been cleverly introduced as a pawn against the crowd." Alexander's shrewd mind had already put the pieces together. "Pilate will pit the men against each other: Jesus or...?" he looked to Julia in question.

"Barabbas," she supplied faintly, her pulse racing.

"Jesus or Barabbas," Alexander finished, shaking his head in disbelief. "Pilate knows these people would be out of their minds to insist on the release of a dangerous criminal." Noticing Julia cringe and Mara's reprimanding expression, he quickly added, "Dangerous by the crowd's standards, that is."

Alexander's uncharacteristic blunder was forgotten when Pilate once more addressed the crowd. "Allow me to be perfectly clear," the governor snarled, towering above the roaring crowd. "One of these men shall be released to you today. We have with us this Man called Jesus, innocent of all wrongdoing. And we have another called Barabbas, a fierce revolutionary."

Julia's heart pounded on overdrive, her eyes darting back and forth between the two prisoners on the platform. Barabbas remained tall and unbending despite his shackles. She noticed that he hadn't offered Jesus a second glance, and it broke her heart.

"Whom do you want me to release to you?" Pilate's voice rang out over The Pavement. "Barabbas, or Jesus who is called Christ?"

***

Melina

Barabbas? Melina froze, instantly recognizing the familiar name. For the first time, she examined the fierce prisoner at Pilate's left hand. He was young, powerfully built, and devastatingly handsome despite his angry wounds. She remembered her last tearful meeting with Julia. Her husband had been arrested, sentenced to death.

She couldn't believe Barabbas stood before her now. This added an entirely new dimension to an already impossible situation! Was Julia nearby, camouflaged somewhere within that roiling crowd? Just looking at the vast sea of people before her made her feel nauseous. She quickly averted her gaze, bowing her head and beseeching her God in fervent, silent prayer.

The aide chose that moment to address the governor.

"Not now, Tertius," Pilate hissed, infuriated by the disturbance.

"But, sir—"

"Not now!"

"It is your wife, my lord."

Pilate's eyes flickered, his stony gaze pinning Tertius, his aide, in place.

"She has sent her handmaiden with an urgent message, my lord," Tertius explained in a rush, sweat dampening the fair hair upon his brow.

Pilate's eyes narrowed dangerously as he turned ever so slightly toward Melina. "You may approach," he snarled, running a hand over the back of his neck in an agitated fashion.

Whispering a silent prayer, Melina approached the fearsome governor.

CHAPTER 62

Julia

Glancing at Malchus, Julia saw that his eyes were fixed upon Melina as she timidly crossed the platform and stood beside Pilate. With little more than a second glance at her, Pilate snatched the scroll she offered him and impatiently flicked it open. His features, already strained, paled as his dark eyes scanned the parchment. Noticeably upset, Pilate thrust the scroll at Melina, clearly dismissing her.

***

Melina

Preparing to flee the imposing dais, Melina turned, clutching the scroll close to her chest. Pilate was obviously unnerved by his wife's urgent message, but would he heed it or fall prey to the goading crowd?

As Tertius led her by the elbow, Melina passed disconcertingly close to Barabbas. Her heart fluttered frantically in her chest as she whispered daringly, "Your wife, Julia, has not given up on you. She prays for you even now. And God has not forsaken you."

Barabbas' fierce eyes flickered, his expression conveying his great surprise. Who was this innocent, soft-spoken young woman? How did she know him? And Julia?

"Come," Tertius hissed, clearly fearing a reprimand. "We must not speak to the prisoners."

Melina offered Barabbas a sympathetic smile as she was escorted from the platform. "God be with you," she finished with great feeling. *Oh, God, be with him. And Julia.*

Clearly baffled, Barabbas watched Melina as she descended the stone steps with a very agitated Tertius.

***

Julia

Julia couldn't help but wonder about the swift exchange that had passed between Melina and Barabbas on the platform. Her typically confident husband's stark bewilderment would have struck her as rather comical had the circumstances been very different.

"What do you think she said?" Malchus asked with great interest.

"She certainly got his attention," Alexander remarked, his curiosity piqued as well.

"If I know Melina at all," Mara mused, "she successfully and poignantly summarized the entire Gospel in three sentences or less."

Despite the great pain in her heart, Julia couldn't help but smile through her tears. *Oh God, open his heart! May he turn to you even now.*

Julia's ardent prayers were interrupted when Pontius Pilate addressed the crowd with a crisp, clear voice, his very stance betraying his fierce determination. It was as if he had been galvanized into further action by the message he had just received. "I shall ask again," his voice bellowed over the crowd. "Which of the two do you want me to release to you?"

The crowd erupted in angry shouts, and Julia was hard-pressed to decipher their tumultuous speech. Clearly they did not appreciate the options Pilate had presented to them.

"Those snakes in priestly robes are manipulating the crowd, instigating Barabbas' release," Alexander observed grimly, watching as somberly clad men weaved their way through the gatherers, vehemently conversing with the people and pressing their point with large, animated gestures.

"Already," Pilate shouted, thrusting an arm toward Barabbas, "this notorious criminal has stolen the life of a promising young man, and who really knows how many victims have perished at his hand? This man is a thief and a murderer. Consider your women, your little ones. Shall I release him to freely roam your streets again?" Pilate challenged, clearly attempting to sway the crowd in Jesus' favor.

The barbarous mob jeered and hissed savagely in response.

Sickened by the violence, Julia reached for the corner of her shawl, dabbing at the cold sweat beading her forehead. Waves of dizziness swept over her as she considered the various outcomes of this impossible situation. Try as she might, she could not conjure up a happy ending. It would seem there were only two possible outcomes: Today, either her husband or her Savior would walk free. The other would suffer a humiliating, excruciating death.

"Do you want me to release to you the King of the Jews?" Pilate bellowed, drawing Julia from her tragic reverie.

"Not this Man, but Barabbas!" came the frenzied reply, and hundreds of voices joined the ghastly chorus. "Release to us Barabbas! Barabbas! Barabbas!"

Nearly drowning in her great confusion, Julia's eyes swept over the foul mob. Hundreds of men and women screamed for her husband, a man they knew next to nothing about! She had heard hair-raising tales about the chaos within Roman arenas as hysterical men and women screamed for their favorite gladiators, causing the arena's sloping walls to shudder. She imagined the godless cacophony of the Romans' bloody arena must look and sound something like this.

Daring a glance toward her husband so very far away, she saw that he, too, was completely mystified by the crowd's response. Jesus, on the other hand, wore an expression of sorrowful acceptance that nearly broke her heart.

"What then do you want me to do with Him whom you call the King of the Jews?" Pilate demanded, great beads of sweat appearing on his bronzed face.

Prompted by the Pharisees, Sadducees, and scribes, the crowd screamed out obscene and violent suggestions.

Pilate look sickened and appalled. "What then

shall I do with Jesus who is called the Christ?" he repeated, dumbfounded. "Shall I not release Him and rather condemn this violent criminal to death?"

"Release to us Barabbas! Barabbas! Barabbas!"

"But what of this Man?" Pilate implored the crowd, clearly attempting to suppress his own alarm.

"Let Him be crucified!" The mob thundered, and hundreds of voices shook The Pavement like a mighty roar from the pit of hell. "Crucify Him! Crucify Him! Crucify Him!"

***

Barabbas

Jesus, the Christ, the King of the Jews?

Barabbas did a double take, strangely unsettled by the knowledge that he shared this platform with the One the multitudes claimed to be the Messiah. This pathetic figure was the mighty miracle-worker hailed throughout all of Judea and Galilee? This was the Man to whom Julia had pledged her undying allegiance? Barabbas had seen Jesus once or twice at a great distance, and each time he had departed from the gathering singularly unimpressed.

He was equally unimpressed now.

The Messiah will wipe out the Romans and rescue His people, he argued silently. Clearly, this Man couldn't even save Himself, much less an entire nation.

"Crucify Him! Crucify Him!" The crowd continued to rage like a rabid beast, growing even more ferocious.

Drawn from his uncertainty by the ferocity of the mob, Barabbas straightened his shoulders, attempting to maintain a confident stance. Even as the mob cried out his name, he knew that they were fickle. They simply demanded his release to vent their wrath upon Jesus of Nazareth. Barabbas recognized Pilate's indecision and realized that his own deliverance was far from guaranteed. This wasn't over yet.

"Crucify Him?" Pilate repeated incredulously, clearly appalled. "Why? What evil has He done? I have found no reason for death in Him."

The mob grew even more insistent, their shouts devilishly ominous. "Let Him be crucified! Crucify Him, crucify Him!"

Stroking his chiseled, clean-shaven chin, Pilate shook his head in amazement, his sharp eyes scanning the crowd gathered below the elevated dais. Barabbas knew what Pilate was thinking: revolt was imminent. He had to give these people what they wanted or risk his own neck.

***

Julia

Confusion swept over Julia when Pilate commanded a basin of fresh water and linen cloths be brought to him. The lines in the governor's hardened face deepened as he observed the mayhem gravely, clearly deep in thought. Several menservants delivered the requested items, ceremoniously setting the basin and pitcher upon a tall marble-topped table they had brought with them.

Pilate stepped forward grimly, pushing aside the lavish material draping his arms. With great solemnity and dignity, he proceeded to wash his hands with the pitcher and basin.

The crowd grew eerily silent, perplexed by Pilate's strange actions. A proud Roman official publicly performing a Jewish ritual? It was as if the entire assembly held its collective breath, awaiting Pilate's explanation.

Taking a pristine linen cloth and carefully drying his hands, Pilate turned once more and addressed the baffled crowd. "You are all witnesses," Pilate declared, his eyes roving over the people with an air of challenge, "that I have washed my hands of this entire matter. I am innocent of the blood of this just Person."

The crowd shrieked their approval, recognizing that Pilate was about to turn Jesus over to them. "He must be crucified! Destroy Him! Destroy Him!"

"You see to it," Pilate bellowed in disgust. "As for me, I am innocent of the blood of this Man."

"His blood be upon us and our children!" The cry of defiance rose like a swelling wave, beginning with the priests at the head of the assembly and resonating violently throughout the entire gathering. "His blood be upon us and our children!"

Julia clutched her shawl tightly about her, trembling in horror. "Surely Pilate understands that his indecision *does* constitute a choice," she said, her voice quavering slightly. "Jesus said, 'He who is not with Me is against Me.'"

Alexander's mouth tipped cynically, his eyes resting upon the scowling Pontius Pilate. "I suppose the governor must have missed that part."

CHAPTER 63

Melina

Lingering near The Pavement's overly crowded borders, Melina observed the trial with a heavy heart. What on earth would she tell Lady Procula? The kindly woman would be utterly devastated by her husband's wavering indecision and cowardice.

Bowing her head, she began to pray. She prayed for God's will to be accomplished. She prayed for the strength to bear it. She prayed for Julia, her heart breaking for her closest friend. And she prayed for Barabbas.

Oh God, snatch his attention by the might of Your hand. Overwhelm him with the knowledge of Your great love. Grant him Your salvation.

***

Julia

Something gently stirred within Julia's aching heart. What was it? *Hope*, perhaps? Instantly recognizing the still, small voice that had faithfully guided her through many heartaches and victories, Julia bowed her head and heeded the call to prayer. Her lips moved fervently as she silently formed the words bubbling up within her spirit. The clamor of the fierce mob faded into the background as Julia drew strength from her Maker, praying for her husband with a fervency she had never before experienced.

***

Barabbas

Barabbas resisted the urge to hope as Pilate stepped forward, his hard expression etched with deep irritation. "You have made your decision," he declared, his voice thundering over the enormous crowd. "Today, I release to you Barabbas, charged with theft, murder, and treason. Jesus, the One you call the Christ, shall be crucified in his stead."

The crowd exploded in shouts and cries of approval, a mighty roar that shook the very Pavement upon which they stood, completely unfazed by the governor's glowering countenance.

It was in that fateful moment that Jesus, the Son of God, turned and looked directly at Barabbas. And in that crucial moment, Julia's prayers of many years, untold tears, and countless sleepless nights were answered.

Barabbas' heart of stone was instantly, utterly shattered, for all the love and faithfulness of the entire world was conveyed in that one look upon the swollen, bruised, and bloodied face of Jesus Christ, the Savior of the world. That one look would be forever etched upon his soul, dispelling Barabbas' hatred and stubborn doubts, casting aside all fear. That one look pierced his very soul, rousing memories of the past – moments when God had reached for him. Moments in which he had stubbornly resisted.

"*If you wish to find a fitting target for your rage, Barabbas, then look no further than the enemy of your soul, the devil. He is a cruel adversary, and terribly cunning. He has earned his title, the great deceiver. He is the one wreaking havoc on this earth while shrouding himself in mystery and lurking in the shadows. You are only hurting yourself by refusing the God who loves you.*" Julia's voice haunted him, and he wondered at the great clarity by which a conversation they had shared years prior returned to him now. Barabbas had taken great pleasure in mocking her disturbing convictions, but she had not been swayed. "*Remember Dan, Barabbas,*" Julia had persisted, her eyes wet with tears. "*He protected you, shielding you with his own body. He came between you and the wicked one. God is like that, Barabbas. He stands between us and the wicked one. He is our shield, our Defender.*"

Oh, how Barabbas had loathed her in that moment. But she had continued bravely, determined to reach him. "*God is for you, Barabbas. He wants to take the hits for you. He wants to be your shield.*"

Barabbas had been quick to retort. "*Then why hasn't He done so?*"

"*How could He? He stands at the door of your heart and knocks, Barabbas, but you must let Him in. Instead, you have barred the door to your heart and discarded the key.*"

Barabbas recalled his attempt to end the conversation, but his wife had persisted even then. *"Perhaps the Lord allowed Dan to make the ultimate sacrifice because He longed for you to understand the love He has for you, Barabbas."* Barabbas could still remember the rage that had coursed through him in that moment. And he remembered the arrogant speech he had flung back at Julia, consumed with his own pain and fury: *"If He loves me so much, then let **Him** suffer for me and take the hit Himself, rather than sending a convenient scapegoat."*

Let Him take the hit Himself.

With Jesus' tender gaze upon him, His body bruised, His skin torn and bloodied, Barabbas could not deny that Jesus Christ had indeed taken the hit Himself.

Pilate's voice reverberated through Barabbas' troubled mind: *Jesus, the One you call the Christ, shall be crucified in his stead.*

In his stead.

Barabbas' throat tightened in aching, agonizing remorse. Jesus would carry the cross intended for *him!* And Jesus would quite literally *take his place,* suffering and dying in his stead.

Oh, God, what have I done? His eyes were opened for the very first time. Looking into the face of Jesus, Barabbas desperately hoped to convey every ounce of his smarting repentance, aching sorrow, and wretched regret.

Tenderly holding Barabbas' gaze, the Savior's eyes glistened with tears, brimming with pure, unfailing love. He saw not a hardened criminal beyond the reach of grace. Instead, Jesus saw a broken and contrite heart. A child of God, a son of the Father.

With a sharp pang in his heart, Barabbas realized

that he was forgiven. He was loved by God, the true embodiment of love itself. Over the process of many hopeless years, the seed had been sown. And despite the enemy's attempt to snatch it away or choke it out, the testimonies and the prayers of many saints had watered it; therefore, the rocky soil of Barabbas' hard heart was gently, patiently cultivated.

By the grace of God, Barabbas, the *son of the father*, was now ready to be conformed into the image of Jesus Christ, the Son of God.

CHAPTER 64

Julia

Weakness coursed through Julia's entire body as Barabbas' shackles were removed and Jesus was led away to be beaten and scourged. Her mind was so muddled with shock and confusion that she struggled to piece together a simple thought. What on earth should she do now? Her heart thundered in her chest like the relentlessly pounding hooves of the stadium's race horses, overwhelming her with a sense of helplessness.

Barabbas had been released! She was elated and terrified all at once. How exactly would her husband utilize his newfound freedom? Would he recognize God's grace and turn from his iniquity or would he resume his dangerous, familiar habits? Despite the fact that it had broken her heart, Julia had accepted her fate as the will of God: her husband would die, her child would grow up fatherless. But now? Her entire world had been turned upside down in a matter of seconds.

Nearly paralyzed with fear, Julia scarcely heard

the raging crowd as they screamed and shouted approvingly. Forcing herself to concentrate, she weighed her options. Should she run? Hide? Attempt to locate her husband in the raging throng? Wait for Jesus' reappearance and the slight possibility that He might still be released?

"God must have great plans for your husband," Mara breathed, interrupting Julia's train of thought. "Dear sister, he's been released!"

Malchus and Alexander were disturbed rather than amazed by Barabbas' good fortune. "What will you do?" Malchus asked Julia grimly, concerned for her.

Sensing Julia's anxiety, Mara took her hand and answered firmly, "She will do whatever God calls her to do."

Attempting to draw strength from Mara's confidence, Julia pondered Malchus' legitimate question. What *would* she do? *Lord, will You show me?* It frightened her to consider sharing her life with Barabbas again. She couldn't bear to endure this torment one more time. *Lord, I don't have the strength to go through this again.*

I AM your strength.

Julia was alarmed rather than comforted by the Lord's clear admonition. *I can't do it, Lord.*

My grace is sufficient.

But don't You see how he has hurt me? Julia argued silently, weary and discouraged. *How can I trust him again? How can I possibly believe the best about him?*

Love bears all things, believes all things, hopes all things, endures all things.

I can't do it, Lord.

Love never fails.

Perhaps not, but he has failed! Oh, God, I can't even describe the pain he has put me through. Not only this, Father, but the years of criticism, of hateful speech and bitterness I have endured! I have tried to do right by him, Lord. I've done everything I know to do. I've poured myself out like a drink offering, trying to be an example to him, trying to help him. I've prayed for years on end. What more can I do, Father?

I desire mercy and not sacrifice.

Oh, God, how can I love him again?

Love one another as I have loved you, dear one.

Julia knew when she'd been bested. Sighing resignedly, she bowed her head in humble prayer. *Thy will be done.*

"What can we do for you, Julia?" Mara asked earnestly, her brown eyes searching Julia's troubled face. "How can we help?"

Attempting to shake the numbing anxiety gnawing at her spirit, Julia forced a confidence she was far from feeling and responded bravely, "Pray for me now. I must go find my husband."

***

Instantly regretting her separation from Malchus, Mara, and Alexander, Julia plunged through the raging crowd of murderous men and women, frightened by the heat of their rage. The mob was like a livid, ravenous beast, and she was caught in the midst of its madness. Protectively shielding her unborn child, she attempted to push through the crowd, ignoring the railing curses of angry bystanders as she passed. People pressed in tightly from all sides, shouting and thrusting angry fists in the air as they waited impatiently for the crucifixion to commence.

"Get out of the way!" one man shouted, shoving her headlong into another tightly clustered group of people. Yelping in pain, Julia mumbled an apology to those she had stumbled into and continued her frantic search, her eyes burning with tears.

Then two strong hands firmly gripped her shoulders, and before she even knew it Julia was gazing up into the anguished face of her husband. "Barabbas," she whispered, tears coursing down both cheeks. "How did you find me?"

Cupping her face in his hands, Barabbas swiped her warm tears away with his thumbs. "You came."

"I had to," she said in a rush, her heart fluttering. "Father discovered your whereabouts and the date scheduled for your–" she halted midsentence, unwilling to vocalize it again.

"My execution," Barabbas finished for her. Shaking his head, Barabbas looked deeply into her eyes. "Julia," he said hoarsely, "He took my place."

Caught off guard by his statement, Julia's heart sprang into her throat. She raised questioning eyes toward her husband, perceiving his quavering tone, the anguish in his eyes, his grief-stricken face.

"*He was wounded for our transgressions, He was bruised for our iniquities,*" Barabbas professed, his tone laced with contrition and grief. "*By His stripes we are healed.*"

Catching her breath in awe, Julia realized that her prayers of many years had been answered – in a way she could have never expected.

***

Melina

Hesitant to return to Claudia Procula, Melina lingered at the border of The Pavement. Procula had urged her to wait until Pilate proclaimed his final decision after receiving her urgent message, but the governor's wavering indecision was still blatantly obvious. Melina was certain that Pilate still clung to the faint hope that the crowd would allow Jesus' release once He had been chastised. If Melina were to return now, Procula would simply send her back to be her eyes and ears again.

Amazed by Barabbas' miraculous release, Melina wondered if Julia knew about it. How she wished to be with her closest friend during this heart-wrenching time. Her own heart was breaking into a thousand pieces, for the thought of Jesus suffering a Roman scourging was too much to bear. Rome had mastered the art of torture, and scourging was just one weapon among their vast arsenal of human torture. In the past, Melina's stomach had turned when she'd glimpsed criminals shortly after a dreaded Roman scourging, their bones and arteries exposed after suffering the cruel punishment. A scourging was ruthlessly intended to both humiliate and weaken the victim to the point of utter collapse. It wasn't uncommon for victims to perish during the violent act of retribution.

Oh, Jesus, I can't bear it. Wrapping her arms about her own slender frame, Melina suppressed a shudder as tears slipped down her cheeks.

***

Julia

When Jesus reappeared on the platform, Julia gasped in horror and buried her face in Barabbas' shoulder, unable to stomach the gruesome sight. Gulping sobs racked her entire frame as she shuddered against her husband's solid form.

"Julia, I need to take you home," Barabbas said, his tone boding no argument, though it was obvious he was torn between loyalty to his newfound Savior and his responsibility to care for his wife and unborn child. "Think of the baby."

Swiping away tears, Julia shook her head, determined to stand by her Savior in His hour of deepest suffering. "I cannot leave Him." Forcing herself to raise red-rimmed eyes to the platform, Julia gripped Barabbas' arm like a lifeline, steeling herself for what was to come. Bloodied and disfigured, Jesus now donned a flowing, blood-stained robe and a crown of vicious, twisted thorns.

"Why is He wearing that?" Julia managed shakily, certain she could feel her own heart breaking.

"It looks like Pilate's guards had their fun with Him," Barabbas said, his jawline hardening in righteous anger.

"I cannot comprehend their brutality," Julia whispered, her own anger rising. "How could they do this to Him?"

Pilate then stood and addressed the crowd, his eyes forming two narrow, angry slits. "Behold, I am bringing Him out to you, that you may know I find no fault in Him," he boomed loudly, clearly repulsed by the grisly work of the Roman soldiers.

Two guards grasped Jesus by the shoulders and

shoved Him forward as Pilate swept a hand toward Him in a grand gesture. "Behold the Man!"

The crowd exploded in shrieks and shrill shouts of delight at the sight of the battered Savior. It was obvious He could barely stand on His own two feet, for He staggered beneath the weight of the Roman soldiers' rough grip. "Crucify Him! Crucify Him!" the crowd shrieked, pumping their fists in the air and screeching loudly in near-hysteria.

"You take Him and crucify Him," Pilate bellowed, clearly at the end of his patience, "for I find no fault in Him."

"We have a law, and according to our law, He ought to die!" Julia realized it was the religious leaders nearest Pilate now speaking.

Pilate crossed his arms over his chest, his hard mouth tipping humorlessly. "And why, pray tell, is that? Have you not heard my decree? Are you deaf? Dumb? Blind? I find no fault in Him. What accusation do you now present?"

Based on the depth and richness of the booming voice that met the governor's inquiry, Julia assumed it must be the high priest speaking. "He should die, because He made Himself the *Son of God.*"

Pilate grew ghostly pale, and for one endless moment, he said nothing. Then, he snapped a curt order toward the soldiers steadying Jesus, turned sharply on his heel, and stormed down the stone steps toward the Praetorium.

CHAPTER 65

Melina

Lingering casually near a row of marble pillars outside the Praetorium, Melina listened intently as Pilate interrogated Jesus yet again. Before vacating the dais with little ceremony, he had ordered the soldiers to escort Jesus back to the judgment hall.

Something about the high priest's calm accusation had unnerved Pilate: *He made Himself the Son of God.* Melina imagined it had something to do with his wife's urgent admonition in correlation with Caiaphas' shocking revelation. Romans were superstitious by nature, and it was likely that Pilate now feared he was meddling in the realm of the gods.

"Where are You from?" Pilate hissed, his voice easily carrying to the grand, pillared corridor where Melina tarried.

Pilate's gruff demand was met by glaring silence.

"Are You not speaking to me?" Pilate snapped in disbelief. "Do You not know that I have the power to crucify You, and power to release You?"

There was a long pause. Then Jesus' voice, greatly weakened in His suffering, drifted quietly upon the air. It was obvious it took great effort for Him to form each word proceeding from His mouth. "You could have no power at all against Me unless it had been given you from above. Therefore the one who delivered Me to you has the greater sin."

The glaring silence that followed was proof enough that Pontius Pilate was deeply troubled by His words.

***

Julia

When Pilate returned with Jesus and his guards, Jesus was still arrayed in the scornful apparel the soldiers had forced on Him. Julia gripped her husband's hand so tightly her fingernails dug into his skin.

Pontius Pilate hovered over the crowd, his formidable countenance tremendously daunting despite his unusual pallor.

Sensing the governor's mounting reluctance, the high priest addressed him before the people, his eloquent voice carrying easily over the crowd. "We hope you have made the right decision, Governor. After all, if you let this Man go, you are not Caesar's friend."

Pilate's face contorted in rage.

"As you well know, whoever makes himself a king – as this Man has – speaks against Caesar," Caiaphas finished grandly, his gray eyes glittering with malice. "Surely you would not allow this Man to walk free?"

Julia felt weakness go through her, for Caiaphas had driven the nail deep into the coffin. He had all but accused Pontius Pilate as an accessory to treason – a crime punishable by a torturous death – before a vast sea of witnesses.

Pilate's face reddened in scarcely bridled fury. Stridently, he crossed the short distance to his judgment seat and sat down, grasping the monumental chair's gilded arms with a white-knuckled grip. "Behold your King," he announced angrily, sweeping one arm in Jesus' direction.

Despite Jesus' critical condition, the crowd screamed pitilessly for His death. "Away with Him!" they shouted, their faces grotesquely contorted, mirroring their outrage and hostility. "Crucify Him! Crucify Him!"

"Shall I crucify your king?" Pilate implored one last time.

But the roiling mob of seething men and women possessed not a shred of mercy or compassion. Instead, they raged all the more. "Our king?" they sneered, teeth bared. "We have no king but Caesar!"

Julia clasped her hands over her heart, trembling. The implication of the mob was crystal clear: *Our loyalty lies with the emperor, Governor. Yours?*

Pontius Pilate finally succumbed, deeply troubled by their accusations against him. Without a word, he delivered Jesus into the hands of the elders and chief priests of the roiling mob. Caiaphas' borrowed soldiers were close at hand, hungry to inflict pain. And the battle for the soul of the governor abated, for Pontius Pilate had made his choice. The cares of the world and the deceitfulness of power and riches had swiftly, effectively choked out the seed that had been planted.

What is truth? Pilate had sneered, careworn and battle-hardened, frustrated and cynical. Yet the Truth stood directly before him, and Pilate had been blinded to all but preserving his own life, his own prosperity and position. In his frantic attempt to preserve his own life, Pontius Pilate, governor of Judea, ultimately lost it forever.

Julia wept bitterly as Jesus was led away to shoulder His own cross and endure yet another inhumane torture: crucifixion.

***

Melina

Claudia Procula rose gracefully from her chair when Melina was ushered into her opulent chambers. "Well?" she asked, her lovely eyes alight with hope. "Has my husband released Him?"

Biting her lower lip, Melina shook her head gently. Tears coursed unashamedly down her cheeks.

Stunned, Procula's hand went to her mouth. "He is to be crucified, then?"

"They are taking Him to Golgotha."

The color drained from Procula's face, her refined features ghostly pale. Slowly, she lowered herself into her gilded chair, clearly weakened by the disturbing news.

"My lady?" Melina went to her, concerned by the fine lady's reaction.

Procula clasped her forehead with one delicate hand, shaking her head in horror. "Great God of heaven," she breathed, her silvery voice quavering in fear, "be with us."

***

Julia

"Where are they taking Him?" Julia cried, nearly frantic as the soldiers roughly prodded Jesus off the platform.

Barabbas watched with steely eyes, his jaw twitching in anger. "My best guess? Golgotha."

Julia blanched, sickened. Golgotha, *the place of the skull.*

"The place where men are crucified," Barabbas supplied stiffly.

"We must go," Julia managed, swiping at her tears. "We have to go with Him!"

"Julia, you can't possibly comprehend the violence of Golgotha. I'm taking you to your father's house."

Julia looked up at him, surprised. "My father's house?" Before she could question him further, Julia doubled over, releasing a startled cry of pain.

Barabbas reached for her, alarmed. "Julia? What is it?"

Gripping her abdomen, Julia gritted her teeth in sudden pain. "Barabbas," she gasped, sweat dotting her brow. "What do labor pains feel like?"

"You're asking *me?*"

Julia moaned, feeling more miserable than she had ever felt in her life. She met her husband's gaze, startled by the near-panic welling in his eyes. What had happened to his cool control, his confident bearing?

"Barabbas, I think the baby is coming."

CHAPTER 66

Mara

"Where have you been?"

Mara's heart skipped in apprehension at the sound of her former husband's voice. Turning her head, she realized that the imperious address was not intended for her.

Lucius stood behind them, his armor glistening in the bright sunlight. His countenance was fierce as his eyes bored into Malchus.

Malchus met his gaze and shrugged indifferently. "Ah, Lucius. Always a pleasure."

Lucius' eyes narrowed dangerously. "You deserted your post."

"Do I look like a soldier to you?" Malchus dared, attempting to remain calm as the throng grew exceedingly, dangerously violent. "Despite your dramatics, I don't qualify as a deserter."

"The high priest entrusted you with a crucial assignment," Lucius sneered, "and yet you fled the scene like a scared chicken."

"Well, you sure know how to make a man feel good about himself."

"It's no fault of mine that you're a coward," Lucius smirked, his tone dripping with condescension.

"What do you want with my cousin, Soldier?" Alexander demanded, annoyed.

"He's coming with me."

"A tempting invitation, really," Malchus drawled, crossing his arms and turning away in disinterest. "Unfortunately, I must decline."

"You have no choice," Lucius snapped, gripping Malchus roughly by the shoulder. "These are the high priest's orders."

"Do you always do as you're told?" Malchus quipped, attempting to suppress his alarm.

"Shut up. I *said* you're coming with me."

"Lucius, you can't do this!" Mara cried, reaching for Malchus' arm.

"Stay out of this, Mara," Lucius hissed, binding Malchus' hands behind his back.

"We're coming with you," Mara said, her very stance daring Lucius to defy her.

"No," Malchus said firmly. "Stay with Jesus. Don't leave Him now, do you hear me?"

"But, Malchus–"

"Stay with Him," Malchus said firmly, looking first to Mara then to Alexander. "I'll return as soon as I can."

"Little chance of that happening," Lucius scoffed as he gave Malchus a rough shove forward.

"God be with you, Cousin," Alexander called after Malchus as Lucius dragged him through the uncompromising crowd.

"What will Caiaphas do to him?" Mara asked, her

voice tinged with deep concern.

Alexander shook his head, his dark eyes boring into Lucius' retreating back. "Do you believe Malchus is in God's hands?"

"Of course I do."

"Then pray. And in the meantime, we will do as he asks. We will stand by Jesus until the end."

***

Barabbas

"Send for the midwife! Now!" A young male servant dashed out of the house, galvanized by Iskah's terse order.

Carrying his groaning young wife through the front entry of Simon's villa, Barabbas followed Iskah's harried instructions, only half aware of his own wooden actions.

Surprised that Iskah had been summoned by the doorkeeper rather than the owner of the estate, Barabbas asked in concern, "Where is Simon?"

"Scouring the city, searching for his daughter," Iskah responded curtly.

Great.

Barabbas followed his stoic mother-in-law down an elaborately frescoed corridor, entering a large room which he assumed must be Julia's former chambers.

"Gently place her on the bed," Iskah directed him, and he was amazed by her state of calm. He knew she must have been utterly shocked by his appearance on her threshold, bearing her weeping daughter in his arms. After all, he was supposed to be dead by now.

Gently, Barabbas lowered his wife onto the lush canopy bed. He cringed inwardly, observing her opulent bedchamber. What must she think of the rough straw mat he had provided for her mattress?

"Julia, you must focus and keep calm," Iskah said gently, drawing a stool along the bedside and dabbing at her daughter's forehead with a cool, damp cloth. Julia's weeping subsided slightly in her assuring mother's presence.

Joanna entered the room in a flutter, her arms spilling over with supplies. "Has the midwife been sent for?"

"Yes. She should arrive shortly."

Barabbas marveled anew at Iskah's calm composure. He was taken aback when Joanna hastily unloaded her supplies then descended upon him, drawing him against her ample bosom in a warm embrace. "How I prayed for you, dear boy!"

Both touched and discomfited, Barabbas was relieved when she released him from her surprisingly strong grip.

"Don't you worry about a thing now," Joanna exhorted him with a sound slap on the back. "Julia is in good hands. In no time at all, you'll be cradling a precious little son or daughter in those strong arms of yours!"

Julia cried out, and Barabbas turned to Joanna in alarm. "What can we do for her?"

Pushing herself up in bed, Julia raised frantic eyes toward her husband. "You must go back!"

Barabbas stared at her, thunderstruck. "Go back?"

"We left Jesus to die," Julia moaned, sweat pouring down her face.

"Julia, you're in labor." Surely Jesus would excuse her absence under such circumstances!

"But *you're* not," Julia groaned.

"That would prove a mite concerning if he was, would it not?" Joanna quipped, stifling a chuckle.

"Please, Barabbas, go to Him."

"Julia, I can't leave you now."

"Please, please, go!"

"No. I won't leave you, Julia," Barabbas answered firmly.

Iskah was concerned by her daughter's distress. "Julia, you must stay calm."

"Barabbas, please," Julia insisted, catching her breath in pain. "Go!"

Torn, Barabbas looked to Iskah for guidance.

Julia was quickly becoming hysterical. "He needs us," she sobbed. "Please, *go! Go!*"

"It's alright, Barabbas," Iskah spoke up, disturbed by Julia's deep angst. "The midwife will arrive any minute, and she won't allow you in the room anyway. Julia's hysteria isn't good for the baby."

Crossing over to the bed, Barabbas bent and planted a soft kiss on Julia's forehead before walking out the door.

***

Malchus

"Loose his bonds."

Caiaphas' smooth command echoed and bounced off the elegant marble walls of his Judgment Hall, sending strange little shivers of foreboding up and down Malchus' spine. Wryly, Malchus lifted level eyes toward the high priest. Had any man told him he would find himself in this position – the accused one standing before Caiaphas in this imposing marble hall – he would have laughed in his face.

Towering above him in his imposing chair, Caiaphas deigned to rest dangerous gray eyes upon his once-favored manservant. "Tell me these absurd accusations are false, Malchus."

The sound of his name spoken by this devil in priestly robes unnerved Malchus. Even so, he straightened as Lucius grudgingly loosed his bonds. Squaring his shoulders, he met Caiaphas' gaze head-on. "And which accusations are we discussing, my lord?" he asked wryly.

Caiaphas' eyes hardened in anger. "You would dare be so flippant addressing God's high priest?"

God's high priest? Malchus wanted to laugh in his pompous face. He could almost see the innocent blood upon the man's hands. "I apologize if I have caused any offense," he said instead.

Caiaphas sighed tragically, shaking his head in supposed disappointment. "The charges against you are serious, Malchus."

Does Caiaphas ever tire of trying innocent men? "Who brought forth the charges against me?" Malchus asked coolly, sensing Lucius stiffen behind him.

"That is of little import," Caiaphas responded tersely.

"How, then, am I to answer my accuser?" Malchus questioned coolly.

Caiaphas' face reddened. "You wish for me to present a witness against you? I have hundreds – you may take your pick! The entire contingent of soldiers – not to mention the vast audience of priests, Pharisees, Sadducees, and scribes present – witnessed your shameful conduct! Any one of them would gladly testify against you!"

"Well, it's good to know where I stand here," Malchus observed snidely.

"I placed my confidence in you, Malchus," Caiaphas continued, his richly bejeweled fingers grasping the gilded arms of his chair. "You broke my trust."

Malchus simply waited, wondering if his life was about to end.

"I assigned to you a very important task."

"A task or a test?" Malchus dared, his eyes challenging.

"I fear you are unaware of the gravity of your present situation, Malchus," Caiaphas hissed, his eyes flashing dangerously. "But I can see you are a fool, utterly worthless to me," he nearly spat, restlessly strumming his fingers on the chair's elegant arms. "This self-proclaimed Rabbi you esteem so highly – He is on His way to Golgotha, shouldering His own bloody cross."

Malchus attempted to swallow the bile rising in his throat.

"Does this surprise you?" Caiaphas challenged, raising his brows in question. "Surely you are not so naïve as to believe that foul Prophet's testimony now! If He were truly the Son of God, would He be suffering a vile death upon a Roman cross? What have you to say about your Messiah now?"

Malchus raised level eyes to his own dark master's. "*He was wounded for our transgressions, He was bruised for our iniquities.*"

Caiaphas' features tightened in rage.

"*The chastisement for our peace was upon Him, and by His stripes we are healed*," Malchus finished boldly. "That's what I have to say about Him. I should think that you, as high priest, would be far more familiar with Messianic prophecies than I."

The high priest's face turned crimson as his eyes narrowed dangerously. "What are you implying? I would think very carefully about your response."

"I reached my own conclusions long before you summoned me," Malchus replied curtly. "And what I'm saying is this: Congratulations, dear priest. You have single-handedly assisted in the fulfillment of centuries-old prophecies, and by your hand the Messiah is now more apparent to Israel than ever before."

"You speak blasphemies," Caiaphas spewed, his dangerously escalating wrath filling the chamber like a malevolent being. Even Lucius and the endless row of borrowed Roman guards lining the long marble hall tensed in apprehension. "Perhaps you have forgotten that I am the high priest of Israel, selected by God Himself to govern His people."

"Funny, I heard you were appointed by the prefect, Valerius Gratus," Malchus mused, his mouth tipping sardonically.

"The power of life and death is mine! Your very soul rests in my hands," Caiaphas finished coldly, his eyes pinning Malchus in place, daring him to challenge his lofty statement.

"My soul is in God's hands," Malchus answered with great conviction, certain these words would surely be his last. "I no longer fear those who kill the body but cannot kill the soul."

Malchus' bold statement was followed by thundering silence. After a long pause, Caiaphas leaned forward in his chair. "Perhaps," he said, his voice low and threatening, "that will change when you see the great power I wield against you."

Malchus stood rigidly before him, unflinching.

Nodding to Lucius, Caiaphas rose slowly from his chair. Lucius stepped forward, proceeding to bind Malchus' hands behind his back once again.

"You will remain on the premises in a holding cell until I have decided what I wish to do with you," Caiaphas commanded airily. "It would seem you are past the point of redemption. And a pity that is, for you have served me well in the past."

Malchus cringed at that shocking disclosure. By capitulating to the wicked whims of this evil priest, he had unintentionally served Caiaphas' dark master all along.

Yet even as Lucius shoved him toward a bleak, empty holding cell, Malchus silently thanked God for His grace. Though condemned by the high priest, he was accepted and redeemed by God.

Despite his dire situation, Malchus experienced the peace he had craved all along – the peace surpassing human understanding – for the very first time in his life.

CHAPTER 67

l

Barabbas

Barabbas found His Savior exactly where he feared he would – nailed to a cross on an ugly little knoll called Golgotha, a prominent mound located just outside the gates on the northern side of Jerusalem. It wasn't difficult to come by, as the Romans intentionally chose a location near a public highway to showcase their gruesome executions – grim reminders for all civilians to think twice before contesting the greatest world power known to man. The place was even more hideous than he remembered. Large vultures circled lazily above three mounted crosses, while throngs of weeping and wailing mourners gathered at the bases. The air was thick with swarming flies, putrid stench, and the agonized cries of dying men.

Many of Jesus' followers had gathered upon the rocky knoll, determined to stand by Jesus until the end. Barabbas noted that most of the followers were women, which didn't surprise him at all. The men were far more likely to be targeted as fellow revolutionaries, which might very well lead to their own executions. Barabbas did recognize one of the twelve disciples at the foot of Jesus' cross, his arm draped protectively over the stiff shoulders of a pale older woman. Tears coursed down her cheeks, though she stood bravely at the base of Jesus' rugged cross. Barabbas couldn't help but wonder if perhaps this was the mother of Jesus. Barabbas also recognized another woman standing with them – the harlot who had purchased Julia's alabaster jar. He marveled at her obvious transformation. She now donned simple garments, her face was devoid of bold makeup, and her abundant curly tresses were covered by a modest shawl.

Despite those gathered to support their beloved Teacher, others had also flocked to Golgotha, showering the tormented with mockery and accusations. Barabbas cringed at the flagrant cruelty of their hateful speech.

Even more appalling than the hate-driven crowd was the shocking sight that Barabbas had been completely unprepared for – the sight of his two friends nailed to crosses on either side of the Savior. At Jesus' right hand was Lem, the reluctant newcomer to the Zealot cause, and at His left, Amraphel, the brazen leader. As his fellow brothers suffered an excruciating death before him, the stunning realization that Jesus was nailed to the very cross that should have been his washed over Barabbas anew. Why had he been spared? He knew he was the least deserving of all men.

Forcing himself to tear his gaze away from his dying brothers and fixing his eyes upon Jesus, Barabbas' color deepened in shame as Amraphel heaped vulgar accusations upon the Man being crucified with him. Lem joined in weakly, though he quieted when Jesus did not return their cruel reviling. The sea of people gathering to watch the horrid display hurled foul insults at Jesus as well, seemingly paying little attention to the thieves on either side of Him.

Had they no fear of God at all?

Closing his eyes and ears to all but the Savior on the cross, Barabbas made a decision that would forever change the course of his life. Even as the enemy pounded his mind with loathsome memories of the childhood nightmare that had occurred upon this very hill, Barabbas refused to dwell on his pain-stricken past. Instead, he fixed his eyes on Jesus and made a conscious effort to surrender it all to Him. It was here on this rocky knoll of death, so many years ago, that his father and brothers had drawn their final, agonizing breaths. Here, his quest for vengeance had begun. Here, as a small, frightened child, his hatred for everything Roman had exploded into an undying flame, driving him to a life of bitter revenge.

And here, Barabbas now offered up his bitterness, committing himself and his future to God. This gruesome place reeking of death and destruction had now become a fount of everlasting life for him. For here, Barabbas surrendered himself entirely to God, stripping off his burning hatred and offering it to the only One capable of transforming it into something powerful, useful, and meaningful.

Kneeling on the ground before the cross of Christ, Barabbas lifted empty hands heavenward in a simple gesture of complete surrender and heartfelt worship.

***

Alexander

Standing upon the dreaded skull-shaped mound called Golgotha, Alexander's heart broke as Mara wept inconsolably beside him. They were surrounded by others weeping for Jesus, loyal followers willing to risk the wrath of Rome to stand by Him in His hour of suffering. Alexander sensed a comradeship with every single one of them, despite the fact that this was their first meeting. The Spirit of God had bound them all together, uniting them in a way that even flesh and blood could not.

Alexander drew a protective arm around Mara's shuddering shoulders, realizing there was nothing he could do to comfort her or anyone else upon this bare knoll reeking of death and gloom. These were the critical times when they must draw upon their newfound faith, believing that God's will would ultimately prevail.

An unnatural darkness had rolled in from the eastern hills, bringing with it roiling, angry clouds and startling flickers of lightning. A hair-raising chill filled the air, and the atmosphere fairly crackled with intensity. It was as if the very elements protested against the godless act carried out on Calvary's hill.

Gazing at the broken form of the King on the cross, a dream of many nights past surfaced in Alexander's mind with the jarring clarity and power of the mighty lightning bolts teasing the rolling hillsides. Caught off guard by the jolting memory, Alexander paled as he recalled the diabolical laughter filling his senses in the midst of his disturbing nightmare. Someone – or something – had gloried in his impending doom. Alexander shook his head in wonder, now fully understanding to whom the devilish laughter had belonged. In that awful dream, the enemy of his soul had sought to destroy him, but Jesus had touched his head with blood-stained palms.

Alexander still remembered the horror he had experienced in his dream when the blood of Jesus had washed over him. He also remembered the screeches of sheer horror as demonic powers were forced to retreat. Were such forces retreating even now? It seemed unlikely, for the very gates of hell unleashed its fury upon Jesus Christ, fully determined to snuff out the Son of God and extinguish the Light of the World.

In his dream, the blood of Jesus had cleansed Alexander of his sin, washing him like a soothing balm. His burden of guilt had lifted. The forces of evil had fled. But he struggled to comprehend how God could possibly banish the powers of darkness now. It seemed as if those malignant forces now reigned, unharnessed and unrestrained.

Forcing himself to abandon his disturbing thoughts, Alexander gazed upon the tortured form of his Maker. His throat tightened painfully. How could he possibly comprehend the love of this wonderful Savior? Jesus willingly suffered the penalty that he, Alexander, deserved. Every sin he had ever committed weighed heavily upon his conscience, for he realized they increased the burden of suffering his Savior now bore for him.

God, forgive me, he pleaded silently. If only he had known and fully understood the cost of careless, petty sins.

***

Barabbas

The hours crept by slowly, each agonizing minute seemingly stretching on for endless ages. Though Barabbas had arrived after the victims had been nailed to their crosses, he knew they had been suffering for over six excruciating hours. Aching for them, Barabbas silently prayed that each ragged breath they drew would be their merciful last. How he longed to put an end to their unbearable suffering.

Pervasive, bone-chilling darkness had settled over the land like a demonic cloud, completely obscuring even the slightest rays of late-afternoon sunlight. Barabbas had never known a darkness so thick. It hung heavily in the air, smothering all hope as well as the light. Many soldiers and onlookers had lit lamps and burning torches, and the flickering flames cast writhing shadows upon the tortured bodies nailed to brutal Roman crosses. Shadows danced and writhed upon the rocky hilltop like gleeful demons rejoicing in the devilish corruption of Golgotha's hill. Soldiers efficiently mounted steadily burning torches about the perimeter, their hammers *pound-pound-pounding* a steady rhythm in the rocky ground. The dancing flames illuminated the hate-stained faces of both committed onlookers and disgusted passers-by with a ghastly, otherworldly light.

Drunk on their own hatred, the crowd appeared unfazed by the suffocating darkness, the thunder rumbling deeply on the distant hills, or the eerie green flashes of lightning that drew nearer to Golgotha with every angry strike.

Barabbas's heart pounded furiously within his

chest. He couldn't help but wonder if he had stumbled upon the very gates of hell.

Soldiers mingled with elders and chief priests, scoffing and snarling stinging ridicules. Jesus remained their sole target, for the mob had little interest in the two thieves hanging on either side of Him. Would they ever tire of harassing Jesus?

"You who destroy the Temple and build it in three days, *save Yourself!*"

"If You are the Son of God, come down from that cross!"

"Let the Christ, the King of Israel, descend now from the cross, that we may see and believe!"

"He saved others; let Him save *Himself* if He is the Christ, the chosen of God."

"If You are the King of the Jews, save Yourself!"

Barabbas wondered if the entire mob was possessed by the evil one. They repeated their cruel taunts and jeers again and again, never tiring of their own wicked barbs. Barabbas imagined the devil himself supplied their foul blasphemy.

If you are the Son of God... If You are the Christ... If You are the King of the Jews... it was as if the very identity of Jesus Christ, the Son of God, was under attack by a slew of demonic forces. And it seemed the forces of darkness had already initiated a backup plan in case their first attempt failed by actively appealing to human pride: *If You are the Son of God, **prove it.***

Barabbas ached for Jesus. His physical body was broken, His heart and mind under violent attack. If Barabbas had ever questioned Satan's brutality, the reality of demonic forces, or the heinous consequences of sin, his doubts were now banished forever.

In the distance, the form of a Roman centurion drew nearer. His red-plumed helmet and broad armor created an odd silhouette against the stark blackness and the flickering torchlight. Barabbas had noticed the shadowy form hours earlier, even before the darkness had settled over the land. It seemed the soldier was satisfied to observe the grisly scene from a distance... until now.

When the centurion crested the mound and drew alongside another soldier guarding the base of Jesus' cross, Barabbas' blood grew cold. For there, at the base of Jesus' bloody cross, stood Cornelius, the man who had unwittingly stolen the life of Barabbas' dearest friend, Dan.

For one brief moment, familiar, barbaric rage coursed through Barabbas' entire being. His blood pounded in his ears as he imagined the centurion's neck between his hands, heard the snapping of breaking bones, the gasping sound of a final, ragged breath...

And then Jesus' gaze was upon Barabbas, piercing, penetrating, shaking him to the very core and clearing the deadly red haze of murderous wrath blinding all his senses. Barabbas' entire body grew cold.

Jesus knew what he was thinking.

Shortly after Barabbas had arrived, the soldiers had cast lots for Jesus' clothing after stripping Him and tormenting Him with both physical and verbal abuse. The mob had screamed their approval, thrilled by the spectacle and eager to witness which of the gambling soldiers would win the cherished prize. Rather than lashing out in condemnation, Jesus' response had been a love-soaked prayer to God: *Father, forgive them, for they do not know what they do.*

Those words washed over Barabbas now, piercing his soul and permeating his entire being. He, too, had lived in darkness, but Jesus had patiently drawn him. Jesus had not forsaken him in his sins. No, Jesus had stood beside him, gently and quietly showing him the way.

When Jesus lowered His loving gaze and bowed his head, Barabbas knew what he must do. He also knew that Jesus was aware of his sudden change of heart, and he was grateful.

Lifting his head and squaring his shoulders in resignation, Barabbas locked eyes with the centurion at the base of Jesus' cross. Recognition flashed across the young man's chiseled features and his knuckles whitened as he clenched a deadly looking spear.

A guttural growl from Amraphel drew the attention of both Barabbas and Cornelius.

"If You are the Christ," Amraphel gasped with great difficulty, "then save Yourself *and* us." Even in his agony, Amraphel's voice was tinged with searing sarcasm.

"Do you not even fear God, seeing you are under the same condemnation?" Lem cried out weakly. "We received the due reward of our deeds, but this Man has done nothing wrong."

His lips curling in a wicked sneer, Amraphel hurled insults and obscenities at the young man dying slowly in his own service.

Ignoring Amraphel's cruel jeers, Lem attempted to turn his head toward Jesus, grimacing in pain. "Lord, remember me when You come into Your kingdom."

Jesus turned his head and met Lem's frightened

gaze, all the love in the world harnessed in that one simple look. When He spoke, His words were so strained from breathlessness and pain that Barabbas had to crane his neck forward to catch His response. He only caught the last few words of Jesus' quiet assurance, but it was enough to fill his aching heart with a strange joy and peace he scarcely understood.

"...you will be with Me in Paradise."

Tears spilled down Lem's cheeks, falling into his short beard. His quiet weeping pierced Barabbas' heart. He rejoiced that the young Zealot had accepted Jesus as his Savior, but he also agonized knowing that Amraphel had willfully chosen to perish in his sins.

When Barabbas' eyes rested upon the centurion again, it was obvious that Cornelius was both touched and confused by the quiet exchange between the sinless Man and the reckless Zealot. At least momentarily, his attention was diverted from Barabbas.

CHAPTER 68

Mara

Clutching Alexander's arm like a lifeline, Mara's lips moved in silent prayer as she stood stoically before her wounded Maker. Her heart filled with love when Jesus addressed the young disciple at the foot of His cross, entrusting His weeping mother to his care.

Even in the throes of a tortuous death, Jesus was far more concerned for others than for Himself.

Oh, Jesus, my precious Savior, how I love You.

***

Barabbas

Cornelius' gaze was cold as ice. It was obvious he desired to question Barabbas or possibly even apprehend him. And yet he clearly hesitated to do so.

Wondering at the calm he was experiencing in the presence of a man who made his blood boil only moments earlier, Barabbas offered a silent prayer for wisdom. He had all but promised Julia to remain with Jesus until the end. But if he did so, would he be arrested again? What would become of Julia and their baby if he were incarcerated or, worse, executed?

Barabbas' thoughts were diverted when a mighty blast of thunder shook the distant hills just as an unexpected flash of brilliant lightning cracked across the sky, striking a twisted and gnarled dead tree and splitting it in two. Men and women screamed in terror as they scattered like frightened mice, covering their heads and faces with trembling hands.

Lightning flickered and flashed across the sky in a brilliant yet terrifying display as Jesus cried out in a loud voice, "My God, My God, why have You forsaken Me?"

The hairs rose on the back of Barabbas' neck as he recalled the Psalm of David sung by the mysterious Azarel: *My God, My God, why have You forsaken Me? ...My strength is dried up like a potsherd, and my tongue clings to My jaws...*

"Look!" Men and women screamed, shaken from their terror by Jesus' unexpected cry. Tentatively, they approached the crosses again, hungry for more violent entertainment. "Look, He's calling for Elijah!"

"Elijah? Will he come?"

"Shut up and see!"

"Elijah, Elijah, come!"

Barabbas was sickened by their callousness. Didn't they realize that an appearance by the mighty prophet would only confirm their vile sins? Had they no fear of God at all?

Dogs have surrounded Me; the congregation of the wicked has enclosed Me...

Jesus spoke, but the crowd's frenzied screams and

shouts drowned out His weakened voice. A soldier offered a sponge attached to a pole, soaked in sour wine.

They pierced My hands and My feet... Barabbas' eyes rested upon the savage nails drilled mercilessly into the tender hands and feet of Christ.

They divide My garments among them, and for My clothing they cast lots... A nearby soldier grinned savagely as he observed the suffering of Christ, the expensive purple robe he had rent from the Savior's body folded and flung carefully over his armor-plated shoulder.

The defiant shouts of the crowd drew Barabbas from his thoughts once more as they rained insults upon the soldier attempting to quench Jesus' thirst. Barabbas noted that Cornelius observed the proceedings with sober eyes, his muscled form tense. His fingers strummed the pole of his glistening spear as if he was deep in thought.

"Don't give Him anything to drink!" one man shouted angrily at the erring soldier.

"Let Him alone," another yelled, his fury illuminated by flickering torches. "Let us see if Elijah will come to save Him!"

"Yes!" others shouted. "Let us see if Elijah will come to take Him down!"

Confused, the soldier lowered the sponge attached to the rod. The refreshment had scarcely touched Jesus' parched mouth. Barabbas wondered if Jesus had received any at all.

And then another blast of thunder elicited more terrified screams as the sky fairly glowed with flickering bursts of crackling lightning.

"Father," Jesus cried out, His voice incredibly, surprisingly steady, "into Your hands I commit My spirit."

Barabbas watched in awe as Jesus lifted tear-filled eyes heavenward. "It is finished." Bowing His head, Jesus breathed His last.

For one heady moment, the incensed mob grew silent as awestruck wonder rippled through the assembly. *That was it?* Jesus was gone? His torment had finally ended?

Barabbas couldn't shake the feeling that Jesus had not merely died – He had departed. Jesus had intentionally, willfully surrendered His spirit into the hands of God. Men had not taken His life – He offered it up Himself.

The sacred moment had scarcely passed when the ground lurched suddenly, fiercely, beneath the feet of those gathered on Golgotha's hill, sending men and women into fits of sheer panic and terror. The earth groaned in protest as it rocked and swayed like the waves of a churning sea, devastating the entire city with a mighty earthquake.

Barabbas and many others were thrown from their feet. Clenching at the moist dirt and grass with steeled fists, Barabbas lifted his head to assess the situation and his surroundings. Men and women continued to scream in sheer panic, rushing crazily to and fro, taking cover. The sky opened and rain pounded the roiling earth as massive rocks split open and the earth shuddered and quaked in violent fury.

It was as if the earth itself protested the death of its Maker with a mighty display unlike anything Barabbas had ever seen.

***

Alexander

"Get down!" Alexander shouted the moment the earth began to rock beneath his feet.

Pale as death, Mara did as she was commanded, dropping to her knees. Alexander threw himself over her trembling form, shielding her from the terror to come. A pounding rain drenched the earth, soaking through his garments as lightning flashed and thunder roared in response to the earth's mighty shaking.

Screams of terror filled his senses, but he determined to stay his attention upon shielding and protecting a very frightened Mara. The wind screamed and whistled past him, sending shrubs and debris flying. The earth continued to rock like the waves of a troubled sea.

Even the thieves upon the cross screamed in fearful torment as the earth raged against the injustice of Golgotha's hill.

***

Caiaphas

Donning resplendent priestly garments, Caiaphas brandished a glistening knife and lifted it high above his head.

Legs bound by delicate scarlet cords, a spotless little lamb wriggled in terror as another priest placed him calmly upon the altar before the austere high priest, Joseph Caiaphas.

Caiaphas relished the bloody performance of this rite. Though other priests performed ritual sacrifices during the festival, he believed this one would be significant. Regrettably, he had missed the first of the daily sacrifices, for the trial of Jesus had commenced at that very hour. But now it was time for the *final* sacrifice, the most important of all. The slaughtering of this lamb would bring closure to the sacrifices offered before it, sealing the redemption of his people by its shed blood.

The lamb bleated in terror below the flickering lamplight, for darkness had closed in on all sides. The entire Temple compound was bathed in darkness, now only faintly lit by flickering torches and dim lamplight.

A smile touched the corners of Caiaphas' lips above his neatly oiled and styled beard. An accompanying priest nodded solemnly, signifying that the ninth hour had officially arrived. It was now time to sacrifice the Passover lamb.

With one vicious swoop, Caiaphas plunged the knife downward toward the slender white throat of the bleating lamb –

BANG! A thunderbolt unlike anything the high priest had ever heard erupted just above the Temple compound. As if in response, the earth heaved beneath him as thunder quaked and lightning flashed overhead with astounding brilliance. Caiaphas was thrown roughly to his feet. He gritted his teeth in fury as his knife clattered noisily upon the tile floor and the compound erupted with the screams of anguished priests.

A mighty gust of wind blew through the compound, extinguishing the flickering torches. Darkness settled over them, but not before Caiaphas glimpsed the frightened little lamb scampering away in triumph. Somehow, the cords binding it must have loosened amidst the mighty fray!

RIP! Another sound tore through the air, raising the hairs on the back of the high priest's neck. It was a thunderous sound, like the renting of the thickest, largest garment on earth.

Despite the fact that the high priest was only permitted to enter the Most Holy Place once a year, Caiaphas scrambled to his feet, rushing at the Temple with the force of a battering ram even as the earth quaked violently beneath his feet. Flinging open massive doors, Caiaphas was assaulted by the unexpected light bursting forth from the seven-branched menorah burning brightly within the safety of the Temple walls. His heart sank like a heavy rock the moment his suspicions were confirmed.

There before him gleamed the Most Holy Place in all its golden splendor, clearly visible to anyone stepping inside the Temple and seeking the presence of God; for the enormous curtain that once barred commoners from God's presence was now rent in two from top to bottom as if by the mighty hand of God Himself. Caiaphas' shoulders heaved, his breath escaping his lips in short, sporadic puffs as his sharp eyes assessed the damage. Once, mighty sword-bearing cherubim had graced that magnificent curtain, jealously guarding the presence of God. But now the towering 30-foot curtain was ripped right down the middle!

The earth continued to rumble, and Caiaphas was thrown to his feet once more as a mighty crash of thunder erupted just outside the Temple's walls. Raising his head in defiance, Caiaphas' eyes narrowed in suspicion. The famous veil before him was a full handsbreadth in width – nearly four inches thick! How on earth had it been rent as easily as an aging wineskin? Caiaphas' taut features reddened in barely contained rage. Why, anyone might access the presence of God now!

Incensed, Caiaphas beat the marble floor with two balled fists and released a savage cry, chilling the blood of the frightened priests huddled closely together outside.

⁎⁎⁎

Julia

Julia was in agonized labor when the earth began to rumble and quake, rattling the walls and dislodging household items from their places. The terrible darkness that had swept over the land deepened as the elements raged outside the safe marble walls of her father's villa.

The plucky midwife attempted to coach Julia and perform her duties despite the raging elements, while Iskah and Joanna desperately strove to comfort and calm her. But their own great fear and apprehension was evident in their eyes even as they spoke soothing words and whispered assurances. Iskah was certainly thankful that Simon had arrived home a few hours ago. She would be consumed with worry over him had he been trapped in the wild fray.

Doused in sweat and consumed with her present misery, Julia scarcely heard a word that was spoken to her and the women's gentle assurances fell upon deaf ears. Closing her eyes, Julia gritted her teeth against the fear and pain, certain she was bringing her child into the world on the very last day of its existence.

CHAPTER 69

Barabbas

Gradually, the earth's fearsome quaking subsided as the rain softened to a gentle patter and the thunder rumbled away toward the distant hills.

Cautiously, Barabbas straightened, his eyes tentatively sweeping the perimeter. Many of the onlookers had fled to safety but a few remained, their features pale and taut with apprehension.

Barabbas was dismayed when he noticed the centurion still gracing the foot of the cross. He had thrust his spearhead into the ground when the earthquake had begun and now knelt behind it, grasping the long rod for support.

Cornelius lifted his gaze and, once again, locked eyes with Barabbas.

The lifeless body of Jesus hung behind the soldier, a gruesome and heart-wrenching reminder of the indescribable severity of sin. Barabbas met the centurion's gaze without a hint of malice. Instead, he offered Cornelius one humble nod of acceptance.

Cornelius understood. Grimly, he returned the gesture. The forgiveness passing between the young men needed no words of expression, for it was carved deeply within their hearts.

Jesus Christ had demolished the bitter barriers of hatred between them.

Cornelius lifted his eyes toward the limp form of the Savior upon the cross, his expression filled with wonder. "Truly this was the Son of God."

***

Iskah embraced Barabbas after the doorkeeper ushered him into Simon's opulent home. Surprised by the reserved woman's unusually warm gesture, Barabbas lifted his brows in question after she released him.

"Welcome, Barabbas," Iskah said gently, taking him by the hand. "Julia told me what happened."

Barabbas was embarrassed by the tears springing to his eyes.

Reaching up, Iskah touched his cheek. "Would you like to meet your daughter?"

Barabbas' throat closed as new, nearly unbearable emotions coursed through his numb body. Attempting to squelch his tears, Barabbas managed a weak nod.

Leading him down the same frescoed corridor he had previously traveled, Iskah escorted him to Julia's former suite. To his great surprise, Iskah squeezed his arm gently then left him alone at the door. Touched by her thoughtfulness, Barabbas cleared his throat nervously, more frightened than he'd ever been in his life. He was certain that his knees were about to buckle beneath his weight.

Tentatively, cautiously, Barabbas pushed open the door.

Julia stole his breath away. Propped against a pile of plush, elaborate pillows in her elegant canopy bed, Julia was washed in a tender glow as she balanced a very small bundle on one arm. Her wavy, abundant hair had been tied at the nape of her slender neck, and loose tendrils curled about her face. He could not argue that she looked exhausted, and yet she had never appeared more beautiful to him than in that sacred moment.

Lifting warm brown eyes to his, Julia managed a wobbly smile and held her free hand out to him.

Trembling, Barabbas stumbled over to the bed, took Julia's hand in his own sweaty palm, and peered down into the sweetest, tiniest face he had ever seen.

"Your daughter, my love," Julia whispered, tears springing to her eyes. "Have you ever seen anything so beautiful, so sweet?"

Kneeling at Julia's bedside, Barabbas drew Julia as close as he dared without disturbing the precious little bundle in her arms. "Yes," he said, his voice sounding choked in his own ears. "You, Julia. You are so beautiful, so sweet to me."

Julia looked at him, stunned to utter silence.

"But I have hurt you and I have mistreated you," Barabbas confessed, the words pouring out from his very soul. "I don't deserve this happiness, Julia. I don't deserve you. I –"

"Shhh." Tenderly, Julia placed a finger upon his lips. "It is forgiven."

"But, Julia, how –"

"*Forgiven*," Julia said emphatically, a single tear

tracing a slender line down her cheek. "Lord willing, we have our entire lives ahead of us to sort through the painful past. For now, can we savor this precious moment together?"

Barabbas looked at his wife in awe, wondering how he'd ever found it possible to loathe this gentle, lovely woman. By the grace of God, Julia had been utterly transformed, a brand new creation far removed from the spoiled, headstrong girl he had married a few short years ago.

Attempting to swallow the lump in his throat, Barabbas marveled at the beautiful baby girl in Julia's arms. "May I?" he asked humbly, and Julia nodded as tears filled her eyes. Timidly, Barabbas caressed the tiny cheek with a tenderness he had not formerly possessed. "What will you call her?" he asked hoarsely.

"What will *we* call her," Julia amended gently, gazing tenderly into the face of her newborn child. "I know the perfect name, but only if her father approves."

Barabbas was certain he would have agreed to anything in that moment. "I'd love to hear it."

"It's not so much the name itself, though it *is* a very pretty name," Julia explained, her eyes beseeching Barabbas to understand. "*You*, my husband, are Barabbas – *the son of the Father*. And by God's blessed grace, you truly have become His child." Reaching for Barabbas' hand, Julia drew it to her cheek. "And this precious little bundle, I believe, should be called Batya."

Batya. A small smile tipped the corners of Barabbas' mouth, for the name was very fitting indeed. Washed in the soft glow of the warm lamplight,

Barabbas, *son of the Father*, bent to kiss the tiny face of his sweet little daughter, Batya – *daughter of God*.

***

Standing in the lovely garden courtyard of his marriage vows, Barabbas marveled as a thousand dazzling stars dotted the early evening sky. Simon's home was still heavy-laden with relatives, and he felt uncomfortable in their presence. Here, in the court-yard, he could think and pray without condemning stares or prying eyes.

"You wished to speak with me, Son?"

Rubbing the back of his neck anxiously, Barabbas turned to face his father-in-law. "Thank you for making time to speak with me, Simon. I don't even know where to begin."

Folding his hands humbly, Simon smiled kindly as his eyes absorbed the dazzling display overhead. "Such brilliant stars, they are," he commented, his tone tinged with wonder. "And to think that our God knows each and every one by name."

"Surrounded by such beauty, one would never suspect that such atrocities were committed on Golgotha today," Barabbas said, his tone troubled.

Simon drew closer, clamping a hand upon his shoulder. "I can't imagine what you must have en-dured. If there's anything I can do –"

"Simon, that's part of what I wished to speak to you about. You've already done so much for me, long before I was even aware of it. Long before I ever met Julia, you hired me and gave me a chance when no one else would. You believed in me, Simon. And yet I treated you with blatant disrespect despite all you had done. Even then, you never stopped loving me, did you?"

Simon's eyes softened as he gazed into the contrite face of his son-in-law. "God's love never fails, Barabbas, and ours shouldn't either."

"But how did you do it?"

"I must admit, you didn't make it particularly easy at times," Simon chuckled with good humor. "But God grows and stretches us by His grace, helping us overcome obstacles we never thought possible."

"Julia said you prayed for me. Is that true?"

"Every single day without fail."

Barabbas shook his head, amazed.

Settling himself on the marble bench enclosing his prized fountain, Simon gestured for Barabbas to be seated beside him.

Barabbas did so, resting his elbows on his knees and folding his hands nervously.

"What's troubling you, Son?"

"I don't even know where to begin," Barabbas admitted with a self-deprecating shake of his head. "God intervened mightily in my life, and I know I can't go back. But I don't even know what to do, where to go from here."

Simon nodded his head in understanding. "I think the first thing to recognize, Barabbas, is that it won't be easy."

Barabbas looked at him bleakly.

"I don't say this to discourage you, but I believe it's wrong to mislead new believers, giving them the false impression that all their problems will be instantly solved the moment they turn to God. True, God does work miracles in our lives, but oftentimes, He gives us the grace to endure rather than providing an easy way out. This is how we grow."

Barabbas winced. "What if I mess up? I can't hurt Julia again, Simon. She's been through enough. And that precious little girl in her arms –" his voice caught in emotion, and he cleared his throat uncomfortably. "She deserves a wonderful father – someone better than me, Simon."

"God gives grace to the humble, Barabbas. Yes, it will be a long, hard road, but God is faithful. I assure you, I will be here for you no matter what. But even more than that, God will walk beside you every step of the way, guiding you along the paths of righteousness for His name's sake."

"I don't even know where to begin."

"God has already begun a good work in you, Barabbas, and He will complete it. Trust Him and lean on Him rather than your own strength. Study the Scriptures faithfully and live by them each day. Pray without ceasing. Fellowship with other believers. And when temptations arise – as they surely will – cry out to God, don't wait. He will give you the strength to resist temptation and gain the victory."

"And if I fail?" Barabbas asked bleakly.

"Barabbas, we all fail. If not for our failures, Jesus, our ultimate Passover Lamb, would not have laid down His own life today in our stead. His shed blood covers our sins, Barabbas. Repent, then ask God for the strength to turn away from that sin."

Barabbas looked away, his eyes wet. "Every time I close my eyes, I see Him up on that cross –" his voice broke and he shook his head in shame.

Simon touched his shoulder gently. "Have you studied the Messianic prophecies, Son?"

Barabbas lifted his head and said wryly, "I haven't

studied much of anything."

"Those passages have always fascinated me. A few years ago, I reached the conclusion that we were looking for the wrong kind of Messiah. We sought a valiant warrior king, one who would free us from Roman oppression. But the Savior I read about in the Scriptures was described as a lamb led to the slaughter, a Man who chose to take the penalty for our sins upon Himself."

"Very few will accept Jesus as the Messiah because the Romans are still here and He isn't," Barabbas agreed, his brows furrowed in deep thought.

"The most marvelous thing about the Messianic Scriptures, Barabbas, is this: they predict that the Messiah will rise from the dead."

Barabbas snapped his head in Simon's direction, his eyes conveying his great surprise. "What?"

Simon's eyes sparkled with anticipation. "I think the best is yet to come, Barabbas."

"But... but *how?*"

"Is anything too hard for the Lord?" Simon asked, his eyes twinkling delightfully.

Considering recent events, Barabbas could not argue that point. "I don't think we should tell Julia," he mused, rubbing the back of his neck in apprehension. "She's already crushed about Jesus' death, although that blessed little one in her arms is certainly a balm to her wounds. But I don't want to crush her hopes again."

Simon did not argue with him. He merely smiled and squeezed his shoulder. "Will you join us for the Sabbath meal? Julia and the baby are sleeping, I believe, and it would be an honor to share the feast with you."

Barabbas hadn't even realized that the Sabbath had begun. How long since he had bothered to observe the fourth commandment, so clearly set in stone? It would be good to share this special time with family and friends, despite his initial hesitancy and discomfort. He knew he must overcome these obstacles, and what better time to start than now?

"I would be honored to join you, Simon, but I do have one last question before we depart," Barabbas dared, and his great nervousness was evident in his voice. "Julia has been through so much, and I know she feels safe and comfortable here. It truly goes against my nature to ask this, Simon, but for her sake, may we stay with you until she is ready to return to our little home? After all I've done, I'm not sure she'll be in any hurry to return to the Lower City with me, anyway."

Simon's eyes softened in compassion. "Barabbas, you are always welcome here. Our home is your home, and I mean that."

Barabbas visibly relaxed, his anxieties relieved.

"Please know that I understand how much it cost you to ask this," Simon continued with great understanding. "I know it would be much easier for you to return to the privacy and familiarity of your own home, but you are considering Julia's well-being above your own, and this is truly evidence of your transformation in Christ. I'm proud of what you are becoming, Barabbas, and I'm thrilled to witness the mighty works God will perform in your life and Julia's."

Rising along with Simon, Barabbas grasped his father-in-law's hand firmly. "Thank you, Simon. Truly, thank you."

"You know," Simon mused, allowing his eyes to travel over the dazzling night sky once again, "it's rather amazing, isn't it? Even in this, our Lord Jesus observes the blessed Sabbath Day. For in six days God created the heavens and the earth, and all the host of them. According to His Word, *it was finished.* God then blessed the seventh day, sanctified it, and rested from His work."

Barabbas' brows rose in understanding. "Jesus suffered upon the cross for six hours, rather like God's creation of the world in six days. And Jesus rested in death on the seventh hour after finishing the work of redeeming His creation, just as God rested on the seventh day. '*It is finished,*' Jesus cried out after restoring the creation to Himself, just as God must have declared after His work of creation was complete."

Simon blew out a low whistle of amazement. "How can we possibly comprehend the ways of our God?" Smiling, Simon turned to Barabbas. "My good friends, Nicodemus and Joseph, received permission from Pontius Pilate to take Jesus' body for a proper burial. With the help of several devoted women, they bound Him in strips of soft linen and laid Him to rest in a beautiful garden tomb. It belongs to Joseph, but he hasn't had an opportunity to use it – until today. The tomb is beautiful and undefiled – the perfect resting place for our Savior."

Barabbas was comforted by this, though he couldn't explain why.

"*And they made His grave with the wicked – but with the rich at His death,*" Simon mused, stroking his graying beard in amusement. "Crucified between two thieves, and yet laid to rest in a rich man's tomb.

If only the prophet Isaiah could see the fulfillment of his words now!"

Barabbas doubted the prophet would have any desire to witness what he had seen today, though he did not voice his opinion.

"Now we must simply wait," Simon said, the faraway look leaving his eyes as he slapped his son-in-law's solid back. "Mark my words, Barabbas – He will rise again. It's only a matter of time."

Barabbas followed Simon into the magnificent villa, now glowing in cozy golden hues beneath the ambient lamplight. He hoped against all hope that Simon's prophetic words would indeed come to pass.

CHAPTER 70

Mara

It felt odd to return to the kitchen of Caiaphas' palatial home. The Sabbath had commenced, and Mara was grateful. After today, she was certain she hadn't the strength to perform even the simplest of tasks. She would sleep by the hearth tonight, far removed from the gossip and speculation surely circulating in the servants' quarters by now.

"Caiaphas locked him up, Mara."

Caught off guard by Alexander's unexpected announcement, Mara wheeled around, clutching a rough straw sleeping pallet against her breast. "Oh, Alexander. You startled me. I didn't see you there."

"You used to accuse me of sneaking up on you, hiding in the shadows like a prowler."

"You still hide in the shadows like a prowler." Mara tried for a smile, but it felt awkward and out of place after the day's appalling and gruesome events. "Who did Caiaphas lock up?"

"Malchus."

Mara's eyes widened in fear. "*Why?*"

"The high priest claims Malchus failed to serve him on a crucial assignment." Alexander's jaw twitched, betraying his anger.

"Malchus' offense was not deserving of incarceration!"

"Tell that to our merciful priest."

"What will happen to him?"

"I don't know, but we must pray without ceasing for his release." Alexander's eyes darted cautiously about their surroundings before he leaned in so close that Mara's heart began to thump nervously in her chest. "I overheard some guards talking. Judas Iscariot – the man who betrayed Jesus for thirty pieces of silver – committed suicide. They found him in a field he'd recently purchased. It wasn't pretty."

Mara's slender brows lifted in surprise. "Oh, my."

"Apparently Judas was torn up with guilt after Jesus was sentenced to be crucified. He returned to the Temple and flung the coins at the priests in the Temple treasury, shouting like a madman. He admitted that he had betrayed innocent blood."

"I'm sure Caiaphas was thrilled to hear that," Mara observed sarcastically. "Are you sure it was *suicide?*"

"Caiaphas is just relieved Judas is dead. After all, dead men don't talk. But the priests are all worked up about what to do with the money." Alexander's mouth tipped in a show of frustration and sardonic amusement. "Naturally, they're far too righteous to break the Law by donating blood money to the Temple treasury."

"Naturally," Mara replied, shaking her head in disgust.

"You'll find this interesting as well," Alexander added, taking Mara's sleeping pallet and spreading it carefully before the hearth for her. "Caiaphas has ordered a slew of soldiers to guard the tomb with Lucius serving as captain of the guard. And this after he already had that thing sealed, not to mention the monstrous boulder set in place, as if a rock that size was going anywhere."

Mara lifted a brow in question. "Why would he do that?"

"He's heard rumors," Alexander responded, his eyes flickering with scarcely contained excitement. "Apparently, Jesus predicted He would rise again on the third day."

Mara's heart skipped a beat. *Rise again?*

"Caiaphas claims he's posted a guard because the disciples might try to steal His body, making it appear like Jesus rose from the dead, which in turn would lead to insurrection. But deep down, Caiaphas fears something far worse than that, Mara." Straightening to his full height, Alexander gripped Mara's shoulders and leaned in close. "He's not worried about *insurrection* – no, he fears a *resurrection*."

***

Julia

"What a beautiful child. You are blessed indeed."

Julia managed a wobbly smile in response to the young woman's compliment, feeling a bit self-conscious propped up in bed with a new babe in her arms. Her mother had escorted this simply clad woman to her private chambers with a brief introduction. "This woman has sought you diligently, Julia," Iskah had explained. "She was relieved when she finally discovered your whereabouts."

After Iskah had fluttered out of the room to see to her Sabbath morning prayers, Julia had gazed at the stranger at the foot of her bed with questioning eyes. "I'm shocked that you remember me at all. We met so briefly," Julia said, fumbling for something to say.

"I have regretted that meeting so many times," the young woman said quietly, fumbling with a worn cloth bag draped over her shoulder. "I am so sorry for the way I treated you."

"You are Mary, yes?"

Mary dipped her head in a humble nod.

"I must apologize as well," Julia admitted, shifting little baby Batya in her arms. "I was rude and impatient."

"I would have responded as you did had a harlot appeared on my threshold asking for my husband – if I had a husband," Mary amended sheepishly.

Amazed by her humility, Julia offered a genuine smile. "It is a pleasure to meet you again, Mary. Is there something I can do for you?"

"Actually, I have come hoping to do something for you," Mary responded, reaching into her cloth bag and withdrawing an empty alabaster jar. "I believe this belongs to you."

Julia drew in a sharp breath at the unexpected appearance of a possession she had once prized. "Oh no, you purchased it and it is yours."

"I had planned to sell it if I ever fell on hard times," Mary admitted, clutching the jar with nervous, fumbling hands. "But then I met Jesus, and He changed me. You understand."

Julia nodded, a lump forming in her throat.

"I thought you would want to know that this lovely jar of yours was put to good use, Julia. I wished to demonstrate my devotion to Jesus. I knew no better way than to anoint Him – His head, His hands, His feet, with the sweet-smelling oil. I was sharply criticized for 'wasting' the expensive oil in that manner, but do you know what Jesus said to me?"

Julia shook her head, her eyes misting at the thought of her precious oil gracing the hands and feet of her Savior.

"Jesus said He would not always be with us, then He said that I had anointed His body for His burial. At the time, I couldn't possibly imagine it would happen so soon."

"Thank you," Julia managed, her heart bursting with gratitude, "for sharing this with me."

"I want you to keep it," Mary said, placing the jar upon Julia's marble topped vanity. "I know it's only an empty jar, but it's truly so much more than that. Every time you look at this empty vessel, Julia, I hope you will remember that God loves even the emptiest and unworthiest of vessels – like myself. He redeems the lives of the outcasts and transforms them into the worthiest of offerings. And we, like this empty jar, must also empty ourselves, daily pouring ourselves out like a drink offering for the good of others. This, in turn, is a sacrifice acceptable to God. This is how we demonstrate our love for Him. And sometimes," Mary added, the slightest hint of a smile gracing her lips, "we must allow the Lord to empty us, to completely drain us of ourselves, so He can fill us up with Himself. As His forerunner once proclaimed, 'He must increase, but I must decrease.'"

"I don't even know what to say," Julia managed, staring at the empty jar on her vanity with a whole new perspective. "Thank you, Mary. You have truly blessed me."

"I'm truly sorry to interrupt your Sabbath morning," Mary apologized, preparing to leave. "But I knew you would want to know about the harvest reaped when you sacrificed such a valuable possession."

"You are welcome at my home or my father's house anytime, Mary," Julia said with great feeling.

Pausing at the entrance, Mary said softly, "Jesus was buried before last night's sunset in a lovely garden tomb. A kind Pharisee named Nicodemus provided over one hundred pounds of aloes and spices to anoint His precious body. Sabbath was close at hand, so we plan to return early Sunday morning to finish anointing His body."

"I know Nicodemus," Julia said, warmed by his bold donation. "Thank you for seeing to our Savior's body, Mary."

"I wouldn't have had it any other way." Mary was about to take her leave when she paused once again, her eyes traveling to the empty alabaster jar on Julia's vanity. "You know, I have a feeling that jar might become famous someday."

Julia lifted her brows in question. "How so?"

"After I anointed Him with the fragrant oil, Jesus said something unexpected. He said that wherever the Gospel is preached, the story of what I had done would be told as a memorial to me. I have thought about it so many times, wondering what it could possibly mean. Perhaps the empty jar will be significant to others in the future, not just to you and me."

Julia smiled warmly, stroking her baby daughter's soft cheek. "I don't think He was talking about the jar, Mary."

Mary looked at her with questioning eyes, confusion evident upon her softened features.

"I think Jesus was talking about *you*. One day, your name will be famous – maybe even to the ends of the earth."

***

Simon

Typically, Simon reveled in the glorious peace of Shabbat, sighing wistfully when Saturday's lovely sunset signified the end of the Sabbath Day. Today, however, a still, small voice reminded him that he had some urgent business to conduct once the sun's final rays vanished beyond the western hills.

After sharing a casual yet earnest conversation with his daughter, Simon realized it was within his power to improve the lives of someone – possibly several – in need. And by God's grace, he would do it.

But first, he must pay a friendly little visit to the high priest. Simon's gray mustache twitched slightly as he adjusted his richly embroidered garments and gave himself a quick once-over in his elegant, gilded mirror. Despite the unexpected nature of his visit, he doubted the high priest would refuse an audience with him. Simon was no prince, but he was certainly wealthy and influential enough to prove a bothersome nuisance if crossed. And Caiaphas, being the sly politico he was, would certainly take this fact into account.

Simon suppressed a mischievous grin as he adjusted his robe and stepped outside the door. An overdone litter awaited him just outside the walls of his villa. He would arrive in style, a subtle reminder of his powerful position.

If Caiaphas desired Temple trade to carry on smoothly as usual, then he'd best be amenable to Simon's interesting proposition.

***

Mara

"Caiaphas has doubled security at the tomb," Alexander divulged, entering the kitchen and seating himself at the massive worktable across from Mara. "He knows tomorrow will mark the third day, and he's all worked up over it. If Jesus really does rise again, it will contradict everything Caiaphas stands for as a Sadducee. The man doesn't believe in a resurrection for anyone, period. And especially not the Man he moved heaven and earth to destroy."

Mara allowed that bit of information to sink in before replying, "Wouldn't it be grand if Jesus proved him wrong?"

"I'm counting on it, Mara," Alexander grinned, reaching across the table to cover her hand with his.

Blushing slightly, Mara withdrew her hand. "Have we heard anything about Malchus?"

"Just now," Alexander said, watching in amusement as her color deepened. "He's gone, Mara."

Mara covered her mouth in horror. "What do you mean, gone?"

"Oh, he's not *dead*!" Alexander amended, regretting the fact that his careless words had frightened her. "Caiaphas has sold his services to another man."

Mara's eyes filled with tears. "Another man? Who is he? Oh, Alexander, what if we never see him again?"

Alexander's eyes sparkled with mischief. "You can relax, Mara. Just wait until you find out who his new master is."

CHAPTER 71

Melina

Perched upon Salome's balcony overlooking the lovely palace gardens, Melina prayed silently, wishing to banish the dull ache plaguing her heart.

Jesus had been crucified. If rumors could be trusted, He had been laid to rest in a garden tomb. The Light of the world had been snuffed out, and she felt nothing but emptiness. Her lips moved fervently in prayer, and yet, she sensed no response. Why this dreadful silence?

She couldn't help but wonder about Malchus. His predictions had come true – the elders and chief priests had succeeded this time. Would this merely confirm his disbelief? The thought brought tears to her eyes.

Oh, Malchus, how I miss you. How I long for you to believe. How I long to share this faith with you. Leaning upon the marble railing overlooking the gardens, Melina wept quietly. *Lord God, can You hear me? Are You still there? Will Jesus truly rise?*

Her heartfelt prayers were met by glaring silence. *Father? Can you hear me?*

Covering her face with her hands, Melina strove for calm. She must have faith, even when she could not see. Or hear. Despite her own assurances, her heart was heavy, her spirit weak.

She wondered if the still, small voice she had grown to love and trust had been hushed for all eternity.

***

Malchus

"You are Julia's father?" Malchus asked in disbelief as a slew of rather intimidating menservants escorted him and the older merchant toward an awaiting litter.

Simon's eyes twinkled in delight. "Yes, indeed."

"Was this her idea?"

"She told me about you and that sweet little maid of yours – whom you are more than welcome to marry and bring into our home," Simon assured him, pausing before the marvelous litter.

Malchus' stomach fluttered as a thousand unexpected emotions assailed him from all directions.

"This," Simon said, retrieving a scroll from the inner folds of his robe, "is the proper documentation. I have purchased your services, and the transaction is final. You will no longer answer to nor reside with the high priest." Flicking open the scroll for Malchus to see, Simon then did something completely unexpected: he ripped the document in half! Grinning broadly, Simon explained, "You are free, Malchus.

I don't believe it is right to own another man. But know this – you are more than welcome to work for me, beginning tomorrow if you wish. I could certainly use a man with your integrity, talent, and abilities, and this would be a wonderful opportunity for you. You would lodge in my home, of course, as would your bride, should you choose to take one."

Attempting to swallow the lump in his throat, Malchus reached out and grasped Simon's hand firmly. "I would be honored to work for you, Simon. Thank you – truly, truly thank you – for this opportunity."

***

Julia

Jesus stood in the Temple, beautiful in His priestly robes. There, before the altar, He made atonement for the sins of His people. The past, present, and future sins of Jews and Gentiles alike were completely covered by the shed blood of the ultimate High Priest.

As if observing from a distance, Julia's heart stirred as she watched the tender scene. Jesus was larger than life in His lovely, colorful garments, and so very *real* she was certain she could reach out and touch Him...

"Julia! Julia, wake up, my love."

Julia murmured faintly in protest, resisting wakefulness. Her dream was so pleasant, so beautiful. She didn't want to leave.

"Julia, wake up!"

Jarred awake by the persistence in her husband's

tone, Julia pushed herself up to a sitting position, rubbing the sleep from her eyes and instinctively reaching for the cradle at her bedside. Suddenly, she realized her family had gathered around her canopy bed – her husband, her father, her mother, Joanna, and shockingly, her new friend, Mary!

Completely embarrassed, Julia drew the blankets to her chin, her sleepiness evaporating in her stark mortification. What a sight she must be with tousled hair and dark circles beneath her eyes! "Has something happened?" she managed, her voice heavy with sleepiness.

One look at the broad grins and beaming faces surrounding her bed, and Julia realized her beautiful dream constituted far more than wishful thinking. Pushing herself up a bit higher in bed, she looked from face to face, her heart nearly bursting with joy within her. Eyes alight with wonder, she didn't wait for an explanation. "It's Jesus. He's alive, isn't He?"

CHAPTER 72

Mara

"He is risen! He is risen, Mara!"

Mara spun around, her heart springing into her throat. Alexander swooped into the kitchen, placed his hands firmly about her waist, and spun her around and around with a jubilant shout.

"Jesus is risen?" Mara gasped when Alexander finally planted her two feet upon solid ground again. "Is He really? You're sure?"

"Oh, I'm sure," Alexander supplied, his dark eyes gleaming with joy and mischief. "A slew of soldiers – the despicable Lucius among them – came running to Caiaphas with their tails tucked early this morning. The earth rumbled beneath their feet, and they all agree they saw supernatural beings descend from the heavenlies!"

"And then?" Mara asked, her eyes wide with wonder.

"The soldiers insisted that a fierce angelic being rolled away the stone as easily as a child's toy. And every single one of them swears that Jesus rose from the dead."

Mara's eyes glowed with joy. "Oh, Alexander! It's glorious! Jesus has risen! He has conquered death! He has defeated the grave! The wicked one could not prevail against Him."

"Praise God," Alexander breathed.

"Now the whole world will know that Jesus is the Messiah," Mara beamed, her face alight with joyful celebration. "Who could argue against a resurrection?"

"Well," Alexander quipped, his expression changing, "about that…"

Mara's jubilation dimmed. "What is it?"

"Caiaphas paid off the guards. They're already spreading their lies like a contagious disease."

"A Man *rose from the dead*! How could anyone possibly refute that?" Mara demanded angrily.

"Caiaphas paid the soldiers guarding the tomb to tell everyone the disciples stole the body while they slept."

"Oh, please," Mara groaned, her frustration mounting. "Who will believe it? Such an admission by the guards will result in their executions. They'll never go along with it."

"They already have," Alexander responded grimly. "Not only did Caiaphas bribe them with a worthy sum, he also swore to protect them."

"But how can he do that?"

"How does he do anything? Through bribery, trickery, manipulation, conniving schemery – who knows?" Alexander remarked sarcastically. "But he'll do anything to hush this thing up."

"I can't even comprehend the gall of that man,"

Mara huffed, pacing about the kitchen in frustration. "Jesus accomplishes the impossible, and still the high priest refuses to acknowledge Him as the Messiah! He will lead so many astray, Alexander."

Reaching for Mara's wrist, Alexander pulled her toward him. "Then we will just have to speak the truth to everyone we know. Those with eyes to see and ears to hear will believe, Mara."

Blushing at their closeness, Mara lowered her gaze shyly. "I never dreamed I would hear you talk like this, Alexander."

Alexander's mouth tipped ruefully. "Neither did I."

When Mara did not place any distance between them, Alexander ventured quietly, "Mara, I must speak with you about something. I admit the feelings I had for you in the beginning were far from honorable—"

Coloring deeply, Mara lowered her gaze.

"But I can honestly say that God has granted me a pure love for you. I accept God's will for us, whatever that may be. But you need to know that I've returned the money I obtained by dishonest gain. Even so, I've saved enough to make a modest start elsewhere. As I initially hired out my own services here, I am free to leave at will."

Shyly, Mara gazed up at him, her large brown eyes filled with questions. "What are you saying?"

"I'm saying *I love you*. I want to be your husband, Mara, if you'll have me."

Mara's eyes filled with tears as she gazed into the earnest eyes of a man she had slowly learned to love.

"The moment you say yes, I'll shake the dust of this lion's den off my feet and never look back. And

I'll be taking you with me, Mara."

"Don't ask me how or why," Mara teased, her eyes dancing with mischief, "but I love you too, Alexander."

Alexander's determination softened as a tenderness formerly unknown to him filled his entire being. Gently, he took her hand in his, a promise in his eyes.

***

Melina

"You foul little witch!" Herodias slapped Melina so hard she reeled backward, her head spinning. "You've poisoned the mind of my daughter!"

"Mother, please!" Salome cried, reaching for Herodias' arm. "It was my idea to go see Jesus at the Temple. Melina simply followed my orders by escorting me!"

"Don't tell me she didn't know I wouldn't approve," Herodias hissed, her nostrils flaring in rage.

Cowering near a row of marble pillars, Melina prayed with all her heart as two cruel women discussed her fate. Somehow, Herodias had learned of Salome's somewhat recent expedition to the Temple with Melina, and she was livid with rage.

"In case you hadn't noticed, Mother, I'm a married woman. I don't need your approval to do as I please!" Salome snapped back.

"You were a guest under my roof!" Herodias argued venomously. "Therefore, you were under my authority, as you are now!"

"Clearly," Salome spat, "it was a bad idea to come

here. I should have stayed with Philip, even if he is so boring that he puts me to sleep on my feet!"

"You are a stupid girl!" Herodias snarled, circling her own daughter like an angry tigress. "You hear one ridiculous rumor about the resurrection of a dead Man and you believe it!"

Despite the fact that her ears were still ringing, Melina's attention pricked at that shocking disclosure. Joy unlike anything she had ever known washed over her despite the stinging pain of her bruised cheek. Had she heard Herodias correctly? Jesus had risen? Blinking back tears of joy, Melina's mind buzzed with a thousand questions. When did it happen, and how? Regardless, Jesus was alive and that's all that mattered! Her hopes had not perished with Him. It took every ounce of willpower she possessed not to break into a euphoric dance.

"By all the gods in the universe, why are you grinning like that?" Herodias growled, her attention drawn from her erring daughter. "Do you, too, believe these groundless rumors?"

Daring a glance at Salome, Melina saw the great interest glistening in the princess's eyes. Despite Herodias' wrath, Melina knew she must bear witness for Salome's sake. Perhaps one day the girl would believe. "Jesus said He would rise on the third day," she said bravely, her heart soaring. "And so He has."

Herodias rolled her eyes in disgust. "People heard Him making such great claims, which is exactly why this ludicrous rumor is swiftly circulating throughout the region!"

Melina lowered her eyes respectfully, wondering how on earth Salome had learned of Jesus' resurrection. Perhaps she had stumbled into Joanna upon her arrival. Tearfully, Joanna had told Melina about her plans to join several other women to finish anointing Jesus' body in the tomb early Sunday morning.

Melina was drawn from her delightful reverie when Herodias gripped her by the arm and flung her toward a large set of gilded double doors. "Get out," Herodias' snarled, her tone dangerously low and clipped.

Melina raised eyes full of confusion toward the brooding woman. "My lady?"

"You heard me! Get out. Leave! You have been a stench in my nostrils from the day you arrived here."

"Mother!" Salome whined, interceding on behalf of her favored handmaiden. "What will she do? Where will she go? Do you expect her to make her way on the streets?"

"I'm merciful to allow her that much. I should have her thrashed and beaten or worse." Herodias glared at Melina, her green eyes glistening with venom. "Get out of my sight, you worthless wretch, before I change my mind."

CHAPTER 73

"Melina! Wait!"

Pausing just outside the walls of Herod's palace, Melina turned to see Elias jogging toward her.

"Elias!" she gasped, tears springing to her eyes. "You should not be seen with me. I have been banished from the palace. They might punish you too."

"Let them," Elias said coldly. "I would be thrilled to be banished. Perhaps this is your key to freedom, Melina."

"I am concerned for Salome, Elias. If not for her presence this morning, I am certain Herodias would have killed me."

Elias' dark brows drew together in fury.

Melina touched his arm gently. "Don't be angry, Elias. God protected me from her wrath. But I hate to leave when Salome is finally showing a bit of promise. When she visits, please be kind to her, Elias, for my sake."

Elias huffed his annoyance, but his eyes betrayed his deep fondness for her.

Melina's eyes spilled over with tears. "I can't bear to leave you, Elias. You have become so dear to me."

"You've told me about your secret hiding place – where you leave notes for friends. When you miss me, look for my words there. We can still speak, even when far apart."

"I will," Melina promised, swiping at her tears with trembling hands.

Leaning in close, Elias whispered with a gleam in in his eye, "You will be pleased to know I have reached an astounding conclusion about your Messiah. I know who He is: Jesus Christ, Son of God, Savior."

Melina's heart sprang into her throat. "You believe?" she gasped, her eyes wide as saucers.

"Joanna was right. The prophet's words came to pass – every single one of them. He is risen, Melina. Joanna was there. She saw the angels and the empty tomb. She's spreading the word even as we speak."

Taking Elias' calloused hands in her own, Melina kissed them. "You have been a father to me, Elias. And now you are my brother in the Lord."

"Always. And nothing can truly separate us. We are bound by the love of Christ."

***

After making a few careful inquiries, Melina located the home of Julia's father, Simon. She had only traveled there once before, and she had been deeply concerned for Julia at the time. She wished she had paid more attention when Simon's manservant had led her there.

Silently, Melina prayed that Simon would not turn her away. She didn't know where else to go. Was Julia still abiding in his home? If not, surely he would know where Julia's small abode was located. Perhaps he would be kind enough to direct her there. She also hoped he would be able to advise her about the best way to find work.

After shyly informing a rather suspicious door-keeper about her situation, she was amazed when Julia's father and mother hurried to greet her, welcoming her into their home with open arms. To her great surprise and delight, she learned that Julia and Barabbas were also in residence.

Washed in tears of happiness, Melina was nearly wild with joy when Julia placed her newborn baby girl in her arms.

"Julia, I've never seen a more perfect child," Melina breathed, her eyes misting with tears of joy as she sat in the elegant foyer with her dearest friend.

"I tend to agree with you, although I'm hardly an impartial observer," Julia teased, smiling softly as baby Batya cooed happily in Melina's arms. "It is such a joy to share this time with you! God is truly gracious – He delivered you from your oppressors, and now you have your whole life ahead of you!" Noting the faint sheen of tears in her friend's eyes, Julia frowned. "Melina, is something wrong?"

Melina smiled through her tears. "It's selfish of me, really."

"Melina, you're the most unselfish person I've ever met," Julia chided in disbelief. "What is it?"

Smiling down at the little baby girl in her arms, Melina tenderly adjusted the delicate little blanket. "After all we've witnessed these last three days, I shouldn't harbor even the slightest of wishes for myself. After all, our Savior has conquered death and provided atonement for our sins. The hope of heaven is ours because of His great sacrifice."

"But?" Julia prodded gently.

"I suppose I had thought – I had *hoped* – that perhaps one day the Lord would grant me the privilege of marrying Malchus and sharing the joy of children with him," Melina said, swiping at a stray tear.

"I see," Julia said quietly, attempting to appear sympathetic and poised. She was relieved when Barabbas entered the foyer, his powerful presence filling the room.

Melina smiled up at him kindly. "It brings me the greatest joy to meet you," she said sincerely. "Your testimony is powerful. I have no doubt that God has great plans for you."

"You threw me for a loop on the podium," Barabbas admitted, standing behind his wife's settee and placing a hand on her shoulder. "I had no idea how you knew me."

"God's timing is incredible, isn't it?" Melina said with great feeling.

"It sure is," Barabbas responded, exchanging a mischievous look with his wife. "As pleased as you were to meet Julia's infamous husband, I think there's someone else you'll be even more excited to meet."

Julia's eyes sparkled with fun as she exchanged knowing looks with her husband. "Melina, allow Barabbas to tend to little Batya and come with me."

Melina looked between them, her eyes filled with confusion. "Julia, you shouldn't be on your feet right now. You should be resting–"

"It's no use, Melina," Barabbas teased, smiling fondly at his wife.

"I will rest in a minute," Julia assured them both,

rolling her eyes in mock frustration.

"You haven't even completed your days of seclusion, and already you run about like an athlete," Melina laughed.

"I haven't left this villa, so you needn't worry about my lack of seclusion," Julia amended with an impish grin.

Less than convinced, Melina allowed Barabbas to relieve her of her precious bundle as Julia took her by the arm and led her from the foyer to the central garden courtyard. Melina was careful to take slow, measured steps. She was certain Julia shouldn't be on her feet so soon after her delivery.

"Oh, Julia," Melina breathed, pausing below a magnificent row of elegantly curtained arches opening into the garden. Her eyes swept over the stunning array of towering palms, vibrant spring blossoms spilling over elegant urns, lush blooming foliage, and a stunning marble fountain at the center of the breathtaking courtyard, "Have I mentioned this place rivals even Herod's lovely gardens?"

"This is where Barabbas and I shared our marriage vows," Julia explained. "It's always been a special place to me. And I have a sneaking suspicion that it may very well become a special place for you as well."

Melina looked at Julia, clearly baffled. "It is a lovely refuge," she admitted, puzzled. But her extreme bafflement evaporated the moment a tall, lithe young man stepped out from a thick grove of trees and greenery. "Malchus!" she gasped, tears springing to her soft emerald eyes.

Closing the distance between them, Malchus took her hands in his own, his warm brown eyes filled with both pain and longing. "Surprised?" he asked gently.

"More than you know," Melina managed as she struggled for composure.

Grinning knowingly, Julia touched Melina's arm and said, "I'll leave you two alone to sort things out." Tactfully, she disappeared behind the gently flapping tapestries separating the courtyard from the house.

Distressed, Melina watched Julia's retreating back before turning to Malchus, her eyes filled with confusion. "What are you doing here?"

"I could ask the same of you," Malchus said lightly, relieved that Melina had allowed him to take her hands without flinching. He held them captive between his own, inwardly vowing to never let her go again. "You were right, Melina," he said softly. "Jesus is risen."

"Oh, Malchus." Tears traced two slender lines down Melina's pale cheeks.

"I was a coward and a fool. I think I believed all along, but I was afraid to take a stance for the Messiah, convinced such an act would destroy my cherished plans for a peaceful future together," he admitted ruefully, repentance etched all over his handsome features. "Melina, in my desire to preserve my own life, I nearly lost it *and* you."

Unable to speak, Melina squeezed his hands, her eyes filled with sympathy.

"I desired peace above all else, but in my futile quest to obtain it, I denied the only One capable of truly providing it," Malchus finished with great feeling.

"How did this come about, Malchus?"

"It's an earful, I can tell you that much." Touching his ear ruefully, Malchus grinned. "Soon I'll tell you all about it. But first, there's something I must ask you." Drawing her a bit closer, Malchus brushed his knuckles against Melina's delicate cheekbone and smiled tenderly. "Apart from God, you are the most precious thing in the world to me. I don't want to lose you again."

Trembling at his nearness and her own insurmountable joy, Melina's silvery laughter filled the aromatic garden, mingling with the gentle patter of cascading waters from the fountain beside them. "You needn't worry about that, dear one. I'm not going anywhere."

Malchus' brown eyes filled with hope, his handsome features bathed in relief. Taking her hands once more, Malchus bent to look directly into the eyes he loved. "Melina, will you be my wife?"

Smiling through her tears, Melina draped her arms over his shoulders, clasping her hands behind his neck. "I would be honored to be your wife, Malchus."

Yet again, God's Word had proven true. He had made everything beautiful in its time.

***

Six months later...

Caiaphas

Donning the glorious white linen reserved for this sacred Day of Atonement, Joseph Caiaphas passed the glowing menorah in the Temple, plagued by a deep, abiding inner darkness that even the steadily burning seven-branched fixture could not dismiss. Perhaps it was the sin of this godless people weighing so heavily upon his shoulders. Today, he would cleanse the nation of unrighteousness. He, Joseph Caiaphas, high priest of Israel, possessed the power of life and death. He alone stood between these stiff-necked, rebellious people and a holy God. He was the bridge, the one to whom ultimate power had been given. He relished, it, savoring the smell of fresh blood upon the altar.

Furrowing his brow in a futile attempt to suppress his fury, Caiaphas mentally dismissed the foolish dimwits who flocked about Jerusalem proclaiming that the pestilent Prophet, Jesus of Nazareth, had made atonement for the sins of all people by His death and alleged resurrection nearly six months ago. The strange happenings within the Temple compound simply fueled the high priest's desire to disprove the rapidly growing sect now called The Followers of the Way. Why, in recent months, the Temple doors often swung open of their own accord, as if beckoning anyone and everyone to enter into the presence of God. One erring priest had commented it was as if the invisible hands of angels flung open those massive doors, beckoning seekers toward the Most Holy Place. Even eerier than that were multiple occasions when the brightly burning candlesticks of the menorah – signifying the presence of God in the Temple – mysteriously blew out, leaving the holy chambers in utter darkness. Caiaphas was certain those cursed disciples of Jesus must be behind the bizarre happenings. Blasphemous fools! Joseph Caiaphas refused to relinquish his power to any man. Atonement was his to grant or deny.

And today, by his own pronouncement, the scapegoat had been led into the wilderness even as the second sacrificial animal was slaughtered. A scarlet ribbon, signifying the bloody sins of the people, was removed from the horn of the sacrificial animal and fastened to the Temple door. In the past, Caiaphas had savored the moment when that scarlet ribbon turned snowy white, indicating that God had accepted the sacrifice and thus cleansed the sins of the people. Moving calmly through the dimly lit chamber, Caiaphas stroked his beard thoughtfully as he considered this sacred act – an everlasting symbol of the power he wielded in his own two hands.

Emerging upon the Temple's graceful marble steps, Caiaphas paused before turning toward the towering, gilded doors. A chill breeze swept through the Temple compound, and the tell-tale ribbon snapped smartly in response. Relishing the sharp sound, a brutal smile twisted the high priest's lips as his gray eyes traveled downward toward the frantically flapping ribbon. Reaching out, he drew forth as his cold gray eyes came to rest upon it–

Shockingly, *the ribbon remained the deepest shade of scarlet.* Scarlet – like the spilled blood of the saints. Scarlet – like the deathly stain of sin. Scarlet – like his own taut features, his color deepening in fierce, ungodly wrath. Gasping, Caiaphas withdrew a trembling hand as if a lethal cobra had sunk its venomous fangs deep into his flesh. Trembling in seething fury, a guttural growl escaped his throat as he recoiled in both fear and outrage.

For the very first time in the history of Temple

sacrifice, the scarlet ribbon had failed to turn white as freshly fallen snow.

Balling his hands into white-knuckled fists, Caiaphas recalled the proclamation that had rung out upon Golgotha's bloody hill the moment before Jesus breathed His last: *It is finished.*

Caiaphas' gray eyes narrowed, forming two dangerously small slits. A low growl resonated deep within his throat as he tore the ribbon from the door in a fit of unrestrained rage, plunging headlong into the Temple. Pacing like a caged beast within the glorious Temple chamber, the high priest clutched the scarlet ribbon in an iron fist.

Instantly, without warning, the flickering candlelight of the seven-branched menorah ceased, encompassing the high priest in utter darkness.

Caiaphas knew only a moment of terror before his mouth hardened in defiance, forming a grim, uncompromising line. The followers of this blasphemous new sect would pay – preferably with their lives and the lives of their wretched children. Blinded by his own fury as well as the inky blackness closing in on all sides, his hard mouth flattened, curving into a wicked, sardonic sneer.

It is finished? Not for him. In fact, it was only the beginning.

CHAPTER 74

Julia

Nestled cozily just outside the open doorway of her small home, Julia smiled wistfully as she watched her sweet little Batya crawling contentedly on the soft autumn grass, gurgling happily as she inspected each individual blade with eager, chubby fingers. Billowy, sun-tinted clouds drifted lazily across a rich blue sky as gentle breezes caressed Julia's cheek. Julia smiled as she watched her daughter play. Batya seemed to find joy in every moment of life, glorying in the simplest of pleasures – the sunshine on her face, a gentle breeze whispering through the trees, the musical call of a bird perched upon their windowsill. Tenderly observing her little daughter, Julia thought she understood why Jesus had admonished His disciples to become like little children.

Enjoying the warmth of the sun soaking through her lightweight garments, Julia sat with hands folded in her lap and her knees tucked comfortably beneath her, marveling at all the Lord had accomplished in recent months. Not only had Jesus borne the burden of the world's sin upon His shoulders, providing atonement for all who would accept it, He had also risen from the dead, appeared to many, and then ascended to Heaven, reuniting with the Father He so dearly loved.

Julia no longer ached or chafed at His absence. Jesus had promised to return at the appointed time. She had long since learned to trust in God's timing rather than insisting upon her own. Oh, but how thrilling it was to be among those who had witnessed the resurrected Lord! In that precious, unexpected moment when Jesus had appeared to many, Julia and Barabbas had hung upon His every word, treasuring them in their hearts. And what a miracle it must have been for those who had witnessed Jesus' miraculous ascension, as her dear neighbors, Isaac and Deborah, had!

Shaking her head in awe, Julia considered how very far her Savior had brought her in these few short – and yet seemingly endless – years. Her beloved Jesus had indeed taken her by the hand, tenderly, patiently guiding her through the hottest fires and the deepest waters. Her sins were forgiven by the precious blood of Jesus Christ, the Passover Lamb. Wondrously, her father, Simon, had been right all along – the great Passover of the ancients had simply foreshadowed something even greater and far more exceptional to come – Jesus Christ, the Son of God, the ultimate Passover Lamb who, in the words of John the Baptizer, *takes away the sins of the world.* Thousands of years ago, the first battle against sin on earth had been waged and lost in a lush garden paradise when Adam and Eve succumbed to the words of a crafty serpent rather than trusting their loving Creator. And now, Julia thought with a warm smile, the ultimate battle for the souls of men had been won in yet another paradisal garden when Jesus Christ emerged from His grave, triumphant.

Oh, the depth of the riches both of the wisdom and knowledge of God! Her heart cried, as if inspired by the very Holy Spirit poured out upon believers shortly after Jesus' ascension to Heaven. *How unsearchable are His judgments and His ways past finding out!* For years, Julia had prayed for the salvation of her reckless husband, and the God of the universe, by the power of His might, had skillfully orchestrated numberless circumstances and events to accomplish that very purpose! As a small boy, her husband had wept at the foot of his revolutionary father's cross, becoming the son of his father just as his name implied by following in his treacherously violent footsteps. But God had already known that Barabbas would later weep at the foot of another cross. There, he would become the true son of his heavenly Father. Julia knew she had witnessed nothing less than a miracle in her husband's transformation, and she was reminded of this as Barabbas' commitment to the Lord deepened each day. How mysterious and marvelous were the ways of her God!

Lifting a delicate hand to shield her eyes from the bright afternoon sun, Julia's heart fluttered with anticipation at the sight of her husband, still dusty from his caravan journey, approaching on the road.

"Where are my lovely ladies?" Barabbas called teasingly, quickening his pace as he approached his little family.

Batya squealed delightedly at the sound of her father's voice, lifting her chubby arms toward Julia in earnest appeal. Laughing, Julia scooped up her daughter and, cradling her close to her heart, ran to meet her beloved husband upon the road.

"Barabbas!" She cried, her heartfelt laughter filling the quiet street. "How I've missed you!"

Closing the distance between them, Barabbas dropped his heavy bag and pulled her close to him, kissing the top of her head before reaching out to nuzzle his daughter's soft cheek.

Contented and sheltered in the arms of her husband, Julia held her daughter close, her heart swelling with gratitude toward the One who had completely transformed her from the inside out. Remembering the Lord's promise to fight for her, she couldn't help but smile as she acknowledged that the Savior had indeed won this battle. And she had no doubt He would win many more to come.

Slinging his bag over his shoulder, Barabbas draped an arm around his wife as they turned and walked toward their small home together, baby Batya gurgling in sheer delight in the presence of her mother and father. Julia imagined that her own jubilation would certainly rival her little Batya's in the presence of her own heavenly Father someday.

Pausing before the narrow door leading into their home, Julia glanced up at her husband with sparkling eyes. "Every time you return from a long journey, Barabbas, I am reminded of the joy and ecstasy we shall experience when Jesus comes again. Whether or not it happens in our lifetime, it will be a day unlike anything we've ever known!"

"That it will," Barabbas agreed with an understanding smile. "I know we all yearn for the day when Jesus will return to set up His perfect kingdom on the earth."

"But until that day comes," Julia added, her eyes shining with hope, "we must share the joyous news of our Savior with all who care to listen."

"And even with those who don't," Barabbas added with a twinkle in his eye. "Take it from me – eventually, they'll come around."

Julia laughed as she took her husband's arm with her free hand, passing beneath the neatly carved wooden sign Barabbas had placed above the threshold: *As for me and my house, we will serve the Lord.*

Yes, indeed, Julia thought, her heart nearly bursting with joy as she placed her squealing daughter into the arms of a loving father. *Whatever trials we may face, we can take heart, knowing that Jesus has already won.* Someday, Jesus would fulfill His promise. On that remarkable day, He would indeed return for those who loved Him. Julia could scarcely wait to behold her blessed Savior descending from Heaven with a mighty shout and the voice of an archangel, as a blast of the heavenly trumpet of God sounded a triumphant song of victory – a glorious melody of triumph and redemption ringing throughout the endless ages, forever and ever, for all eternity!

A LOOK AT: FINDING THE WAY
BY RACHAEL C. DUNCAN

Get swept away by this beautifully intense story of the infant church of first-century Judea in the captivating continuation to the beloved Crowning Crescendo series.

Sheltered from the brooding turmoil sweeping through Jerusalem lives Mary—a savvy, independent businesswoman of the Upper city who is assured of her life's course. But when the disciples of the controversial Rabbi appear at her doorstep requesting the use of her Upper Room for the Passover, she has little idea that God's plan for her is about to unfold.

When Mary's life comes crashing down, she is determined to walk in the will of God—despite fierce opposition from all sides. She throws herself into action as the fledgling church explodes into an unstoppable force that sets the world ablaze with the power of gospel.

Meanwhile, Mary's favored maidservant, Tabitha, agonizes over her inability to walk in the spirit. She must learn to entrust the pain of her past and an unknown future in the hands of an all-knowing God. But when a fiery Hellenist is hired to fill a vital position in the household, Tabitha's resolve is tested.

Finding the Way may be more challenging than Christ's followers ever imagined as Mary, Tabitha, and a cast of familiar characters from the New Testament stand firm for the church of God.

AVAILABLE AUGUST 2023

ABOUT THE AUTHOR

Rachael Duncan is a passionate follower of Christ. Her goal is to reach as many people as possible for the sake of Christ and His kingdom. She believes that God has gifted each of His children with different gifts to be used to strengthen the body of Christ and fulfill the Great Commission. (Matt. 28:19-20; 1 Cor. 12)

Rachael was blessed to be raised in a strong Christian home, and she accepted Jesus Christ as her Lord and Savior at a very early age. Since then, she has determined to live her life in accordance to His Word and to share the love of Christ through the gift of writing.

Rachael has been passionate about writing since she was a small child. She especially loved writing plays and short stories. At the age of fourteen, she wrote her first play, which was performed as a dinner theatre production by a local school.

She has been actively involved in both women's and children's ministries for over a decade. Currently, she enjoys teaching a weekly girls' Bible study, writing plays for a local homeschool group, and participating in local ministry outreaches for women and children.

Rachael currently resides in Texas with her husband and their first "child" – a playful rescue puppy named Riley! In addition to her writing, she is an enthusiastic "keeper of the home" and "helpmeet", as well as being actively involved in ministering to the women and children God has placed in her life. (Titus 2:3-5; Gen. 2:20-23)